IF
YOU
LEAVE
ME

IF
YOU
LEAVE
ME

A NOVEL

CRYSTAL HANA KIM

WM

WILLIAM MORROW
An Imprint of HarperCollins*Publishers*

HarperCollins books may be purchased for educational, business, or sales promotional use. For information, please e-mail the Special Markets Department at SPsales@harpercollins.com.

First William Morrow hardcover published June 2018

FIRST EDITION

Designed by Leah Carlson-Stanisic

Library of Congress Cataloging-in-Publication Data

Names: Kim, Crystal Hana, 1987- author.
Title: If you leave me : a novel / Crystal Hana Kim.
Description: First edition. | New York, NY : William Morrow, an imprint of HarperCollinsPublishers, 2018.
Identifiers: LCCN 2017039672 (print) | LCCN 2017049776 (ebook) | ISBN 9780062645203 (EBook) | ISBN 9780062645173 (hardcover) | ISBN 9780062645180 (softcover)
Subjects: LCSH: Korean War, 1950-1953--Fiction. | GSAFD: Historical fiction. | Love stories. | War stories.
Classification: LCC PS3611.I45295 (ebook) | LCC PS3611.I45295 I35 2018 (print) | DDC 813/.6--dc23
LC record available at https://lccn.loc.gov/2017039672

18 19 20 21 22   LSC   10 9 8 7 6 5 4 3 2 1

사랑하는 엄마와 아빠에게 이 책을 바칩니다

And for my sister, Diana

I the self
longing for cloud
the earth
and man
stand dreamily
like haze
on my eyelids from where
the war has scattered

—Chon Pong-gon, "Hope"

IF
YOU
LEAVE
ME

Part I

Haemi

1951

KYUNGHWAN AND I MET WHERE THE FARM FIELDS ENDED and our refugee village began. I waited until my little brother was asleep, until I could count seven seconds between his uneasy inhales. I listened as Hyunki's breath struggled through the thick scum in his lungs. If he coughed, I'd stay and take care of him. On those nights, I imagined Kyunghwan waiting for me by the lamppost with cigarette butts scattered in a halo around his feet.

Everyone in our village whispered what they wanted to believe: the war would end and we would return to our real homes soon. Mother and the other aunties chattered in the market. They had survived thirty-five years of Japanese rule and the Second World War. They had withstood the division of our Korea by foreign men. What was a little fighting among our own compared to past misfortune? *We can stitch ourselves back together,* Mother said. I believed her.

When Hyunki's breathing was steady and slow, I slipped out through the kitchen entrance and went in search of Kyunghwan. He and I were celebrating. We celebrated every night.

❀

A year ago, when the 6-2-5 war between the North and South began, everyone in my country fled, propelled by confusion and news in the form of unexpected sounds—bullets, airplanes, the cries of the dying.

The mothers, daughters, elders, and children of my hometown stampeded south, hitching ourselves onto trains, scrabbling up mountains, wading through paddies, and treading rivers. Mother, Hyunki, and I wore white and carried loads on our backs and on our heads. We walked until we reached the southeasternmost tip of our peninsula, where shelters gathered around markets and landmarks to form crude villages. All along the coast, people I knew from childhood lived crammed up against strangers. Most settled in the center of Busan, where houses and churches and schools and salvaged structures packed the streets. Refugees thronged together as tight as bean sprouts, as if closeness and the East Sea equaled protection.

Mother separated us from the others, planting us farther out in the fields, away from the ocean and its currents. She said it was foolish to live so close together. "They'll be killed clean in one day if the Reds come. Swept into the sea like a pile of dead fish."

She often spoke of luck and what happened in its absence. We were lucky to have been among the first wave of refugees. We were lucky her great-uncle had died soon after our arrival, so we could claim his straw-roofed home as our own. It was small and timeworn, but less fortunate families sheltered beneath scraps of steel. We were lucky the others, displaced and adrift, had not dared to crowd us out—and lucky to have found this place where life persisted, where news of fighting arrived on leaflets but didn't yet invade our days.

I felt lucky for nothing except my nightly distractions—for Kyunghwan, whom I had known since childhood, and his desire to erase my fears, and our secret hours together.

I arrived through the field to find Kyunghwan waiting. He blew a stream of smoke in my direction, and the clouds curled toward me, hazy and warm. I breathed in their bitter scent. "What took so long?" he asked.

"Hyunki's sick again." I grabbed the cigarette from his lips. "It took him a while to fall asleep."

He nodded at the hanbok I wore. "You still want to go?"

"Would I chance coming out here for no reason?" I blew a smoke ring in the dim glow of the lamppost. His gaze lingered on my long wraparound skirt and short jacket top. I shrugged. "I don't want to wear the men's pants anymore. We'll be careful."

"I don't know." He stared at the road connecting our market to the other makeshift villages. "What if someone catches us?"

"No one will hear us if we're quiet." I started toward his bicycle, partially hidden behind the thick barley. "Let's go."

"We'll head east," he said, catching up to me. "Found some extra money this time."

"Can we buy food? I'm so hungry I sucked on one of Hyunki's tree roots today."

Kyunghwan held the bicycle steady as I scooted onto the handlebars. "We'll see."

I didn't care where we went, if we only cycled around in the open air. But Kyunghwan liked to hunt for the hideaway bars rumored about among the men. These establishments moved from alley to alley, avoiding detection. Even when we found one, they rarely allowed two sixteen-year-olds like us in—so we'd beg drunkards and homebrewers to pity us a bowlful of makgeolli. We'd drink in fields and forests and behind buildings. On lucky nights, we'd find a bar and pretend we were wounded orphans.

As the dirt road raced toward us, I closed my eyes and listened to Kyunghwan's steady breathing. "I've got you," he whispered whenever he felt me tense. But when we were drunk and cycling back, I'd loosen and stare at the black sky, my hair whipping into his face—and he'd tell me to straighten up, that we'd fall into a ditch one day.

In the next village, everything looked the same as in our own. Mud and grass-built quarters, an open road where a market assembled every morning, scrap-metal shelters scrounged together from what people could find. "We'll cover the bicycle here and walk," Kyunghwan whispered as we reached a standing tree.

At the first hideaway, the men joked that I was a poor man's whore and refused us entry. Eventually, we found a narrow shack made of wooden planks and blankets cramped into a back alley. Kyunghwan wrapped his arm around my shoulders. When a man tried to stop us, I touched Kyunghwan's cheek the way I thought a lover might.

"I got drafted. This is our last night together," he said.

The man let us in with a warning. "Don't bring attention to yourselves."

A few men looked up as we ducked under the blanket entrance. The makeshift bar was composed of makeshift objects. Upended tin drums were packed tightly together to form tables. A plank bolstered by metal dowels acted as a serving area at one end. Crates, bricks, and the ground were used as seats. We wove through the unwashed bodies to a corner spot with two crates. I tried not to look at the others, to feel the heat of their gazes. I hoped it was too dim or too late in the night for them to care that I was a girl.

Once we were seated, it was too dark to make out Kyunghwan's face. I could see only the shadow of his thick, straight nose and thin lips. I liked it this way. I knew him already—the smooth arc of his forehead, the turn of his wrists, the freckles along his right arm and how, when traced to his elbow, they formed an ocean's wave. His face was beautiful when he wasn't using it to charm others. He tilted his head toward the lone candle burning in the center of the room and closed his eyes; he knew me, too.

We listened to the sound of bowls hitting drums. We sipped cloudy-white makgeolli until our eyes adjusted to the dark, and we talked about the drunks all around us. A lonely grandfather with drawings of women and children lining his table—his family, perhaps. Another man with a jagged scar running across his face. In the flickering candlelight, it shone like a streak of fat.

"What do you think her story is?" Kyunghwan nodded at the only other woman in the bar. She was older and wore a short hanbok top that exposed her breasts. I watched Kyunghwan's gaze sweep over her body. Her companion reached out a hand, but I couldn't tell if he meant to touch her or cover her up.

"She's clearly not his mother." I glanced at my own hanbok top, my hidden chest. "She has nice breasts."

"They're saggy."

"Big, though," I said.

Kyunghwan turned back to me with a wide grin. I stood, saying, "I want food. The alcohol's hitting me too fast." I hadn't eaten since morning and knew he probably hadn't, either. We were stupid, wasting money like this, but I didn't care. I placed a hand on his shoulder when he tried to stand. "Stay. Pour us another bowl."

I ordered arrowroot porridge and fried anchovies, a small lick of red pepper paste. The barman squinted at me from across the wooden stand. "Your father know you're here with a man? How old are you?"

"Old enough." I tapped my knuckles against the scrap of wood that separated us and tried to look as if I didn't care.

"You shouldn't be in a place like this."

"I already paid." I jutted out my chin. "The porridge, please?"

He shook his head. "Wait here."

When he returned, I told him, "He's leaving for Seoul. He's drafted."

The man bent over and sank a bottle into a large pot of makgeolli. Milky clouds swirled through pale moony liquid. After he filled the bottle, he wiped it with a brown rag. "Here," he said. "I don't understand this war, this fighting our own."

I dropped the makgeolli on our tin drum and held out a plate piled high with small fried fish. Kyunghwan pinched one by the tail and sucked it down. "Got thirsty on your way back?"

"The barman took pity on us. Can you get the other dish?"

Kyunghwan brought over the porridge and raised his eyebrows. "Who orders mush?"

I shrugged. "Steal more money next time."

"You know what the barman said? To take good care of you tonight." Kyunghwan grinned. "Now I feel bad for lying."

"Me too. We shouldn't joke about that."

He scooted closer. I watched his hands and mouth, how he only smudged a drop of pepper paste onto a spoonful of porridge.

"What if you *are* drafted?" I asked.

"What does it matter?" He sipped, smacked his lips. When he exhaled, I smelled the spice and fish collecting on his tongue. "The man's watching. Let's act like a couple."

I let Kyunghwan feed me an anchovy but made a face when the barman looked away. "That's not what couples do. And what do you mean it doesn't matter?"

He wouldn't answer. I let it go.

We poured each other bowls the formal way, with bowed heads and both hands. We talked in old drunken man accents until our stomachs hurt with laughter. He recalled our hometown and our grade-school teacher, the one with the cluster of moles on his cheek. How we two had been the clever ones, yet only Kyunghwan was ever praised. I asked if he remembered how Teacher Kim had made the girls wash the floors with rags that rubbed the skin from our fingers. Kyunghwan reminded me that even if I hated him, Teacher Kim was dead, so we sipped makgeolli in his honor. We quieted until Kyunghwan no longer liked our wistfulness, until he tried to get me to raise my top like the lady in the corner. We drank until it was hard not to touch each other. Then he answered me.

"It doesn't matter if I get drafted or if I don't show up tomorrow night because you're letting Jisoo court you. He told me."

"That's not true." I pushed my bowl against his, until our rims touched.

"He's my cousin."

"Your fathers are cousins," I said. "And that doesn't make what he says true."

"Don't lie to me."

I had forgotten about Jisoo. I didn't want him in the room with us—not even the mention of him. I looked up. I could use my face to charm, too. "Pour, Kyunghwan."

He sighed and filled my bowl.

They kicked everyone out an hour later, in time for us to scurry home before national curfew. I hated leaving, the sudden plunge back into our lives, but I liked how I felt scraped clean with alcohol, painted over with indifference, until I was a wash of emptiness inside. We stumbled into the street, and I watched the sadness drift out of us. "There it goes," I said, pointing as it floated away into the riven sky.

"What are you talking about?" Kyunghwan tugged my arm. "Get on the bike."

As we raced through Busan's dirt streets, I thought of our hometown. The boys' middle school had stood along its western edge. When we were younger, when boys and girls were still allowed to be friends, Kyunghwan and I spent our free afternoons there. A stone wall enclosed the property, and on one side it cornered around a tree. The tree's roots had broken through the ground, causing the stones to loosen and form a nook. This was where we sat, our backs to the sunken slabs, our feet propped against the trunk, as Kyunghwan taught me what he'd learned that day. After the Second World War, when we were liberated from Japan and students were taught to replace their foreign alphabet with our own Korean, he was the one who showed me. I was no longer allowed to attend class, but we still believed we'd go to college together someday. Until then, Kyunghwan wanted to share all he knew.

Northeast of that school was my real home, waiting for my return. Wild and yellow forsythia bushes grew along the wall that enclosed our property. I remembered the smooth slab of stepping-stone that led to our thatch-roofed hanok. It was just wide enough for four pairs of shoes. I used to place flowers in Father's sandals to rid them of his smell. Above the step, a planked wooden porch ran the length of our home. Even then, Mother had insisted on living apart from the others, if only by half an hour's walk and a few fields. I imagined the structure now. Packed full of Korean and American soldiers, or worse—the Reds, our rooms ransacked and gutted.

"Do you miss home?" I turned on the handlebars to catch a glimpse of Kyunghwan's face.

"Don't wobble." He thrust his head forward, his voice heavy with effort. "And you should dress as a boy next time. I don't like how those men stared."

"They were my father's pants." I kept my head straight and still, watching the texture of black trees on black sky. My hand searched for Kyunghwan's fingers on the handlebars. "I had to wear them when we fled."

"I didn't know." He paused. "Haemi?"

"Keep cycling, Kyunghwan."

I listened to his breath as he pedaled up the hill. It was a habit I'd learned from Hyunki, this concentrating on steady beats of air. Some nights, after a day of watching my little brother ache and Mother hunger, I wanted to wrench the stars from the sky and fling them at our feet. But tonight, soaring through these streets, I imagined reaching for the clouds, swirling them around a stick and licking them down.

"Let's do this even when we go home," I said. "Meet in the night and explore. Do you want to?"

Kyunghwan, quiet and distant, cycled on.

The next morning, in the dirt plot behind our house, Mother stood with her hands over her eyes, her head tilted to the sky. She looked as thin as a mahwang plant. Her body's angles sharpened with each season. Her face, though, held on to its pancake shape—round and almost fluffy in the cheeks. It lent her the guise of youth.

"Don't you say anything," she said from behind her hands, her face still canted to the sun. The washed skirt she was holding hung across her chest, dampening her top.

I continued stretching the wet laundry over our clothesline, smoothing the long sleeves and strings of a worn hanbok jacket. I wished Mother would stop her superstitions.

This strange ritual had begun years ago. That first day, she'd huddled above a large clay pot, massaging red chili powder into the hulls of salted cabbages. I sat beside her, brining radishes. Suddenly, she stood, with those spiced hands covering her eyes. I wondered if she'd go blind from the heat. Even the underbeds of her nails were red. I asked her why she was standing like that, if I should call for help.

"I'm talking to your father," she said.

"He's dead."

Her hand was quick and hard against my face. Some of the chili went up my nose. The burn was fierce, but I didn't dare wipe off the powder until she looked away.

Six years had passed since she began consulting the skies, since Father's death.

Mother cried when she found out. I held Hyunki in my arms and watched her fall to the ground. We were in a different war then—the Pacific War, the Greater East Asia War, the Second World War—the name didn't matter. Only Mother's voice when she'd told me: "Your father is dead." I was ten and old enough to understand only the words.

Father had been conscripted in 1944, to labor in mines for the country that ruled over us. He died somewhere in the hills of Japan a few months before the war ended and we were declared free. His body was never returned to us. Maybe he was blown to nothing in Hiroshima or Nagasaki. Maybe he suffocated under a mass of coals. If only he could have survived another hundred days. If only we could have brought him home. Mother had loved him. "Not all arranged marriages are so lucky," she used to say.

I peeled the laundered skirt from Mother's arms and draped it over the twine, stretching it into its rectangular shape. One of the arm straps connected to the high skirtband needed stitching, and the cotton ties that wrapped it around the body and across the chest had ripped.

I touched her elbow. "I'll sew these once the cotton's dried. Mother, should I leave you?"

"Yes," she said, her hands still covering her eyes.

I walked past the outdoor kitchen and through the rear entrance. In the back of the house, I found Hyunki sitting on the floor of our shared room. I couldn't remember Father's face anymore, but I liked to pretend my brother was him in miniature. Hyunki's curved forehead met large, creased eyes and a nose that bridged and jutted where Mother's and mine flattened. The strangeness of his features made him look too serious for a seven-year-old boy.

He opened his fist to show me the mash of bark and herbs knotted into his kerchief. "This smells bad."

"I know, but you have to breathe it in. Remember what the herbalist said?" As I retied the kerchief around his neck, I heard a rattle in his lungs. "Were you running around?"

He shook his head. "I wasn't!"

"Let me see," I said. "Breathe for me."

He exhaled slowly, and his throat scudded at the end.

I touched his chest. "Hyunki."

"I went to the market really quick. Don't tattle." He pushed the kerchief to his nose. "I'll breathe it in, no complaining."

I opened his mouth. No blood, only mucus.

"I'll tell you a secret if you don't say anything." He scooted closer until his lips brushed my ear. "I saw Jisoo-hyung at the market. He gave me stone candies. I saved some for you." Hyunki rooted around in his pocket and pulled out three white spheres. "He asked if he could come to dinner next week."

"Dinner?" I smoothed Hyunki's sleeping mat with my palm. Jisoo had come for tea before, as if we were Westerners who didn't need matchmakers, but he'd never mentioned what would happen afterward. "He wants to meet with Mother?"

"He said dinner with all of us. Me and you, too."

"Here? What'd you say?"

"I said I don't know. Then he said he'd bring something delicious for us to eat, so I said yes." Hyunki grinned, threw a candy into the air, and caught it.

"Maybe we shouldn't." I gestured to the treats. "You can keep these, but tell him not yet."

"Why?"

I pushed my thumbnail into one of the candies. Hard as stone, pure sugar. "I don't know what it means." Before the war, Mother wouldn't have allowed a boy to enter our home without a matchmaker. All my life, I had watched girls wed without meeting their husbands before the marriage day. Now, our customs seemed to have changed. Kim Hasun, who sold sesame oil in the market, said she wanted to marry a white soldier. There were rumors of wives shedding their clothes with strangers for extra bags of rice. Men and women who had met fleeing south now lived together for warmth, a room, shared comfort. "You wouldn't understand," I said.

"It's free food." Hyunki jabbed my cheek with a candy, rolled it down my shoulder. "Who says no to free food?"

He was right. Only a reckless person would refuse. And I knew Jisoo would come one way or another. He was willful, different from his cousin. "Fine," I said. "He can come."

Hyunki dropped the sweet into my mouth and popped another into his own. "I wonder what he'll bring."

"Next time, don't say yes until you ask me first, all right? A boy asking to eat dinner with us is more serious than you think."

Hyunki cocked his head. "Hyung said we could go to Seoul with him one day."

"You'll say yes to anyone with candy, won't you?" I asked.

He smiled, careful not to laugh himself into a cough.

"Mother's talking to Father again. Go tell her the news and convince her to come inside." I swatted his back and he scampered away.

Hyunki had tried to copy Mother's prayer-talking once. But when Father didn't respond, he cried. I tried to explain that Mother was only pretending. That there was nothing to believe in except for the ground and sky we lived between. He didn't understand.

I watched my family through the open back door. Hyunki placed his palm on Mother's hip until she looked down. He mimicked eating and rubbed his belly. She smiled, shielded her eyes against the sun, and called my name. I pretended I couldn't hear, that some greater sound was filling my ears.

Mother and I shook a sheet of fabric between us that evening. The laundry had dried, stiff and warm with the summer's heat. We lined up the edges and came together. I released my side to her fingers and picked up the dangling corners to fold it again. Once we had a small, neat square, we reached for another sheet.

"Yun Jisoo asked to come to dinner next week," Mother said. I nodded.

"We should formally accept. I can send word to his elder."

"Kyunghwan's father?" I shook my head. "I don't understand. Jisoo's from Seoul, and the fighting could end soon. I don't want this dinner to mean anything."

Mother lifted her chin to the withered barley, the holes in our roof. Her fingers touched mine as we folded the ends together. "You need to help."

"I'll work at the market."

"Selling what?" She swung around, gesturing again to what little we had, then she came close. "Pull."

"I could ask if any of the aunties need help."

We held the sheet tight between us and shook out the ripples and creases, even though we would have to smooth it again with sticks tomorrow. "I scrape bark off trees to get sap for you two," Mother said. "I harvest from barley stalks that don't want to give. Hyunki hoards tree roots as if they were precious meats. You know what I'm saying, Haemi. The dinner is a good sign."

I dropped the sheet and turned away, hating that she spoke the truth. The skies looked yellow and powdery on the days I gave my meager portions to Hyunki. When I lay down, the walls around me changed shape, like melting layers of clay. But we were hungry before the fighting, too. "Jisoo could go back to Seoul in a month if the war ends."

"And if that happens, maybe he'll take you with him as his wife."

"I'm only sixteen." I picked up a shirt. The thought of marriage seemed far off, a part of the world we had left behind. "We don't know him. We've only had tea with him four times."

Mother laid the laundry across a nearby sedge basket and turned me to face her. She touched my hair, the slight waves that swelled with the heat. "I know he's kind from the way he treats Hyunki."

"There are a lot of kind men in the world. Why do you care for this stranger?"

She closed her eyes. I knew she was asking Father for guidance. When she looked at me again, she spoke slowly, as if she could lull me into understanding. "We don't know what's happening with this fighting. If it's true that we'll be able to leave or if we'll be taken over. Yun Jisoo from Seoul? In any other circumstance, someone of his standing wouldn't look at us. We are lucky, Haemi. You're lucky you look like me." Her grimace gave way to a smile. The rare, openmouthed kind that buckled my resistance. "Even with Father's curls," she added, with a laugh.

"I'm prettier," I teased.

She tucked a loose strand into my braid and returned to the laundry. "Then use it for something good. Go inside. I can do the rest."

I left the yard but watched her from beneath the straw eaves. I knew she was right. We were lucky. I imagined the pride and elevation and security that would come from such a fortuitous match. Without turning to me, Mother called out, "Be kind to him. There's no harm in that."

Four nights later, Kyunghwan and I rode homebound, high and soaring. I wanted to touch him, not merely his sharp cheek against my back or his hands gripping the metal handlebars but all the little spaces in between. It was almost midnight, and we cycled through the mist. He'd stolen three bowls of makgeolli, and the alcohol had fuzzed the world around us.

I pulled off my cap and unraveled the bandage that held my braid coiled. I rocked from side to side and felt Kyunghwan try to steady me. "I'm drunk!" I yelled. "I'm drunkest! I don't want to go back to my little house!"

He pulled on my unleashed braid and hissed. "Want them to find us?"

I stared down the road. There were no soldiers, no policemen. "What can they do, anyway?" I asked.

"Force us to enlist, throw us into a prisoner camp, kill us right here." Kyunghwan spoke fast. "Don't pretend you don't know."

I lifted the long pouch that hung around my neck. "We have identification."

"You think they care after curfew? When you're dressed as a boy?" He was right. I already knew. There were rumors of girls snatched from roadsides for the pleasures of men and killed without mercy, without the decency of clothes to cover their bodies.

"Ahn Dongwook got roped by the hands and dragged off to fight while he was walking to the outhouse," Kyunghwan said.

"He was a mean little boy, anyway."

"Haemi."

"*Kyunghwan.*" These horrors occurred in the middle of the day as other refugees watched in hordes. Night offered us no magical protection, and I didn't want fear to control our world. I leaned back on the handlebars. "Don't be cross. Be happy with me."

"Don't be so careless, then. You're not the one who could go to war."

We hadn't seen each other in four nights, and I wanted Kyunghwan here with me, easing into the salty, thick breeze. He wasn't drunk enough. As he spoke, I surveyed the field hospital along the southern shore, where they treated prisoners from the North.

The tents jutted up like rows of slippery gray teeth. We were on a hill. We were safe. We were better off than those prisoners—and I wanted to be kind to the boy I'd known all my life. "Do you remember that Pushkin poem, the one Teacher Kim taught us when we were eight? *Even if life deceives you . . .*"

"Are you listening to me, Haemi? Did you hear what I said?"

The fear in his voice whistled clean through the alcohol.

"What?" I asked. "What were you saying?"

Kyunghwan spoke too fast and held my back so I couldn't turn around. The word *enlisted* stuck.

"You're enlisting?" I turned and pushed against his hands, trying to catch what I had missed. Trying to touch his face, his forehead, where sweat clotted his hair together in spiky clumps.

"Haemi, watch—"

"Are you leaving?"

The bike swerved wide, yanking us apart. My body unlatched from the handlebars and flew through the open air, through the night, into nothingness.

Kyunghwan yelled my name. My voice was silent, nowhere in my throat.

I grasped for the wind.

And then, I hit the ground too soon. A hard thud jolted through me.

"Haemi?"

I opened my eyes to slopes of rolling grass looming above, the sky packed in between. I laughed. "Kyunghwan? You were right. You said we'd fall into a ditch someday and look at us." I tried to sit. "Where are you?"

"Are you hurt?" His voice came from underneath me. I realized I was sprawled on top of him, his knee jerking into my backbone.

Our bodies pressed together like planks. I felt the warmth of him, the muscles of his legs touching mine. I tried to clamber off as heat rose in my chest and my palms grew slick with a sudden sweat.

"You're jabbing me. What are you—? Hold still." He rolled me by the shoulders until we lay side by side. In my father's pants, instead of my usual billowy skirt, my legs felt exposed. We rode together in the night, sat across from each other in fields, and yet, lying down, the small space that separated us felt different. We were too close. I wanted to be closer.

Dirt smeared his forehead. I smelled the smoke trapped in his clothes, whiffs rising in the cramped, heated distance between our bodies. I reached out a hand to wipe his face. He shrugged me off. "I told you not to swing around. Look." He raised his knee until it brushed my hip, and he parted a tear in his pants to show stringy bits of skin curled around a gash. With his knuckle, he smudged a blot of blood into a wave.

"Does it hurt?" I licked my thumb, ready to help.

"It's not too bad." He laid his head on his arm, settling into the ground as if we were always this close to each other. His face was calm, almost distant. I wondered what I looked like, if my eagerness was obvious. I stared up at the stars, hating his easy indifference.

"The curfew siren will go off any second now," I said.

"Do you remember what I was saying about the enlistment?"

"You enlisted?" Fear spread through me, sweeping away any budding resentment. Kyunghwan tried to speak. My voice carried over his. "We shouldn't have joked so much. It snuck into your head."

I could feel it—the unhappiness ruining our night. I followed the hairs of his eyebrows to steady myself. Thick, black, running away to his slender ears. "What if I told you to stay?" I asked.

"I don't know," he said. "Should I stay for you?" The night was brighter than I wanted, the moon casting its glassy, curious light all over us. I could see Kyunghwan clearly. His wide, pleased grin. "What do I get if I stay here for you?"

"I hate you," I said. "You're awful."

"I don't hate you." He pulled at a clump of grass. "But if I go, maybe I'll find myself a pretty nurse."

I shoved his shoulder. He fell onto his back and pointed to all the stars crowding the sky above. "Look how clear it is."

"Kyunghwan?"

His fingers didn't clasp mine when I placed my fist in his palm. He didn't move when I crept toward him. I bridged the space between us until my pant leg touched his. His motionless face drank in the sky. I wanted to pull him close. Instead, I pretended he was in an open field alone. That this was the reason he lay so still, as if I were no longer beside him.

I woke to Kyunghwan clutching my hip, his fingers curled into the fold of my pants. The smeary heat of him surprised me, how comforting it felt. I wanted to push my back against him. Then I noticed the sky. It was nearly sunrise, and we were still in the ditch, in a field where anyone could pass by. The smell of dust and dew rose as I quickly straightened.

I pinched his arm and whispered, "Wake up," until he opened his eyes. "We need to get home."

He stood, scanned the ground and sky. "Shit. How did we fall asleep?"

I stood, too. The ditch only came to our knees. It had seemed higher in the night when we were drunk. I crouched down. "What if someone sees us?"

"No one's out yet. We're close." He pointed, and I saw the outline of my house. "We can go through the fields. If your mother finds you here—or the soldiers—"

"Meet me tomorrow night," I said, turning to him. "I don't want you to go without saying goodbye."

Even in the dark, I saw Kyunghwan's face color. "You didn't hear me right. I'm not leaving."

"What do you mean? You were lying?"

He dragged his knuckles across his eyes. "I never said I was going to enlist. You were talking about—you heard me wrong."

I touched his collar where the dirt had rubbed in. "You're going to stay?"

"Haemi." Kyunghwan cupped my shoulders. "You pretend like you don't know what's happening. You pretend we'll all be fine, like sneaking around couldn't get us killed. It's Jisoo who's enlisting. Not me."

I shook my head. "He would have told me."

"Why? Because you're letting him court you?"

I opened my mouth, but I didn't know how to explain Jisoo to him or even to myself. "Don't talk to me about him."

Kyunghwan weighed my braid in his hand, smoothed the strands that had unraveled as we slept. "Is that why I haven't seen you lately?"

I whipped my braid away. He was so stupid. "Hyunki's sick. He's the only reason."

"It doesn't matter. Let's go."

"No." I pushed against him until his back hit the grassy slope. His knees pressed against my thighs, and his closeness thrilled me. His lips were as red and shriveled as a dried goji berry. I raised my face to his. "Kiss me."

He grabbed my waist and hoisted me out of the ditch. He pulled himself out, too. "Jisoo talks to me about you," he said, already striding toward his bike.

I followed him. "Why won't you do it?"

He stood the bike upright and shined the handlebars with the cuff of his sleeve. "Jisoo's an ass, but he's my elder. He's here because of me, and if it weren't for him, Father and I would be living in a C rations box. Besides, you decided to let him court you."

"If you don't want to kiss me, say so. Don't be such a coward." I knocked over his precious bicycle and searched for something to throw at him. "He's coming for dinner in a few days. Did he tell you that?"

Kyunghwan grabbed my hands. "His parents care about money, class. He's having fun with you."

A fresh gust of anger. "I'm a girl to play with and discard, then?" I tried to push at his chest, but he held on to my wrists.

"That's not what I mean and you know it." His fingers loosened, climbed up my arms. Warm and careful, his rough palms slid along my skin. The raised burn on his lower right heel, the callus in the shape of an acorn's hat. His mouth so close. The tang of his breath against the damp of the morning. I arched closer. When he reached my shoulders, he stopped.

"Get on," he said, and gestured to the bicycle.

I stared at him, then turned and ran toward the fields, as fast and fierce as I could.

He wouldn't follow me.

He was a coward.

He was an idiot.

He was always afraid.

Jisoo

1951

TEACHER SUNG SCRAWLED OUR COUNTRY'S HISTORY ONTO sheets of scrap paper ripped out of used books. Every day, he went on about the 6-2-5 and blamed other countries for cutting us to our knees. "The United States and Soviets in Seoul, 1945." He pointed to a student in the last row. "What came next?" When the student hesitated, Sung picked up his ruling cane and strode toward him.

I slid out the newspaper I'd hidden in my notes. Whoever we blamed, the war was happening all around us, and here we sat doing nothing, huddled inside our makeshift school, a long stretch of tarpaulin hoisted over a wooden frame, as if we were supposed to ignore the world and continue our education.

But my friends were already fighting. I knew them. They would have enlisted from the beginning. As soon as the Korean People's Army invaded Seoul. I imagined what they would say to me. *Your family is missing. You haven't heard from your mother, father, or sister in months, and you, Yun Jisoo, what are you doing? Almost eighteen years old and chasing a girl. Come fight,* they would say.

Soon. Soon I would have a wife and I'd join them.

"Yun Jisoo." Sung knocked his cane into the back of my head. "Share your thoughts with us. What requires so much of your attention?"

Sung had a limp. He tried to disguise it, but his right leg stiff-

ened as the day wore on. It was said that he'd done it to himself
so he wouldn't have to fight in the war. Not only dickless, he was
unimaginative, too.

I held up my newspaper for the other students to see. "I'm thinking about how I should be filling ditches with Northerner KPA
bodies. I'm thinking I should be out there instead of listening to
you go on about what I already know."

He struck me across the left temple. His cane was thick, hard,
and wooden. It made my eyes water. Classmates snickered. I tried
to sneak a look at Kyunghwan, who sat a few rows behind me.
Sung turned my head to face him. "The smarter one can't help you
now. You're done."

"You asked me what I was thinking, sir."

"You think you're clever?" He came so close I could see where
his chinless face met his wide neck. "Typical. A smart-ass that isn't
so smart."

"I never said I was smart." I nodded at his leg. "Just able."

One more blow across the face, and he kicked me out.

Outside the school tent, I massaged my temples and waited for
Kyunghwan. We were on the highest hill of our village, and I
sat along the ledge with the best view. Leaning against a thrash
of trees, I stared down at the mass of shelters, their rusted steel
and moldy cardboard outlines. Villages like ours spread west to
the Nakdong River, north to the mountains, and east to the sea.
Tucked inside Busan's borders, we remained safe.

I watched the pin dots below, a handful of the millions who'd
fled. Their smudged outlines hustled between markets, shacks, and
streets. I imagined my parents and Hyesoo in another makeshift

village, only a few kilometers away, safe and worrying about me. When Kyunghwan, Uncle, and I had first arrived, we searched for them, sifting through conflicting reports of aunts and uncles and cousins who'd survived, been arrested, killed. The news—of Communists massacring civilians, of the government masquerading as Communists massacring civilians, of bombings, rapes— eventually quieted us, and we stopped asking altogether. News from the mouths of strangers was never reliable.

"You're still here," Kyunghwan yelled as he emerged from the tent with his usual saunter and wide grin. "Sung asked when you were leaving for good. He was foul to us all morning because of you."

"Tell him I'm leaving as soon as I can." I moved aside as Kyunghwan sat down with his lunch. "Here come the others." We watched the boys exit in a huddle. They whooped as they saw us and ran over.

"Nice ragging," Youngshik said.

"'You asked me what I was thinking, sir,'" Ilsung mimicked.

Youngshik grabbed him by the neck and wrestled him to the ground. "*Yun Jisoo, I will beat that pride out of you.*"

"We were laughing in the back," Kyunghwan said.

"Yeah, but it was costly. You can't make fun of Sung's leg and get away with it." Ilsung picked himself up. "To the radio man?"

"Go without me," I said. "Call if anything's changed on the stalemate line."

"Kyunghwan?" Ilsung asked.

"I'll stay here." He tossed my lunch at me. "If I leave Jisoo alone, he might try to kill Sung."

The boys headed to the almost-blind man who lived on the other side of the hill. He owned a radio and listened to it every day. We mostly heard static, but sometimes news of battles and casualties came through in bursts. There were never any updates about civilians, though. The announcer wondered aloud about how many were alive, how many had been slaughtered. All useless conjectures.

"You don't want to listen today?" Kyunghwan asked.

"I have things to do. A favor to ask," I said.

"More for us then." Kyunghwan held out a handful of roasted ginkgo nuts. "I got these from Sung's bag."

"Little thief. If you close your eyes, someone will steal your nose—that saying's about you."

Kyunghwan split one open. "Do you want some or not?"

"Sung's going to find out it's you and stop loving your goody ass."

"I'm too slick." He dropped a few nuts in my hand. "He'll blame you before suspecting me."

"True," I said, laughing.

We cracked the green nuts from their white shells. As we ate, Kyunghwan rewrote his morning notes on a new sheet of paper. "Why do you do that every day?" I asked.

"Helps me study." Kyunghwan nodded. "You could do it, too. Stop pretending you're stupid."

"I don't care what Sung thinks."

Kyunghwan shrugged.

"I need your help," I said.

"Let me finish."

He drew little images along the margins to match his notes. A waste of time. What was he studying for? The exams that would transition us from one year to the next at a school for refugees? I took a bite out of his boiled potato as punishment for making me wait. I walked around the yard, almost abandoned him for the radio man. "You ready over there?"

"Done." He slipped the pencil behind his ear.

"I need you to help me find some food after school," I said.

"You're the rich one." Kyunghwan gave a seated bow. "'Oh, thank you, sir, for spending all this money today. Please come back anytime.'"

I flung my empty shells at him. "Hasn't anyone told you we're in a war?'"

Kyunghwan waved his papers at me. I didn't understand how he could care so much about schoolwork and so little about the real world. He hadn't once complained as we fled south, not even when there were only five beans to eat between thirty men, but he hadn't asked any questions, either. Not—why don't we cross the hills instead of the rivers and paddies? Or why don't we wait for Hyesoo and my parents? Instead, he stared at the sky and studied for a high school exam he'd never take. Even when we listened to the radio during lunch, he sat silent as reports came through of the North, China, and the Soviets' aggression.

He reminded me of my mother. How she'd groan when there was any political talk in the house. After we were freed from Japan, Father and I were forced to sit in the courtyard when we wanted to talk about what might happen to our country. As we stared at Mother's garden—the twisted limbs of the pine tree and the bright peonies—Father had argued that this was the beginning of the end. With the general election and a new president in South Korea, he was certain our halves would remain permanently divided. I'd picked up slices of sashimi, white squid and fresh salmon, and eaten them whole, laughing at his fear, naive enough to disagree. But what I remembered most was Mother's humming as she sat in the large sitting room across from us with Hyesoo in her lap. Kyunghwan, with his studying, was just like her.

I looked at him, how complacent he was with his orderly notes and common stealing. It didn't occur to him to venture beyond his own preoccupations. Maybe that was the consequence of growing up an only child—he was the kind of man who cared only about himself.

He arced a pebble into the air. "So why do you need this food?"

"I'm bringing dinner to Lee Haemi's family tonight. I want something special."

"You're putting a lot of work into courting her." Another pebble. "Have you done this before?"

I shook my head. "They're having a hard time finding food. They're a good family." I slung my arm around his shoulder. Haemi was the only aspect of my life that seemed to follow any semblance of order these days. Thinking about her calmed me— her long, thick hair and slow smiles. The low duck of her bent head when her mother poured us tea, and how she made faces at Hyunki when she thought no one was looking. "I want to do something nice for them. Help me. What would impress her?"

Kyunghwan shrugged. "You know her better than I do now." He ate the last remnants of barley rice and dried potato vines in his lunch tin. "I haven't talked to her in years."

"What did she like to eat when she was young?"

He laughed. "Whatever was around. Anything will do." He ran his finger along the corners of his container until the tin gleamed. Then he peered into mine, which was also empty. "Everyone was hungry then and everyone's hungry now. *I'm* starving."

I showed him a few won. "Help me today and I'll give you some bills."

"You'll give it to me anyway. I'm the only cousin you have left."

"That we know of, you dog."

He nodded at the school tent. The others were returning for the afternoon session. They yelled Kyunghwan's name, and he stood.

"Already?" I asked.

"Shortened lunch for all of us because of you," Kyunghwan said. "I'll help you after class."

"I'll wait here," I called after him.

He saluted as he walked to the tent. "I didn't mean what I said about the cousins!"

"You're still a dog," I yelled back.

I watched the skies as I waited for class to end. Shaded from the summer heat, I pictured my parents and Hyesoo again. They could have fled before Seoul's fall. They could be somewhere in Busan waiting for the end. It was possible.

After class, Kyunghwan and I walked through a small knot of trees. I broke a branch and held it like a rifle. "You'll come with," I said. "We'll shoot Reds and force them to surrender. We'll be victors."

He cocked his fingers into a pistol, shot back at me. "Glory whore."

I laughed. "Don't you want to reunite?"

He shrugged. "Sure, I do."

"We have to beat the Reds first. Join the ROK with me."

"What about the killings in Sancheong and Hamyang?" Kyunghwan snipped a leaf off my branch. "They say the ROK killed those civilians for no reason."

I stopped him. "We don't know anything." I looked past the trees, but we were alone. "Even if people are saying that, you shouldn't. And if that happened, then the civilians were probably Reds."

Kyunghwan kept walking. "The fighting will be over before I'm of age, anyway."

I was surprised that he cared. That he was listening at all. He was still an idiot, though, repeating rumors aloud. I caught up with him. "We can fake your age, easy. Don't you want to get out of here?" I gestured at the trees, at this place I hated. The stench of the shit pits behind overflowing outhouses, the thatch-roofed buildings with no electricity, the vendors hawking buckets of water for heartless prices. The pity I felt watching Uncle wade through seawater searching for driftwood to bundle and sell.

"I like this place," Kyunghwan said.

"No one likes being a refugee but you."

"Coming here saved you, also, didn't it?"

It was true. I had missed the KPA's invasion of Seoul by less than a month, but it had split me from the world I knew. "I'm enlisting," I said.

"Then why are we hiding from the recruiting convoys? Why don't you let them cart you off now?" Kyunghwan pushed aside the tree's branches and gestured at the streets beyond.

"I want to do it right," I said, ducking until he let go.

"What does that mean?"

A legal marriage, money set aside for Uncle. Only then did I want a proper enlistment. I wanted a wife and a family that would wait for me through the war. How did Kyunghwan, so smart in his studies, not understand this?

"Soon," I said.

Kyunghwan sighed, pointed to the open-air market beyond the last group of trees. Haggling voices rang through to us. He stooped to pluck some flowers and signaled that I should do the same. "Come on then."

We bowed deep and low at the first stall. The local vendors were wary of me, as if my laced shoes and neater clothes meant I was a swindler, and those passing through tried to flip me for more than an item's worth. But Kyunghwan was beloved. The few women from his hometown clung to him, eager to see a face from their past. They carried his childhood stories like stones in their pockets, passed between hands and mouths. Little Kyunghwan would cry for hours, they recalled to their new neighbors. He would sit in front of whoever was responsible for him that day and weep until his father returned. The chopped wood left behind as payment would soak with his tears until they turned into bloated and useless logs. Kyunghwan had won their loyalty by being a weepy, motherless kid, and he culled their memories to suit him.

"Auntie," Kyunghwan said, holding out a flower, "this is my cousin, Yun Jisoo."

"I know who he is." The woman kneaded a small ball of dough. "What do you boys want?"

"He has a request." Kyunghwan nodded to me.

I nodded back. He was supposed to ask, to sweeten them with his familiarity and pretty face.

She rested her elbows against the high wooden table. "Well?"

"It's your request, Jisoo." Kyunghwan bent a flower stem. "Ask her."

"I'm looking to buy a meal for four. No trading—I'll pay money." I showed her my bills.

She clucked her tongue and whispered something to Kyunghwan. Knuckling her dough again, she said, "Money doesn't create food, you know."

"He doesn't know any better. They aren't taught modesty where he comes from," Kyunghwan said.

The woman laughed, looked me up and down. "The only thing I have is relief aid flour. I can make you some noodles, but that's all I can offer." She signaled to the vendor one stall over, a man with a thick scar across his face. "He's selling dried fish. You could have a decent dinner with that."

"I'm only here for today. If you want anything, I'd take it now," the man said, slicing tentacles off a dried squid.

"That sounds perfect." Kyunghwan pinched the dough and tasted it.

"I don't think Haemi would be impressed with that," I said.

"What are you talking about? It's *food*," Kyunghwan responded.

"Lee Haemi? This is for the Lees?" The woman peered at me. "I wouldn't have thought you'd get matched with her."

The suspicion on Auntie's face annoyed me, even if she was right. A year ago, considering a girl like Haemi wouldn't have occurred to me. But here, Haemi spoke like someone with an education. And while others carried their desperation around like an extra limb, she seemed to float above it. She had a wide, pale face that was somehow both graceful and sharp—and when her eyes met mine behind her mother's back, it unnerved me. "That's why I need something delicious, Auntie. To represent my Yun family."

"Haemi's a sassy girl." Auntie wiped her face with a rag tucked into the band of her pants and turned to Kyunghwan. "I remember you two kids begging for peaches in the summertime."

He played with the tacky dough between his fingers and laughed. "You used to give us the sweetest ones. We'll take the noodles, Auntie."

"Not yet." I knocked his elbow. "I want to keep looking."

"You interested in this?" The dried fish vendor held up a squid head. "Also have these here." A small pile of anchovies covered in salt lay on the wooden board behind him.

"We'll come back if we need to," I said.

"I'm leaving in an hour." He bit into a squid leg and beckoned at Kyunghwan with his knife. "I've seen you before."

"In the market, Uncle?"

"You live in the next village over? You wander around at night with the drunks?"

Kyunghwan shook his head. "I live here, Uncle."

"You'd remember a face like this," the man said, pointing.

Kyunghwan bugged his eyes at me with a smirk. He slid a flower to the man, another to Auntie. "Thank you. I'm sorry my cousin's so picky."

I shoved him once we were far enough away. "You're being a jerk."

"I'm helping you like I said. That man was crazy, wasn't he? Where do you think he got that scar?" Kyunghwan walked ahead, gifting flowers to the aunties as we passed. They cooed his name in sentimental tones. It was disgusting.

I shoved him again. "Try harder. Pick a good stall this time."

He looked at me, annoyance on his face, his nostrils flaring. "If I knew it'd be this much work, I wouldn't have said yes."

I counted out three bills and slapped them into his hand. "You have a test tomorrow I don't know about? You on your period?"

A small smile. "I've been bleeding all week." He folded the bills and slid them into his pocket. "All right, I'm a jerk. Let's try this one. She knew my mother."

We went to all the aunties he recognized, from wooden stalls to mats on the ground displaying meager piles of vegetables. The market was emptier than usual. Most of the vendors had gone to the water supply station, and those who remained had barely any-thing to sell. Straw shoes, limp carrots and squashes, a palm-sized square of rice cake. But we became better at asking until finally, miraculously, we found a young chicken for sale. Auntie Bae had caught it in a dead man's yard that morning. She offered to cook the bird into a soup that'd be ready in a few hours.

Kyunghwan and I walked home chewing on strips of cornhusk. We stopped in the kitchen between our rooms and squatted against the stove. Constipated groans came from the outhouse behind us. We laughed.

"You think that's Uncle?" I asked.

Kyunghwan shook his head and pointed at a hole in the wall. We could see Uncle in the room he shared with Kyunghwan. He was wrapping rope around the back carrier he used to haul firewood.

"I should go in and see how he's doing," Kyunghwan said.

"Thanks for today."

He nodded, and then asked, "What does this mean? Don't you need to wait for your parents' approval?"

I looked at him, surprised. I would marry Haemi. Focusing on this goal steadied me, but it wasn't worth articulating for Kyung-hwan. He thought ahead to the next day and no further. I saw his future clearly. He would become one of those college students who married by accident.

"She's real good-looking, don't you think?" I joked.

Kyunghwan smiled. "She's smart, too. Stubborn, though, if she's anything like she used to be." He whipped me with his soggy strip of husk. "I have to study. Enjoy your chicken."

"Haemi will."

He pretended to kick me from his door. "Lucky bastard."

———

The fields that surrounded the Lees' home appeared hopeful from a distance. Flooded with amber light, the barley swayed in the wind. On closer inspection, it was clear how brittle the stalks were, and how slight the house with its cracked mud walls and ragged straw roof, its splintering wooden beams and poles. No gate guarded the property. Everything in Busan was made of shit. Even the rooms I had secured for Uncle and Kyunghwan weren't much better, though they weren't as pitiful as the corrugated metal shacks littering the streets, crammed with too many families.

I'd come for Haemi after the war. We would find my family and live together in a proper hanok home. We would return to a life with ondol floors, tutors, imported toothpaste, and white rice. We'd help Kyunghwan and Uncle settle in Seoul, too.

"Hello?" I set the jar of chicken soup on the ground between my feet. "Auntie Lee?"

Haemi came to the door. She wiped her hands on a washcloth and looked at me with that tilted head. I wanted to know what she was thinking. I could tell she was the kind of girl who evaluated before giving consent, and that she didn't yet approve of me. I liked that. I would prove my worth.

"The view's pretty here, isn't it?" She gestured at the sky, which had turned red and orange with dusk, then pointed to a small figure cutting a path through the fields. "Mother's coming. We'll wait."

"You think I'd enter your house without your mother present?"

"Who knows with you? You could be bringing meals to all the girls in Busan, for all I know."

I laughed. Haemi had arched eyes and a sly, skeptical mouth. I liked how curved her face became when she smiled.

This meal would do it. I would win her.

"Is that Jisoo-hyung?" Hyunki skipped past Haemi. "Jisoo-hyung! My friend is here!"

"Oh, he's your friend now?" Haemi teased.

Ignoring her, Hyunki ran to my side. "What'd you bring for us?"

"Don't be rude," Haemi said.

"It's all right." I picked up the jar and removed the cloth cover so Hyunki could see. Red, bloated jujubes floated around a perfectly boiled chicken.

"Chicken?" Haemi asked. "You bought a chicken? How?"

"This is the best thing I have ever seen!" Hyunki yelled. "The best thing I will ever eat!"

Haemi edged closer and sniffed the center of the jar. "You're really showing off, aren't you?"

"Impressed?" I asked.

She returned to the door.

I couldn't tell if she was happy—or if she had been expecting even more. "Do you like it?"

"*I* like it." Hyunki jumped in place. His shirt was too long and stained around the neck. He was small for his seven years. "Haemi-nuna likes sucking on the bones."

"Everyone likes samgyetang." Haemi straightened as her mother reached us, already shouting.

"Look at that fat chicken!" Auntie Lee took the jar and eyed her daughter. "Come in, come in! Haemi could have let you wait in the shade, at least."

In the entrance room, I bowed formally. "It's nice to see you again, Auntie."

"Call me Mother."

"Don't," Haemi said.

Auntie cradled the jar. "My daughter's embarrassed. Let me

prepare the barley rice. You two keep Jisoo from running away."
She walked past a strung-up blanket that separated the entrance
and small sitting room from the rest of the house.

On my earlier visits, I'd never been allowed beyond the front
door. I'd waited at the low table outside while Auntie brought us
tea. The sitting room was spare, more miserable than I'd expected.
The hanji paper had been ripped off the walls and windows, revealing bare clay and open frames. But I appreciated their effort to make
it a home. A bowl of dried flowers decorated a small desk. Straw
floor cushions were piled neatly in a corner. The open windows
brought in a soft breeze. I smiled. "A real home. You're lucky."

Hyunki pretended to lift something heavy from the ground.
"I'm going to eat this chicken and grow strong."

"Are you going to share with the rest of us?" Haemi asked.

"Nah." He poked her stomach. After a moment, he decided to
poke mine, too. "Are you my brother now?"

I spun Hyunki around. "Maybe if your nuna's lucky. Or is it
maybe if I'm lucky?"

Haemi grabbed his legs. "Put him down. He's not feeling well
today."

"I'm fine!" Hyunki reached for the ceiling. "Lift me higher?"

"Just once, before your nuna gets too mad." I threw him into
the air.

"I'm serious, Jisoo. Stop it or leave."

I set him down, surprised by her anger. She pulled Hyunki behind the blanket partition. They whispered together. I couldn't
hear their words. He bowed to me when he reemerged. "I'm sorry,
Hyung."

"You don't need to apologize." I turned to Haemi. "What's
wrong?"

She squeezed her braid between two fingers. "I told you he didn't feel well."

Hyunki rubbed his face against her hip. "Mother said chicken's good when you're sick, so I get the biggest serving. Right?"

"Always." She hugged him, and the image made me soften. I could picture her as a mother.

"You can have a whole drumstick, Hyunki," I said.

Swinging his sister's hand, he smiled at me. "You should bring us chicken all the time."

I laughed. "I'll try."

"Let's sit." Haemi gestured to the low table in front of the house. "It's nicer to eat out there."

As we waited outside, Hyunki unrolled a large rush mat and asked if I was comfortable before I had even found my seat. He slipped a knot of straw under the table's rickety leg, tested its steadiness with a grim look on his face.

"Looks like he's courting you," Haemi whispered.

When he finally sat, a quick throat clearing turned into a loud heaving, and his tiny body curved over until his head touched the ground. Haemi caught him in her lap, stroking his back and whispering as spasms rattled through him. The coughing sounded like more than a cold. "What's wrong with him?" I asked.

"Can you get some water?" She pointed to a jar beside the front door. A hollowed-out half gourd hung from a nail on the wall. I dipped it into the shallow supply of water and brought it to her.

Once Hyunki finished drinking, Haemi held a strip of cloth against his mouth. "Breathe slowly and spit it all out," she said. Each hack brought up thick green mucus, some tinged with red.

"Is that blood?"

She shielded him with her shoulder. "You shouldn't have swung him around so much. I'm going to lay him down until Mother's ready."

"No!" Hyunki wriggled in her arms. "I want to stay and talk to Hyung."

"I'll take you. How about that?" I glanced at Haemi. "Is that all right?"

She touched my wrist. "Be gentle."

"I will." I picked him up. "I'm sorry."

Inside, Haemi swept the first blanket curtain aside. They had partitioned the rest of the small house into chambers using cardboard and more blankets. Haemi guided me to the only real room in the back. "Put him in here. I'll tell Mother he's not feeling well," she said.

In the room, I laid Hyunki down as carefully as I could on a thick sleeping mat. I felt his bones, the sweat on his neck and legs. "I'm sorry I threw you around like that."

"I'm sorry I'm sick." He picked up a knotted handkerchief and held it to his face. "I wanted to play."

"We can play when you're feeling better. After the war, you can meet my little sister in Seoul. Hyesoo's younger, but she likes games, too."

"I could teach her how to spin tops." Hyunki rubbed his face into his pillow. "Wake me when the chicken's ready?"

I fingered the handkerchief he held under his nose. Herbs, roots, and twigs. "How long have you been sick?"

"I don't know." He squeezed my hand. "Will you stay with me?"

I looked around the room. There was no furniture, yet the space felt cramped and messy, with scraps of twine littering the floor.

Haemi's hanboks were stuffed into a corner. "Does your nuna sleep here with you?" I asked.

Hyunki nodded.

"I should go back outside. They're waiting, but I'll wake you soon." I found a cornhusk doll and laid it by his head. "You should rest."

Outside, I found Haemi arranging wooden chopsticks on the table. Her curved spine pressed against the fabric of her white top. I stared at the round knobs of bone aligned in a row. They seemed too sharp and distinct for her small body, as if her skeleton were stretching through her skin. I wanted to press each bone back in. I wanted to bring her all the food I could find.

I shuffled by the door until she straightened. "Hyunki's napping now," I said. "Is he getting medicine?"

"We're taking care of him. We spoke to an herbalist."

"Medicine from a real doctor," I said.

"Where would we find one of those?" She fiddled with a chopstick. "You can sit."

I walked toward her. "You could try the field hospital."

"Get past the guards and then what? Speak to the Americans? Swing my hands around until they understand what I'm saying?" Haemi's shoulders stiffened around her pale neck. "The barley rice is almost ready. We can eat without Hyunki and save his portion."

"I said I'd wake him."

She looked at me, her chin jutting with annoyance. "I know how to take care of him, all right? We're going to let him sleep. Sit down, please."

"You're upset," I said.

"You didn't listen to me." She gestured to the cushion across from her. I sat next to her anyway. "What are you doing? Go sit over there."

"I'll behave." I smiled. "I'm a gentleman."

She moved to the other side, but it seemed her resistance was waning. A small smile tugged at her lips. I pulled the sweet potato I had saved from my pocket. "I brought this for you. Your favorite."

"Who told you that?" She tried to sound angry as she grabbed the treat.

"You. When I came for tea last week. You said if you had to eat one thing for the rest of your life, it'd be sweet potatoes."

Haemi bit into the yellow flesh, hunched and eager. I touched her shoulder, for the first time, and she smiled. She was tiny, nearly as frail as Hyunki. It affirmed what I had felt upon first meeting her—that she was a girl I wanted to care for.

"Slow down. I can get you all the sweet potatoes you want," I said.

She raised her eyebrows, gave a mock bow. "Show-off." Then she held out the treat, offering me a share.

Once the meal began, Haemi's mother ate loudly and hurriedly. She asked questions while chewing openmouthed, slivers of jujubes mashed against the molars she still had. Haemi was quiet, though. She concentrated on the chicken, shredding each portion with precision. She didn't suck on any bones.

"My daughter tells me you know a lot about the war," Auntie said.

"I try to stay informed, but it's hard to say what's really happening. The radios only tell us so much," I said.

Auntie spooned barley into her soup. "I think those radio men speak a different language from us. I never understand what they're saying."

Haemi raised her head, her face warm with color. "I heard the United States is talking about a truce."

I tried to nod at them both, to even out my attention. "There are talks in Kaesong, but I don't think a truce will happen."

"Pessimist." Haemi squinted at me. "Let us believe what we want." Her braid fell across her shoulder as she picked at a side dish of soybeans. She jerked her arm away from her mother. A secret pinch, maybe.

"I'm an optimist," I said, smoothing an imaginary knot on their wooden table. "That's why I'm here courting you in the middle of a war. Family and future over fighting. We don't even need match-makers."

"That's because they're all dead."

Auntie slapped the table. "Haemi—"

"You're eating without me?" A little voice.

We turned toward the door, where Hyunki stood with the herb handkerchief still against his nose.

"Come join, now that you've rested," Auntie said.

"You promised to wake me." He stamped his feet. "I wanted to eat with you all."

"We saved you the biggest piece." Haemi rose from her seat. "Guess who gets a whole drumstick?"

"But you didn't wake me."

She wrapped her arm around his shoulder. "You'll turn into a statue with all that anger." She tickled his neck until he loosened. "Come eat with us now."

It surprised me, how easily a child's temper could change. He walked to the kitchen on his tiptoes, talking about the chicken. Haemi followed.

"I'm sorry about the difficult behavior tonight," Auntie said once we were alone.

"Haemi's a good older sister," I said.

Auntie touched my elbow from across the table. "You treat Hyunki right, and Haemi will follow."

I separated the rest of my money into stacks the next morning. If we were careful, the bills would last a few more months. I should have paid better attention last year, when Father had given me too much for one summer. It was frivolous, even for him. "Go take care of our wayward family," he'd said. Kyunghwan had moved out of their home, leaving Uncle alone, and I was supposed to reunite them. I'd accepted the money without a thought. We had heard about the border skirmishes by then, and Father suspected danger with an intuition even our own ROK had lacked. And I, eager to see my younger cousin for the summer, had left without thinking.

I added three extra bills to leave behind. Without me here, Kyunghwan would steal from Uncle. For myself, I counted out enough for the medicine and a week's worth of travel. The thin paper of the won felt weightless in my hand, insubstantial. I understood what the auntie in the marketplace had meant—money guaranteed nothing.

I found Kyunghwan facedown on his sleeping mat in the room he shared with Uncle, the stink of makgeolli in the air. "We're going to be late. Wake up," I said.

Kyunghwan rolled over and groaned. "I feel awful." He pinched the sides of his nose.

"Where'd you get the alcohol?"

He nodded at the wooden planks separating his sleeping area from Uncle's. "Go look. I'll be ready in five minutes."

Emptied bowls cluttered the floor on the other side. Uncle slept around the mess. He was a small brown man with drool crusting his lips.

Before I left, Father had told me his cousin was a drunk. That he was the kind of man who would rather piss in his rice bowl than leave his alcohol. Father had been wrong. Uncle had changed in a different way. He had become the kind of man who couldn't see beyond the hour, who didn't believe there was a point.

"Let's go!" Kyunghwan called from outside. "The sun's killing me."

"Piece of crap wall." Uncle covered his head with his arms and turned over.

I nested the bowls, pulled a blanket over Uncle's shoulders, and left the money at his side.

As we walked to school together, I imagined what Kyunghwan would say. That I was rushing into an uneven match. Or that I was trying too hard. I could ask her mother and she'd approve. But I wanted Haemi to say yes. I wanted her to see that I could help her and her family.

"So." Kyunghwan held his hand above his eyes and squinted into the light. "How was dinner?"

"They loved the chicken. I'll find something hearty for us to eat, too."

"That'd be good. Father's getting frail. I think he might be staging a hunger strike." He elbowed me until I chuckled with him. "We're all staging hunger strikes, right?"

"I wanted to ask you about Hyunki," I said, once we were climbing the hill. "He's sicker than I thought."

"He's been like that for a while." Kyunghwan wiped his face on his sleeve. "You and them. What's next?"

"Hold on." I stopped. The school tent stood ten meters away, its walls flapping with the wind. Trees hid us from Teacher Sung's view.

"Don't be late!" Youngshik called as he passed.

"I'm not going to class today." I handed Kyunghwan my note. "Give this to Sung."

He stared at the tent, then back at me. "Don't be stupid. You don't want to end up a one-day officer."

"I'm not enlisting yet. I'll only be gone a few days."

He studied me, trying to concentrate despite his hangover. "Where are you going?"

"To find Hyunki some medicine. Make sure Uncle stays alive while I'm gone, and don't let him drink too much." I offered Kyunghwan a few bills. He ignored them.

"You're doing this for her," he said, using my note for Sung to pick under his fingernail. "You're serious about courting her."

"The kid's really sick." I tucked the bills into his pocket. "Don't steal from Uncle."

"Don't lie to me, Hyung."

"I'm doing it for them both. Why do you care?"

Kyunghwan shrugged. "I don't. I'm going to be late."

I caught the back of his shirt as he turned. "What is it?"

"Get off me."

We walked a few steps like that, me slowing him down, him desperate to pull free. I was stronger than him, though. I pushed him against a tree. His shoulders thudded against the bark and he hit his head harder than I'd intended. I winced at the blow. His face, sallow moments before, mottled red.

"Tell me. What're you upset about?" I asked.

"Get off." He grabbed my arms and, when that didn't work, kicked at me like a child.

I let go, more from surprise than pain, and then a thought—so obvious—came to me. "You're jealous?"

He straightened his shirt, tried to force a laugh. "It's a good idea. The medicine. Must be nice to have the money to go around saving sick kids."

I grabbed his collar. He smelled like a drunk. "Admit it. You're jealous."

Kyunghwan's bloodshot eyes blinked at me. "It's pathetic, how hard you're trying for someone you won't get. Go ahead, good luck." He pulled his collar from my grip and walked toward the school.

"I'm going to win her," I yelled after him. "You don't know anything about her anymore!"

Under the last bit of shade before the entrance, half-shadowed by the long branches, Kyunghwan stared back at me with that same expression on his face—like *I* was the dumb country kid.

Haemi

1951

HYUNKI WAVED HIS STRAW BAG AND PRETENDED TO CATCH invisible dragonflies as we strolled to the market. With him, the walk took twenty minutes instead of ten, but he prized the visits, the chance to leave the house.

"Can I look for Jisoo-hyung when we get there?" he asked. "Watching you trade is boring."

"No wandering away." I hadn't seen the boys in days. Maybe Kyunghwan had finally confessed our nighttime adventures. Maybe they had given up on me. I caught Hyunki by the shoulders and tickled him. "I don't want you to get lost in the crowds."

Hyunki jumped and tried to tickle me back. "Hyung doesn't like me because I'm sick?"

"No, I probably scared him with my crankiness at dinner," I said. "I don't want to see him anyway."

It was true, for both of them. If Jisoo or Kyunghwan was at the market, that's what I would say. *I don't want to see you anymore.*

Hyunki wove from one side of the dirt path to the other, kicking stones. "But Jisoo-hyung's my friend, too."

I hitched the strap of my bag of barley higher on my shoulder. "Too bad. Nuna says no."

He swooped in front of me and pulled my hands through his bag's handles. "Caught you." Then, holding me captive, he led me along the path. "When I'm old, I'm going to boss you around. Come on, cow. This way."

I bellowed like a bull calf. "*Eum-meh.*" Hyunki laughed and copied me.

As we lowed back and forth, a sallow cat slunk past with a mouse gripped in its teeth. I felt closer to that rodent than a cow, caught between Jisoo and Kyunghwan, Hyunki and myself. "If you could boss me around, what would you make me do?" I asked.

"Order you to get meat this time! I'm sick of bones."

"Then you need to stay by my side and look hungry for the butcher," I said.

Hyunki unlooped my hands. "But I *am* hungry." He stared at me, his face lusterless, even in the sunlight.

I touched his high forehead and tried to push aside my guilt. "Always so hungry!" I squeezed his stomach. "Do you have tiny creatures in there eating up your food?"

He laughed, wormed out of my grasp, and skipped ahead. I let him. He drank his ginseng tea without complaint these days and had slept easy for three nights straight. Three nights I could have snuck out but didn't.

"We're almost there." He clutched a tangle of twine that was tied around the lamppost. It marked the beginning of our village, where the marketplace stalls eventually opened into crowds of shelters. An orange strip of fabric woven into the twine slapped in the wind.

The wooden lamppost looked frail and ordinary in the daytime. Bleached by the sun, it blended into the surrounding fields. As I ran my hands across its knots, I noticed that a smattering of cigarette butts, half-hidden by the grass, circled the base. Kyunghwan. He hadn't forgotten about me, then. I hadn't joined him since the night we fell asleep together, but he had still come and waited.

"Help me pick these up," I said.

"Why?" Hyunki pinched a bitten stub. He peered at it with one eye closed, his head cocked.

"Do it for me and I'll try to get you stone candies."

He sniffed one ashy end and then helped without asking more questions. I hugged him for his silence. One of the cigarettes was barely smoked. A few others were stubby, wet licked, tamped down at the ends.

"Ready, Nuna?"

We were done, the ground picked clean.

Hyunki pointed to the market. "Let's go before people leave."

As he walked ahead, I watched his small, round head of hair ruffle in the wind. "Come on," he called, from farther along the path.

I stroked my hip, where Kyunghwan had wound his fingers that night in the ditch. I didn't understand him. He acted jealous of Jisoo, and still he refused me. Embarrassment heated my face and chest. I wanted to slough away the memory of that night. The way Kyunghwan had turned his head—how pitiful I must have looked with my eyes closed. I wouldn't ask him again.

"Nuna?"

I hurried on, wondering if Kyunghwan would be at the market, and if I would show him the proof I had found on the ground.

The market was crowded with vendors from nearby villages and neighbors in search of bargains. Grandmothers in hanboks laid their found aluminum cans, driftwood, and careful mounds of red pepper flakes on large square wrapping cloths. Crouched over their goods, they yelled out the prices in strident, whittled voices. We walked past fish dangling on strings and wove among women carrying children on their hips or wrapped in podaegi slings on their backs. Always, whispers of the war thickened the air.

Auntie Chyu, a seamstress from our old village, called us over to her stall, a wooden plank on two boulders. She handed us small squares of cloth dyed a bright blue. "For a bit of good luck." She held one against Hyunki's shirt. "Doesn't it make you happy to look at color?"

We bowed our thank-yous. Hyunki pointed to Auntie's sons. Three boys kneeled by the roadside with dark bottles and greasy cloths. "Can I help them?" he asked.

"Sangchul," Auntie Chyu called to the eldest, "show Hyunki how you shine shoes." She turned back to me. "I told them no one has leather shoes here, but they want to help." She leaned against the stall and stared into the crowd. A man sat on an overturned bucket selling woven bags. A grandfather advertised battered and fried carrot slices at high prices. "Just yesterday Uncle Han was beaten over there and carted off, and today we're milling around." She clucked. "We can get used to anything."

"Yes, Auntie." I traced the end seam on a swath of red fabric on her table. She spoke to me like I was a friend. It made me shy.

Auntie nodded at a woman breastfeeding an infant while she bartered for anchovies. "You know what she told me?"

I shook my head. I didn't want to hear the latest gossip. It scared me, how easily I clung to the slightest hope of returning home, and how swiftly the rumors proved false. "Do you have any new stories to share instead?"

She stretched her fingers and cleared her throat. I lost myself in the sound of her unbound voice as she told me about her middle son, who dreamed that she had turned into a fox, and upon waking, believed she was a kumiho monster. She laughed openmouthed, without hiding behind her hand. When I was with her, I did this, too. The sharp crack of our laughter turned the heads of those around us.

"Oh, that hurts." She massaged her stomach, still chuckling. She pulled at her laugh lines with two fingers. "What I really wanted to tell you is that new soldiers arrived yesterday. Be careful, especially once it's dark."

I nodded. "Thank you. We should go before it's too late." I called to Hyunki, who stood with one straw shoe held out for the boys to shine.

"What is it you have there?" Auntie pulled the bag's strap off my shoulder and peered at the barley inside. "You have plenty! I know there's going to be more of that for you. Can I get a handful? For a lonely woman and her children? Boys, come over here and beg!"

The three sons and Auntie Chyu offered up their bowled hands.

Hyunki dipped his fist into their curved palms, thinking it was a game.

We found the butcher's stand in the market. His wife snatched my bag before we even bowed. "You two are lucky," she said, evaluating the weight with her hands. "We don't have much to give."

"Leave them alone." The butcher walked around the wooden stand that separated us. His large stomach bounced as he squatted before Hyunki. "My wife's heart grasps when it should try to share. We've got enough for your family."

When we arrived in Busan, the butcher had searched for us. He claimed to have known Father in Japan. I didn't trust him so easily, even if Mother did. She would believe anything about her husband. She still set aside a bowl for Father at every meal, six years later and now in a new war. A few grains of barley, never cooked food we could eat—but still, she was consistent.

"Do you have any meat for us?" Hyunki asked.

The butcher smiled. "I don't think you'll have to worry about that for too long." He glanced at me. "Am I right?"

The wife returned my bag. From the way it rattled, I knew she had given us bones. "Yun Jisoo has been courting you." Her eyes flicked down to my neck and chest and hands before she smiled. "What good news. Your mother is pleased?"

"Where did you hear that, Auntie?" I folded my hands and stared at my knuckles. "Is that what people are saying?"

"What's courting?" Hyunki asked.

"That boy wandered from stall to stall asking for that chicken. He even had his cousin help him," the wife said.

The butcher nodded. "Did you enjoy it, Hyunki?"

"I ate a whole drumstick!" They bent their heads together as Hyunki described the broth, the elaborate meal.

"Yun Kyunghwan helped?" I asked.

She touched my shoulder and leaned in. "That isn't all people are saying. You be careful with yourself. Young people think they can do anything these days. War doesn't mean decency's been killed off, too." Her lips curled into a closemouthed smile. "Think about your mother's shame."

Heat prickled my hands. I tried to tamp down my sudden blush. "I don't know what you mean, Auntie."

"The night's darkness does not make you invisible. You think a poor disguise can hide you?"

"You must be mistaken." I glanced around. It seemed no one else had heard. "We should get back to our mother."

"I'm only telling you what's already being said throughout the stalls. I wouldn't be surprised if some refused to sell to your family now."

"Hyunki," I called. "Let's go."

"Already?" The butcher and Hyunki asked at once, and then laughed.

The wife nodded at her husband. "Time for us to get back to work."

The butcher patted Hyunki's head and my arm. "Come again soon. We'll give you even more next time."

I shook the bag as I slung the straps over my shoulder. I watched the butcher's face, avoiding his hateful wife. "Thank you for the bones."

The fields at the back of our house were dying from heat. Yellow-white barley swayed and bristled in the dry wind. It was the hour before sunset, when reds and oranges and a hazy pink light spilled over the country.

I rolled a cigarette butt in my hand, feeling the tobacco shift inside its slim body. Kyunghwan had helped Jisoo find the chicken. Someone had found out about us and whispered to that wrinkled woman that I was a girl who crept out in the night.

"You have hairy wrists!" I yelled, flinging the butt. "You have no friends! You smell like soot and dog sweat!" I hoped my words would soar through the air and into Kyunghwan's empty head. "I know you stole that bike! I know who you get your money from!"

"Haemi!" Mother yelled from the front of the house, her voice a knife cutting my name in two.

Punishments surfaced and sank in my mind. The backs of my legs beaten. Arms held up to the skies for hours. My hair hacked to the scalp, so anyone I encountered would know I'd shamed my family. I stuffed the remaining cigarettes into my underwear. The butcher's wife had told, or Mother had found out from someone else. The village had turned against us.

Mother came charging, dragging Hyunki by the arm. "Tell me! Why weren't you watching him?" She waved a broken cigarette, still lit but dying. "He was smoking. He said he picked it up on the road to the market."

"He was smoking?"

Hyunki ran to me. "I did it when Haemi-nuna wasn't looking," he said, words muffled by my stomach. "Nuna didn't know."

"I didn't know," I said, my voice a weak echo.

Hyunki turned to Mother. "I'm sorry. I won't do it again." He pushed out his bottom lip and widened his eyes into the pout that made Mother soften. He coughed and buried his face in my skirt again.

She grabbed his shoulder but spoke to me. "You can see the sickness as well as I can. Haul your eyes out from inside your head."

Hyunki twisted under her grasp.

"No more going to the market," she said to him.

"Please! I'm fine."

"I'll watch him better." I tried to pry her hand away. "Mother, I'll watch him."

She stooped to Hyunki, her fingers still clawed around his shoulder. "You think you're healthy enough? Then you get treated like the other boys. I see you at the market or with a cigarette again and you'll be fetching me sticks."

She released him, then squatted and crushed the cigarette beneath a gray stone. There was nothing left, only ash and brown, but she kept grinding anyway. "I'll whip you. You know I will."

Hyunki rubbed his shoulder and avoided my gaze. He hurt so easily these days. I felt the wing bones of his back, how delicate they were. He was weakening, and here I was thinking about a boy.

"It's my fault. I'm sorry." I squatted beside her. "Mother, I'm sorry." I wanted to show her somehow.

"I'm putting him to bed, and then we'll talk," she said.

As they walked inside, I pictured little Hyunki smoking. The cigarette's blistering tip, the coughing that followed.

I had been careless. It was Kyunghwan's fault for making me so curious. I had to be better.

I pulled off my underwear and the hidden remains fell to the ground. I rubbed them all out as Mother had done, until there was nothing left to hold on to, only gray ash in dirt and grass. Kyung-hwan's lips, those chewed-up bits that pressed together when I asked him to kiss me—I rubbed it all away.

Days had passed since the smoking incident, yet Hyunki's cough still flamed through him. Every afternoon during his naps, I searched for enough herbs to grind into a paste. I hiked and scav-enged the hillsides, avoiding the slums, the ROK campouts, and the prostitutes' huts.

As I climbed the tallest hill, I passed the elementary school Hyunki wasn't allowed to attend because of his sickness. Children sat on the grass in neat rows, reciting the alphabet. Farther up, I looked for the boys' high school tent, for a glimpse of Kyunghwan or Jisoo, but I saw no one.

With my hanbok skirt scuffed green and five paltry herbs in

my woven sedge basket, I walked home. I had picked the land clean, and I didn't want Hyunki to wake up alone. But as I returned through the fields, I noticed a figure waiting in the entranceway. Jisoo. He wore a dark, Western-style jacket I'd never seen before. The fabric looked thick, almost shiny. He had a wide smile on his lips.

"Why are you dressed so nicely?" I asked.

"I don't even get a welcome?"

"You haven't been here in more than a week. I forgot about you." I walked into the house. He followed me with that smile still on his face.

"You've noticed I've been gone, at least." He nodded at my basket. "Are those herbs for Hyunki?"

Something about his probing, the satisfied knowing that threaded his words, made me want to lie. I shook my head. "I'm making tea for myself."

He raised a hemp bag. "I brought something for your family."

"I don't want your charity, Jisoo."

I walked toward the kitchen, but he snagged my elbow and pulled me back. His eyes were small but so evenly placed in his broad, square face that it suited him. I remembered why I'd let him walk me home that first time. "I'm here to take care of my cousin," he'd said. Carrying a paper cone of sunflower seeds, he had spat empty shells through the air as if nothing scared him. Even though we were powerless, hungry, and abandoned, he'd acted as if he were in control, as if he'd come to this city of his own wanting.

"Hyung?" Hyunki emerged from the back room and shyly hugged Jisoo's hip. "Where did you go?"

"I went on a little journey, but I'm back now. Are you feeling better?"

Hyunki curved his arms above his head. "I'm a shark. I feel great." He squiggled around the sitting room and pretended to eat us up.

"Don't run around too much," I said. Hyunki had no sense of his own weakness. He spent all his energy in a few hours only to lie limp for days afterward.

He gobbled Jisoo's stomach with his hands. "I don't want to. I rested all day."

Jisoo found a floor cushion. "Why don't you sit with me?" He curved his arms, too. "I'm an even bigger shark and I'm hungry for tiny Hyunki fish unless he sits right here," he growled.

Hyunki laughed. "All right, but first, I have something!" He ran into the back room, calling, "Wait!," and returned with a note. "For you, Nuna."

"For me?" I snatched it quickly. From the way my name was written, the letters all crowded into one another, I knew it was from Kyunghwan.

Jisoo watched us. "What is that?"

"Just a letter." My fingers itched with want. I folded the note as carelessly as I could and flicked it into my basket.

"Hyung came while you were gone." Hyunki sat and leaned his arm on his upright knee, copying Jisoo's pose. "I made sure to keep the letter safe for you."

"He came here?" I asked.

"Who? Which hyung?" Jisoo asked.

"Kyunghwan-hyung," Hyunki said.

"Kyunghwan?" Jisoo studied me. "Why is he writing you?"

"I don't know." I turned to straighten the cushions, but they were already in order. "I have no idea."

"I thought you two didn't talk anymore."

I spun the basket around, watched the letter flutter among the dead herbs. "Sometimes we do. Why does that matter?"

"He steals things."

"You know Kyunghwan-hyung, too?" Hyunki asked.

"Do you two still talk?"

"I can do what I want, Jisoo."

"Then maybe I should leave." He stood and brushed his knees, as if our floor had dirtied his pants. "I don't need to stay here with a liar."

"Leave then." I thrust my head at the door. "You don't get to call me a liar in my own home."

"Why is everyone mad?" Hyunki hugged his knees.

Jisoo grabbed his bag. Hyunki asked again. I strode to the entrance. Right then, the door slid open and Mother appeared.

She walked in with a bundle of wood gathered in her skirt. "Yun Jisoo! We were worried not seeing you for so long. What are you doing here?"

He turned to me. "What *am* I doing here?"

No one spoke. Hyunki watched with his curious, wounded eyes. I wished I were alone—in the ditch, or on the hillside still looking for herbs. Even on the open sea. But I hadn't been allowed the space or time or means to truly be by myself in years, and we were far from home.

"I should go," Jisoo said.

Mother set down the firewood. She stopped him with one hand. "Haemi hasn't even brought you a cup of tea. You can't leave before you're offered a refreshment." She guided Jisoo to the cushion and pricked my side. "Be good, Haemi. Get some tea."

I set down the basket in the outdoor kitchen and rattled items around, pretending to lift pots and search nearly empty sacks.

When I was sure Mother wouldn't follow, I opened the note. Hating him and wanting him, I read Kyunghwan's words:

> *Come tonight, Haemi. I won't wait around anymore. I'll be at the market today, so find me.*
> *I need to see you.*

His command, the sudden assurance in his words, surprised me. I folded the note so I couldn't look. So he couldn't tell me what to do. I didn't know where he fit in my life anymore.

As I stood there, Jisoo's broad, weighty laughter came through the door. Mother laughed, too, and Hyunki's earnest voice tried to climb above theirs.

I thought of the day Jisoo and I had met, a month after my family had arrived in Busan. He'd approached me with such confidence in the center of the market. Like a man who knew how to move through the world. I'd listened to his greeting but hadn't heard him mention Kyunghwan's name, instead focusing on the deep grit of his voice. With each new word, I'd felt myself loosen. A simple, whole sense of release, like how I felt on wash day after Mother's scrubbing—raw and thankful.

I heated a stone pot of barley and water over the fire pit, and I decided.

I wouldn't go.

I wiped down our tea tray, the cups.

I would be good.

As I waited for the water to boil, I watched the summer rays collect in a patch of trees in the distance. I wished I were underneath that cluster, in that small haven of light. A swallow floated from leaf to leaf and I pretended it was Kyunghwan. I would be firm and tell him there would be no more drinking.

The coward. He hadn't even signed his name. *Yun Kyunghwan.* He was clumsy when he drank. Lean and tall and always too quiet. The smell of persimmons, that ripe chalky sweetness, rose from his skin when he stood too close. Handsome. His beauty rooted in his gaze, his focused stare. When he smiled, looser, drowsy, and unassuming, I wanted him near, always.

It seemed the world was moving away from me, as if I were expanding and dissolving all at once. I thought I heard his horselike breathing, the way it turned shallow yet thick when he cycled us uphill—but it was me. I was breathing too fast.

I knocked over a cup.

In its clacking, I again heard Jisoo's laughter. It seemed like a small bit of dust that had come in with the wind, or like the clatter of pheasant bones in a tin can. Why was it that as soon as Kyunghwan came into my mind, Jisoo turned to nothing?

"Nuna?" Hyunki stood at the door, scratching his ankle. "Mother says hurry."

"Get me a pencil."

I wrote on the back of Kyunghwan's letter. "Go to the market and find the hyung who gave this to you."

"I don't want to." Hyunki rocked on his heels. "You're doing something bad. Mother and Jisoo-hyung are mad at you."

"No one's mad." I forced the letter into his grip. The muscles on my cheek twitched. I covered my face. "We're just talking. It's fine now."

"Take this back." He thrust the letter at me, but I clasped my hands around his.

"You got me in trouble before, now do this for me. I'll tell them you have a stomachache, that you're in the outhouse. Walk quickly," I said.

He scrunched his nose. "I didn't mean to get you in trouble."

Sweat rimmed his small, serious face. I parted his damp hair and wiped his forehead. "I'm not angry with you, but I need you to do this for me. Please. The sun's setting soon."

He shrank from me. "I want to stay here."

I smiled, too wide, and tried to breathe cheeriness into my words. "Do this for your nuna and I'll do something nice for you, all right?"

Mother appeared then, arms crossed against her chest. "Why is this taking so long?"

I stooped to the fallen cup. "I'm pouring the tea right now."

"Hyunki?"

He curled his toes into the dirt and glanced my way, the letter tucked behind his back. "I don't feel good. I'm going to the out-house."

As he left, he whispered something to me, but I only saw the new layer of sweat that shone across his big, rectangular forehead. His lips were so pale they seemed invisible, like bellflower roots sunk in water. He was too sick to walk alone.

"I need to check on Hyunki," I said.

"He can go to the outhouse by himself." Mother seized my arm. "Jisoo is a good boy."

I turned to her. "When you say good, you mean rich. What if I don't love him?"

"No one's telling you to love anybody." She released me with a look of agitation. "What do you think will happen to our country? To us? I'm telling you to bring the boy some tea."

She dumped our saved rice cakes into a bowl and turned to leave. At the door, she stopped. "Your father and I—the first time I met him was on marriage day. Affection grows between a woman and a man. You can't expect it from the beginning."

I walked into a room of happiness. Beneath the open window, Jisoo and Mother sat on our best straw cushions. White square packages lay before them on the floor. Mother picked one up and held it far from her chest, as if it was both precious and dangerous. "Jisoo's brought medicine."

"This is why I've been away. The field hospital couldn't help, so I went farther north. These are modern medicines for Hyunki. I took as many treatments as possible. I'm hopeful that one of them will help."

Mother clutched the package. With two fingers, she pulled out a brown tube of liquid, a bottle of pills. She was shaking. Even her bones seemed to tremble. "This will work, Haemi."

I looked at Jisoo, at his assured posture, his open hands, and saw the kindness in him that I'd ignored. My instincts had been right. He took care of those around him. Even though I'd told him to leave, he had given us the medicine. "Thank you." The quiet in my voice shamed me. I cleared my throat. "Thank you so much. Thank you."

"I wanted to do this, for all of you. There's one more thing." He rooted around in his bag. Two wooden objects emerged. "I have some news, too."

They were carved ducks, the outlines of their wings and beaks crudely formed.

"Oh, Jisoo," Mother said.

"Wedding ducks?" I asked.

Jisoo kneeled in front of Mother. He folded his hands into a neat triangle. "I have a proposal."

Mother beckoned to me.

I didn't move. I couldn't.

Mother and Jisoo had always wanted this. I knew, had known all along, and still I'd continued with the courting, willing myself to disbelieve. I thought I would have more time. I thought we were living in an uncertain world, one without rules. But Mother and Jisoo were not reckless. They were not me, blindly groping through the war without expectation.

"Haemi?"

Outside, the whistle of leaves. A sudden mass of thick gray clouds. I thought of the swallow I'd seen flying through the trees. How he had soared, slanting toward the sun.

Kyunghwan

1951

ONE YEAR AGO, HAEMI AND I FOUND EACH OTHER AT THE entrance to our village. I was tying a piece of wrapping cloth to the lamppost out of boredom and fear when I heard her call my name.

"Kyunghwan—is that you?"

I had wanted to touch her, to feel the flesh of her face and confirm she was real. She hadn't been caught by the Reds or taken to the hills on her way south. She was standing before me, safe and whole. The year before we had fled, she'd stopped speaking to me, punishment for some senseless argument, but her anger seemed to dissolve as soon as we saw each other.

She bowed, aware of the searching gazes of strangers. "You're here," she said. When a crowd of new arrivals surrounded us on their way to the market, calling out the names of relatives they hoped to find safe in Busan, she touched my wrist. "No more fighting."

I concentrated on the feel of her fingers. How cool they felt against my pulse. She had changed. I could see the soft humps of her breasts underneath her hanbok jacket. The small, gritty Haemi I'd known all my life had been winnowed into this new person—a woman.

She drew a map in the dirt with the tip of a twig. "As soon as the fighting ends, we'll meet here and go back together. All right?"

"All right." I tried not to smile. She was speaking to me again. She was here.

That night, we snuck away to explore our new village in the moonlight. We stood on a hill and looked south at the jumble of tin-roofed shacks, straw-thatched homes, and brick buildings turned into shelters. Haemi gasped at the mess of muddy alleys, outhouses, walls scribbled with messages—*Looking for Jungsoon from Gang-neung. Little boy Younggi in blue jacket, have you seen? Migyeong, we are with Uncle Kang.* Farther out near the sea, we saw the field hospital, tented and foreign. Haemi leaned her head on my shoulder. We could smell the salt, but she didn't want to go any closer to the water. Afterward, I followed her through the fields to her new home. She walked parallel to the road, never on it, and raised her hem so it wouldn't graze the ground. I think she liked the prickle of grass and barley against her ankles, the feel of the earth on her bare skin.

❦

With a letter for Haemi in my pocket, I looked in on Father. He sat on his side of the room, smoking his long reed pipe. He bit the brass mouthpiece as I entered. "What is it?"

"I'm going to the market, but I've brought you lunch." I set a bowl of millet grains covered in bean sauce on the small square table in front of him.

"What about yours?" he asked.

"I ate already."

He adjusted his glasses and inspected me. The whole shape of him had changed since our march south. He was gaunt of hope and body. Even the glasses Mother had given him years ago slipped down his nose, as if his features had shrunk from the inside out. "You're lying," he said.

"You shared your portion yesterday." I burped to convince him and pushed the bowl until it was directly below his chin.

He dragged his chopsticks through the smeary brown sauce. Thick paste clung to the lines of his knuckles as he dug in. He offered me a bite. I took it.

"How was the water line this morning?" I asked to fill the silence. Father grew quieter with each month. It unnerved me. His life had become a cycle of sleeping, drinking, eating—all alone. On the days he peddled wood at the market, he silently bargained with the villagers, using hand signals.

"Long line, as usual," he said.

"At least it's free."

Father snorted and then clutched his jaw. A back molar had loosened in his mouth, and pain shot through him with any sudden movement. I went to make him a cup of tea.

When I returned, he held a bowl of bartered makgeolli with both hands. "It's too early," I said.

"I'm not collecting wood today." He gestured to the window. "It's going to rain."

I watched his toes as he sipped. He always squeezed them on the first gulp. Mother had loved this habit because of its whimsy, and he'd always kept his feet clean just for her, even now.

He passed me the bowl. I drank with my toes clenched, too. Dirt packed the undersides of my nails, though. He noticed and swatted me. "Wash your feet."

"Do you know when Jisoo's returning?" I asked.

"Jisoo-hyung," Father corrected. "He's your elder." He lay down on his side. His hair, white at the roots, still black at the tips, puffed up on his cylindrical pillow. "He wants to take you to Seoul when the war's over. What do you think about that?"

"Will we go with him?"

"You know where I'm heading."

Father would return to our clutch of earth, to our farm, which was nestled in the rabbit's back of our country. When I was little, he'd traced a rabbit in profile onto the borders of Korea. The tapered ears the northeasternmost point, encroaching on China, the paws jutting out into the Yellow Sea. Seoul tucked safely beneath its belly. We the humped back, and Busan its soft tail.

"We'll go home together. I won't leave you," I said.

"You'll be smart and follow the money." Father turned over. "Wake me in a few hours if there's anything to eat."

It was barely past noon. I covered the hole he used as a window. "I'm staying with you," I said again, but he had already fallen asleep.

I circled the perimeter of Haemi's fields with the note in my hands. I wanted to leave it somewhere for her to find. I'd sneak it onto the doorstep or set it against the front window. Entering the house didn't seem like an option, I don't know why. Maybe I really was a coward.

When confronted with the silent structure, though, I was disappointed. There was no Haemi slipping past or cooking outside. Since reuniting in Busan, I took pleasure in the look of her—a flash of throat as she thrust out her chin at one of my pert comments, her hair brushing my face when she tilted back on the handlebars, her open lips when she sang up to the clouds. Even when she dressed as a boy, her thin legs swishing in her father's old pants, I watched her.

I sat on a rush mat in the yard behind her house and turned my words over in my head, in my mouth, really. I conducted imaginary conversations and sifted through the meaning of my letter. I had rewritten it three times—first mean, then apologetic, and then as simply as I could.

A head poked through the window beside me. Hyunki waved. "Hi. What are you doing here?"

"Looking for your nuna. Are you home alone?" I asked.

"Wait for me." He disappeared into the room and resurfaced at the back door, still in his bedclothes. They were green, and his neckline was stained with saliva. He lay beside me and rested his head in my lap. "I don't feel good. Do I have a fever?"

I touched his forehead. He was warm and sticky, his sweat dampening my pant leg. I didn't know what a fever felt like on a kid. "I'm not sure," I said. "I think so."

He peered up at me. "What kind of adult are you?"

"I'm not an adult."

He mulled that over, rolling his head until his nose touched my knee, as if that would tell him something new. "Do this." He lifted my hand and motioned for me to brush his hair.

"I'm Yun Kyunghwan," I said. "From your hometown."

"I'm Lee Hyunki. I'm seven years old."

"I know." I laughed. "We've met before." I brushed his hair. He didn't look much like Haemi, but they had the same funny hairline. It peaked at the temples like mountains. I wondered if this was what Jisoo did when he visited—act like a big brother to Hyunki. Jisoo was less than two years older than me, but he was the sort of adult Haemi and her mother could trust.

"I want to go back to my room," Hyunki said. "Will you carry me?"

I gathered him in my arms. He was so light I almost hoped

Jisoo would hurry back with the medicine. Hyunki rubbed his face against my shoulder and directed me through the back door. When he closed his eyes, I shook him. "Are you all right? What should I do?"

"I'm tired. Inside, on the right."

Haemi's belongings were scattered throughout the small room they shared. The palm-length strips of twine she used to hold her braid were strewn across the floor. On our rides home, I'd graze my finger against their roughness. In a corner, there was a rumple of blankets, and a set of clothes—her bedclothes maybe—lay on top. Hyunki's side of the room was immaculate, everything folded into piles.

"You're neat." I jostled him in my arms. "Hey, stay awake."

He shook his head. "Nuna cleans for me."

"Why doesn't she tidy her things, too?"

"Mother gets mad and Nuna thinks it's funny." I set him down, and Hyunki crawled onto his sleeping mat and dragged a sheet over himself. He coughed hard. His face looked paler, his features larger than they'd seemed moments ago.

"Should I find someone?"

Lying on his stomach, he patted the space beside him, where I imagined Haemi sat on the nights she wouldn't come to me. "I'm going to sleep and then you can leave. Can I hold your hand?"

I cupped his fingers as best I could. "I know you," I said. "I grew up with your nuna. I met you when you were a little baby." I touched his shoulder. "Hyunki?"

He pushed his cheek into his pillow, crunching the buckwheat husks inside. "I'm sleepy."

"Does she talk about me? Have you heard my name—Kyunghwan?"

"I'm tired, Hyung."

"Will you give her this letter, then?"

He blinked a few times, staving off the lure of sleep. "Why don't you give it to her yourself?"

"I have to go. Make sure she gets it, all right? As soon as you see her. It's important."

"I promise." Hyunki slipped the note under his pillow. Seriousness suited his face. It made the boniness seem a natural part of him. "Once I fall asleep, you can leave. That's what Nuna does."

I tried to think of a song or story to soothe him. I patted his back and listened to his breathing. "Steady and slow," Haemi would say. "I can only meet you if his breathing is steady and slow."

※

I didn't want to lose her again. One day, two years ago, during the peaceful lull between this war and the last one, Haemi stopped talking to me. We were fourteen and we had been friends for years.

On that day, I found her waiting in my middle-school nook with an empty wicker basket on her head. "Mother wants me to find acorns. Come help?"

She spun the basket and tried to keep it from falling. As she flailed her arms for balance, I noticed her fingernails—they were stained orange. "You're spending time with *girls* now?" I asked.

"What?" She started walking our usual way, still spinning the basket. We had an elaborate route to the crossroads where we split and went to our separate homes. It began at my school entrance, trailed down the stone steps of a hilly cemetery, wound around a small pond that was more mud than water, and crossed a deadened field no one had claimed in years. Old folks said a leper colony had once lived there and contaminated the whole area, but no lesions ever formed on our skin.

"Coloring your nails with rose balsam petals?" I yanked her wrist and flicked her fingers. The basket fell off her head. "Are you finally turning into a proper girl?"

"This is nothing. I was only playing." Her embarrassment came through in the volume of her denial. She whipped out of my grip. "I could still beat you in arm wrestling."

"Nah." I fluttered and pretended to braid my hair. "You're a good little girl."

"You're a babo."

"I think it's smart you're learning to be more feminine. How else will you find a suitable husband?"

She punched me, her small knuckles driving into my chest. I pretended to fall backward from her great strength. She didn't watch. She crossed the cemetery path, jumping from stone to stone. "You're an idiot." She threw the words back lightly, across her shoulder.

I wish I could remember her face, the other insults she'd lobbed at me. I wasn't paying attention because I hadn't realized how angry she was at the time. She sucked her fingers and spit orange-tinged blobs onto the ground. I thought she was renouncing her dip into girlish ways. I spit, too, to show her I approved.

"Who'd you stain your nails with?" I asked as we approached the small pond.

"No one. I was watching Hyunki." She said something about the neighborhood girls and their schooling, how they weren't interested in her. She didn't say what she really meant—that she was smarter than them, that if her father hadn't died, she'd still be in school, and if she ever returned, she would slaughter their haughtiness with her intelligence. Haemi shrugged off my question and returned to an old conversation about tadpoles. Every time we reached the pond, she talked about the almost-frogs. She thought there was something beautiful about their bodies right before transformation, when they were thick and round and alert, like an eyeball with a small tail. I thought they were about as exhilarating as larval amphibians could get.

"I go to school," I said, "and we're friends."

"You aren't too snooty to teach me."

She stuck her hand into the mud pit and caught a tadpole. It was black, slick with water, and its back legs were two nubs, just beginning to grow. It squirmed against her flesh. Viscous. Disgusting. I threw it back in the water.

"Why'd you do that? You probably hurt him," she said.

I couldn't explain.

Instead, I wiped Haemi's palm against my chest.

My teasing that day wasn't any more vicious than usual, but Haemi stopped coming to see me afterward. She no longer snuck away from her mother's constant chores. She acquired a few girl-friends. With my words, I had spurred her to create a world without me.

❧

After leaving the letter with Hyunki, I sat on a wobbly crate a few meters from the market entrance, under the lamppost where we always met. I waited for a reply, for her to come running with an apology.

I missed her. I missed having her all to myself. I had lost her before to a meaningless spat, and I didn't want to lose her to Jisoo now.

Jisoo was Seoul born, from a different class than us. When he first asked me about Haemi, I hadn't thought anything of giving him her name. New refugees arrived every day, and he was seeking reports of his family. When he began to court her, I dismissed it again. He hated our rural life; he was desperate to return to his precious city; his parents and sister were missing. Haemi was a distraction, nothing more. As soon as the war ended, he would leave.

Now, I wasn't sure, and I didn't want to watch any longer. I would tell her so, if she came. *You are like the moon,* I would say, getting romantic. *Your upturned eyes are the color of unearthed soil. When we sat across from each other that night in the hideaway bar, I only pretended I wasn't paying attention to you. I was watching your face. Wide like an apple. Your ears poking through your hair, sharp like the first sweep of January pine.*

I should have kissed you when you demanded it in the fields, I'd say. *But I was surprised by your forcefulness, the clever look of your mouth.* I'd thought about Jisoo, too. He was generous and took care of me and Father without coveting money or means for himself. But I didn't care about that sort of loyalty anymore. "Jisoo doesn't know you the way I do," I practiced. The words sounded small even to me.

"Hyung!" A high-pitched voice. Hyunki rushed toward me, his face both pale and blotchy at the cheeks.

I sat him on my crate and squatted beside him. "What's wrong?" His shirt was sheer with sweat. A dark birthmark across his right rib cage showed through like a stain. "Are you sick?"

"Everyone's mad."

From his pocket, he retrieved the letter I'd written.

"She didn't read it?" I circled around him. "I don't want it, then."

"She did. She wrote 'yes.' See?" He showed me the single word, pencil soft and written in quick strokes.

I laughed. Relief crawled up my back and into my cheeks. I sat on the ground and read the note—my words and her one—again and again.

I had found her before Jisoo. She would come to me.

Hyunki coughed, his frame shuddering with each breath. I rubbed his back, asked him what I should do. The wet scraping sound continued. He pointed at the path and tried to say he had to go back.

"I'll walk with you. We can try to find some water," I said.

He shook his head and spoke between hackings. "Everyone's mad. Tell Nuna I did a good job." His breathing slowed to a gummy hiccup. "I can go now. Bye, Hyung."

Partway down the road, he waved. I listened to the faint rumblings of his cough as he walked on alone.

When I returned home, the smell of meat drew me to Jisoo's room. Rice topped with slices of thin, almost translucent meat waited in three bowls. Father raised his arms as if he were a shaman. "Let's eat."

"Is Jisoo back?" I asked.

"How else would we have gotten this?" Father settled onto a floor cushion. "He said he'd eat his later."

"Where is he?"

Father caught my ankle before I could look. "I need to talk to you."

"About?" I asked.

"Sit. Let's eat first."

We bit into real rice that stuck to the grooves of our teeth. There was even a strip of fat in one of my beef slices. I held the meat on my tongue and imagined it melting into me.

Father sighed and closed his eyes. "Savor this. We don't know when the next time will be." He gave me half of his boiled quail egg. "I spoke to Jisoo. He's joining the ROK."

"Good," I said. "He's been talking about it for months." I tried to sneak an extra slice of beef from Jisoo's bowl, but Father caught me.

He snatched it back. "You should join with him."

I withdrew my chopsticks, surprised. "I'm only sixteen."

"He's going to look for his family. I found these under his blankets." Father set a pile of newspapers on the table. He pointed to a headline from a few months before. NO SHADOWS OF HUMANS IN SEOUL. "His family's dead. I can feel it." I didn't want to look at the image below that headline, but Father jabbed his finger at it. "This is what's happening." The picture showed mounds of debris strewn across the streets, and above that, a tall building being bombed. A large hole gaped like a wound. Rubble exploded outward like broken teeth.

I hadn't brought up Jisoo's family in months. I didn't want to remind him of their unknown state, but more than that, I didn't want to dwell on the unknown myself. "They must have paid someone to get out of Seoul safely. They're probably fine. They might even be nearby."

Father sucked his teeth. "Don't be an idiot. You two should stay together."

"Other fathers try to save their sons from the war, and you're telling me to join?" I picked up my spoon. "I don't understand."

"We're in a stalemate." Father sighed. "The fighting's almost over. You'll be fine. Jisoo's here because of you, you know."

"Then I saved his life."

Father looked away. He spat a piece of gristle on the floor.

Jisoo had come to us in the summer of 1950, because I'd run away earlier that spring. When he arrived, he beat me up and dragged me home. But I wasn't the one who needed to reexamine my life. Father had given up first, drinking and no longer working. "Don't be so self-centered," Jisoo had said as he dabbed at my face. A week later, Seoul fell and we headed south. He came with us. He had no other choice.

I looked at Father across the table. "I'll help Hyung find them after the war. Enlisting doesn't make sense. They wouldn't even take me."

"It would be the right thing."

"Do you really want me to leave?"

"His family is our family." Father leaned back from the table, gazed at the ceiling. A slow, quiet drizzle tapped against the roof. "You've always been this way—concerned only with yourself. What about your kin? What if Korea's overtaken?"

I wanted to tell him that I remembered our years under Japanese rule. How we were perpetually hungry, how we weren't even allowed to speak our own tongue. We had no power in this fight, either. We were pawns, tossed around by Japan, then the Soviets and the United States. I didn't want to join their cause. And above all, I was too weak, untrained. I would be killed.

"A man who doesn't care isn't worth his place in our nation," Father said.

I snorted. "You haven't cared about anything besides your drinking in a long time."

He finished his meal in silence, set Jisoo's on a crate on the other side of the room, and left.

I brought Jisoo's bowl back to the table. I would eat it. I didn't care. Thousands of people had died. Millions more were starving. It wasn't my fault.

A throat cleared behind me. "Hungry?"

Jisoo leaned against the wall in a fancy jacket, his smugness stamped all over his face. It was part of him—in the shape of his thickset nose, his meaty mouth, and his tiny eyes. He had the body of a high school boxer. "I didn't know about your family," I said.

"Never mind."

I pushed his bowl to the other side of the table.

"You can have my share." Jisoo glanced at my hands, my empty bowl, and his full one. "I'm not hungry. Really."

I lifted a slice of meat and he smiled. Dangling it from my chopsticks, I ate.

Later in the night, I left Jisoo and Father to confer between themselves about what a selfish son and cousin I was. I went to see Haemi.

We sat across from each other on unsteady crates in an alley where a man sold local brews. Soaked and skittish with alcohol, we grimaced at each other inside the narrow tent. Haemi's hair was wet from the rain, and her peaked hairline made her look like a balding boy. Her fingers, scavenging the anchovies I'd bought with Father's—no, Jisoo's—won, were greased and impatient.

"You're a delicate eater tonight," I said.

"I'm a delicate, graceful woman." She held her fingers up to my mouth. Flecks of fish skin stuck to her nails. "Don't you think?"

"Is that why you didn't dress as a boy?"

"What good does that do? Do you think anybody believes us?" She swept her arm, knocking into the other end of the tarp. She held her fingers up to me again, oblivious and daring, and then pulled away. "When a girl does that, you're supposed to lick her fingers."

"I thought you were a woman now." I pretended to devour my own knuckles, gnashing my teeth. "Is this how to do it then?"

She drank makgeolli quickly with little exhales. "Tell me why you came to my house."

"Because you said yes," I said.

She looked up, her crescent eyes focusing. "To?"

I nodded at the small bowl we shared, her fingers gripping the rim. "Coming here. I missed our adventures."

Her gaze skimmed over me, and her mouth loosened as she raised the bowl. "You joke and you pretend. Hyunki's sick and it's my fault, so stop playing."

I took away the makgeolli. She was already drunk. "Fine, I asked to see you because I've made a decision," I said.

She slapped the table and swayed. "Today's the day of big decisions. Big decisions!"

"Jisoo's going to enlist, but I'm going to stay right here."

A loud, openmouthed laugh shot out of her. "Your decision is that you're staying?"

"To stay with you."

She tilted her head as if the alcohol could leak out of her that way, a stream of makgeolli pouring from her ear to the ground. "Nothing's changed with you."

I showed her my bundle of papers. "These are school notes. I wrote them for you. We can go back to studying together."

She riffled through the papers. Her fingers traced the words and numbers I had written. The sketches that could help her learn. Her lips moved to the rhythm of history, science, arithmetic.

I caught the smell of grass and rain that had swept in from the sea on her clothes. She was beautiful, even with that hair. I wanted to tell her—how her gaze gnawed at me until I turned mocking, how she unsteadied me. "You think I don't care, but I've been re-writing my notes for you for months now," I said.

"Kyunghwan." She pressed her fingertips to the back of my hand. "You were right about Jisoo. He came to my house today."

I nodded. "He's going to enlist. He and Father tried to convince me, but—I want to stay here with you."

"Before he leaves, he wants to marry me."

I stood. Too quickly. The end of the table knocked into her. "You're lying."

It was Jisoo's nature to care for others, but he couldn't marry someone he didn't know. Without a matchmaker, his parents, a date-setting ceremony. Even if he was serious, he would have to wait until the war was over.

"Tell me you're lying."

Haemi, with her apple face and small breasts that pressed against the table, with her braid that she released on drunken nights and the curls I wanted to run my fingers through. I couldn't say any of it. We were sixteen, in a city where we didn't belong, and I had nothing to offer her.

"He asked me." Haemi spread her fingers, examined them. "He asked my mother."

"I saw him," I said. "A few hours ago. He didn't say anything."

"Kyunghwan—" Haemi's gaze shifted behind me. "Look—"
She stood and pointed.

But I couldn't hear anymore. I didn't turn.

All I could see was the shape of the alley we occupied—a bottle upright on our small share of table. Makgeolli puddles swirling with miniature clouds, a bowl wobbling on its curve. I stayed inside the silence, seeing only what lay in front of me for a flushed, precious second—until she yelled, "Behind you! Kyunghwan!"

I turned and ducked as soon as I recognized the boxy face. Jisoo's fist raged past where my head had been, his arm arching from anger.

"You want to fight?" I shoved, but he was beyond me.

He grabbed her wrist. "What're you doing here?"

Haemi tried to sit back down. "I'm getting drunk. I'm celebrating all of today's big decisions." She cast him an indifferent gaze, but her knuckles were white and shiny as she gripped the table.

I seized his shoulder. "Did you do it? Did you ask her?"

He pushed me off, easy. "We need to go, Haemi."

"I don't want to." She tried to dump makgeolli on her wrist, as if that could loosen his grip.

He pulled, gentler this time. "It's Hyunki. He's sick. Your mother had to go for help." He turned to me, his gaze resting on my wet collar. "Her brother's sick, and you brought her here."

"Hyunki?" Haemi looked at me, asked me. "Where is he?"

But I didn't know. Only Jisoo knew. I tried to grab Haemi's other wrist. "I can find him."

"You left him, Haemi. You were supposed to watch him tonight," Jisoo said. "I'll take you."

"You can't marry her." I looked from Haemi to Jisoo, trying to pin them with my stare. "You can't come here and do this."

He glanced past me. "Stop being an idiot. This is serious."

Haemi touched his shoulder. "Let's go."

I called her name as they walked out, but when they turned back, I had nothing to say. My mind was an empty, murky blank. Haemi let Jisoo pull her through the tent's flapping tarp and out into the street—a blur of loose hair rounding a corner.

They were halfway across the alley when she looked back at me again. A quick, blanched face I couldn't divine. I tried to work my mouth, ready my words. If I could say the right thing. If I knew where Hyunki was. If I hadn't let Jisoo treat me like a child.

I sat back down at our table.

I stayed alone.

The papers I had copied for Haemi lay scattered. They leached up the makgeolli puddles. Charcoal markings thickened and spread, like worms surfacing after a long night's rain.

Part 2

Haemi

1952

LUCK SPILLED BETWEEN OUR FINGERS AND POOLED around us. Mother spoke of the others—the sullied, unlucky women. "By the Chinese, the Japanese. Mongols. Americans. Korea's girls have been snatched up since the beginning." She dipped a dirty shirt from the field hospital into the stream that tendriled from the Nakdong River to our refugee village.

"That doesn't make me feel any better," I said.

"My job is to prepare, not comfort." She rubbed the shirt against a boulder until the bloodstain loosened its grip. Women we knew from the Busan markets waved at us from the other side of the bank. Mother ignored them. "They only want to take our jobs."

We squatted together, our long skirts bunched, our hands full of other people's laundry. "The sullying happened to Kim Hasun up on the hill," she said.

"Auntie Chyu told me Hasun was in love with that white soldier. Does that still make her a tainted woman?"

"What does the seamstress know?" Mother clucked. "Besides, that's just as bad."

I snapped a sheet in the water. "Let's finish the washing. No more gossip."

I didn't want to discuss these marred women or their men any longer. I could too easily imagine myself in their place. Jisoo and

I had married before he left for the war, a quick but formal cere-mony. If he returned, we would lie with each other just like Hasun and the American, and yet Mother wouldn't call that a shame. It was strange, how marriage turned the act into something good, something natural between a man and a woman.

I stretched a nearly dry shirt across a flat stone and pummeled it with wooden sticks. Mother saw our work as luck, too. Before he left, Jisoo found us jobs washing and drying for the field hos-pital. As long as the war continued, even in this stalemate, we had security.

She raised her arms and made thumping noises. "Hit the shirt harder. Rhythmic, constant, for an even shine."

The nurses' outfits were the most tedious. They wanted pristine seams and their Western-style shirts had buttons that broke easily under my careless pounding. "Hyunki loves pressing clothes," I said. It was true. He liked to hold one wooden stick between his hands and match my rhythm.

"Let him play."

Hyunki—alive and shin deep in the almost-summer water. Mother and I watched him together. At the stream's bend, where a group of boulders formed a small pond, he splashed with a few vil-lage boys. Wet and speckled by the shadows of the trees, his body flickered like glass glinting in the sun.

"After this load, you can relax," Mother said.

"Can I swim, too?"

"What we do isn't so bad, Haemi." Mother rubbed the good luck pujok she kept tucked inside her skirtband. Ever since another washer introduced her to these yellow-papered talismans, she had covered our bodies with them.

Mother cycled through superstitions with more fervor than

anyone I knew. They kept her hopeful, and maybe they worked. We *were* lucky. The stalemate continued, far away from us. I was married yet still remained with my family. I had not been taken away to tend the groom's relatives for the rest of my life. It was a calm April morning, and we squatted with our bare feet in cool running water, a wealth of whitened clothes swimming around us.

Relaxing meant an hour's walk to the hospital tents southeast of our village, where the soldiers had cordoned off the area for the sick and dying prisoners of war. "Come back with next week's sets," Mother said. Hyunki, still swimming, splashed me as I left.

From the top of the hill, where the old blind man relayed his radio announcements, the field hospital could be seen in its entirety. Beyond that, the sea that roiled against the sand. And farther out, Geoje-do, the island the prisoners returned to once they'd healed. Stories of uprisings there had crossed over the strait, circulated by village women content with the war's standstill. I didn't pay these stories much attention. If it didn't have to do with Kyunghwan or Jisoo, I didn't want to know.

The first time I delivered clean laundry to the field hospital, I had spoken to everyone I encountered. The Military Police that demanded my entrance papers, the foreign doctors who strode so purposefully between the indistinguishable tents. I'd repeated two names into their blank, uninterested faces.

The boys had left me for the war. Jisoo had gone the right way, enlisted and eager. I never understood Kyunghwan's departure— whether he was forced or had joined to spite me. He'd left without saying goodbye. Nearly a year later, I didn't care about his reasons any longer. I only wanted them both to remain whole.

I stopped an American soldier with eyes the color of gosari. He wore a belt with too many pockets and boots I wanted to steal. "Yun Jisoo? Yun Kyunghwan?" I asked.

The soldiers all responded in English or with apologetic shakes of their heads. This was a space for injured Reds. Jisoo and Kyunghwan could be anywhere, and I was only a girl.

I tried not to think of them, and the hospital provided a decent distraction. I liked how the soldiers' attempt at order butted up against the chaos of their days. They had laid out the grounds in neat sections, separating their half-moon huts from the guarded lodgings of the prisoners and the hospital's surgical tents. But, in reality, the doctors, Military Police, and patients continuously crossed all these constructed borders.

With the fresh laundry, I passed the guards with a bow, walked down the array of tents, and entered the one reserved for clean supplies. I searched for a Korean to report to. "Nurse Minhee? I've come with this week's sets."

"Oh, damn." She stood beside a rack of towels, her arms laden. "I forgot you were coming today. The dirties are still in Recovery. Leave those here and follow me, will you?"

We walked to the middle of the pathway, where the tents were laid out in a grid. "I have to go into an operation now," she said.

"Is everything all right?"

She focused on me, a sudden flutter of attention. "We're a nurse short today, so it's a bit more hectic than usual. You see that tent?"

"I could help," I said. "What do you need me to do?"

She smiled but shook her head. "Go to the Recovery tent. Dirties will be there."

I watched her walk away. She was the nicest of the Korean nurses. Twenty and unmarried, she'd been in college when the war began. Fluent in English, French, and Japanese. She wasn't pretty, too tall, but she was sharp, and foreign words fell from her lips with precision when she spoke to the Americans. She was better and smarter than me, and everything she had, I wouldn't. It made me hate her.

On my way to Recovery, I heard a man's cries coming from one of the surgical tents. Chinese curses flew through the air like birds. I pictured a man about to lose a part of himself—a leg, a hand, a full arm. His screams peeled away my frustration. Only meters away, our doctors worked metal instruments through the bones of our enemies. I had all my limbs intact. I had a free life. I could pick up the laundry without fuss.

The dirty satchels waited inside a tent that smelled of iron and vomit. I peered through the sacks, looking for the easiest items to wash. Mother preferred sheets, towels, prisoners' uniforms— simple fabrics without buttons or complicated seaming. I preferred the doctors' clothes. Sometimes, inside their pockets, I found half-eaten biscuits, letters, an ink pen that Hyunki could use to scrawl across leaves.

As I nosed around, I heard a whimper crawl up the corners of the room. I touched my chest, where Mother had laid a pujok that morning. I didn't believe in her death ghosts, but I stilled with fear.

"Is someone here? I'm the cleaning girl," I said.

The whimpers continued, harsh and uneven. I followed the sound like a fisherman's line, from one section of the tent to the next. Behind a wooden pallet, I found him—a man all in white. He shoved his shoulders against the wall like a caught animal.

"Are you hurt?" I asked.

He opened his mouth and blood spilled out, red and trickling and staining his teeth. Hunched over, he tried to suppress his coughing. He was a prisoner, and I'd caught him in a room where he didn't belong.

"Let me help you." I turned him on his side and pounded his back. When another fit overtook him, I stuck my finger in his mouth to check for choking. The soft insides, the rough terrain of teeth. A familiar act.

I called for help. I couldn't tell if the man looked like Hyunki or if I only imagined it. Round eyes. A raked, naked look to his gaze. His body twined in and around itself, as if the smaller the space he consumed, the smaller the pain.

An American nurse found us, gasped, exited, and returned with doctors and soldiers. English chatter crowded the room, and the prisoner looked up at them with his large, alarmed eyes. A Korean man in a flat military cap guided me from the room before I could see what happened next. With a firm grip on my elbow, he led me into one of the endless tents and sat me at a wooden table.

"My name is Major Kim," he said. "Are you a girl-san?"

I twisted in my seat to look out the entrance. I could no longer hear the prisoner. "I'm a laundry washer. My name is Lee Haemi, and I have identification."

"You should face your elder when you speak," he said.

I rose from the chair and half bowed, still stunned by the prisoner's coughing, the blood flooding from his mouth like a pond after heavy rain. "What will happen to him?"

A cup appeared. My hands were red, but I didn't care about the stains I left on the tin. I drank. The water slid down my throat like a fish. I remembered the dirty laundry sets I had left behind. I saw Mother at home, wondering why I was late.

Major Kim closed the tent flap, dragged a chair to the other side of the table, and sat down. He gazed at the stacked papers and the driftwood branch acting as a paperweight. Blood stained my clothes. The prisoner—he'd had a leg wound, too. The memory came to me as I touched the hem of my reddened dress.

"Did you know him?" Major asked.

"How could I?"

He stared at me as if I hadn't helped a sick man. Graying eyebrows decorated his saggy, jowled face. "He was trying to escape. Why didn't you call for someone first? How did you know he wouldn't hurt you?"

"Am I in trouble?" I glanced at the entrance again. It seemed to have moved farther away, stretched out at the other end of the tent.

"Please answer my questions." The major picked up the driftwood paperweight and rolled it in his hand.

I stood. "The man couldn't breathe. Wouldn't you have done the same?"

He stood, too, still grasping the branch. He was tall, maybe the tallest Korean I had seen in a year. "You don't scare easily."

Mother's words about men and their strength and what they could do to women returned to me. I gripped the aluminum cup, my fingers looped through the handle. We were alone in a tent I'd never been in before. At least ten paces to the entrance, and I couldn't remember which direction he'd taken me.

"Let me go," I said.

He stepped back. "I didn't mean to scare you." He gazed at the branch, set it down, and motioned at the air between us. "No one's keeping you here. I meant you're not frightened by the sight of blood."

Heat crawled up my skin. I wasn't ashamed of my thoughts,

only at how easily he'd deciphered them. I loosened my fingers but didn't release the cup. "You can't blame me. We've all heard the stories," I said.

"You have a brazen mouth for a girl."

"My mother says the same."

His face broke into a smile like a watermelon cracking open. He chuckled as he eased back into his chair. A soft ripple of laughter revealed a gentler man. He offered me his handkerchief. "I'm only curious as to how a laundry girl would know what to do in that situation."

I wiped my hands, the cup, my face. I left my hem as it was. "My brother was sick in the lungs. Sometimes he would cough so much he'd choke."

"I'm sorry."

"He's better now."

Major Kim pushed himself out of his chair. "Come." At the other end of the tent, beyond a trio of stools and a smaller desk, someone had tacked a map onto a post. He gestured toward it. "Where's home for you?"

The map was unmarked, peaceful compared to the truth of the war. I found my hometown below the line that had severed our country after the Second World War. On the eastern side of South Korea, my village was a speck of brown encircled by mountains. "Here." I pointed.

"When did you flee?"

"Late July, two years ago."

I remembered it too clearly. The day we learned of Seoul's fall, Hyunki and I had been catching grasshoppers. Mother ran to us with her hanbok skirt clutched in one hand. She didn't speak, only motioned for us to follow. Snippets, flaring and incomprehensible, wove through the crowd as the whole village gathered in the market. The Northerners had crossed the thirty-eighth parallel three days before. The Chinese were with them. No, the Soviets. No, both. Whoever they were, they were Reds. Seoul had fallen in less than an hour. Our country would be reunited. We would be killed. The hysteria was contagious, congested with too many emotions. I didn't want to catch their panic, didn't want to understand.

"What's happening, Nuna?" Hyunki held his string of chirping grasshoppers above his head.

I turned to my brother. "Let's go back and cook up these critters. Mother will tell us later." As we walked home, I helped Hyunki pluck their wings one by one.

Major Kim pointed to Busan. "How long did it take to get here?"

"Weeks. It felt like years."

In the days afterward, our young men began to disappear. Some left freely to fight, others were forced. The families with teenage boys, like Kyunghwan and his father, were among the first to flee. After our own ROK soldiers absconded, and the whispers of piled bodies had frenzied our neighbors, Mother decided to leave.

"We left together—the families with children and girls. There were so many of us, at first," I said.

With beans, rice, hollowed gourds, and a few garments wrapped in bojagis, we'd gathered in the market before sunrise. The mothers had argued over the best path south. Hyunki, excited by the idea of missing school, had tugged on my pants and laughed because I wore Father's old clothes. I felt anger at his innocence, so clean and simple, and leaned close to say, "I'm pretending to be a boy so men won't rape me." The bewilderment on his face as he tried to understand. My immediate shame. I'd hugged him and said, "Don't listen to your mean old nuna. I'm sorry, Hyunki. Tell me what you want to see in Busan."

"The ocean," he'd whispered.

"Let's go now. Let's head to the water."

Then the walking, a mass exodus of bodies. Not only our village, but all the villages. The mood wavered between community and competition whenever shelter or food appeared. Tanks and soldiers swarmed the roads as if they sprouted from the ground. Our feet were splintered and raw, and hunger shone in our faces. I remembered the dead, how the summer heat pitched the old, young, and sickly into roadside graves. Their bodies decomposed quickly, and strangers stole the clothes that covered their limbs. Fear marked us more than our desire for food—fear of others, ourselves, the soldiers, planes, death, of finding Busan occupied. Mother and I feared for Hyunki the most. He was always near death, and yet always managed to hold on.

I touched the map again. "We ate the beans inside Hyunki's favorite cornhusk doll and he hated us." It was strange to speak about those first days now. I'd never shared this story with anyone, not even Kyunghwan.

"I'm sure your brother understands."

"How would you know?" I asked.

"That mouth again."

Major Kim stood behind me, close enough that I could feel the heat of his breath. I was no longer afraid of him. I knew this type of man. He wouldn't hurt me. He touched a spot of land to the west of my hometown. "This is where I grew up. I went away for middle and high school, but I remember my father's house."

I turned to him as he spoke. He thought I was pretty. I could see it in the way he avoided my gaze. I smiled at my earlier fear, at how hastily I'd accepted Mother's beliefs. I didn't want to be like her, walking through the world fearing the evil in all men. Since Kyunghwan's and Jisoo's departures, it was too easy to despair, to see only how senseless living had become. I had to resist such thinking.

"We need another house girl," he went on, "for the mess hall."

"The mess hall?" I asked.

"Extra money. Extra food. A job here."

"A girl-san?"

"It's a term of endearment. The Americans don't mean to offend."

"I want to be a nurse." I straightened. "I've been watching them."

He laughed again, flashing his glossy pink gums. "You're not qualified for that."

"A secretary, then."

"No." He wandered to his desk, perhaps losing interest in me. He picked up two slim cardboard boxes that fit in his palm.

"I can be an assistant to the nurses. I don't scare easily."

He smiled, and I knew. "All right, an assistant to the Korean nurses."

"Can my mother keep her washing job?"

"Yes, of course."

I approached him and thumbed the edge of his desk. "Why are you doing this?"

"You made me laugh today. You saved a man's life without fearing for your own. You remind me of my wife with your face and smart mouth." Behind his desk, he looked like a man who belonged. "Here. Some cookies for your brother. Come back tomorrow."

———

I imagined Mother's reaction when I returned home with the news. She would sing and dance with Hyunki. She'd say, *Because of you, we'll be all right.* I found her in front of our house and told her about the position as she rummaged through the new load of laundry. She looked up, her round chin shadowed against the sun. "Why would this man help us? What did you do?"

I'd hidden Major Kim's sweets to avoid this—her flaring suspicions, her fear that I involved myself with men. I knew how Mother thought. She hadn't forgiven me for that night last year, for drinking with Kyunghwan and fueling gossip, for almost ruining my prospects at a respectable marriage.

"I saved a prisoner's life. He was coughing and choking. I thought of Hyunki and I saved him."

Mother dropped the bag. "A Red?"

"We wash their laundry," I said.

"Saving a Red's life is different."

"What about your family up in Ongjin? What if they're Reds?"

"You don't talk about them with anyone down there, do you?"

"I'm not stupid." I gathered the straw scattered at our feet. We were supposed to erase Mother's family in the North from our public memory, as if the war had suddenly made us two countries with no shared history. She was cold, heartless. "If you don't want the extra food, that's fine with me. I'll tell the major we don't need his help."

"I want to know that it's honest food."

I found a rusty crate and balanced it in front of the house we'd lived in these past two years. I stood on the crate and tried to fling the straw back onto the roof, but the pieces fluttered down again, useless.

"I hate it here," I said.

I strode past the open entrance, tossed the blanket door aside, and went to change out of my bloodied hanbok. I heard Mother move to the backyard, where she thrust grains into the metal cauldron we'd dug into the ground. I wanted to go home. On days like this, the stalemate felt worse than the fleeing. I felt as if I were suspended on a bridge, waiting for someone to let me cross.

Hyunki entered our room with mugwort leaves gathered in his shirt. "I found these by the river. We can burn them tonight." He dropped the mugwort on the floor beside me. "Stink away the mosquitoes."

"We aren't supposed to build fires at night. You know that."

Hyunki buried his face in my skirt. "If we start a little fire in the back and put the big jar and the rock and crate around us, no one will see the light from far away." He looked up at me and cupped his hands. "A baby fire. We could roast chestnuts."

"And where would we get chestnuts?" I asked.

"I forgot about that part." He threw a leaf into the air. "We'll roast something else then."

I stroked the back of his neck. This was my favorite part of him, where the hairs grew soft and tender. "I have some treats for you, but you can't tell Mother. All right?"

He patted my skirt, searching. "What is it?"

I sat down. "Turn around."

He pushed his face against mine until our noses touched. "Why?"

"Fine." I stuck a hand underneath my chest binding.

Hyunki laughed and pretended to mold breasts on his shirt. When he saw the treats wrapped in paper, he squealed. "Can I have them all?"

"You better share."

"Give over!" Hyunki quickly unwrapped one and bit into the golden cookie sandwich inside. He rolled on the floor, kicking his feet. "The Americans make the best sweets!"

I grabbed his toes. "Let me try."

We split the cookie in two and licked the sugary middle layer until it crumbled. The sweetness coated our teeth and tongues until my head hurt.

"Should we save some for Mother?" Hyunki asked.

The smell of her barley rice and boiled radishes heated the air. I shook my head. "Let's eat them all now."

We burned the mugwort, too. A baby fire, like Hyunki had said. While Mother slept, we breathed in the medicinal, sooty scent and imagined all the mosquitoes dying from the smoke. We didn't have chestnuts, but we had runty potatoes. We roasted them on sticks and pretended we were eating better things.

"When we go home," Hyunki said, "I'm going to make song-pyeon rice cakes."

I jabbed my stick at him. "You mean you'll beg me to make them for you."

"Maybe." He stuck out his tongue. "Will you tell me how you got the cookies now?"

"Only if you won't repeat it to anyone."

Hyunki kissed his palm and I did the same. "Sealed tight," we said, with our hands, warm from the fire's heat, pressed together.

I told him about the sick man from the morning, how I'd helped a Red regain his breath. I told him about Major Kim and the map stuck to the tent's post. Hyunki gasped at the right moments. He was only eight and I don't know if he understood, but I loved him for the effort.

When he fell asleep, I carried him to our room. For a moment, I pretended he was my husband and hugged his small body to mine. I would miss him, my little man, when Jisoo came to take me away. I gripped him tighter and tried to avoid the course of my thoughts. I wanted the stalemate to continue so I could remain my own person. I didn't want the men hurt, only far away from me. That way, no affection would grow between me and my husband. I could remain a daughter and sister.

I sat by the burning mugwort until Mother appeared to use the outhouse. She stared at me. "You'll get us shot."

When she finished and returned, she said only this: "It'll be hard for you, but if you want, go work for them. Bring back as much as you can. Food, money, whatever they give you. If you see dying men and can't bear it, there's no shame in that."

I brought home pears, hard biscuits that left a sweet tang in our mouths, rations chocolate and real chocolate, a plastic spinning top, tins of jam, and coins slipped into my hands by both the injured and the dying. I was closer to the violence of our war now, and I loathed the screams and blood and sheathed bodies of the dead. Even so, I went every day. The chattering nurses, the heavy-footed steps of men, the chaos of stitching prisoners back together—these things made my days feel useful, defined. I no longer had time to linger over Jisoo and Kyunghwan and their unknown state.

Mother nodded her approval when I returned home each evening, and Hyunki greeted me, perched on his knees, ready to hear my heroic stories. They gave my weariness worth.

Every morning, I returned to Major Kim for my day's assignment. He was generous and sent me to work on the gentlest cases.

I entered his tent and bowed. "Good morning, Major. Which nurse should I follow today?"

He waved me over to his desk, where he had a plate of boiled eggs and thick, shiny slabs of pink meat. "Who were you with yesterday?" he asked between bites.

I stared. "Is that pork?"

He laughed, covering his mouth with the back of his hand. "You look like you'll steal this from me even if I say no." He pulled out another plate. "Come eat with me."

"Are you sure?" I asked.

"You're drooling."

I sat and ate quickly, before he could change his mind. Fat and salt and saliva lingered on my tongue, and I closed my eyes, pretending to eat it all over again. I hadn't seen pork in more than two years. Major Kim ate with measured bites, as if there were no such thing as time.

"It's called Spam. Almost like the real thing, isn't it?" he said.

"If this isn't real, it's better."

He smiled. "You've forgotten how good samgyeopsal can be."

"You're from a different, richer world, Major."

"Haemi," he warned.

I paused with my chopsticks in the air. "It's the truth. I've never had samgyeopsal." I let my braid fall down my shoulder to my chest the way he liked.

He glanced at me, amused, uneasy, and cleared his throat. "One day your husband will buy a pig for you, and you'll understand what I mean."

"Until then, I'll keep thinking about this pretend pork." I bit into a boiled egg, nodded at the new papers on his desk. "Are there any updates?"

He unrolled a map, and I looked for the stalemate line. It was north of Seoul and south of Ongjin, where Mother had lived before her marriage. I never told her what I'd learned about her village, how it was battled over from the very beginning. She hadn't returned since marrying Father, and Ongjin was no longer her home.

"The war continues, but we're holding our own." Major Kim skimmed his finger down to Busan, then to Geoje Island. "Tomorrow, I'll return to Geoje for a few days. Today, I'm preparing."

I studied the island's jagged borders. "Can I go with you?"

"What I do there isn't for girls."

"I'm a woman." I straightened in my seat. "I know about the prisoner riots. I heard someone was killed."

He ran a finger across his jawline. This tic reminded me of Kyunghwan. I liked the major even more for his slips into nervousness.

"I'll rephrase." He sliced his remaining Spam with the length of his chopsticks and offered me half. "What I do there is for men."

"If I were your daughter, would you take me?"

He shook his head, a frown aging his face. "You shouldn't wonder at our fighting so lightly. Hundreds of thousands have died. You're smart enough to know that."

I couldn't even hold a number that large in my head. I stared at my tin plate, its surface slick with grease. "I'm sorry. I was disrespectful."

"Be mindful of the dead." He plucked his egg and set it in front of me. "Minhee needs help in the recovery wards. Finish eating and go."

I found Nurse Minhee in Tent Thirteen, where the postsurgery prisoners were held. She sat beside a patient, coaxing him to eat. Some days, I still hated her despite myself, but she was the best nurse to work with because she treated me like a partner.

"Haemi," she said, smiling. "Nurse Ahn isn't here yet, and Kwak Chul says he's in pain. Could you massage his right arm?" She pointed to a patient with a stump that ended below his right shoulder. He tried to wave. She lowered her voice. "He's been irritable and delusional all week. Pretend until I can get to him."

I strode over to the patient and began squeezing his shoulder and the air below. Chul wriggled. "You don't look qualified."

"My name is Lee Haemi. I'm an assistant." I tried to mimic Minhee's slow, even cadence. "The upper arm looks like it's healing well."

He eyed me. "You probably think I'm disgusting, don't you? Is it because I'm a KPA? They picked me off the street! I'm not a Red any more than you are."

"Please, I think you're fine." I pretended to squeeze and avoided his gaze.

He turned away, stared at the other prisoners, and then rolled back to me. "You have breasts like my sister. You must have tiny little nipples. How are you going to nurse with those things?"

I looked at Minhee, but she hadn't heard. Kwak Chul was only nineteen and already a filthy dog. "It's better if you close your eyes and sleep," I said.

"I don't know where she is. My sister. My brothers and parents, either. I heard your side shot everyone in my town."

I looked beyond Chul to the man who lay beside him. He hummed with a towel over his face and raised his arms, swaying to the music inside his head.

"Are you still massaging? I don't feel anything," Chul said.

"Yes, be quiet, please. Just shut up."

He jerked away. "You're angry." The indistinct look slipped from his face, and he sat up. "What's going on? What's wrong with me?" He wailed, loud and garbled, as I tried to clamp him down.

Minhee walked over with her ease and confidence. She petted Chul's cheek as if he were a child. "Everything's going to be fine." She handed me a cool compress. "I think our friend has a fever. This should help."

I laid the compress over Chul's forehead and eyes. "Your arm will feel better once your fever breaks." I used a calm voice and stroked his hair. As Minhee returned to her patient, I spoke to Chul about rebuilding the strength in his arm, about returning home one day.

The dancing man pulled the towel from his face. "Can you help me next?" Fat water blisters covered his eyelids and cheeks. Swollen and disfigured, he didn't look human. I concentrated on his lips, on how they hummed.

I couldn't blame these men, whether they were liars or Reds or innocents. They were sick. I bent close to Chul, so my chest pressed against his half-limbed body. So he could feel a woman against him, at least this once. "I don't know where my husband is, either," I said.

The Korean nurses and I took our lunches to a spray of beach beyond the tents. I didn't like the waves, how they loomed and crashed, but the others didn't seem to mind the ocean's vastness. Minhee dumped the ash from her pipe into the water. "So long, tobacco. No more until tomorrow." She stretched out on the sand beside me.

"I had a dream about him last night," Jeongja said. When food wasn't enough, we filled ourselves with Jeongja's tales of how it felt to be loved, and how a baby could form. Full of Seoul haughtiness as she told these stories, she collected our attention like pebbles in her hand.

"I want to go home," Kyungah sighed. Like me, she was a wife without any news of her husband. With no postal system, we were left with only our imaginations.

"At least we're working," Minhee said, fierce in the mouth as she reached for my pipe. "I'm almost glad the war came."

"You don't mean that," Kyungah chided.

I hadn't told them about marrying Jisoo, about the quick ceremony or how he was marched to a truck full of soldiers that same evening. It happened so swiftly. Some days, even the memory felt flimsy and unreal. Mother had borrowed a simple wedding hanbok from Auntie Chyu, and as I'd walked around our house wearing it, the short green jacket and full red skirt seemed far too saturated for our daily lives. Contrasted against our home's bare wooden beams and Mother's determined air, the colors had revealed our truth— the life we'd once known had been taken from us. We were pitiful now, mere husks of ourselves bundled into a presentable form.

Jisoo had entered in his black suit and gaped. "I didn't think you would wear a hanbok." He'd touched the white buttons on his shirt. "I don't know what I was expecting, I guess."

I'd laughed. The oddness of our union evident in our dress. "What you wear today doesn't matter to me."

There was no matchmaker, proposal letter, or official date setting. Instead, we'd exchanged scraps of blue and red cloth as a promise of future gifts. Jisoo had offered me the wooden ducks he'd carved with a shyness I'd never seen in him before.

"We'll have a proper wedding with my parents when I return," he'd said. "We'll find them and hold a feast. Long noodles to ensure our long lives together." In that moment, as he careened between happiness and hesitation, I felt protective of him, my new husband.

The doubt set in only after he left. When I realized what it meant to be married during a time of war, when news would never reach a nameless, inconsequential citizen like me. Jisoo, his parents, his sister. Mother, Hyunki, Kyunghwan. Me. Who among us would survive this war?

"What're you thinking about, Haemi?" Kyungah tossed sand in my direction.

"A patient told me my breasts looked like his sister's." I balanced a seashell on my finger. "Isn't that strange?"

"That's disgusting," Minhee said. "Was it Chul? Don't let him talk to you like that again. We're too nice to them already."

"Next time, tell the guards," Jeongja said.

"But the guards are just as dirty sometimes," Kyungah replied.

When it was time to walk back, we dipped our chopsticks in the ocean and tied up our lunch tins. On the way, we smelled him before we saw him—the shit-shoveling man. He balanced buckets on a plank and carried a shovel on his back. He bowed hello.

"He's friendly and all," Jeongja whispered as we returned his bow, "but who would want to marry a man who carries away your shit?"

"He profits off something we all make. It's smart," I said.

They laughed. "Selling our shit for fertilizer is smart?"

"You're too good, Haemi." Jeongja flicked my braid.

I resented their misunderstanding. I knew I was bad and unkind and selfish. I felt it in the absence of my actions, in how I always wanted the opposite of what was expected. Sometimes I found myself wanting Major Kim to touch my hip. He reminded me of Kyunghwan and our easy pleasure, of drinking under the night sky. I forgot that Jisoo was generous, assured, right. My husband. I confused myself.

That evening, Minhee and I walked home along a path lined with trees. "Do you want to come over?" she asked. "We're making pajeon for dinner."

"I won't be allowed." I mimicked Mother's peaked face and spouted the excuses she would give. Minhee laughed and imitated her own mother's sandy voice. As we turned a corner, her chatter quickly turned to a hush. She nodded at the fork in the path. "I hear something."

Whispers of women being taken wove through the nurses' circles. Even the prisoners warned us to be careful. We strained together, struggling to hear beyond the rustle of trees.

"It's nothing," I said. Minhee pointed to a shadow as it moved into the light. A man, walking down the right-side path.

She grabbed my hand. "I have a knife in my satchel."

"Let's turn back," I said, but then the man cleared his throat, releasing a familiar cough. "Wait, I think—"

"Haemi?"

Major Kim. He slipped his hands into his pockets. "Nurse Minhee and Miss Haemi."

"It's you," I said.

Minhee relaxed her grip and bowed. "We were helping the overnight shift, sir."

I watched him pull out a cigarette, look at it, then return it to its case. There was something strange about seeing him in this setting. He seemed ordinary. "Do you need an escort? You don't want to be here alone once it's dark."

"We'll walk quickly. Thank you anyway." Minhee bowed, and I followed.

He touched my crown as he passed. "I'll see you when I'm back from Geoje. Good night."

Minhee raised her eyebrows once he was far enough away. "You know, right?" She pointed at the fork.

We always took the left path, and Major Kim had come down the right. I followed Minhee's thinking. "The prostitutes?" The last time a drove of soldiers came through Busan, the village women to the right of the fork had disappeared into the mountains. Whispers had candled into flames, but when the women had returned, they appeared unchanged. "You think the major was with one of them?" I asked.

"You don't? Those whores are famous," Minhee said.

Major Kim. He was a man who doled out sweets to the nurses, to the soldiers in pain. He'd offered me a job because of my smart mouth. I sometimes caught his gaze skimming my features, but he had never done more than look.

"He's spent too much time with the Americans," Minhee said.

Of course. He was also a man who slept with prostitutes. With women who weren't his wife. My mouth filled with spit, metallic and sour. I pointed to the nearest house we could see. "Do you think it was that one?"

"I know about her. Kim Yejin. They say she gave birth to a white man's child and drowned it in the ocean." Minhee tugged me along. "Let's go. Are you jealous?"

"What?" I stared at Minhee, then back at the house. "Of her?"

"He touches you. A little pat on the head, the shoulder. Do you like him?"

I pulled away, my face rushing with heat. "Don't be stupid."

She laughed, looped my arm with hers again. "I'm only joking. You have to come with me now." She tugged me along, despite my protests. "Jeongja and Kyungah will love this."

The air was cool as I left the nurses' boardinghouse later that evening, ignoring their insistence that I stay until morning. I was tired of them. They'd surprised me with their gossip, their insults jagging sharper against the women than the men.

"Men are disgusting," Kyungah had said, "but the women are unforgivable, selling their bodies for money."

"They prey on men's weaknesses," Jeongja had added, then nipped my arm. "What's wrong?"

Minhee had pinched my cheek. "She's jealous. She's in love with Major Kim."

But I wasn't jealous. I'd only wanted to feel pretty. Clever. There was no harm in Major Kim's affections. I'd wanted distraction and comfort and some attention, just as he had. It had been the same with Kyunghwan and Jisoo. Yet they were still men, protected and forgiven, while women were not. I turned those facts around in my head.

"You will not sneak out with Kyunghwan again," Mother had said, last year, the night Jisoo took me home from the bar. Hyunki was the sickest we'd ever seen him, yet Mother focused on purity, reputation, on whether Jisoo still wanted me for his wife. "If he doesn't take you, we'll never be able to return home." She didn't call me a whore, but I felt it shimmering her every word into a threat.

Why was it that Kim Yejin was sullied and shunned, if she wasn't married and the major was? Why had I been called a fox by the aunties in the marketplace, while Kyunghwan walked on without shame?

I watched the moon, its chaste white glow. The nurses' words reminded me of my place in the world. Even if the next day brought the end of war, I was still a seventeen-year-old girl married to a man I barely knew, a man who could be dead even now.

I passed my home. I turned down the road and walked back to the fork, following the clouds until I stood before her house. Kim Yejin. I knew about her, too. She was tall and slight with one rolling eye.

A thick metal cylinder lay by her gate. I picked it up and wondered if it had to do with Major Kim and what they'd done together. Its body was cold and strange, with a lever at one end. I knew the nurses would have told me not to touch it. I wondered what would happen to me if my husband died. A widow. I would never lie with a man. I would live alone, at the mercy of the goodwill of others. Or perhaps Mother would move us to a new town and present me as an unwed, marriageable girl again. I rolled the cylinder between my palms.

"Don't push it. It might explode."

Kim Yejin. Shaded by the trees at her front door, she stood in a white dress with a chamber pot in her arms.

"A chamber pot in May?" Jealousy flexed in me as I imagined this woman with Major Kim. I *was* jealous—not of their sex, but of her ability to choose. The control she must have felt while disrobing.

"Drop the grenade."

"If my husband comes back, will I ever see my family again?"

"Who are you?"

I set my thumb on the lever. "Do I press here?"

She hissed and held the pot in front of her face. "Are you crazy?"

I pointed it at the sky above. "What will happen?"

"Don't—"

I pushed.

She screamed.

Clouds.

Clouds came out in streams and caught on the trees. Mist and a grenade and smoke and the whore and the sliding open of doors and the smell—artificial, burning, unfamiliar. It wasn't a bomb at all.

"What's happening out there?" a woman's voice yelled. "What's going on?"

A slow clearing.

The world returned in layers. Sky. Shadows of humans. Trees. Ragged breathing. Watery eyes. Whispers from the awakened, from those who'd emerged from their homes. Kim Yejin's white dress. Her fear.

It was only mist and smoke. One of those cans used to distract the enemy or signal to your own.

"Just smoke," I said.

"What's wrong with you?"

Nothing. Nothing was wrong.

We were fine. We were undrowned, awake, not strung across the trees in pieces. We were fine.

Jisoo

1953

YURI WOKE ME. HER FAMILIAR BODY LEANED OVER MY
narrow cot. Right away, I could tell she looked different. As I tried
to place the change, Jongyul whooped from the cot beside mine.
No curtains divided our corner of the hospital, and I saw his lips
widen into a floppy grin.

"Tell me it's true, Yuri. I can see it on your face," he said.

That was it. Serious, grim Yuri was smiling. She nodded and
swept a screen of black hair behind her ear. "You'll be discharged
tomorrow."

"We're leaving?" I braced myself against the wall. "How many
of us?"

"There's a whole list. Definitely the two of you." She adjusted
the pad that supported my arm, and it felt like a mattock swinging
into my shoulder. I looked at Jongyul's face, at Yuri, at anything
except myself. Yuri's hairpin had loosened, and I tried to touch it
through the blur of pain.

"Don't force it." Yuri was gentle with her reminders, even when
she shouldn't have been. "It'll be good for you to leave. Get used
to moving around."

"I'm going to get a girl pregnant tomorrow!" Jongyul yelled,
smacking his cot's metal frame.

Yuri pretended to cover her mouth, but she was used to our

crassness. A hundred of us lay on cots in the one wing of the hospital that remained usable. Parts of our bodies were buried around us. Not just parts, the remains of commodity lieutenants and one-day officers, too. At least I'd kept my arm. I was lucky, they said. I didn't think so.

"Even if you're given duty, you could ask for a pass in a few weeks for Chuseok." She placed her pinkie in my hand. I tried to squeeze as hard as I could. "Your grip's getting stronger." She searched my face. "You could celebrate the harvest festival at home, make sure your family's all right."

"My family's gone." I squeezed again and tried to feel the strength she insisted was returning to me.

"Your wife and her family," she said. "They'd want to see you."

Jongyul lifted his casted foot off the cot. "I'm going straight home to my parents. The agreement's been signed, the war's over. I'm not working a day longer."

"It's not over yet," I said.

"Armistice, truce." He shrugged. "The fighting's done. We've been waiting around for a month already. We should be allowed to go home."

I stared at Jongyul's half-burned, disfigured face. It looked like someone had spooned out his left eyeball and patted extra skin over the hole. He'd lost a thumb and two fingers and broken his foot. "You'll be fine."

He kicked my cot and explained what else he would do once he was out. Yuri left to tell the others. The hospital filled with the noise of grown men crying and cursing and yelling.

I lay back down. I could go home for a day—south to Seoul or farther east to Haemi's hometown, where they'd returned once the fighting passed. To a disappeared family or to a wife I hadn't seen in two years. I didn't know what I wanted anymore.

The next morning, they loaded the too damaged and almost recovered into trucks without ceremony. I stood outside the hospital in used fatigues. Going home to become a civilian—the thought of life as an ordinary man felt slippery, dangerous.

I couldn't imagine myself back in Seoul. I didn't want to see our square hanok home, the courtyard where Mother and Father used to watch Hyesoo fly her kite in the afternoon. I squeezed my shoulder until the pain pierced my thoughts. My useless arm. I would return to my wife as a man no longer whole.

Jongyul limped to my side. "My mother's going to cry when she sees me." He squeezed his milky, shiny cheek. "I'm disgusting."

"You look fine," I said, but I looked away.

Yuri called to us from the door. In the late-summer brightness, her dress was almost sheer. The silhouette of her thin legs, the intimate revealing, reminded me that I understood her only within the hospital's confines. A nurse, a kind woman. She bowed. "Were you two going to say goodbye?"

Jongyul bent his head to hers as they bid farewell and then scrambled past me with his crutch and half-blind face. "I'll save you a seat on the truck. I got a dirty magazine." He was like a monkey—always joking around and a little stupid, but in a tolerable, winsome way.

Yuri offered me a cloth-wrapped bundle. "Tofu for lunch. I had to sneak it from the kitchen."

"Thanks," I said. Her red pin had loosened again, and her bangs swept over her eyes. "You should let your hair grow."

She shook her head. "They might not recognize me then."

Her brothers were almost certainly dead, but I didn't say this; we all needed our own logic to withstand the war. "Leave your address. Your brothers will find you."

She smiled for my sake and rewrapped the binding around my arm. "Keep the sling on for another two weeks at least." I counted the seconds, concentrated on her hair, on the buttons of her uniform. Perfect yellow circles with tiny holes. "Breathe. Stop being stubborn. I know it hurts."

"How would you know, with your two whole arms?" I tried to joke.

"You stare at my pin when you're in pain." She unclipped it. "Take it. Give it to your wife."

I turned the pin around in my hand, unsure what to say. It was lighter than I'd imagined. Red and palm sized and sweet, as if it were made for a child.

"Take these, too." She handed me my release papers. "My turn to give advice. Tell her about the injury. Let her share your burden. She'll understand." Yuri saluted. "Corporal."

All the things I once would have said—to find me if she was ever in Seoul, that I'd treat her to a good meal—I could no longer offer. My family, my home, my money—they were all gone, and with them, my generosity. I bowed. "Be safe, Nurse Yuri."

The truck led us to an overcrowded officer center an hour away, where Jongyul and I waited together in line. When we reached the front desk, the staff sergeant eyed me as he took my information. "Crippled arm?"

"Partially, but I don't want to be discharged yet. I'm able," I said.

"Stay here." He returned with my work papers. "You're stationed in Daegu."

"What about Seoul? I have people I'm searching for."

He looked beyond me. "Next!"

Jongyul hobbled up, already asking about the best train home. I waited outside. A few minutes later, Jongyul staggered through the entrance. "They're keeping me. I got blown to pieces and they're keeping me." He leaned his head against his crutch. "Goddamn Daegu."

"Daegu?" I asked. "They put you there, too?" Of course. We were injured but still able. Our government didn't want cripples like us in the capital when we could still serve.

We trudged to the train station. Inside an unroofed container, we stared at the wispy, pathetic clouds. As the rails led us to our new city, we quieted with our different angers. I didn't know which one of us was right.

In Daegu, I stamped and signed official papers that held no meaning. Some retained corporals got to patrol the DMZ border. Others watched prisoners while the brass argued over a decent arrangement. They gave me a job at a desk.

"Lunch?" My partner, Taeil, stood from the chair beside mine. "Let's get out of here." He said the same thing every day, and every day, we walked to the mess hall to meet Jongyul, and there we ate the same meal—a handful of rice and a bowl of vegetable soup that wouldn't satisfy a child.

I fumbled with my jacket on the walk over. Though I had worn the sling for a few extra weeks as Yuri recommended, the pain in my arm had taken on a new form. Sometimes it was now a blistering worm that grubbed from muscle to muscle without reason. Other times, I felt nothing at all, as if no limb hung from my shoulder socket. I didn't know which was worse.

Jongyul, already seated in the hall, waved us over to our usual table. An eye patch covered half his face, and a man we didn't know sat beside him. "This is Kim Kwangseok. He's new in my division," Jongyul said.

Kwangseok bowed. He seemed needlessly nervous, his hands shifting from his pockets to the front of his shirt and then down to his belt.

Taeil nodded at Jongyul's eye patch. "New fashion accessory?"

"A girl sold it to me. She said it made me look handsome." Jongyul thrust out a hip and posed like the women in clothing advertisements.

"Let me try." Taeil snapped the band and pulled off the patch.

From the look on Kwangseok's face, it was clear he hadn't yet seen the mass of grooved skin over Jongyul's eye socket. He let out a loud, ugly sound that made me want to punch his childish face.

"What're you looking at?" I asked. "Can't keep your eyes on the ground?"

Kwangseok stopped gaping at Jongyul and turned to me. "Him, sir, I'm looking at him."

"Be nice," Jongyul said to me.

Taeil returned the patch with a shrug. "I think it looks good on you."

I shook my head. They were too easily content with the life given to us. We were half-formed and useless in the minds of our government, and these boys accepted it as fact.

Taeil nodded at the line forming along the back wall. "Let's get our meals."

As we ate, I realized I wasn't any better. I couldn't look away from Jongyul's hands, even if I tried. He squeezed his spoon between his pointer and middle fingers as if he'd always eaten that way. I was the one who'd struggled to learn how to use my left hand to use chopsticks, to wipe my ass, to stamp the damn documents.

At the end of the meal, Jongyul stomped his healed foot and cleared his throat. "I want to make a toast. There's a reason Kwangseok's here. He's replacing me."

"What do you mean?" Taeil asked.

"I'm leaving tomorrow." Jongyul grinned. "They're finally letting this cripple go home."

We whooped. We slapped him on the back and knuckled his head. "You have to become a lot funnier if you're going to be the next Jongyul," Taeil said to Kwangseok.

Kwangseok's scrawny build annoyed me. He reminded me of Kyunghwan. After I'd enlisted, Kyunghwan tried to knock down the plank walls dividing our rooms. He couldn't even do that right. "Father signed me up. Did you convince him?" He had kicked at the rice bowls, pathetic, ineffectual. "If I die, she won't forgive you." But he was wrong. I had nothing to do with his enlistment. I had won Haemi, and I didn't need a traitor in my life. Staring at Kwangseok, I saw Kyunghwan's weak limbs, the sly face of a liar.

We walked out of the hall after lunch, still celebrating Jongyul's news. Taeil blew a thin line of smoke from his pipe. "Lucky bastard. Eunmi writes every day asking when they'll let me go, why we have to stay when the war's been over for months."

"Our wives should get together and commiserate," I said.

"They let me go home for a weekend," Taeil said. "You should ask."

"Jisoo's too honorable to leave before anyone else." Jongyul turned to Kwangseok. "You know about this guy?"

"No, sir."

"Jisoo's an unsung hero." Jongyul cleared his throat. He loved this story. He told it as if he'd been there fighting beside me. I let him. I wondered if Haemi would think me heroic, too—and if I could mimic Jongyul's gusto when I returned to her with one working arm.

✿

When I had first arrived at the hospital, I wanted medications they didn't have or refused to give me. "What kind of place is this?" I yelled. The doctor ripped off my right sleeve and cleaned my wound with a metal rod, a cotton swab stuck on one end. The rod swiped up and down below my skin, like a foot kicking under a blanket. I passed out. When I woke up again, I was in a different room with a nurse.

She cut off the rest of my shirt with a pair of scissors. Her lips were a tight, closed line as she ignored my screams. "Breathe," she said. I closed my eyes and tried to concentrate on the feel of the metal edge sliding against my chest. The scissors' cool, sleek snaking. "You'll have to wear buttoned shirts from now on."

"What are you doing?" I asked when she pulled off my pants.

"You need a wash."

I tried to stop her. She was stronger than she looked. "You have an arm that's probably crippled. Don't make this so difficult."

"I can do it myself," I said.

"No, you can't, or you wouldn't be here."

Yuri. She moved with assurance and it made me want to hurt her. "When do I get to bathe myself?" I asked.

"When you can manage." She softened as she swept a wet cloth across my chest. "You'll be all right. I can tell from how annoying you are already."

When she brought me to my cot, a disfigured man lay in the one next to it. He was crying and I couldn't understand his face. Seeing Jongyul for the first time, I felt spineless for my earlier yelling.

I offered him a cigarette later that night. He tried to grab it and missed. "My thumb, my thumb," he said, as if that were the worst of his injuries. He hadn't stopped crying.

Yuri came over as soon as we lit our cigarettes. "You can't smoke here. Give me your pack."

I didn't care. They weren't mine. She threw them in the garbage and turned to dress Jongyul's face. I couldn't stop watching. The skin that was no longer skin but not nothing either and the blasted shape of the eyehole and how he whimpered.

"Damn." The wrapping stuck to the wound. "I need to clean this before it gets infected." She grimaced. "It'll hurt, all right?"

He screamed as she pulled at the stuck gauze. Yellow and red oozed out. I couldn't look away. "Distract him," she said to me. "Tell him a story."

Jongyul held on to the cot's metal rim. "Tell me how you got hurt. Tell me something bloody."

A fight in a small village with wrecked trees and ruined homes. A surprise attack from the Chinese PLA. My commander shot in the leg. A little boy and a girl, separated from their family. The girl hit in front of us, clean through the cheek. A sharp spray of blood. Her brother's cries cutting through the air. As I scrambled to reach him and the commander, a Red had pounced on me.

"Did you kill that Chinese Commie dog?" Jongyul asked.

"I killed him."

"Describe it," he said.

I told him about the soldier's gun against my neck, and how we'd rolled over the girl's body, her eyes still open, by accident. The boy's shrill and endless bawling, my commander's panting. How the soldier's shots missed me, but the shards ricocheted and bored through my arm. I described the rage of pain and how I'd killed him with his own gun, without remorse or thought or pity.

Yuri didn't look up until she finished. Jongyul had sweated through his shirt. She stared at me as she changed him into a new one. I hadn't looked at her before, directly. A small, blunt nose. Disarming eyes. They seemed too tender for a nurse. The diamond cut of her face tilted away, and I wondered if she knew that I'd lied.

✿

Jongyul, Taeil, and I strolled through Daegu's streets that evening, still celebrating Jongyul's news. We passed civilians talking about their preparations for winter in loud voices. Families had been shorn and lost in the halving of our country, and yet these villagers continued on, as if the years of stalemate had lulled them into dullness. Or perhaps they were too frightened to speak about anything but the commonplace.

It disgusted me, how easily people accepted the armistice. They seemed to confuse the end of fighting with the end of war. To see the continued presence of the United Nations as a comfort rather than the violation I knew it to be. But for one night, I tried to act like them, mindless and content.

We went to Little House. It was a wooden hut fit for twenty people and had the best naengmyeon in Daegu. "Come in, boys." Auntie Kang waved from the back counter.

"Three naengmyeons and a bottle of whatever you have hidden away," Jongyul called as we claimed a table in the front.

A man in the corner yelled, "They're delicious. Exactly like the Northerners make them."

Taeil turned to reply, and that's when I saw him—the bastard from my platoon. The real reason I was a cripple. Lee Mansik.

He sat across from the yeller. Too tall and thickly built, with the same crooked nose and small, shapeless chin. The same dumb look in his eyes. Hunched over his bowl, he slurped noodles into his fat mouth.

Auntie brought a bottle to our table, obscuring Mansik from my view. "What are we celebrating, boys?"

Taeil poured corn whiskey into tiny cups. "Jisoo, give us a speech."

I forced my thoughts back to the group. I raised my drink, winked at Auntie. "To lucky Jongyul finally getting out. He's going home!"

We cheered and joked and when our food arrived, we ate in noisy gulps. I wavered between caring and not. What would happen if he revealed the truth about my injury? I decided that I did care, that I would go to him. He would notice me anyway on his way out, and I wanted to confront him on my own terms.

I stood from the table and yelled. "Lee Mansik!"

He froze when he recognized my voice. And then he was moving—excusing himself from his group, looking toward the back door, wiping his mouth with his wrist.

I crossed the room quick and caught him by the back of his shirt before he'd reached the kitchen. "You say hello to me now," I said.

He followed the command, turned and bowed. "Corporal. I didn't know you were in Daegu."

I stood close. His chest rose with his heavy panting. It was true. He was fine. I gripped him by the neck. "I'm here with my good arm and my injured arm," I said.

"The commander—"

"You lied."

"I couldn't remember. When they asked me—"

"You're lying now."

A knife lay on the kitchen counter. Auntie pretended not to see us. I was close enough to gut him until his insides—shiny, bubbling, and wet—bled through his uniform. I tightened my hold on his neck. I could wrench his arm from its socket, batter it to pieces. Relish the sound of his pathetic squealing. But as his sweating face gazed down at mine, I realized I didn't want to hear any excuses from him. I didn't want to look at his giant, whole body. I didn't want to remember.

I stepped back. "I wanted to tell you that it's done. Sit down and enjoy your meal."

I left Mansik, stunned and unmoving, and returned to my table. Jongyul whistled, eyebrows raised. "What'd he do to you? Was he in your division?"

"Forget him. He's a piece of shit on my shoe." I ordered another bottle. Jongyul distracted us with his jokes, and Taeil again spoke of his wife. We drank until the corn whiskey tasted like water.

On his way out, Mansik hesitated at our table and bowed. I didn't watch him leave. I'd meant what I said. I didn't want anything from him anymore.

Later that night, Jongyul came to my barracks with two envelopes. "From the hospital," he said. We both recognized the handwriting.

"How'd she know where we were?" He sat on my cot and read his letter aloud. Yuri spoke of his eye and leg, asked about all the women in his life, and hoped that he would be able to go home soon. He folded the paper into thirds with a heedfulness I'd never seen in his movements. "I'd marry her. I really would." He nodded at my envelope. "So?"

I didn't open the note. "I'll read it later."

"You guys having an affair?"

"Shut it."

"I'm joking. Yuri's going to be mine. I'm going to tell her to find me in my hometown." He patted my good shoulder. "I'll come say goodbye in the morning."

I read Yuri's letter once I was alone. She was growing out her hair and didn't want to be around hurt people any longer. The country would never reunite, and she'd decided to accept this fact. She didn't want to grieve forever. *All that matters are the people who loved us before the war,* she wrote. *My family in the North are gone. My parents are dying from the waiting.* She asked if I'd visited Haemi, if I had told her yet. *I miss my brothers,* she wrote at the end. No signature or goodbye.

I threw the letter away. It annoyed me. How she insisted on the truth to someone like me. It made me feel like a liar.

❀

Yuri was the only person who knew the real story—the one where I wasn't a hero but an idiot. I had promised myself I'd never tell anyone. Then a month into my stay, she and I sat on a bench outside the hospital, watching the patients with intact legs walk around a fifty-meter yard. A barbed-wire fence encircled us, as if the Reds might come for the injured. Yuri held an unlit kerosene lamp between her arms. "I'm restless," she said. "Let's walk."

Along the way, she told me about her family. "My parents want me to quit. My father wants to head south to his sister's. He thinks we'll be safer there."

"He's right," I said.

She glared at me. "My grandparents are buried here. And my brothers—they'll come here to find us." The last she'd heard, her younger brother was in Japan, and the older one in the Military Police. "He could be anywhere," she said.

She walked with a slight lopsidedness I hadn't noticed before, and I wondered if she was becoming one of us. Yuri was able-bodied while we were not; still she seemed so fragile, as if I could break her wrist with one hard tug.

"I was an MP, too," I said. "Your brother will be safe. They keep us away from the front lines."

She glanced at my bandaged arm. "Like you were safe?"

In that moment, I felt as if I'd known Yuri all my life. I woke to her bent frame each day—her thick eyebrows and pale face, her hurt gaze as she checked my stitches. It was as if my pain were hers as well. I couldn't keep the truth from her.

When we were far enough from the others, I laid out my story for her to judge.

I'd been a watcher of my own people. By June, I was anxious. Every day we heard news of the war coming to a close. I wanted to join the fighting before it was too late.

"Your request is denied." The major sat at his table carving the skin off an apple. He slid a slice into his mouth. "You're good at this. Don't complain again. You should be on patrol right now." He pointed his knife at the door and watched me leave.

It was misty and cold for a summer night. I walked the perimeter of our camp, and as I rounded the eastern edge toward the parked trucks and entrance road, I heard mumbling. I aimed my flashlight at the sound. A drunk soldier. I recognized the man's height. "Mansik?"

He raised a hand to his eyebrows and squinted. "Who is that?"

I grabbed his arm and hauled him behind a group of trees that ran along the entrance road. "What happened to you?"

He crouched to his knees and moaned a long, low bleating. The stench of alcohol spilled from his mouth. "I was due back yesterday."

I squatted beside him. "Sober up. I'm on duty."

"Don't turn me in. I'll be jailed if you do." He showed me a ring of keys. "I could take a truck and leave."

"Don't be stupid. Wait here until you feel better. You can explain tomorrow."

He held on to my sleeves. "I can't, Jisoo."

"I need to make another round." I sat him behind the trees and walked on. The commander's office was quiet, the lamp still lit.

When I circled back ten minutes later, Mansik was smoking. Anyone could have seen the glow. I fought the urge to stub the cigarette out on his face and threw it on the ground instead. "You're an idiot." I stuffed his pack into my pocket.

"I can't think without smoking," he whined. "Give it back."

"I'll call you in if you don't stop." I pushed him against a tree. "I'm already shoveling myself into shit for you."

"You goddamn MP. You think you're special, monitoring us?" He sniggered, his head lolling against the trunk. "You're nothing. You hide and send us out to fight. You're not worth the dead skin falling off my dick."

I cuffed him hard. He was pissed and strong. But so was I. He swung back, connected with my cheek, and lost his balance. I punched him again. He lurched toward me, grabbed my neck, and we fell.

A stupid, useless fight.

We tumbled onto the entrance road, deaf and blind until suddenly, we weren't. A truck. Lights. Honking. Metal and rubber and heat coming straight at us. A wheel and my shoulder. Cold dirt in my face, my mouth, up my nose. Everywhere, pain. My voice screaming out a high, strange wailing.

And Mansik, that ass, running away just in time.

❦

Taeil walked into the office late one cold November morning. He didn't wear a jacket and stared at me like I was somebody else. His lips, blistered from the sudden frost, opened and closed like a fish's. He staggered to his chair and pounded its back with his fists.

"What is it? What happened?" I asked.

He sat and then stood again. "I can't believe it."

I followed him around the room. "Tell me."

He wrung a note in his hands. "Jongyul fell off a train."

"What?"

"He was going to visit some girl."

We read his parents' letter. They said Jongyul had always talked about us, and they wanted us to know about his death. They thanked us for being his friends.

I wanted to burn their note. Taeil refused. We didn't stamp papers for the rest of the day. The next morning, I asked the office for a weekend pass.

"To visit Jongyul's parents?" Taeil asked.

"To visit my wife."

When I had first joined the war, I'd wanted to send Haemi an envelope with my fingernail and hair clippings as a precautionary memory. I was desperate to act, to understand the significance of *honor*—this word that Father had disciplined into me when I was a child. I was ready to fight and defend my country. Instead, I watched maggots eat at the sores of prisoners, punished my own for the smallest of infractions, and listened as other men shared their battle stories. I injured my arm in a meaningless argument. Jongyul was dead. I was ready to go home.

With a weekend bag over my good shoulder, I left Daegu, passing the half-razed buildings and empty fields. I walked until it was dark, and then I found a bus headed northeast toward Haemi's hometown.

The village had changed. There were markings of war but of reformation, too. Gravel had replaced some of the dirt paths. Rubble lay beside newly built homes. Some villagers recognized me from my summers visiting Kyunghwan, but most didn't. I didn't stop at Uncle's home. I didn't ask about my cousin. I thought only of Haemi. I wondered if Yuri was right, if my wife would understand.

A few days after I'd confessed to Yuri, she'd approached me with a nervous look. She patted her hair and hesitated. "What is it?" I finally asked. She revealed that there was a different version in my hospital entry papers. Not the hero story I'd made up and not the truth I'd hidden. After the fight, as I lay unconscious, they'd found Mansik and asked him for an explanation. His warped response blamed me, claimed I had started beating him without reason. This became the official answer. There was no way to erase his words.

I practiced telling Haemi each version as I followed her directions, unfolding and refolding the first letter I'd received from her in the hospital. *We've returned home. I never want to see Busan again. Find us soon. Hyunki misses you.* At the very least, I could show her what had happened to me, even if I couldn't manage the truth.

At an entranceway decorated with flowery yellow bushes, I knocked. A thin boy opened the door. "Hyunki?" I asked.

"Jisoo-hyung?" He whooped and ran inside, yelling, "He's here! Jisoo-hyung!"

He returned with his mother, both of them shouting. Her greeting was high-pitched and happy as she stumbled down the stairs. Tears filmed her eyes. It moved me—how much they cared that I had made it back alive.

Haemi came last. Slender and sharp, she stood by the door, her hand against the frame, surprise showing on her face.

Mother guided me to the planked porch beneath the eaves. She bent to remove my shoes as Hyunki brought me water. Haemi hovered, paced from one side of the porch to the other. As they gathered around me, I noticed they looked older, darker. Hazy. Like people I almost didn't know. It chilled me. They were my only family now.

"Food! We need to feed you. Look at your bones. Say hello to your wife while we cook you a meal." Mother hustled Hyunki inside.

Haemi moved closer. I watched her arched eyes, her mouth. She no longer wore her hair in a braid but piled high in a bun. I could see her slim neck. Her face, still beautiful, had shifted somehow. Weariness had settled over her features and narrowed her gaze. I hesitated, glanced at the door Mother and Hyunki had disappeared through. When I turned back to Haemi, she smiled. "I'm glad you're alive."

"Me too."

"Sometimes when I couldn't sleep at night, I'd think someone was pretending to be you, writing me, and that you were dead this whole time. A cruel joke." She laughed. "But you're here now."

She stared at me with the sharp, discerning look that had lured me to her from the start. She touched my eyebrows, temples, arm, the ruined shoulder. She touched me freely. "I saw it right away."

"I was hurt."

She frowned. "Not one of your letters—"

"I didn't know what you would say."

"So?" She raised her chin and crossed her arms. "Tell me."

Watching her, I understood. Haemi was no longer the girl I had met in Busan. She was already a wife.

Kyunghwan

1954

TWO LINES HUGGED THE LIBRARY'S EXTERIOR, WITH THE women and men separated by the width of the sidewalk. I was late, and I couldn't find the Whimoon boys. They'd probably claimed their usual table already.

A high school girl with clipped hair nodded at me. "They're over there." She pointed. In their dark caps with serious faces, the four boys compared notes near the entrance. "You're always studying here. What's your name?" The girl wore an ankle-length coat, even though it was May and too warm. She threaded the top buttonhole with her pinkie. "I see you watching them every Sunday."

"I'm no one, really. Thanks." I snuck my way through the line as best I could.

The National Library was three stories high and rested on a block of land large enough to fit ten hanoks. It no longer astonished me the way it had my first day in Seoul, but it was still my favorite building. The rounded dormers gazed down upon the hundreds who retreated inside. If I could have chosen where to study, I would have crept up to the highest floor and sat by one of those eyebrow-shaped windows.

Instead, I filed into the main reading room on the first floor, where the rows of tables cramped with students leached the splendor from the space. I sat at a table behind the Whimoon boys. Kyungho asked mathematics questions and the others took turns explaining their answers. Namil, with the fish mouth, snuck a look at me across his shoulder before he responded. I copied down everything they said. When they switched from group studying to their individual writing sections, I did, too. I didn't care if they knew. I had been studying off them every Sunday for weeks.

Even so, I was surprised when Kyungho approached and nodded at my notebooks. "You're preparing for the entrance exams?" He whirled a pencil with his pale, clean hands. A boy who hadn't ever worked, fought, or tackled fear.

"Studying like you are," I said.

"What school do you go to?"

Namil swung around. He tucked his chin against the chair's high back. The wood flattened his face and made his mouth seem even larger. "You know about the National Unified Test? They added it this year."

"I know," I said.

"It's to make it harder for guys like you to get in."

Kyungho rubbed the back of his head. "Guys like who, Namil?"

"Unqualified guys, ex-military guys, refugees-who-missed-a-year-or-two-and-are-trying-to-make-up-for-it-too-late type of guys. So, which kind are you?"

All of them, I should have said—a one-day officer who somehow survived the war. In a secondhand U.S. Army uniform, I'd fought to gain land for an armistice while these kids ate oranges at home and worried about their fathers' factories. "I don't know what you're talking about," I said. We had only two days before the exam and I couldn't afford to waste any time.

"I'm not trying to be rude, but you're obviously not in high school." Namil looked at the others in their group. "Why else would he be listening to our lessons?"

"I'm only nineteen," I said.

"So I'm right." Namil shrugged and turned to face the others. "I don't care. You're not the competition."

"Ignore him." Kyungho gestured to a stack of books on their table. "Our teachers told us to review these the week before the test."

I copied down the titles and thanked him. "I can study off other groups, but you guys are the most focused."

"We don't mind. I'm Park Kyungho."

"I know. I'm Yun Kyunghwan."

"Of course." He smiled. "We're here tomorrow, if you want to join us."

I went to search for the books he'd recommended. I didn't want to tell him what I did on Mondays.

Cheonggyecheon was a river of waste, squatters, disease. Huts on stilts stood rickety and fragile like flock-lost birds along the river's edge. Women in stained shirts poured buckets of laundry water from their windows. Others threw out their shit and urine, their vegetable ends, their children's vomit. Everyone's noses and mouths and asses leaked from sickness and no one could escape it.

My life was consumed by filth. Four days a week, I dredged trash out of Cheonggyecheon. Two days, I wheeled a garbage wagon through Seoul. One day was mine. Always, the test lodged itself in my head, distracting me. If work ended early, I would walk past Whimoon High School. I couldn't hear anything, but being close to the studying inside made me feel better somehow, smarter.

If You Leave Me

Byungwoo was my dredging partner. Bald, with joints that swelled without reason, he steadied the boat while I maneuvered the hoist. Sometimes we found items worth keeping—an undamaged celadon-glazed plate, a waterlogged lantern, a knife with a chipped hilt. Mostly we picked up refuse and weeds.

"On the left. That sheet," Byungwoo said, steering toward a crumpled piece of tarpaulin wrapped around a hut's half-submerged leg. I dropped the hoist and the attached bucket into the water.

As we approached, a woman with a slim, horselike face leaned out the open window. She wore a blue tee shirt showing a cartoon mouse holding its own tail. "What do you men want?"

"What do you think?" Byungwoo asked. "Look at this junk. We're cleaning up."

"You'll knock down my house with that thing! Government assholes!"

"What else are we supposed to do?" He nodded to me. "Go on, Kyunghwan."

I tried to rake the bucket against the tarp, but it was too slippery. Sloshing with the river's waves, the tarp only twisted further around the hut's leg. I adjusted the hoist, and as it butted the canvas, a smell hit us—rancid, putrid, almost sweet at the edges of its noxious weight. I stopped. Instead of knocking me over, the scent had an uneasy familiarity.

Byungwoo sniffed. "Lady, you have something to tell us?"

She dusted her windowsill with her fingertips. Thick splinters of wood fell into the water. "I have three kids here and they're sicker than before the war. If you take that plastic, you take what's underneath it, too." There wasn't a papered window for her to slide shut, so she walked away with loud, angry calls to her children inside.

· 133 ·

I knocked the hoist against the hut. Again the smell circled the air and seeped into our clothes. It seemed to coat us, not with its scent, but with its power to recall memories we no longer wanted.

"You know what I think?" Byungwoo asked.

I nodded. We both knew—the scent reminded us of war. As I'd waited in the trenches for nightfall, I'd breathed in the stench of decomposing bodies, those not yet burned. Afraid the pungent odor would poison my insides. Afraid the Reds would smell it, too, and find me.

Byungwoo stepped back to the rudder. "They don't pay us enough for that."

"Dead husband?" I asked.

"The tarp's too small. Dead kid?"

"It can't be that bad, right?"

We stood on our tiny boat in our shit river. Slow waves from the other dredging vessels rippled the water. A cluster of children downstream jumped on a narrow bridge.

"Someone else will come around," Byungwoo said.

"Not today." I covered my nose with my shirtsleeve. "Get closer. I'll do it."

I tried to use the bucket's weight to drag the sheet to our boat. The bulky stretch of tarpaulin didn't provide any grip. When we were almost under the woman's hut, I sank my arms in and pulled.

The sheet came off easily.

A mountain of rats. A reeking cloud of decaying bodies on a rotting wooden raft.

Byungwoo raised his arms. "I quit."

"They're just a few rats."

"A few?"

Some were more skeleton than animal, others were tinged with green muck. Dimpled eyeballs and knotted fur. It was disgusting, but at least they weren't human.

"This is why her kids are sick. They're all savage country idiots." Byungwoo kicked a piece of trash into the water. "I hate this job."

"Am I a country idiot, too?" I asked.

"Yeah, take them all with you and leave."

Sludge dripped from my arms, and the stink made my stomach clench. I grabbed our largest pail. "Let's get this done."

We tried to use the tarp as a barrier as we carried the rats to the hold. They slid around the slick canvas, jostling against one another and falling over the edges of the sheet. Eventually, we used our hands. We doubled our gloves, but still, we felt them—delicate and thin boned, teeth larger than expected, feet gaunt.

"It's the cats." The woman leaned out her window again, this time with a baby against her hip. It looked sick, too yellow. "They keep bringing them into the house. My other boy's four. He feeds the strays and they repay him. Don't get me in trouble."

"You're going to have to vacate sooner or later," Byungwoo said.

I hefted the raft onto our boat. "Whoever you're waiting for, he's not coming back."

"You don't know that," she said.

"Look around you." I lifted my arms at the sludge, at the trash I was shoveling for her and all the other beggars who lived along the river. Here in Seoul, the city of dreams and opportunity, I'd been reduced to this. I thought of the Whimoon boys, their pristine minds and bodies. "Look at where you are. It's pathetic. No one will save you."

The woman cursed. The baby started to cry. It, too, had a horse face.

Byungwoo turned the boat downriver, and we floated away. After a long silence, he grunted. "You were a little mean there."

I shrugged.

We both knew I was right. The widows of Cheonggyecheon were delusional.

After discarding the rats and the rest of the waste, Byungwoo checked the dock line. We changed out of our gloves and our work uniforms. "Let's get something to eat," he said. "How about some sea squirts? We deserve a treat after that mess."

Three dredgers whose names I hadn't bothered to remember waited for him on the street. "Come on, little hick." Byungwoo smiled. "Join us."

"I can't." I opened my empty wallet. We weren't friendly enough for any of them to offer me food.

"Walk with us to the main intersection, at least."

"Let's go," the tallest dredger called.

"I have to tell you what happened," Byungwoo said as we joined them. "Kyunghwan and I got the lousiest luck today."

"You always say that."

"I mean it—not like today."

Byungwoo was elaborate, detailed. The men spat as he described the rats. One snorted. They laughed and cursed in sympathy. I watched pedestrians shuffle around us. I didn't want to end up like these old men, pathetic and crass and hopeless. As we walked toward the city center, a fat woman in a pink dress rode by on a rickshaw.

"I'd rather pull her than shovel any more crap," Byungwoo said.

"She'd crush you with her huge ass!" the tallest one replied.

The dredger who walked next to him nearly tripped over a girl washing pants in the gutter. He yelped. "Country bastards coming here with nowhere to go."

Byungwoo agreed. It was a common, easy topic.

"Let them take our useless jobs," the one beside me said. A purple birthmark covered one of his hands. He pulled his cuff low. "Know what my brother thinks?" He gazed at the others and then me. "He said the money's in the factories. Cotton, paper, sugar, flour. The whiter, the better. What do you think?"

"The whiter, the better? That's funnier than Byungwoo's rat story."

"We have rice. Why would we need flour?"

The men went on like that, bouncing from one topic to another. When they looked at me, I said the first thing that came to mind. "I'm going to take the college entrance exam tomorrow."

They all stopped to stare at me with fresh interest.

The birthmarked one nudged. "You think you'll pass?"

"These hicks and their dreams."

"What're you doing that for, anyway?"

"You didn't tell me that." Byungwoo tugged at himself. "Is that why you're such a dog at doing your job? Your head in the books?"

I didn't know why I'd said anything. They were older and set in their ways. They wouldn't understand. "This is where I turn." I pointed to a side path that shot off from the main road. "Enjoy dinner."

I didn't watch them continue on, but I heard them. Byungwoo's thick, nasal voice chafed against the birthmarked one's insistence on the future of factories. The angry one railed at the beggars on the streets again. The tall one: "Rats and cotton and roads and all that. What does it matter to us? All we can do is eat and live."

I walked half an hour before I reached my real home. My shack was one of hundreds jutting up against the side of Namsan. There was no order to these shelters flanking the mountain. They sprouted around shared outhouses and any available space. A little boy handed me a pebble as I passed. I'd killed a cockroach for him once. "The rock looks clear in the sun," he said. His sullen older sister, nursing their youngest sibling, bowed hello. Inside my shack, I turned on my battery lamp. Across from my sleeping mat, I rolled up my canvas curtain to let the breeze in. The evening sky was bruising already. That meant the library would close soon. The Whimoon boys in their crisp black uniforms and caps, with their new books and their tiled hanok homes—they would take the test tomorrow, just as I would.

I opened my notebooks. From a tin can, I took out a fresh pepper and held it on my tongue until the heat burned me awake.

The test took place in an open amphitheater where leveled rows of grass ringed a circular field. I felt my inadequacy as I found my seat in one of the upper tiers. The other students seemed like a different breed—ease an essential part of their being. Boys wearing jackets with band collars joked as they found their spots. Their shirts underneath were probably stiff and clean. Mine was loose, stained. A rope cinched my pants. A grandmother who lived in the hut beside mine had sewn on the flapping soles of my shoes with gray thread.

A boy with thick black glasses bragged about his girlfriend taking the women's entrance exam less than a kilometer away. He didn't say *wife* or *match* or even *engaged*. He chose that particular word and looked around to catch his friends' reactions. I tried to spot Kyungho or even Namil.

A proctor approached my seat and scanned my papers. "Yun Kyunghwan?"

"Yes, sir."

He inspected my identification, checked off my name. "No high school certificate?"

"I lost it in the war transition, sir."

He handed me a packet. "Don't start until you're told." He continued climbing, marking the students in my column until he reached the top. The kid in front of me smelled of garlic and sweat. He was already balding. I concentrated on the skin peeking through his whorl of hair and felt better.

A sharp laugh kicked through the air. It was the boy with the glasses. He whispered something, probably about his girlfriend, to the student next to him. I imagined her. A smart, educated girl with her hair cut short in the high school style, her shoulders bent over test papers, wearing a crisp white blouse and a neat navy skirt. It could have been Haemi. No, not her, with her long, wavy hair subdued in a braid and her penchant for traditional hanboks. Her fierce intelligence. How she used to sit on her knees in class, the right answers perched and ready for our grade-school teacher. Her loose, listing handwriting. No, Haemi would have been like me— determined despite the odds, hoping to keep up with the others once the world quieted to pencils on sheets of paper.

As I thought of her for the first time in months, a man below yelled through a bullhorn, "You may start!" I picked up my pencil and began.

Afterward, I wandered. The tests had been as hard as I'd expected. I had stayed until the absolute end when the proctors yelled to stop, and then I'd rushed outside. I didn't want to hear the stragglers compare their answers. A few blocks away, on a street occupied by secondhand stores and food stalls, I ran into Kyungho and Namil.

Namil looked at his watch. "Did you just finish?"

"I've been walking around," I said.

"Come join us. We're about to eat." Kyungho gestured to one of the noodle stands.

"I didn't bring any money." I waved at a secondhand bookstore farther down the street. "I was heading that way."

"To buy something with your imaginary cash?" Namil grinned.

I wanted to tell him we didn't know each other enough for him to joke. Instead, I responded, "To browse," and tried to move past them.

"I've got it tonight." Kyungho clapped my back the way Jisoo used to when his privilege cloaked his pity. "We should celebrate."

We sat on wooden pallets and ate braised chicken stew that had simmered for hours over a small fire. I ate one starch noodle at a time. They avoided all the obvious questions about me. Instead, they discussed specific test problems with the same intensity they had in the library.

"This"—Kyungho wrote in his notebook—"was how I solved it."

"It's faster this way." Namil presented both calculations. "What do you think?"

They erased all the pleasure of eating. I hadn't done it either way and was sure I was wrong. "Let's talk about something else."

"What, the election?" Kyungho asked.

"How about the war?" Namil nudged. "Were you part of the ROK?"

"Forget the 6-2-5. Do either of you have girlfriends?" I asked. Kyungho reddened. Namil shook his head.

"Let's return to this," Kyungho said after a pause, pointing to their written problems.

I stood as soon as I finished. "Thanks for the meal. I have to go."

Kyungho wrote his address on the back of his notes. "The study group is meeting at my house the morning of the results. You should join."

It was Namil who stood when I tried to make an excuse. "Don't let an asshole like me stop you from coming. We might be classmates in a year."

I took the address in order to get away from them. They watched me leave, and at the end of the street, I entered the secondhand bookstore to escape their gaze. Inside, a man leaned against a shelf with a cigarette between his fingers.

"Can I have one?" I asked.

"If you buy a book."

"I don't know if I can."

He gave me one anyway. "Look around, at least."

Towering stacks covered the tables. There didn't seem to be any order to them. I wanted clean, new books like the ones in the library. I laughed.

"What is it?" the man asked.

"This is the first time I've felt spoiled in a long time," I said.

"What does that mean?"

"Nothing at all."

Lewd comics, foreign paperbacks, novels, clan registers, slim slips of poetry, almanacs, literary magazines, short stories, a few translations. I wanted to rummage through them all, to indulge in their words, to keep moving, to avoid the hut where I lived alone. Haemi had needled herself into my mind, and it made me restless. As I'd read question after question during the test, she'd floated through my head—the swift motion of her arms when we used to strip pine trees as children to get to their edible inner bark, her figure on my handlebars, the pressure of her shoulder against my collar as I cycled through shantytowns. Her face, apologetic and defiant, the last time I truly saw her, when she had let Jisoo lead her away.

Maybe she would have preferred the boy with the glasses, his arrogance. Maybe she was here in Seoul, a wife and mother of a higher class who had forgotten about me. Maybe it was because of her that I wanted to take the test at all. She was the one who'd whispered the dream of college into both our minds. But her presence, now, annoyed me.

She and Jisoo had abandoned me. After the war, Jisoo hadn't gone beyond asking Father if I'd survived, and Haemi hadn't sought me out, either. As I lived in a hovel, they continued on—comfortable and without any thought for me. I had meant nothing to them in the end.

"So are you buying or not? I need to close soon." The man walked to a shelf. "These comics are cheap."

"I'm still looking." I held a short story pamphlet in my hand. *Cranes.* I walked to the back of the store. As the man smoked, I slipped the slim volume into my pocket. It was easy; it had always been easy for me to lift.

"Nothing?"

"I don't have enough money," I said.

He blew smoke circles toward the ceiling. "This is my brother-in-law's store, and he's a jerk. Here." He extended another cigarette. "Enjoy."

I smoked with him, but the cigarette reminded me of Haemi, too. She wetted the tip too much and had scowled when I tried to teach her the right way. "I know what I'm doing," she'd said, walking ahead of me on the narrow footpath. We'd been in the woods looking for something to do. With the cigarette between her fingers, her sharp elbow angled to the ground, she'd swung toward me, her mouth billowing. "See?"

A week later, I hesitated at the entrance to the doctor's office with a shirt held up to my face. The bleeding had stopped, and the idea of asking for help embarrassed me. Since the day of the test I had felt as if Haemi was following me, watching me at work, in my hut, and now here with a shredded cheek, ready to beg for care. I imagined her pity at the unraveling of my life.

A nurse stood by the front door, careful to avoid direct sunlight. "Do you need help?"

I lifted the shirt off my face. "Should I go in?"

She squinted. "Come closer." I waited for her to flinch. She only nodded. "Yes, definitely."

"I can't pay."

"The doctor might help anyway. Better to get it checked out than lose your handsome face." She smiled at my surprise. "Come in."

She led me to a small waiting room with a few chairs and a desk. "He's with a woman who lost her baby," she whispered. "Sit. Let me see the damage."

A strand of her hair had caught on her earring, and I concentrated on that tangle as she leaned over me. Even so, I felt her. She touched my forehead with the tips of her fingers, walked the length of my brow down to my right cheek, where I'd bled the most. I couldn't remember the last time anyone had touched me. It felt strange, like I was underneath someone else's skin. I wanted her to continue.

She found some gauze and held it against my face. "These are bite marks. From what?"

"Rats," I said, almost laughing at the pathetic story. My throat tightened, and I closed my eyes as her fingers pressed against me. Ever since that raft, with its death mound stink that still made my nostrils flare, I saw rats everywhere—around street corners, in my dreams. They taunted me. "I woke up to them. Gnawing on my cheek like I'm nothing."

"That sounds awful. Here, use your fingers to apply pressure." She tucked the tangled strand of hair behind her ear. "I could fix you up myself, but the doctor won't let me."

"I don't mind waiting."

She crossed her arms and held up one hand, as if weighing an invisible object. "He wasn't here during the war, so he doesn't think women can do anything."

"Where was he?"

"He's rich. His family probably shipped him off somewhere."

A low wail floated through one of the screened doors behind us. "She's all alone. Her husband's away and the mother-in-law's watching the other kids."

I imagined the faceless woman, a dead infant in her arms. "I'm sorry."

"I'm not the one who lost the baby." The nurse pushed herself up. "I'll tell Dr. Kim you're waiting."

A few minutes later, the nurse, doctor, and woman emerged. The woman's dress was stained, and I tried not to look. She moaned and yelled when she saw me. "Who are you?"

"Me?" I asked.

She looked ruined as she pointed at me. "People like you."

"Mrs. Jo, please." The doctor shifted her to the nurse, and as they walked out, he shook my hand. "I'm sorry about that. She's a little hysterical. Let me examine your wound."

"It's not that bad," I said. "Could you just give me some bandages?"

"Come with me."

The treatment room was small but clean. So was Dr. Kim. "I can stitch these up in a few minutes," he said.

"I can't pay."

"It's all right. Lie down." He gave me a circular board covered in cushiony fabric to hold against my chest. "In case the cream anesthetic isn't enough. I need to ration it, unfortunately. How did this happen to you?"

His smooth face didn't flinch as I described waking up to rats with my blood on their dirty mouths. He hummed and continued with his almost painless stitches. I saw myself from his perspective—unwashed, nearly homeless, a vagrant. I closed my eyes and tried to swallow my resentment.

Afterward, he guided me to the waiting room and suggested ointments. He showed me a few examples on his table. "I'll write down the names for you. Your wound will look bad for a while but it should heal well. A small scar, at most."

"What did you do during the war?" I asked.

He stopped writing. "I was studying for my medical degree abroad."

"Why didn't you do it here?"

"There are less than ten, maybe five, real medical schools here. And in a war? That wouldn't have been the right way."

"I listened to the Chinese attacking in the night, banging their gongs and playing their flutes to disorient us. I thought I was going to die as I waited with a rifle in my hands. That's what I was doing," I said.

"Excuse me?" he asked.

The nurse sat behind the desk, watching us.

I touched my face. "I'm curious. I wanted to know how you become a doctor."

"It's hard here. I'd suggest going overseas."

"With what money? Were you listening to how I got these bites?"

The doctor finished writing with a sheepish, annoyed look on his face. The nurse frowned. "Here," he said. "Come back if you get an infection."

When I exited the doctor's office, there was some sort of parade celebrating Seoul's continued recovery. Women and men hoisted neat, round children on their shoulders for better views. I watched through a gap in the crowd. A man in a suit yelled the city's accomplishments from a moving truck. Kids in colorful matching outfits cheered in formation. Boys cartwheeled. A done-up woman wearing an elaborate hanbok rode in a flatbed and waved.

The lady beside me didn't hide her stare as I raised my bandaged face for a better view. She turned away when I held her gaze. The test had peeled back a layer of the world for me. I noticed more. The way the richer folk moved around and away from people like me. When we were children, Jisoo had described Seoul, and I'd been jealous. I was still jealous.

Hours before, I woke to rodent teeth digging into my face, their damp, mushroomy smell all over me. Their flicking tails. The tent I'd once shared with Father ridden with rats. The pot of rice I'd so carefully saved overturned. I chased them out, waving Father's long pipe. The one indulgence I had allowed him to bring. When

I retrieved him from our hometown in the middle of the night, refusing to live near Jisoo and Haemi, Father had wrapped his pipe in Mother's red bojagi cloth and slipped it into my pack. He apologized for enlisting me, for being foolish enough to think a stalemate meant the end of war. I used his guilt as leverage and pushed him out of our home, only to watch him shrivel to death a month later.

In my pocket, I found the doctor's note and the tube of ointment I'd taken from his desk. "It's a stupid habit," Haemi had once said about my stealing, with a cluck and a twelve-year-old girl's sincerity. "You don't think it's stupid when I get you food or schoolbooks," I'd replied. That smile. It was her. She was the reason I had taken the test. Haemi, who had left me for someone sturdy and predictable, who hadn't waited long enough for sixteen-year-old me to shed my pride, to understand the circumstances of our upturned lives. I would defeat Haemi and Jisoo both. I would go to college. Then I would find them and show them what I had become.

The days were the same. I dredged. I picked up shit. I kept track of Results Day and loathed myself for caring. I rubbed *Cranes* and the ointment tube between my fingers as I wheeled my cart through different neighborhoods. These lifted items made picking up garbage seem like a choice. When I pulled the bell on my wagon, the aunties waved at me with their pails.

I dumped their buckets into the cart as the women blushed or looked away or tried to hide their embarrassment with chatter. When I reached the last woman in line, she tapped my shoulder. "Is he calling you?"

Someone across the street yelled my name. It was too dark, but as the shape came closer, I recognized the mouth. "I thought it was you," Namil said. "Yun Kyunghwan, right?"

"What do you want?" I sounded angrier than I'd intended and realized I hadn't spoken all day.

Namil shrugged, as if suddenly aware of the wagon, the garbage uniform, the garbage boy. I wondered if he could see my face. "We haven't seen you since the test. We still go to the library on Sundays."

"The test is over," I said.

"That's probably why I was thinking of you. The results will post tomorrow."

"I know." I handed the last woman her emptied bucket. There wasn't anyone else. I didn't know if I was relieved or embarrassed. "I have to go."

"Will you meet us in the morning? At Kyungho's?"

I shrugged, picked up the handlebars, and pulled the two-wheeled wagon along.

Namil walked beside me. "His parents are having a little party—whether it's a celebration or mourning, we'll have to see. You should come."

I felt better with the weight of the wagon steadying me. We passed a streetlamp, and from Namil's face, I could tell he saw my marks. He looked around, as if I were dangerous.

"It was a rat," I said. "Rats, plural. A whole family of them."

He smiled, uncertain.

"Tell the others I said congratulations."

"How do you know we'll get in?" he asked.

"You said it yourself. I'm not the competition." I started down the road, yelling "Garbage day!" for Namil and all the aunties to hear.

———

The next morning, I smoked Father's pipe. I put on his shirt. It was thick, wheat-colored. He hadn't ever graduated from middle school, and he had always regretted it.

Crowds of parents and boys surged against the bulletin boards. Their rumblings stitched together into a mass of deep-throated waves. I walked past with my face averted. I didn't want to see Namil or Kyungho or the bragger with the girlfriend. I wanted to feel ready. A few streets down, the girls with dreams of getting into a women's university gathered together with just as much ferocity as the boys. When I could no longer hear either group's shouts or stand the wait, I turned back around.

From across the street, at the top of the amphitheater where I'd sat a month before, the names on the boards looked like little rivers, like the wormy parasites that squirmed out of our asses when we were young. Boys hugged their mothers. Some rested their hands on their knees. A few turned away with shocked, unreadable expressions.

I waited until everyone left. I missed work. I didn't care.

I walked up to the bulletin board. At the top, the word *PASS* stood in bright, black strokes. I started at *Ga*. Family names. I read one after another. Student identification numbers, exam scores. I read it all again.

Still, it was true.

There was nothing that resembled my name.

Part 3

Haemi

1956

ON THE DAY SOLEE WAS BORN, A STICKY SUMMER MORNING in 1954, Jisoo gazed at his first child and said she was a wonder. That she was worth more than any son. Despite the pain in his arm, he hefted Solee into a cradle so he could smell the sweet-rice scent of her newborn skin. He kneeled beside me. "We're a family now," he said.

As he held me in his arms and whispered to our child, I made myself a promise—I would love my husband.

So I fell in love with Jisoo. I didn't run away. When his nightmares turned him around, I didn't imagine covering his face with a heavy buckwheat pillow. I stopped all that and loved him.

❁

Jisoo entered the kitchen, smelling of spring and grain, and dipped me into a half swing. He'd won the fight against his tenants just in time for this year's planting season, and this victory buoyed him still, a month later. *This man*, I thought. His broad, square face and those evenly spaced eyes that almost disappeared when he smiled. I smiled with him.

"I'll come with you to the market," he said when he saw my water jug. "I want to parade my pretty wife around."

Hyunki, seated at my side, groaned into his meal. He was twelve and didn't want to see me that way. "Does that mean I don't have to go with you, Nuna?"

"You get to stay and help Mother with Solee and Jieun." Jisoo snatched Hyunki's spoon and scooped a mound of rice into his mouth. To me, he said, "Let me change my clothes." He wore a suit when he spoke to the tenants, but for the market he favored light cotton. He sauntered away, hooting with happiness.

The walk to the market was my daily exercise. With Solee, returning to the tasks of regular life had been easy. But since Jieun's birth a few months ago, I tired quickly. Jieun's mulish character had revealed itself with the earliest birth pangs, and I still felt an aching in my bones.

I touched Hyunki's hair, shorn close to the scalp like his friends'. "There's more rice in the back."

"Chickens and beef and pork. That's what I want for every meal," he said.

"Soon." I tugged the round curl of his ear and left.

❀

When Jisoo returned to us after the war, he found me in my hometown. As soon as the armistice was signed, Mother, Hyunki, and I had left Busan. Prisoner uprisings had swept Geoje Island, and when the American general was taken hostage, the field hospital turned oppressive. It dismantled as soon as it was allowed, and everyone dispersed. Without saying goodbye to Major Kim or Minhee or the other nurses, we were gone.

Jisoo had considered taking us all to Seoul. I'd refused. I wanted to live in the house where Hyunki and I had been born. I wanted to relish the seclusion of rural life. We compromised and settled in the

closest town. We were ready to move on from the war, to start anew
with each other. As we packed our belongings, I was grateful for
Jisoo's parents—for their disappearance or death or capture. It was
merciless, but true. It meant Hyunki and Mother could live with us.
With our country broken, we clung to any type of blood, even if it
came from the wife's side.

Our new hanok, a long structure that cornered into a right angle like a scythe, was unlike our squat makeshift house in Busan
or the square hanoks with inner courtyards to which Jisoo had
been accustomed in Seoul. We had the traditional planked porch,
though, which led to five rooms. In the back, a lone tree, an addi-
tional outdoor kitchen, and a large yard completed the property. A
stone wall bordered us in, leaving a breath of field between us and
the neighbors. Once we were settled, Jisoo guided me to the farm-
land he'd purchased a few kilometers away—more space than I'd
ever thought we could own. "A person can get used to anything.
Even you," he'd said.

It was true. Habit cloaked us now in an easy rhythm. Jisoo
charmed the tenants as if he'd been born here. I knew how to clutch
Jieun to my chest while carrying Solee on my back. Even gangly
Hyunki fell into the routine of home as if we'd never left.

But two years ago, everything between us had been new, and
with Solee's birth, I became a mother. The first time she needed a
wash, we filled a deep basin. Jisoo layered cold and hot water. He
tried to find the perfect medium. I teased him for turning soft, for
not treating me with the same gentleness. He smiled. He skimmed
his wet finger down my forehead and paused at the end of my nose.
I let him slip his finger into my mouth. He touched and turned until
he knew every surface of my tongue, the textures of my roof, the

ridges of my teeth. He marked me. Solee watched from the floor, blinking up at us with her small, slight eyes. We crowded into each other. We wanted to wash our firstborn daughter together. We counted, "One, two, go," and lowered Solee into love-warmed water.

With each passing year, Jisoo wanted more ease, more rhythm.

"Solee's still teething and Jieun's not even six months. I need time," I said as we walked to the market.

He was talking about a son.

"I'm getting old. How do you know I'll be able to last much longer?" he asked.

I laughed. He was twenty-three. I was twenty-one. There were others our age with larger families, but we weren't too far behind.

"Give me a year," I said. "Then Jieun won't need milk, and I'll be ready."

"We'll try tonight." Jisoo grinned. He walked with a surety that aroused me, even with his arm.

"I get to decide," I said.

"I'll seduce you. Maybe they'll be selling popped corn." He glanced over, cunning written on his face. "You'd love that, my USO girl." He tugged at my sleeve.

I had pulled on a yellow-dyed sweater over my hanbok for the walk. It was American, with buttons down the front and green trim along the wrists. When he'd first brought it home, I danced around our room, pretending I was one of the Kim Sisters. He said I was even better than the USO ladies, all tarty, with their pale, coiffed curls. "The color of piss," he'd joked.

I danced again for him, up the road and back. I fluffed my hair, took the jug, and used it as a partner. It was this part I liked best, when we laughed together without undressing. A bee stalked the air around me, and Jisoo swatted it.

"I'm the only one allowed to taste your honey," he said, then turned away, embarrassed by the sentiment.

"A bee's stinger only works once."

"Not mine."

"Dirty man." I knocked him with the bottom of the jug. He held on and swung me closer. Over the jug's open mouth, he kissed me. Right there on the road.

I leaned down to pluck a pink cosmos flower and stuck it in his top buttonhole. "I wish you'd walk with me more often." I held his good arm so tight he laughed and asked if I thought he was going to run away.

We were almost at the open market's entrance when Jisoo pointed to the ditch that ran along the roadside. "Look." He slid down the slope and pulled out a bicycle with a crate fastened to its back fender.

It was rusted in all its bends. Clumps of old metal flaked onto Jisoo's hands as he inspected the body. Palms stained orange. He toed the wheels until they spun. A bicycle, conjured up from the earth, from the air.

He whistled. "Ugly and dented but once expensive." Checking the sturdiness of the crate and its lid, he said, "Sit and I'll ride."

I shook my head.

I hadn't been on a bike in years, since Kyunghwan.

I didn't even want to look at the thing—it tore the day open, flooded the good with memories I thought I had discarded. Even the scent of its rust overwhelmed me. It smelled too close to blood.

To distract myself, I filled my head with as many English phrases as I could. I'd been practicing, and the soldier who poured clean water knew my name. I knew his, too. *Jonathan*. He had mesmerizing hair—reddish brown, like dried jujube berries—and the fleshiest nose I'd ever seen on a human. It started out predictably, protruding with a high arch, like all Americans', but then bulged in the middle and flattened at the nostrils into the shape of a leaky dumpling.

"Good morning, Haemi." Jonathan stood on the bed of a white truck and poured water from a plastic container into our jug. "Is this your husband?"

"Yes," I said. "His name is Yun Jisoo. He is a landowner."

Jisoo stepped in front of me. "Hello. Good day." He pointed to me and then at himself again. "She is my wife."

Jonathan laughed and put his hands up by his ears. "I'm not trying." He pulled a photograph from his shirt pocket. Within its white border, a pale, freckled girl with chin-length hair sat with a book in her hands. She wore a necklace with a *J* pendant. The round curve of the letter's bottom rested at the hollow of her throat. "My sweetheart," he explained.

When Jisoo turned away, satisfied, Jonathan winked at me. "Jealous husband."

I understood enough to smile. "Thank you. Have a good day."

"Let's go," Jisoo said.

I waved at Jonathan a beat longer than I needed, gave a slow "Goodbye."

"Freckle-faced dogs." Jisoo strode ahead with the jug, past the line of women waiting. When we were alone, he turned too fast, spilling the water. "And when did you learn all that English?"

I smoothed the cosmos flower in his buttonhole. One of the petals had torn. Its juice bled onto my fingers. "Didn't you want me to be a USO girl?"

"Not for him."

"I thought I get to decide."

"You don't." He set down the jug and leaned close. From the red in his cheeks, I knew I'd pushed him too far.

But he didn't yell at me. He didn't throw anything. He walked to the corner shack and squatted to pull out the bicycle he'd hidden. "The Americans will steal it," he'd said. Watching him stoop over, I was embarrassed for him.

"I'm sorry," I said.

"You carry your own water."

He walked ahead with the bicycle.

"Do you know what men say about chatty women?" he asked once I caught up with him.

"I was only teasing."

He shoved the jug into the crate. "Let's go."

I followed. We passed broken buildings overtaken by wild azaleas. Thick bunches of oranges, pinks, and reds poked their heads between slats and through empty windows. Wide swaths of dirt fields butted up against newly built homes. It was too warm, but I still wore his sweater, hoping another bee would unite us.

We stopped with every neighbor's greeting. I was tired, and Jisoo took his time to spite me. I smiled politely at all his people. If he wanted my anger as validation, he wouldn't get it.

It was the bicycle that felt like a punishment. He made me push it along the road. Sunlight threw wheel-shaped shadows across the dirt. I concentrated on the spokes, elongated and transformed in their silhouettes.

I didn't want to think about him. His thin lips drawing from a rolled cigarette, the narrow cheeks sucked in. His tall body against the lamppost, his freckled arms. I didn't want to wonder what had happened to his bicycle, if he even rode one anymore. What he was doing now, away from us. I didn't want to remember all those years ago, how I'd sit on his handlebars and we'd cycle so hard the earth seemed to peel away, one dusty layer at a time.

"You," Jisoo called to a boy carrying a load of grains. "Who do you work for?"

The boy hiked up his back carrier by the straps. "The Sungs, sir."

"How much do they pay you?"

I kicked the wheel, hoping some of the dirt would land on Jisoo's trousers. I blamed him—for picking up the bicycle from the ditch, for ruining a happy day with his jealousy, for being a man who couldn't hold my whole attention.

Beyond the boy, Mun Soonhee and Son Jongho walked up with a jug of their own. I waved. "Son Jongho and his wife are coming," I said to Jisoo. I needed a distraction, and Mun Soonhee, always flouncing around in her Western tops and skirts, would do.

"Hello, hello." Soonhee tapped the leather seat and raised her eyebrows.

"He found it in a ditch." I shrugged.

Jisoo dismissed the boy and accepted tobacco from Son Jongho. They walked away from us, talking about the election campaign with pipes in the corners of their mouths. I leaned toward them. Jisoo retreated in the evenings with his newspapers and radio. He didn't speak to me about what was happening in our country, but I read his scribbled notes, the editorials he bunched into balls. "Take these to the outhouse," he would say as he handed me the articles on President Rhee. "We can wipe our asses with his lies."

Soonhee stepped into my view and placed her jug at our feet. "Eavesdropping?"

I smiled. "Listening. My husband never talks to me about politics."

Soonhee shrugged. "The government shouldn't be trusted. What else is there to say?"

"Do you think Rhee will win again, now that Shin's dead?"

"Don't ask me." She placed her hands on her hips and looked me up and down. "You and your hanboks."

I turned my gaze to her. "I know. I should be more like you." I fell easily into the talk she liked—complimentary and mindless. "You're so modern. Men like that."

"If I had a perfect moon face like yours, I wouldn't have to try so hard." She covered her chin with a sleeve. It was true that it stuck out like a shovel.

As Soonhee talked, I caught a glimpse of Jisoo. He rested one leg on an abandoned box. From the way he leaned into Jongho, his face hard with pride, I knew he was retelling the story of his tenant victory. His left arm clutched his bad one at the elbow, in a stance of natural ease. He grinned at me for a brief moment. Jisoo was driven by his desire to appear whole. While other landowners granted more rights to their tenants, he'd increased the share of rice ours had to provide as rent. "Five seoks more," he'd said. Jongho clapped a hand onto Jisoo's shoulder. Only Jisoo and I noticed his bad arm anymore.

Soonhee waved at the smoke wafting toward us. "How're the girls?" She widened her downturned eyes, glanced at my stomach. "Trying for a boy again?"

And just like that I was annoyed with her, with her shovel face and her mushrooming family, and her short, styled hair that curled around her neck. Soonhee wore American clothes, even bared her ankles and shoulders at times, but she was as wearisome as all the other women in this town with their talk of motherhood.

"It's getting late." I pushed the bicycle forward. "We should go."

"Let me hold this. Sit down." She grabbed the handlebars and clucked. "You look terrible. Have you been sleeping? That's probably why you haven't been able to, you know." She glanced at my stomach again.

As I turned to respond, I realized why her face looked so strange. She'd cut her eyebrows into thin, curved lines. A ridiculous woman.

"It's true! Rest and heat your stomach every night," she said.

"Maybe you're lucky." Sitting on a boulder, free from the strain of balancing the bicycle and jug, I felt a pulsing pain spread through me. I leaned forward. Motherhood seemed to tilt the space around me, leaching the energy from my mind, even clenching my muscles into knots. I panted, touched the ground. "We should go, Jisoo."

"Boys aren't so wonderful," Soonhee said. "Mine are always eating every last bit of rice. Look at me. Jongho says I'm getting too thin." She turned to show me her slim waist and bent closer. "He's trying to fatten me up. If I have another one, you can have him." She clucked. "Poor Haemi."

"Poor Soonhee," I clucked back. "Trying so hard to please her husband with those new eyebrows."

She opened her mouth. Then with an ugly, nose-flaring pout on her face, she turned to the men. "Jongho! Let's go. Sharp-tongued woman, Jisoo. You need to watch your wife."

"He knows," I said.

As the men emptied their pipes, Soonhee fingered my sweater. "You and your yellow."

I shrugged her off. "I prefer white."

She leaned in. "Last time I saw your husband, he was buying a yellow dress. It looked expensive, like something you wouldn't ever wear." Before I could respond, she called to her husband. "Time for this lucky family to go."

"Jisoo met Dumpling Nose today," I said to Hyunki later that evening. We leaned against the tree in our backyard.

"So?" Hyunki passed me a circular slice of glass with smoothed edges. It was useless but beautiful, deeply blue with a swirl of gray. I liked to think the glass had come from a rouge case that an American girl had given to her sweetheart as a keepsake. Hyunki thought it had once been the lid on a soldier's pocket watch.

"I was better than him at speaking English." I smiled. Hyunki had been teaching me, even borrowing extra workbooks from school.

"I'm going to get a first in mathematics. I'll know more than both of you soon."

"So conceited." I swatted him. "You have a few years before you catch up to Jisoo at least."

Hyunki swung an arm around my shoulders. He was lengthening in all directions—his hands, legs, feet, the expanse of his chest. "Teacher Lee said I'm the best in class." He smiled almost the way he used to, a slip of tongue showing between his teeth, pink gums bared. "He said if I keep it up, I could be good enough for a better high school. Maybe even in Seoul."

"Seoul?"

"Can you imagine?"

I ran the glass along his arm, from palm to elbow. Seoul was too far. I needed him close to me. "I'm still the one who checks your homework," I said. "Don't forget that."

I watched the swirl of gray balance on his elbow and let myself be jealous for a moment. When I was twelve, I studied in secret in the middle of fields. I sat with books scattered around me in a half-moon as Hyunki, three years old, toddled between the barley stalks. *Mathematics* had a thick black cover that smelled like moss. A boy strode through the stalks with a basket in his hand. "For Hyunki to play with. It'll keep our little chaperone from bothering us," he'd said with a grin, slick with slyness. Pacing in front of me, careful to step only on dirt and spare the barley, he had a thick, straight nose and a handsome face. Kyunghwan. He recited his homework problems, and I solved them as fast as I could.

I nudged Hyunki with my shoulder, as if that movement could push my thoughts away. I'd been happy this morning. I tried to recall that lightness—in the comforting weight of Jisoo's good arm slung across my chest as he'd slept, the girls snoring beside us. How I had wakened early and imagined Hyunki studying in his room and Mother heating her first cup of tea in the back kitchen.

"I feel awful today," I said.

"You've been saying that for months." Hyunki pretended to be me, one hand squeezing his temples, the other pounding his back.

I smiled at his teasing. It wasn't the exhaustion. Or even the sadness that sometimes flashed through me as I stared at my girls. I was unexpectedly jealous. Of Jisoo and what Mun Soonhee's words might mean. He was my husband, after all.

Hyunki squeezed me into a hug. He liked it when he could take on the role of the older, wiser sibling—but only when it was easy.

I peered at the sky through the glass's blue film. "Do you think Jisoo has other women?"

Hyunki caught his surprise in his mouth and shot a spit bubble into the weeds.

"It's common enough. I'm just curious," I said.

When I finally looked at him, he shrugged, his gaze on an object in the distance. "How should I know?"

"You're a boy. You're awake when he comes home, when he's drunk. Does he say anything to you?"

Jisoo seemed to consume more alcohol with each passing season. Often when I woke in the night to tend Jieun or Solee, I'd find him gone. He said he had nightmares, that drinking helped, that for all he did for us, he could get drunk every night if he wanted to. But disfigured, bloodied bodies wormed into my dreams, too. I'd thought he was making excuses. But maybe there was more to it.

"Haemi-nuna?" Hyunki touched my arm.

I imagined Jisoo with another woman. I wondered if she'd felt the thick, raised scars that tracked his injured arm, if she'd pleasured with him.

Hyunki held my hand, called my name again.

I passed him the glass. "Jisoo bought a yellow dress," I said. "An expensive one. For someone else."

Hyunki rolled the glass between his fingers. "Maybe it's a surprise?"

"Mun Soonhee told me, so who knows if it's even true."

"A surprise," he said, nodding. "A present for you?"

"He didn't even notice Soonhee telling me, he was too busy talking about himself."

"It's getting cold." We turned to find Mother at the back door. She nodded to Hyunki. "You better go inside before you get sick."

"The doctor told me that it's fine if I'm careful," Hyunki said.

"Inside, now," Mother said.

Hyunki pressed the warmed glass into my palm. He scurried down the stone path that led from the tree to the back kitchen. Mother frowned as she slid the door closed behind him. Always fierce, she'd hardened with each war.

I walked to where she stood beneath the roof's eaves. "We were talking about a dress," I said.

"I heard. You are filling your brother's head with badness."

"*The birds and rats are always listening.*" I rolled the glass along my wrist. "Don't spy on me in my own home, Mother."

"There are wives who roll boiled eggs over their bruised faces every night. You're lucky. If Jisoo has another woman, you pretend you don't know."

I turned away.

Mother was slowly dying. I could tell from the stench that roosted in her mouth. I concentrated on that smell and the way her skin hung loose around the curve of her ribs, how fragile she felt beneath my hands when I scrubbed her on wash day. It shamed me to wallow in these images, but it was the only way I could tamp down my growing resentment. I thought about her dying until I could forgive her enough to turn back around.

"I don't want to pretend," I said.

She held my hand in hers, followed the lines on my palm. "You hear everything as an occasion to cry, as an event that will ruin you."

"So what if I do?"

"It's not practical."

"I don't care." I turned from her again. *Practical.* When I was young, before Hyunki was born, Mother would knot flowers together for me to wear around my wrists, my neck. She'd adorned me solely for the pleasure of beauty, without any other purpose. "I'd rather be this way than like you."

Mother sighed. "He bought it for me. New members are standing in front of the congregation next week. I needed a proper dress for church. If none of you will come with me, at least I can look presentable." She brushed my shoulders with short strokes and nodded. "Done. Out of your mind now."

It wasn't true. I slipped into Mother's closet while she prepared the fish for the next morning. I searched her small wardrobe of neatly folded clothes, from summer ramie to double-layered cotton for the colder months. There was no yellow.

"So?" I walked around her room. He could meet other women if he wanted to, I decided. I retrieved Mother's sleeping mat from the wardrobe and unrolled it across the floor. I found her pillow. I didn't care. I would flirt with Jonathan. I would even flirt with Son Jongho. I would retaliate against Mun Soonhee and Jisoo both.

"Mommy?" Solee stood shirtless at the door with pillow marks lining her square face. I watched her plump stomach rise with each inhale. "Jieun waked up."

She beckoned me to our room with her tiny hand.

I couldn't think if I wanted to. Jieun wept until I untied my top and she bit down. Solee hovered, always fascinated by this process. Jieun's tight, assured mouth on my nipple. How my breasts leaked with milk. The pain of gums sucking and clamping.

"I help." Solee sat beside me and stroked Jieun's arms. "You tell story."

"Mommy's tired today."

"Bird bridge. Stars. I want hear."

"You tell it then," I said.

"No. I no want."

"I don't want to, either."

She scooted away from me. "You, Mommy. Please?"

"Leave me alone, Solee." I wished Hyunki would walk by. He would hold his shadowed fingers against the wall and transform his voice into a threatening tiger or bear or goddess. But he was probably studying, readying for a world away from us.

"I want story," Solee said again. She kicked at her blankets.

I slapped her feet. "Fix those blankets immediately."

She cried out, wet and resentful. She petted her soles as if I'd actually hurt her and screamed higher and louder until Jieun joined in with her relentless infant shrieking. "Silence from both of your mouths," I yelled. I slapped Solee's feet again.

Among all the noise, I almost felt better.

"Why are they so upset?" Jisoo stood at the door. Solee saw him and quieted. Jieun stopped, too, as if in chorus with her sister.

"I thought you were out," I said.

"I was. I am. Just need to change." He crossed the room, searched his wardrobe, and pulled on a silky purple button-down shirt. A shirt that would match a yellow dress.

"Who are you voting for next week?" I nodded at him to sit beside me. "I heard you chatting with Son Jongho."

"I don't want to talk about that stuff right now. I'm going out." With his good arm, he slung Solee onto his hip. He petted her wispy hair. "Be nice for Mommy."

"She not nice." Solee burrowed her head into his neck. "Me nice."

"Maybe Mommy's cranky. Should we make her feel better?" Bending low so she'd squeal, Jisoo said, "Kiss her forehead. Ten should be enough."

Solee laughed as Jisoo counted each of her kisses aloud. It was easy for him. To make her happy, to leave. At the door, he said, "I'm celebrating the tenant win tonight," and closed me in.

Solee crawled to the blankets. "Come, Mommy."

I slid in beside her and held Jieun tight to my chest. With one hand on Solee's face, I told the story. The right way, with the princess and the stars and the birds that built a bridge with their bodies so the princess could cross the Milky Way to reach her shepherd boy.

I told the story again and again, until she fell asleep.

I walked in the dark, through fields, over new seedlings. I walked past the market, the watering line, Hyunki's school, the tiredness that had settled in me with Soonhee's and Mother's and Solee's words—with Jieun's small, slathered body coming out of my own. I walked until I was sure. The stalks were gone, but this had been the field.

It was a brown and dry scrape of land now. I retraced our positions. Here little Hyunki, here my open books. I remembered the smell of barley. How it mixed with our sweat. Here, Kyunghwan. Here the pencil holder I'd made for him with orange string and a sun-whitened watermelon rind. I'd dyed the threads in a pool of water tinted with rose balsam petals. Here, me.

"My father's meeting a new woman," Kyunghwan had said one afternoon.

I'd looked up from my mathematics paper, the numbers floating away. His interruption had annoyed me. Then, I'd parsed the meaning behind his words. "A woman? Which matchmaker did he use?"

"I guess it's all right." He'd twisted a barley stalk. "It's been a year."

I had known he was upset, that I should comfort or distract him. But instead I'd felt relief—relief that his father and my mother had never encountered each other by the water mill over the past year.

"Maybe it's a good thing," I'd said.

"Maybe. I saw her. She's pretty. Breasts like this." He had squeezed the air in front of his chest, and I'd swatted his leg.

A dog barked in the night, and Hyunki's little round glass tumbled from my hand. I sat on the ground in the middle of this same empty land. I imagined barley, rose balsam, him. If Jisoo had a woman, I could have my memories.

Jisoo

1958

I DID EVERYTHING RIGHT. MY TENANTS DEFERRED TO ME
without complaint. The neighbors shared their oxen, workers, and
hospitality, and the elders listened to me at town assemblies despite
my lack of local lineage. I was ascending in the world in which
Haemi had wanted to live—all with one good arm. And so, if I
wanted to spend my time elsewhere, I could do as I pleased.

Yuri, in a blue woolen dress and white sneakers, came to the
door. "You again?"

"I need a break," I said.

"They're about to eat dinner, but come in. Sangwoo's been asking about you." She led me to a playroom cramped with children.
It was a cold winter day, and the sound of sniffling filled the space.

Sangwoo, a curly-haired boy of six, ran toward us. "Uncle! I've
been practicing cards so I can beat you."

"Grandmother Lee's going to announce dinner soon," Yuri
said. "You only have a few minutes while we set up. Go on."

Sangwoo and I wove between the groups of kids to his favorite
corner. Settled on floor cushions, I asked, "Have you been studying? Eating well?"

He pushed out his belly. "I'm growing fat!"

I laughed. "You can get even fatter!"

"Look." Sangwoo balanced a box on his knees and thumbed

through it with intent. "We got these yesterday." He displayed a piece of clothing I'd never seen before. It was an all-in-one garment with a hood and the feet attached. "One of the babies peed in his in the middle of the night. The soldier-man gave me the orange one because I was the nicest."

"Which soldier-man?" I asked.

Before he could answer, Grandmother Lee called from the kitchen. The children around us dropped their toys and ran, yelling their predictions. "Tteok-bokki!" "Miyeok-guk!" "Rice and fish!" "Spinach soup!"

I held on to Sangwoo's belt loops. "Wait a second."

Yuri teased us from the door. "Is Uncle keeping you hostage?"

"I have a gift for him," I said.

"Quickly then."

I showed Sangwoo the package I'd brought. He fingered the twine. "For me?" He ripped the paper wrapping with both hands. Inside, a wooden duck on wheels, painted yellow with a tiny brass bell around its neck.

"You pull it by the string," I said.

"Look!" He marched in a circle, dragging the duck. The wheels turned with a loud, satisfying rattle.

"Say thank you to Uncle and go eat," Yuri said.

He hugged me and ran through the door with the yellow duck rolling behind him. A cheer came from the kitchen. Sangwoo's happy shouting.

Yuri crossed the playroom and leaned against the main window with a mug on her lap. Snow collected on the glass behind her. She sipped. "You favor him."

"He looks healthier each time I visit."

"Why don't you adopt him then?" She straightened and walked around the room collecting toys. "Only the Americans will. They won't all get adopted, you know."

"I know it's hard." I picked up the last of the toys and brought them to her. She let me touch her arm for a second. "Come sit with me. How have you been?"

"Go back to your own children, Jisoo."

Melancholy clouded her movements, and I was here for a break from that. Even so, Yuri looked just as young as she had five years ago. I rubbed the sleeve of her blue dress. "Remember how Jong-yul whistled the first time he saw you in regular clothes? We were worried that all you nurses would abandon us overnight."

She smiled but lifted her arm out of my reach. "I need to help in there. The kids are inside all the time now that it's cold. It drives Grandmother Lee crazy."

"I'll help, too."

"It's after six."

"I can stay a little longer."

She shrugged, picked up her mug from the sill, and walked away.

In the kitchen, the children sat at two long tables. The older ones held babies in their laps; the crippled sat close to the door, where they could be easily helped; and the half-breeds grouped together at the other end. Grandmother Lee served soybean soup in tin bowls. Yuri poured water into cups.

Sangwoo sat with the other orphans his age. Some had been found during the war, some afterward. Others were the offspring of lepers. All of them were skinny, scabby, and slowly returning to a more human form.

A boy with a lazy eye tapped my hand. "Where's my toy, Uncle?"

"And mine?"

"I want a duck!"

The children looked up with their spoons dangling. Yuri saved me. "Uncle needs to pass these waters. The duck is for everyone."

We worked our way down the tables. "I told you," she said above the children's heads. "You can't give to one unless you're going to give to them all."

"Sangwoo knows how to share."

"Do your daughters always share?"

I set a cup in front of a little girl. "Of course they do."

Yuri smiled. "Fine. Your children are better behaved than mine. Time for you to go home, Jisoo."

"I like being here." I watched her lift a crying toddler to her chest. She moved around the orphanage as if the children were all her own, with a simple ease I admired. But I came for them, too. The way they stilled sometimes, lost, and looked at the door as if waiting for someone. They were without parents. I understood this loss.

"I don't need people talking," she said.

"Does it matter if it's not true?"

She raised her eyebrows. "What do you think?"

"Fine, I'll go."

"Bring your wife next time."

I nodded. This was how we always parted. She extended a hand, and I set it aside for another day.

The winter darkness made it seem later than it was. I entered my home and immediately felt Haemi's anger. She followed me to the dining room with Jieun asleep in her arms. "You're late."

I smelled grilled mackerel, rice, kimchi-jjigae. The table wasn't set. Not even the hot tea poured. Her irritation caught me in the throat. "Where's dinner? I'm hungry."

"We're hungry, too."

"Then go get our rice. We can eat together," I said.

Haemi paced, bouncing Jieun as if she were an infant rather than a two-year-old. "She cried all day. I don't know why she's so sensitive."

"Let me hold her." I carefully lifted Jieun. For a moment, Haemi leaned her smooth forehead to me. She nestled into my chest and her body relaxed. I stroked her curls, her pointed ears. I wanted her to stay, for the weight to be an apology for her crabbiness. She straightened.

"Solee's been asking for you. I'll call her," she said.

Haemi returned with steaming rice and our first daughter. Solee ran to me with her thick open arms and happy smile. She squeezed my side, careful not to jostle Jieun. "I counted the beans in Halmuni's jar! To forty, Daddy. She gave me a rice cake and said I was the best granddaughter in Korea."

"My smart girl! I think your halmuni's right." I settled onto a floor cushion. "Were you nice to your sister?"

"She was grumpy because a tooth's growing in." She reached for Jieun's lip. "Want to see?"

"Don't wake her," Haemi said as she arranged the table. "I just got her to stop crying."

"You wouldn't want Jieun to do that to you while you're sleeping." I stuck a finger in Solee's mouth. "How does that feel?"

She laughed. "Not good."

"Someone must be hungry!" Mother entered with a tray full of food, her sickled frame trembling from the weight. "The mackerels you bought were perfect, Jisoo."

I rose to help. "I can get more tomorrow. Let me take that."

"We'll trade." She lifted Jieun from me and squeezed my hand. "You all eat first. I'll wait for Hyunki."

"Come sit." Haemi gestured to the banchan and chopsticks. "Hyunki stays at school so late these days."

"I'm not hungry yet, and this one's waking up." Mother hitched Jieun with a calming croon and walked back to the kitchen.

"She must feel more comfortable back there," I said, once we started eating.

Haemi snorted, ripped her fish into small pieces. "She's old and she knows it. She's scared of being thrown out of her own home."

"It's custom to eat separately. She probably prefers it."

"If we were following custom, I should be eating back there, too," Haemi said.

"I'm a baby bird." Solee raised her head and flapped her mouth like a beak. "See? *Bbi-ak! Bbi-ak!*"

"Stop playing and eat." Haemi yanked Solee's chin down to her bowl. The noises died in her throat.

"What's wrong with you?" I pointed to Solee, who held a palm up to her face. "You're angry at her because I was half an hour late?"

"Forget it, Jisoo." Haemi ate loudly and quickly. She mutilated Solee's fish, portioned it into circles. She exaggerated their hunger as punishment. "Tell me something interesting at least. What's happening with the tenants?"

"It's winter." I slurped the kimchi-jjigae as if I were starving, too. "It's all paperwork."

Haemi stared. Her hair was neat, her clothes pressed, but still something in her face made me uneasy. I didn't understand her. If the smallest thread in her happiness loosened, she followed it without reason.

"You don't need to concern yourself with my work. Why do you care?" I asked.

She yawned in a theatrical, false way. "Because I need something to keep my head busy so I don't die of boredom."

"What I do is complicated." I offered my last square of tofu to Solee. "I don't want to talk about it when I get home."

"Fine." Haemi took my empty bowl. "I'll get you more stew then."

She turned my appetite around. I didn't understand her discontent, how she was bored without justification. She acted the part of a dutiful wife yet had no real concern for me. "I don't want any more jjigae. Get me a drink," I yelled, but she was already gone.

"The mommy bird eats up the food and then mushes it and gives it to the babies," Solee said, quieter, talking only to me now.

I hugged her. Her chin was fine. "What's wrong with Mommy today?"

Solee poked my knee. "Can you ice-skate? I want to learn."

Haemi returned with a full bowl. "Learn what?"

In front of my wife, I wanted to be the better parent. It was silly, but I felt the need. I crouched to Solee, expanded my voice and energy. "Some of the smaller rivers in Seoul freeze over so thick you can skate all winter. I'll teach you." I eyed Haemi. "I've started looking into getting back my father's land."

"In Seoul? Closer to the dictator?"

"Rhee will be gone in two years." I pushed the bowl away. "I heard one of my father's uncle's cousins is doing well in the yeon-tan business. Maybe I could get into that, too."

"You want to move to Seoul and sell coal briquettes?" Haemi laughed. "We're not leaving. That's a promise you've already made." She heaped spinach onto Solee's rice.

"My tummy's full," Solee whispered.

"Eat it anyway." Haemi turned to me. "Mother would be scared. You think she'd survive that trip? And everyone we know is here."

"You don't socialize with anyone," I said.

"And if there's another war? They wouldn't call you now, not with that thing." She nodded at my arm. She wouldn't even look at it. "But Hyunki could be in trouble."

Anger spiked in me, blunt and full force. A heat in my chest I wanted to thrust at her dismissive hands. I threw down my spoon. It skittered across the table, hit the chopsticks. "I can't eat with you in this house." I grabbed Solee, straining my arm just to show Haemi.

She knew, though, and clucked, "You're being stupid. It'll hurt later."

"Let's get something sweet to eat. Daddy wants a treat," I said to our daughter.

Solee squeezed her ears.

"It's cold out, Jisoo. She'll only get sick."

"Don't fight," Solee yelled, louder than us both. I swung her onto my back. I would handle the hurt later.

We walked to the main road, where the evening was alive with hunched vendors and idling neighbors. I'd remembered Solee's jacket and hat but not her gloves. Still on my back, she stuck her hands underneath my shirt collar and collected my heat. I told her the stories I'd learned at the orphanage, imitating the characters Yuri acted out so well, and clung to the sound of my daughter's laughter. When the pain in my arm flared, I let her down, and we walked aimlessly. I knew she was cold, but she didn't complain.

I watched her as she pulled her jacket sleeves over her fingers and packed snowballs. She looked nothing like her mother. Haemi, that sixteen-year-old girl I'd chosen in Busan. I had wanted to confirm that life's rituals continued before leaving to fight, to find comfort in this during the war. But with each passing day, I realized the truth. Haemi didn't fit the life I'd envisioned.

"Mommy says your arm hurts and it makes you grumpy." Solee cocked her capped head, the words so easy in her mouth.

I swept her bangs to the side. "What else does she say?"

"A president speaks from the moon." She dusted snow off her sleeves.

"Which president?"

She shook her head, but I understood. Eisenhower. Haemi focused on the good of other countries over our own. "We're going to make Korean radios. We'll catch up."

"I sing to the radio," Solee said. "Mommy listens to the bad man."

I sighed. Rhee had become an oppressor in his third term, but we would force him out soon. We would move to Seoul and live there as our country rebuilt itself. I knew it. Korea would recover quicker than any American thought possible.

At one of the market stands, I bought a roasted sweet potato wrapped in foil. I broke it into pieces and fed Solee. "You'd want to move to Seoul, wouldn't you?"

She licked her fingers. "Seoul?"

"It's where I grew up," I said. "We can buy you real ice skates. We could buy a Korean radio as soon as they're for sale."

"I want to go there." She pointed to the elementary school at the end of the road. After the war, they painted it bright colors—blue walls, a red roof. A poor attempt at cheeriness.

We walked to it and Solee peered into one of the snowy windows. "Mommy says I start in one year. I know my letters and numbers."

She was only four and already so smart. Jieun would grow to be smart, too. But a son would be smarter and have more chances in our world. I imagined us, a man and his wife, two girls and a boy. Maybe two boys. One raised to be a scholar, and the other a doctor. A hanok in Seoul near the Han River. The girls with Haemi's delicate face and someone else's temperament. They would go to college and meet the right husbands, men who would be their brothers' peers.

Snow collected between Solee's reddened fingers as she clutched the windowsill. She had my square jaw, my slight eyes. She looked up at me. "Can we go home now, Daddy?"

Haemi woke when I entered our room. Her curly hair, released from its bun, stuck to her face as she blinked awake. Seeing her with that dim sleep in her eyes, I wanted her to forgive me. I crouched beside her and stroked her head. "Solee wanted to stay with Hyunki," I said. "He's still studying. She's asleep in his room."

"Jieun would only go with Mother." Haemi rubbed her face. She wore the yellow sweater I'd bought her in Daegu.

"We'll get a decent night's sleep then," I said.

"Why is age two so much harder for her? I try to remember what Solee was like then, and I can't." She closed her eyes. "I'm not as good with Jieun."

"Don't say that. You're doing fine." I slid in beside her, and she shifted away. Her eyes were closed and I couldn't tell if she'd meant to flinch. "I was serious about Seoul," I said.

She turned to the wall. "Let me sleep."

"Haemi?" I studied the angle of her shoulders without touching her. It was hard. Unless I was drunk, I had become too aware of her growing indifference. I twisted a curl of her hair into a tight circle. "Solee and Hyunki. Eventually Jieun. They'll all have a better education in Seoul. They have universities for women there. If we have the means, why should we stay here?"

"You'd let them go to college?"

"I want our children to do better than us. Don't you?"

I slid my hands under her clothes, up her back, and touched each ridge of her spine. She was always cold during the day—she wore layers and socks, and sometimes even a coat indoors—but her skin flamed in the night. Come morning, her sweater lay inside out by her head. Sometimes even her shirt. She'd blush if I woke before her, if I saw her that way.

Her shoulders loosened when I pressed into the muscles of her back. I skimmed up to her neck, my palms warmed with her heat. Haemi turned to me, her face relaxing into a smile. I touched her, her ribs, the stretched stomach and small breasts with their sweet, nutty milk. She laughed a little at how cold my hands were. Haemi was a soft creature. I forgot it too often.

She raised her arms for me. I pulled off the sweater and shirt, kissed her neck down to the long, flat bone between her breasts. I listened to her soft panting as I raised her skirt. With my hands on her hips, I told her the truth. "I miss my home. I miss seeing the city where my family raised me."

"I know." She threaded her fingers through my hair, trailed her nails down the tendons in my neck. She unbuttoned my shirt and touched my bad arm. "I was mean about this." She held me by my shoulder joint. Underneath the skin, the cup and ball-shaped bone, the withered muscles. She felt it all. "If you promise about the girls, then we can go. Next year."

"I promise." I pulled her closer. It surprised me every time, how small she was. How easily I could carry her, and yet how easily she held me in her sway.

She kissed me. "One more thing. The way I felt after Jieun's birth—I don't want that ever again."

"It's not always hard. Solee only took a few hours, remember?"

"No. *After.* It still hasn't gone away, even if you don't believe me. I'm tired, my joints ache. I'm—" She shook her head, a laugh limped out. "I feel like something's breaching inside me, like I've left something undone all the time. I don't like it, Jisoo."

She was right. I didn't believe her. She touched me only when she wanted comfort, when she wanted her way. She placed her moony fingernails on my face. I pulled away. "You don't want more children? A son?"

"I don't want to feel the way I did, that I do still."

A sound like a laugh escaped me. "You know what I'll say."

"Then I won't go to Seoul."

"You can't do that."

"I'm doing it now."

She made me want to hit her. I crushed a pillow in my hand instead. I threw the chamber pot against the wall.

"You'll wake the girls," she said.

I pulled the blanket off the soft, bare body she used as a weapon. My fickle wife. "You can't do whatever you want. We don't live in a world of your making."

"Oh, but we live in your world?"

"You don't get to choose how many children we have."

"That's all I have to choose." She reset the chamber pot. The piss had spilled and she sopped it up with the shirt I'd taken off her moments before. In the darkness, she seemed smaller than she had in years. "Leave me alone, Jisoo."

I crouched beside her. "You'll feel different. Once you're pregnant again." I could hear the appeal in my voice. I couldn't help it. I tried to touch her stomach. "The way you were when Solee and Jieun started kicking. You were so happy."

Haemi lay back down, the piss-stained shirt still in her hand. "I don't feel twenty-three. Do you? Like you're twenty-five?"

"What are you talking about?"

"I feel like an old, old lady with an old, old husband."

I left so I wouldn't yell. I heard her call after me, "Where are you going now?" But she didn't mean it. She didn't care.

Hours later, I walked up the muddied, slushy path to the orphanage. Leaning against its wooden, slatted walls, I knocked. Yuri opened the door with just as much anger as the wife I'd left earlier in the night. In a thick gray robe, American style, with a fuzzy belt looped around her waist, she glared. She shouldered a kerosene lamp against the wind. "What are you doing here this late?"

"I was angry." I propped myself up with my good arm, bowed until the ground seemed too close. "Now I'm drunk."

She looked past me at the night's shadows. "You can't come in here."

"It's dark. Who would see me?"

She stood in my way. Behind her, the playroom and kitchen were silent, empty. "You'll wake the children. Grandmother Lee's room is right above us."

"Let me in for a little while." I held on to my shoulder and remembered the chamber pot, Haemi's threats. "My wife's driving me crazy."

Yuri lowered the lamp. I searched for a sign of jealousy, but I couldn't see her face. She touched my shoulder, probing with her sharp, knowing fingers. I tried not to show any emotion. But the alcohol had weakened me. I groaned.

"You would be hard to live with, too," she said. "You think of that? Acting like you're able when you're not. I'll get a warm compress and then you're leaving."

In the kitchen, she undressed me in the swift, efficient way she had years before. The uneven muscles of my arms were now visible, no longer covered by clothes. I wondered what she thought of me now. What she'd thought of me then. She slathered a dense paste on my shoulder. The kerosene lamp's light spilled across the table beside us, revealing long strips of cloth, herbs, a mortar and pestle.

"Nothing for the aching? Some pills or an injection?"

"This is all I have." She wrapped a bandage over the salve, and I remembered when her hair was short. The red pin. The pain that had dulled but never went away. She acted indifferent, but she was a compassionate woman. I'd always seen that in her. How she winced with each patient's suffering. She turned to the table and formed a mound with the remaining paste. Her robe was too large, trailing the ground and hiding her body.

"Hey, Yuri?"

"I know it hurts, and that it's been hard to get used to, but you can't act like your arm is fine," she said.

"I don't want to go home."

She didn't look at me. She wrapped the paste in cloth. "Don't overexert the muscle. Your nerves will deteriorate."

"They already have." I grabbed her hand. "Yuri, I don't want to go home."

"You don't mean that. Put this on every night." She placed the bundle by my side and handed me my shirt. She didn't help me when I struggled to put it on. She retrieved my coat instead. "Your wife's waiting."

She wouldn't even give me a cup of tea. She lent me a scarf and kicked me out. "Come tomorrow. I need to tell you something when you're sober," she said.

I leaned into her at the doorway. She had a good, wholesome face with a small, round nose that rumpled when she laughed at the kids. "I don't know where I put the red pin. The one you gave me. Do you remember?" I asked.

"Go home, Jisoo."

"It's all right." I touched her cheek. She was wearing new earrings. Dark blue buttons rimmed in silver. "I'm here with you."

She laid her hand against my elbow. Then gently, she pushed. "Good night."

My footprints disappeared behind me. In the falling snow, I felt small, invisible. Even my grunts were eaten up by the winter's thickness. I walked in the middle of the road and didn't care who saw. I'd done nothing wrong, not with Yuri, at least. I wondered if she and Haemi had heard of the others—nameless bar girls on nameless nights—and if that was why they guarded themselves from me. The town passed by in clumps. Unusable winter fields, common stores, houses upon houses. I had left Seoul for this.

"Jisoo!" Haemi waited in front of our house. With my coat over her shoulders, her hands stuffed inside the pockets. "I watched you," she said, as I approached, her voice heated and fierce.

"Get inside." I pointed. "I can't even see you."

"See me then." She surged toward me. "Don't lie to me. Do you want to adopt or do you want to fuck that woman?"

I shoved her. I pushed her shoulder with one hard sweep, and she tumbled. Frail, a little thing swept up in snow. As soon as she hit the ground, her elbows sprawling and her head snapping back, I feared she'd disappear, smothered in all that whiteness. I kneeled down and crawled to her.

She might have been crying. It was too dark, too hazy. I watched her mouth open and close and tried to say I was sorry.

I picked her up. She clutched my neck as I walked us through the gate, past the snow that clumped all around us. I felt the bandage around my shoulder tear open, but I couldn't feel my arm. I couldn't hear anything.

In the morning after breakfast, I led the girls to Hyunki's room. Solee slid to a stop beside his desk, where he sat studying. "I need you to watch these two," I said.

Hyunki placed his finger on an equation before looking up. "I have a test tomorrow, Hyung."

I picked up his book—physics, at fourteen. The subjects seemed to grow harder each year. "Get out of the house for a few hours. Why don't you all go with Mother to church?"

"Let's play the number game! Can we?" Solee asked.

Hyunki stood as Jieun grabbed his legs. I wondered if he'd heard us arguing in the night. "All right," he said, sighing. "Let's see what Halmuni's doing."

When everyone left, I told Haemi to get dressed.

"Why?" she asked, listless. There wasn't a mark on her, but she glared at me like she was hurt.

"Because I'm asking."

We walked to Yuri. On the way, I told her what I could about the hospital and how Yuri had helped me recover. "She wrote last year saying she had no one, and the orphanage needed another hand. That's all." I didn't feel guilty. I ended with "You're the one with the bad mind," to prove it.

Haemi gave a humorless laugh. "That's true."

One of the older children answered the door. "Uncle." He bowed and brought us to the playroom. "Would you like a chair, Auntie?"

"I'd rather sit on the floor."

"Get Yuri for us," I said.

The little ones ran to Haemi as we waited. They watched as she untangled her scarf. They touched her hands, her wavy hair. I remembered that she was beautiful. She didn't wear makeup like the other women in town. Her features were perfect already, with a pale, wide face that made her eyes seem larger and darker, a shapely mouth. The bold stare and arched brows that held me to her. She rustled her shoulders, finding pleasure in their bright, loving attention. The children poked fingers through her curls.

Sangwoo ran in with his toy duck. "Uncle's here!"

"This is my wife," I said.

He bowed, the way I had taught him. "Hello, wife. Nice to meet you."

Haemi smiled. I imagined Sangwoo as our own. He and Solee and Jieun could chase one another around, trailing the rattling duck behind them.

When Yuri entered, she didn't hide her surprise. She touched her hair, a nervous habit I hadn't seen in years. She spoke only to Haemi and motioned away the children. "I would have put on a nicer outfit if I'd known." She wore the same blue dress she always wore.

"I don't see what that would have done," Haemi said.

Yuri smiled through the remark. She dragged over a low table and fetched a tin of cookies. "It's perfect that you're here. I've asked your husband to bring you so many times, and I thought he never would."

"I wanted Haemi to know we weren't having an affair," I said.

They both turned to me, similar in their anger. Rigid seething that quickly returned to impassive faces, even while their cheeks flared red.

"I can't believe you," Haemi said, lightly.

"I'm sorry." Yuri broke a rectangular cookie in two. "I don't know what's happening here, or what you mean, but—" The halves disintegrated in her hands. "These are butter cookies."

Haemi grabbed one and, staring at Yuri, fractured it into pieces. "What are we doing here?"

Yuri skirted her gaze. She surveyed the children at the far end of the room. The older ones were playing house, adding details from their lives before this place. "I get to be the mama this time," a tall girl whined.

"I never found my brothers after the war," Yuri finally said. "Your husband helped me. He's been kind. I asked him to come today because I wanted him to meet Andrew." She gestured behind her. "He's here now."

"Who?" I asked.

Haemi straightened. She motioned to the closed doors. "One of the soldiers. I thought I heard English."

It was true. American voices came from the kitchen—male, deep, unfamiliar. Grandmother Lee laughed among them. A child yelled in accented English.

"Am I right?" Haemi asked.

Yuri nodded. "He comes on Sundays, and Jisoo doesn't usually." She looked at me. "I wanted you to meet him."

"Are you going to marry him?" Haemi bit into a cookie beaded with sugar.

Yuri's face flushed. "He's working to get me a passport. A visa." She laughed. "He wants me to move to California with him."

"When?" I asked. "A white man? One of the Americans?"

Haemi took another cookie. "You'll go?"

"I think so. He wants to leave before the New Year."

"You're brave enough?" Haemi asked. "California? With his foreign family?"

Yuri touched her hair, her ears. "I'm scared. An American and everything. I won't know anyone."

Haemi nodded, said something in return. They loosened in each other's presence as I tried to understand. Yuri, relieved, fluttered her hands and unraveled the story of this soldier. *Andrew.* "He's volunteered here for the past few months, but he's ready to go home. We'll leave by the end of the month, if it all works out."

"How do you communicate?"

"He knows a little Korean and even some Japanese."

"Is he kind to you?"

Haemi and Yuri went on. They forgot about me.

Watching them, I realized we were lurching toward a new world—one where women could disappear with foreigners, where Americans would never leave us alone, where they didn't simply provide us with money, but with their ways of living as well.

We weren't rebuilding. We were shaping ourselves into a different form.

I felt duped by my own blindness. Like a man who doesn't know he's soaked until halfway through a creeping storm.

Hyunki

1960

WHEN I WAS FIVE AND HAEMI FOURTEEN, I WANTED TO capture a hundred dragonflies. In the late summer evenings, Haemi would sit as I hopped from rock to rock, slipping into river puddles, trying to catch those tiny creatures with their flashing wings.

"Splash some water on them," she said. "They'll fly slower."

Wet and discouraged, I stretched out beside her. "They're too fast."

Haemi sat with a pile of fluttery rose balsam petals. She layered them on her fingers, careful to stain only the nails. I helped her tie a long leaf around her pinkie to hold the crushed petals in place.

"If the orange color stays until winter, you marry your first love," she said.

"Marry me," I responded. "I'm going to be rich."

She laughed. "It doesn't work that way."

"Why not?" The idea of another man in our lives didn't make sense to me. I pierced a petal and tried to drag the juice across her face. "I want a dragonfly."

"Let me dye your nails and I'll catch one for you."

"I'm a boy!"

"Just one hand."

I thought of my friends and how they'd tease me, but I wanted the dragonfly too much. I would hold its skinny, straight body in my hand. I would pin it to my wall. "All right, just one," I said.

She lined my nails with petals and leaves. She pressed each finger and counted to twenty. "To make sure the juices bleed onto the nail," she said. "Now you keep these on while I catch the dragonfly."

As I waved my leaf-covered hand, Haemi pulled the back hem of her long skirt forward and between her legs, tucking it into her high skirtband. I laughed. Her pale ankles were knobby beneath her billowy makeshift shorts. She picked up a branch, broke off a thin twig. "Get the rice," she said.

Haemi used a few grains from our lunch and my spit to form a gluey blob. She stuck it on the end of her stick. At the river's edge, where the dragonflies buzzed, she slid into the water. "The trick is to jab upward."

The creatures teased her, hovering around the stick and shooting away, but she was patient. Finally, with a majestic thrust into the air—she caught one.

The dragonfly wriggled against the trap, its body stuck, its wings fluttering. I flew into a shrieking happiness. It was beautiful, helpless, and mine. Even though I wasn't supposed to—I was already sick in the lungs—I screamed. And Haemi, she did a wondrous thing. She jammed the dragonfly stick into the ground, sat down beside me, and screamed, too.

We sprawled our legs into the river and splashed, raising our orange-dyed nails to keep them dry. The water lapped up our knees. Haemi held out her hand toward something unseen. "If I were a boy," she said, "I'd do this every day."

I laughed. "But you're a girl."

Her forehead, shiny and white, caught the sun. "Of course I am." She smiled. "Let's go home."

She pitched herself forward. With one turn of her wrist, her pants released and billowed into a skirt again. She stretched herself outward, all limbs and skin. I thought it was wonderful. How she was able to expand the world just for me.

🙣

Youngho and I whooped with excitement as we sprinted toward home after my last meeting with Teacher Lee. The August heat coated our shirts and shoes with a muggy dampness, but we didn't mind. I rolled my hands in waves at the cemetery, slowing to copy the humps of the burial mounds. In one day, I'd leave this place, and I wanted to impress each image in my memory.

"I heard Seoul girls are different," Youngho said with a grin as he caught his breath. "They'll let you put your hand up their skirts."

"And there'll be Americans. I bet those girls would let me get a finger in." Their flesh would be pink, and the hairs down there curly, springy, and yellow.

"They're probably older," he said. "Eighteen or nineteen."

I grinned. "So?"

He threw a pebble at me with a laugh. "If you really want it, tell them you're sick. They'll sleep with you out of pity." Youngho's hands fluttered to his face. "Oh, Hyunki, you brave boy. Come here and let me breathe into your poor little lungs to make you feel better." He pretended to untie his shirt and hitch up an imaginary skirt. We hunched over, laughing again. "Seoul tomorrow!" Youngho hooted. "You, a city boy!"

I imagined my first day. The walk from my boardinghouse to the high school was supposed to take half an hour. Along smooth, paved roads lined with trees, enormous brick buildings would sell brand-new American goods behind glass-paned windows.

"That's what I get for being poor and stupid, you lucky worm." Youngho shoved me. "You think there'll be any demos left for you to join?"

I shook my head. The spring had been filled with protests after Rhee's reelection. Youngho and I had heard the news on the radio, steaming with jealousy. As the Seoul students forced Rhee to resign, we'd turned the dials of our wireless and imagined the crowds. "We got the Second Republic we wanted, right?"

"Yeah, but can you imagine?" Youngho twisted a leaf off a tree. "To be part of the action."

"You only want me to suffer here longer." I punched his shoulder. After the election and news of the violent protests, Haemi had forced me to stay and miss my first semester. "You jealous?"

"Maybe a little." He smiled. "If anything happens, write me and I'll get on the next bus. Promise?"

"Done."

We shook hands and passed the center of town without saying anything more. I wanted to tell Youngho that I'd miss him, that we could explore Seoul and seduce its women together if he came along. I ran my hands over hanging leaves, a cat lounging on a stone wall, and hoped that somehow he understood.

At the corner where we parted ways, he glanced toward my house. "Seems like a calm day."

I stared at the stone wall and shrugged.

"I'll see you later tonight. It's going to be great," he said.

"I hope we can handle it."

"We will. Drinking with Jisoo-hyung!" Youngho threw his book into the air and caught it as he ran down the road, all grins and ease.

It was calm inside because no one was home. In the common room, I ate leftover fish and skimmed through a short story Haemi had given me. I thought "Rain Shower" would be about Seoul, but it followed two children in the countryside. I wondered if she was trying to make me feel guilty or giving me a way to remember our home.

I heard little-girl chatter blow through the front gate, and I set down the book. Soon after, bare feet slapped on wood as Solee ran across the porch and slid open the hanok doors. "Uncle!" She skidded into my room, plopped herself on my lap, and pushed the sweaty strands of hair from her forehead. "Guess what I saw today!"

Haemi waddled in next with her enormous stomach, steering Jieun in front of her. "Not right now. Do I look like someone who can do that right now?"

Jieun stared at Haemi's looming belly and set her lip. She tucked her long, narrow chin to her chest and hitched her thin shoulders. We knew what would happen next.

Haemi blew out a groan. "Please don't—"

"Come here, Jieun." I shifted Solee, who was chattering about a certain chicken she'd seen, to my left knee and coaxed Jieun to my side. "Uncle Hyunki's here."

"Mommy's mean," she said.

"This baby's jerking my insides. I need a moment, please." Haemi lowered herself onto a cushion, bags still dangling from her arms. The handles cut into her swollen wrists, leaving strips of reddened flesh. "Did you eat?"

I nodded. "Fish and rice."

She kicked a parcel in my direction. "Another present for your trip."

A sleek tin box emerged from carefully wrapped paper. Solee flurried with excitement. "This looks like my teacher's pencil case." She opened the lid and Jieun stuck her fingers inside the compartments.

"What is this?" I asked.

"It's to hide your medicine. Mother said you were worried about the boarding mates."

"It looks like a jewelry box," I said. "The girls can keep it. I feel good, strong."

"You need to take the pills with you, just in case."

"Jisoo-hyung said I'm fine."

"He's not a doctor. Anyway, at least thank Mother. She's sick again and still out shopping for you." Haemi shut her eyes and wiped her nose on her sleeve. "And how are you? Ready to run off to the big city and leave us all behind?"

I closed the lid and imagined it full of white pills. "I guess."

"What does that mean?" Haemi snorted. "Don't pretend you're not excited."

I focused on Solee, who'd returned to her story about chickens. Haemi was cranky with pregnancy, and it poisoned all her conversations. She snaked between crying and yelling, sleeping and marching through rooms with a wooden spoon she rattled against the walls to get our attention. She wrung our words around until even hardy Jieun felt guilty for an innocent remark. I tried not to speak to my sister more than necessary.

Jieun stuck her slim feet into one of the empty shopping bags. "Mommy?"

"Not right now." Haemi lay down and dragged a floor cushion over her face. "I'm feeling awful. Watch the girls for a bit?"

"I'm going out. Saying goodbye to friends," I said.

She lifted the cushion. "You've been saying goodbye for weeks. You can spare an hour for me, Hyunki."

Solee looked up, her hands in the form of beaks. "Are you listening? The chickens were trying to eat each other!"

"Fine. An hour." I lifted Solee and pulled the bag off Jieun's feet. "Time to leave cranky-monster Mommy alone."

Haemi frowned. "Don't be like that in front of them."

The girls giggled, aware that I was somehow making fun of their mother. I shut the door on Haemi with a large gesture, as if I were trapping a monster within.

My room was in the corner of the house and received the most light. In that sunny crook, on my desk, I laid out the items I would take with me to Seoul—the first chocolate bar I'd bought with my tutoring money, still uneaten; a collection of notebooks I'd kept since middle school, categorized by subject; a wooden pencil set I'd won at a local writing competition; clothes that wouldn't mark me as a country boy. I ripped sheets of paper from one of the old notebooks and handed the girls some peelable pencils. When the point flattened, they liked to pull the string and watch the paper shavings fall to reveal the waxy core.

Solee lay on her stomach, curling the edges of her paper. I sat in between her and Jieun, rubbing their backs in turn. "What are you drawing there?"

Jieun pointed to her blotty image. "This is Mommy."

I touched the large circle inside the squarish body. "Is that the baby?"

"Baby baby." She scribbled over the circle, squeezing the pencil in her fist. "Gone! Mommy don't want baby and I make it go." She dragged the pencil across a final time, leaving a thick black gash.

"That's not nice, Jieun," I said. "Don't make up mean things like that."

"I not making up." She drew spirals around the body. "She *told* me. She want baby dead."

Solee looked up from her work. "That's a lie. Uncle, she's lying."

"Mommy say so." Jieun furrowed her thick eyebrows and again pointed at her drawing. "No sister. No brother. It dead."

"Uncle, tell her she's being bad!"

Jieun poked Solee with her pencil. "I not bad!"

Solee pushed Jieun's face with one hand and snatched at the pencil with the other. "You are!"

All of a sudden, they were wild, yanking and hitting and screaming at each other. Their high, shrill voices pierced the air. Solee's hair fell out of her ponytail and Jieun grabbed a thick handful.

"Hey!" I squeezed between their bodies and pushed Solee's reaching arms away from Jieun's red face and fists. They weren't fast, but they wriggled without any fear of me.

I caught their shoulders and howled along with them. "Stop yelling right now!" I steered them to separate sides of the room. "Face the wall or lie down for a nap. No speaking for twenty minutes."

"You mean, too," Jieun whispered. "Mommy said so." Sniffling in her anger, she settled onto the folded sleeping mats and crossed her arms. "I not sleepy."

"Close your eyes anyway." I smoothed her rumpled hair. "It'll make you feel better."

Solee watched us with her attentive gaze, as if I were the one in trouble. She was smart, intuitive. If Haemi had said anything that awful, she would know. When Jieun fell asleep, I returned the papers and pencils to her. "You need to be nicer to your sister."

"She started it." Solee rubbed her arm. "She poked me first."

I sat beside her. "Did your mommy say anything to you? About the baby?"

"She didn't say anything like that. Jieun's lying." She grabbed my hand. "You're leaving tomorrow?"

"I'm going away to study. You know that."

She squeezed my fingernails one by one. "Come visit a lot."

I wondered if I would have time. If Solee would hold it against me if I didn't. She was usually the accommodating sister, but in rare instances, she could hold a grudge with more ferocity than Jieun. "I'll come back," I said.

Solee drew a circle with eyes, a nose, and a mouth, a patch of hair and a lanky body. "This is you." From the figure's hand, she traced a line that wormed away. "This is me." She pointed to a small dot at the far corner of the page.

In the kitchen, I watched Mother's curved frame as she cut the stems off green chili peppers. She wore a handkerchief across her mouth to stop her coughing, and it reminded me of the mashed herbs she used to force me to inhale. She seemed as small as I used to feel back then. She hunched close to the counter, squinting. I wondered if it was worth mentioning what Jieun had said. But it was my last night, and I didn't want to fight. I tucked the picture in my pocket. "Can I help?" I asked.

"I thought you were going out." She stuffed half the cut peppers into a jar. "Look in those boxes over there. I bought some items for you."

I opened the cardboard lids near the kitchen door. Thick button-down shirts in white, pale gray, blue. A folded suit wrapped in sheets of lightweight paper. "This is all for me?"

"I asked Jisoo for your measurements." She smiled a flash of yellowed teeth. "They're custom-made. The same tailor he uses. I wanted it to be a surprise."

I stroked the jacket between my fingers. It was too nice, better than Jisoo's suits or anything Mother had ever sewn for herself. I shouldered it on and touched the buttons on the sleeves. "Was it expensive?"

She clucked. "Don't you even ask. Bend down so I can see." She smoothed her hands across my arms. "My son in a modern suit. Your mind's just as good as those city folks' and I want you to look good, too. The wool's nice, isn't it?"

"It's fancy city wool." I laughed, rubbing the silk-lined pockets, the invisible seams. My name embroidered on the inside pocket. I felt myself standing taller, straighter already. "It's too much, Mother. Thank you."

I bowed low to the ground and felt her cup my neck. I held her hands, the crimped skin. She was shaking, her cheeks flushed, but she smiled again for me. "You should rest. Have Haemi-nuna cook dinner," I said.

Mother patted me once and shuffled back to the chili peppers. "I like cooking. It's the only thing keeping me alive."

"You're sick. I'll go wake Nuna."

"Hyunki." She frowned. "Be kind. She's having a hard time."

"She's just pregnant." I folded the jacket back inside the box. "She's not even good to you most days."

"You don't know what it's like to carry a baby for months, and now you're leaving." Mother raised a chili dipped in gochujang. "Eat this and go. Tell her you'll miss her."

I found Haemi sitting outside on a low stool, her legs apart and her wide stomach pushing her back. She smoked a cigarette beneath the evening sky. Her curly hair, loosened from its usual bun, hid her face from my view. I crossed the yard, stepping on the flat stones that led to the tree in the corner, and sat on the ground next to her.

She inhaled, deep and slow. "Do you remember our old place, where we grew up?"

"Sure," I said, adjusting my seat on a spare rush mat. "I remember."

"Describe it to me." She stubbed out her cigarette with her foot. "Describe what you remember from before the war, when it was only us and Mother."

"Why?" I picked up her stub, passed the warm, smashed cylinder between my hands. She didn't respond.

"There were forsythia bushes everywhere," I started. "In the spring, it was all yellow. We had a bark roof, I think. The house was cramped, and you'd complain that I kicked you in my sleep."

"I walked there this morning."

"It's at least five kilometers away." I touched her knee. "That's why you're tired."

"I wish we were back there," she said. "That I hadn't let Jisoo convince me to move into town."

"Why?" I turned to her, but she curtained her face with her hair. I couldn't decipher Haemi anymore. "What do you mean, Nuna?"

"All these people with their talk and gossip. The homes all close together." She gestured to the houses beyond our stone wall. "This isn't what I wanted."

"Korea's changing," I said. "It's exciting. We're rebuilding and modernizing."

"Don't talk to me like I'm a child." She tried to hold her knees, but her stomach was too wide. "I don't need you treating me like that, too."

"I'm not trying to talk down to you."

"Then don't." She raised her head to the sky, as if the clouds could part a path of understanding for her. "Jisoo made me feel like I was winning. He said I could get a job if I wanted to. Did you know that? He said living in town would provide me with more opportunities."

"You want to get a job?" I scooted closer, almost hugged her. "You want to work?"

"No—never mind." She massaged the back of her neck. "What'd you come out here for? What do you want?"

I pulled the drawing from my pocket. I unfolded it slowly, almost regretting the decision. "I wanted to show you this."

"What's that?" she asked.

"You," I said.

She tugged her dress over her stomach with a small laugh. "Looks just like me."

"Jieun drew it. You see this? She said that you didn't want the baby. That you wanted it to die."

For someone so pregnant, Haemi's face was all bone. She tilted her head to the sky again and sighed.

I got on my knees and touched her arm. "Is it true? Do you feel that way?"

"What kind of mother do you think I am?" She took the drawing and examined it, grimaced. "I'll talk to her."

"I want to make sure. If something's wrong—" I grasped her hand. "You can talk to me."

"Enough." She cut me with her voice. "Don't make me into some monster. I get enough of that from the girls." She folded the drawing, set it on the ground, and finally met my gaze. Her dark eyes were impenetrable. "Are you hungry? What do you want for dinner?"

I sat back on my heels, not wanting her to shift the conversation, yet not wanting to fight. "I'm going out with Jisoo-hyung."

"Oh, right." She raised her eyebrows. "Your last meal with Jisoo. Is he going to teach you how to be a man tonight?"

"I came out here because I was worried." I sat back on the mat. "Don't be mean. Why can't you be excited for me?"

"Mean mommy. Mean sister. I'm always so mean, right?" She shifted on her stool, edging farther away. "I *am* happy for you. We're all so happy for you."

"Stop it." I kicked her stupid cigarettes. I didn't know why I bothered. "Shut up."

"My smart, brilliant brother ready to move to Seoul and make his family proud." Haemi thrust her arms in the air. "Hurray for Lee Hyunki," she shouted.

"Are you avoiding this?" I grabbed the drawing. The paper creased as I stood and I held it up to her again. "You don't even want this baby, do you? That's why you've been so miserable."

She yanked the picture from me. "Don't throw that in my face." She stood with effort, her hands bracing her hips. I didn't try to help her. "And don't be so stupid. I didn't say anything about the baby."

"I'm not stupid."

She sighed. "Of course you're not." She touched my cheek, brushed my hair back with her fingers, tenderly, like she used to when I was a sick little kid. "Maybe you shouldn't go. What about that poor high school student in Masan Harbor? Can you imagine finding him dead like that?" She sucked in her breath. "You only saw the picture. That tear-gas canister slicing his head open—I've seen that kind of evil with my own eyes, Hyunki. Maybe Seoul's not safe enough yet."

I wanted to laugh. She careened from mood to mood. I wouldn't let her sway me. "The revolution's over. Hyung said it's fine."

"Then why don't I come with you tomorrow and help you settle in? I could stay with you." She squeezed my hand, her voice rising into girlishness. "It'll be fun. Just us. I could sneak into your classes and see what it's like to be you. I've never been to Seoul."

It was too late. I picked up the picture, now torn at the edges, and heard the petulance in my voice. "I don't want you to come. I don't need you."

Haemi released me and straightened her shoulders. "I'm joking anyway. I'm going to be right here." She lit another cigarette. "Be careful tonight. You won't be able to keep up with Jisoo."

She walked to the house and sang over her shoulder, "Trying to be a big man," light and airy. She didn't turn back around.

I ran to Youngho's even though it left me winded—my lungs tight from the exercise, heat, and humidity. I ran until Haemi's taunt hardened into a little stone I could kick around in my mind. Outside Youngho's hanok gates, I called his name until he came to the door. He held a spoon in one hand and a bowl in the other.

"Let's go," I said.

"Already?"

"Yeah." I jerked my head at the road behind me. "I don't want to be late."

Youngho looked at me. Arguments always left their record on my face. This time I didn't care. It was my last night in this tiny town and then I'd be rid of Haemi's moods. I wouldn't have to live with her inexplicable anger and feel guilty for wanting to leave. I'd go to Seoul and become my own person.

"All right, let's go," he said.

But when we arrived at the bar where we were supposed to meet Jisoo, the barkeep wouldn't let us inside. Of the two of us, Youngho looked older. Dressed in a large button-down shirt, he argued with the man. "This guy's brother-in-law is Yun Jisoo."

The barkeep spread his arms. "Well, I don't see him. Get out of here until you have someone of age with you."

Down the street, Youngho and I stole nuts from the vendor with the lame leg and cut a deal with a street hawker selling photographs of naked women. I bought Youngho one of a girl showing her nipples. They were dark and large in contrast to the small verve of her tits. Jisoo found us hunched over it and clapped a hand on my back. He snatched the photo and showed it to his friends.

"You'll like the ladies here, then," he said, laughing.

Jisoo spoke in a large, rounded voice whenever he was in town. He held on to the edges of his syllables until they became generous. Around him, I found myself speaking this way, too.

"Let's get drunk," I said.

Jisoo grinned.

At the bar, we crowded up the painted stairs, past closed doors that seemed to vibrate with laughter. Jisoo led us to a private room where a long, low table was stocked with makgeolli and bar girls. Youngho had told me about these women, how they would pour drinks and laugh at your jokes all night. They wore matching modern dresses, dark blue and tightly cut. Their faces were painted with makeup.

"Come join us," a girl in red lipstick said.

The others, at the corners of the table, tilted their heads at us, bowed and beckoned with their hands. Jisoo strode in and sat on the floor beside the one who'd spoken. His friends greeted the girls they knew. Youngho and I were given our own girl, one who looked as young as us.

She bent her head, a small bow. "You can call me Sookja. Would you like a drink?" She poured us two bowls of makgeolli and wiped the rims with her pinkie finger. Her nails were painted a pale pink. "Aren't you going to ask if I'd like one, too?" She sat between us and touched our wrists. Youngho poured before I could, and I wondered if Sookja wanted both of us, if this night would unravel like one of those stories where men slept with girls in entwined, many-limbed groups.

She was pretty enough. With a small nose that didn't thicken too much and a sharp little chin to match. She guided the bowl to my mouth. "Drink up now, handsome."

I wasn't prepared and almost sputtered. Makgeolli looked creamy and sweet, but its taste was clinical. I tried to smack my lips like Youngho had. "It's good," I said. "Did you make it?"

Sookja laughed, her hand covering her mouth. She held up a bowl for Youngho but spoke to me across her shoulder. "Do I look like I work in the kitchen?"

Jisoo and his friends ordered snacks. We all raised our bowls in cheers. The girls replenished our drinks as soon as they emptied. I gulped a whole bowl, then another, and the room covered itself in a sticky wash, like sap clinging to my vision.

Jisoo wiped his mouth on his wrist. "I wish it hadn't taken your leaving for us to do this, Hyunki." He turned to the girl at his side. "My little brother-in-law's going to Seoul tomorrow."

"Maybe we should be doting on him instead of you," his girl teased. Her lips looked even redder, parting to reveal white teeth, a pink tongue. She touched his ear and leaned in close. I couldn't make out what she said.

He laughed at her comment and winked when he saw me staring. "Maybe we should go visit little brother together."

The girl sniffed and thrust back her shoulders. "What about your wife?"

"She's pregnant. You're pretty and young and, best of all, not pregnant."

The girls laughed. Youngho did, too, swiping glances at me until I chuckled. *Trying to be a big man.* Haemi's taunt, that little stone, rattled around in my head. I would show her. I slurped more makgeolli. We cheered again and there was more stickiness.

"Am I right about Haemi or what?" Jisoo signaled to me from across the table. "She's huge and always complaining about the girls, Mother, you." He whistled. "She grouses about you a lot."

I opened my mouth to speak, but whether to defend Haemi or agree with Jisoo, I didn't know. She complained about me? I stayed out of her way and hadn't done anything to her. I stared at my hands. They didn't feel connected to the rest of my body. She terrorized us, and she complained about me? I looked up. Jisoo, his friends, Youngho, the girls—they were waiting for me to respond.

"You know it's true," Jisoo said. He spoke easily, shrugging, as if his words held no weight. I felt him leering in my direction. "Right, Hyunki?"

I nodded, working my anger until it heated through me. I wiped my face. "Yeah," I heard myself say. "What a bitch."

The red-lipped girl and her friends snickered. I nodded again, surging with the attention. I wanted Sookja to join in on the laughter. "She's miserable to be around."

"I told you," Jisoo said to the red-lipped girl at his side.

"She's not even happy for me. She doesn't know how to be happy," I said.

"I hear her and the little girls yelling all the time," Youngho added, looking around the room.

I clinked bowls with him. "She hates being pregnant."

Jisoo laughed, head thrust back. "She really does."

"She wants the baby to die."

Someone gasped. I followed the sound to a girl's gaping face. I thought someone had spilled the makgeolli, the room became so quiet. Sookja shook her head, clutched my arm. "That's terrible." Another girl nodded. "Awful." "Who would say that?" Everyone turned to me, their bowls left on the table, their faces drained. They looked at me like I was the one who wanted to kill the baby.

"She said it, not me."

"That's crazy," the red-lipped girl said. "Is she crazy?"

"Shut up." Jisoo's voice shot across the room. He cocked his head at me. "Hyunki, did those words come out of her mouth?"

Everyone looked away. Jisoo rustled his shoulders, as if readying for a fight. He seemed too big next to the girls. If he stood, he could touch the ceiling. He could smash right through it. "She said that?"

I palmed a spoon in front of me. I didn't know how it had gotten into my hand. I'd never seen it before. Makgeolli crawled up my throat, burned its acid taste into my mouth.

"Speak, Hyunki."

"I think I'm drunk." I glanced at the door. "I think I'm sick."

No one looked at us, not even Youngho. Jisoo's eyebrows and lips twitched. His face seemed strange, as if someone had stretched the skin wide and tight.

"I don't know what I'm saying." I stood, and the room seemed to move with me, snatching away its walls. I clutched at the air. Sookja steadied me.

"He's so drunk," someone whispered.

"He doesn't know what he's saying," the red-lipped girl said to Jisoo. "He's a kid."

"I'm sorry." I searched for my shoes. "I can go."

"Sit down." Jisoo grabbed the red-lipped girl's waist. "You're right. He's a stupid kid." She tittered, a small, high giggle, and glanced between us. He barked out a laugh and smiled at her, his teeth gritted into a grin. "My little brother made a stupid joke. He doesn't need to leave for that, does he?"

"No." She widened her eyes, rubbed his arm. "It was only a silly joke."

He let her stroke him for a moment and then nodded at me. "Sit down." His voice smooth, easy again. "Drink with me, Hyunki." He pointed and Sookja placed a new bowl in my hand.

Jisoo cleared his throat. He stood and raised his bowl to everyone in the room. He gave a loose, indifferent smile. Using that big-room voice again, he said, "Let's drink to my little brother-in-law. To Hyunki leaving for Seoul—here's hoping some poor girl will let you stick it in."

A trickling, testing laughter around the room. "He's cute enough," a girl with short hair said. "With more makgeolli." The laughter came louder then, full-bodied, and their chatter erupted, eager to eat up the silence.

As Jisoo sat down, I caught a glimpse of his glare, the tendons of his neck raised tight. He slipped on a smile and nuzzled his head into the red-lipped girl's hair. He kissed her ear, made her giggle, but he stared straight at me.

"I should leave," I said to no one.

Sookja touched my hand. "Forget it, Seoul boy." She rubbed my back. "Stay. I'll make you feel better."

Jisoo caught his girl's necklace and pulled her closer, no longer paying attention to me. I didn't want to watch any longer. The town rumors about him were true, then. Youngho, beside me, surveyed Jisoo as if taking notes. I concentrated instead on Sookja's palm digging into a knot of muscle in my neck. When she leaned in, I smelled her clean, floral scent. "Let's drink," I said.

She slipped a loose strand of hair behind her ear. "Yes, let's."

I liked her crooked teeth. She was mine and not the others', and so she was better. She was good. We struck our bowls together before swallowing the liquid down.

❀

Beneath the streetlamps, Sookja danced. She lifted her skirt above her knees and kicked her feet. She ran ahead then circled around the road as I held out my arms for balance. Her blue dress, cut at the shoulder, revealed such softness.

She looped her warm, thin arm with mine. "So are you really sick?" She stood right beside me, her skin sticky with sweat, but her voice seemed to come from everywhere. "What kind of sick?

Not bodily, I hope," followed by a hard, streaky laugh. She was too loud, too disorienting for the night's quiet.

I put a hand across her mouth. "I'm healthy. Youngho's stupid."

"I think he was taking care of you," she whispered against my palm.

"We're here." I led her to the back of the house and opened the kitchen door. "Watch the fire pit," I said as we ducked inside. I didn't know if I liked her or if I was just drunk, but her fingers were laced with mine, and her perfume had changed somehow, into a stronger, muskier scent.

"I can't see. I don't even know why I'm here." Sookja followed me past the piles of kindling, the earthenware jars, our rice chest.

I blinked with purpose, tried to adjust my vision to the kitchen's darkness. "You have to be quiet now."

"I'm not actually supposed to leave the bar. Just entice you to come back for more. The men are usually so old." She laughed. Her breath was warm against my neck.

I hit something hard and familiar and couldn't understand how Sookja could be in front of me and behind me all at once. I stepped forward again. There was flesh and movement and a different laugh. Haemi.

She lit a kerosene lamp that blazed the room with light. Bending over her jutting stomach, she set the lamp on the counter and sucked her teeth. "This is what you're doing on your last night?" She held a stick with a dried corncob stuck on one end—our mother's back scratcher. Her top's ties were loose. I remembered how she'd complained during the other pregnancies of an unbearable, roaming itch that lived beneath her skin.

Sookja, behind me, whispered, "Is this your sister?"

Haemi pointed at the door. "Go away, you silly girl."

I held Sookja's hand. "Don't tell her what to do. She's my guest." I tried to sidestep Haemi, but she blocked me. She'd always been the strong one, protecting me from schoolboys and Jisoo's ricocheting tantrums.

She pressed the whole length of her arm into my chest and used her stomach as a barrier. "What did you say to Jisoo?"

I pushed her arm away. "Nothing."

"He came home angry. Usually those girls"—she flicked her stick at Sookja—"make him feel so good he falls asleep as soon as he takes off his shoes."

"Leave us alone." I gripped Sookja's hand tighter. "Get out of our way."

"What's the point?" She wiggled the cob between Sookja and me. "You wouldn't know what to do with her anyway."

Sookja giggled, soft but present. Haemi laughed, too. I felt the heat return to my cheeks, my feet, my chest.

"Maybe," I said, shaking them both off, "if you weren't such a *bitch*, if you knew how to keep Jisoo *happy*, he wouldn't have to visit bar girls like her. Have you thought about that?"

They both caught their breaths, a sharp intake that silenced us all. Haemi's scratcher dropped to the floor. In the lamplight, her face seemed inflamed, almost red and purple with anger. A thick vein ran down her forehead.

"Oh." Sookja pushed me aside. She picked up an egg lolling on the counter and strode to Haemi. Neither of them spoke as Sookja held the egg to Haemi's cheek with a softness I didn't understand.

"What are you doing?" I tried to ask, my voice cracking out half the words. Sookja shifted in front of me so I couldn't see them. "What's going on?"

I stood there, watching them murmur to each other.

Finally, Sookja picked up the fallen scratcher, placed it on the counter by the lamp. She didn't meet my gaze and spoke only to Haemi. "I should go. Good night."

We listened to the back door close, and then we were alone. I wished Haemi would yell or cry or hit me. She stood still, the egg in one hand.

"I didn't mean what I said." I moved toward her. "I'm drunk and I'm stupid. Nuna?"

I wanted to hold her, to tell her I was sorry. Her wet face looked strange, almost swollen, as if she'd been crying for years, as if she were someone else. I wanted to touch her cheek, the way Sookja had done.

Haemi stepped back, her hand a blade in the air between us. "You think you're so smart, but you don't know anything. You, Hyunki," she said, slow and precise, "you—weren't worth this life."

She turned and left. Tiny, hunched over, belly hidden from my view.

Alone, I picked up the scratcher and raked it across my hand and tried to understand. The hardened husk left red marks across my palm.

The next morning, dense clouds cloaked the sun and sky. I folded and refolded my clothes, ate two bowls of rice, and finished all the vegetable dregs of my stew. I looked around for Haemi, but she wasn't in the kitchen or the dining room. By leaving time, I still hadn't seen her. Mother called from the front yard, prodding me to hurry before I missed the bus.

In the common room, Jisoo held Jieun in his good arm as Solee tugged on his right leg. I wondered if Haemi had told him about our fight, if he'd berate me before I left. He grimaced at the girls' high chatter but smiled when he saw me. "That was a fun last outing. Are you feeling all right?"

I nodded. "I have a headache."

"Me too." He laughed. "You'll be great in Seoul, you know that? You'll fit right in." He shook my hand. "You ready to go?"

Jieun squeezed Jisoo's ears. "Daddy, you stay today?"

"Say goodbye to Uncle first," he said.

"Bye for only a little while," I added. "I'll come back."

"I'll miss you," Solee said, and hid her face in Jisoo's pants when I tried to hug her. Jieun didn't understand. She bowed her head dutifully and again asked Jisoo to stay home.

"Don't let Mother worry you. We're in the Second Republic now. A parliamentary system, the way it should have been since the beginning. I'm jealous of all the fun you'll have." Jisoo thumped my shoulder, his mind already drifting toward matters that didn't relate to me. "You should go before the bus leaves."

I looked out the front door. Mother stood alone. "Have you seen Nuna?"

He squeezed Jieun's narrow face left and right, like a puppet. "Nope. I woke up and she was gone. Right, Jieun?"

"Hyung." I shifted my bag between my hands, feeling panicked all of a sudden at its weight. "I haven't seen her. I kind of argued with her last night."

Jisoo breathed out his nose. "Then we both did. She's probably mad, hiding somewhere." He set Jieun down next to Solee, ignoring her protests, and shook my hand. "I have work. I'll see you soon."

I shepherded the girls to their room, hoping to find Haemi there. I wanted to apologize, to ask for her forgiveness. She wasn't there.

"Where's your mommy?" I asked.

"She said I have to watch Jieun until you leave. She went walking." Solee cuddled Jieun. "I'm being a good sister."

"She said that?" I searched the room for any sign of where she might have gone. I'd been drunk and mean, but how many hateful words had she thrown at me in the past months? I always let her taunts slide off. I never held her words against her.

"Will you visit soon?" Solee asked.

"Visit visit?" Jieun echoed.

"Of course. In the meantime, I'll send lots of treats and letters. Now, back to sleep." I sang a song and they fell asleep quickly, the way only children can.

Watching them clutch each other as they dreamed, I decided I would come back for the girls, but no longer for my sister. If she planned to hold a grudge and disappear on my last morning, if she was going to make me feel guilty for leaving, I could be that way, too. She wasn't the only one.

On the bus, I devoured Mother's carefully packed gimbap without much chewing. Fingers slick with oil, I handled the slim box I'd found tucked inside my bag, between layers of shirts and pants. I almost ripped open the paper wrapping, thinking it was money. The seal stopped me.

I watched as millet fields, rebuilt towns, mountains, and large patches of land still marked by the war passed by my window. I touched my seat's frayed stitching, the clouded glass separating me from the world, my unsteady legs. I left a glistening trail of oily fingerprints.

I held out as long as I could, and then—I tore open the box.

Inside, a dragonfly lay pinned to a scrap of ramie cloth. Tiny, withered, preserved whole. The wings—sheer and netted, except for a darkened panel at the corners—felt like crystallized air.

Kyunghwan

1962

THE WHITER, THE BETTER. I CHASED IT LIKE A RESTLESS
dream. One year in sugar, three and a half in flour, another half
in cotton, then the past three in paper. I knew how to work all the
sections, but I liked the calenders best. They were simple. Two
rollers leveled out the lumps until smooth and finished paper reeled
toward you. After shit work, the creation of something so white
and clean was enough.

Donggeon and I sat next to the reel chewing on dried squid legs.
His wife roasted them perfectly, until their suckers were burnt nobs.
"Want to see a movie today?" he asked.

"Which one?"

"Does it matter?" Donggeon was twenty-seven, the same as
me, but also a father with a movie obsession. He folded the squid
leg into fourths against his tongue. "*Farewell Duman River* or the
American one—*West Side Story*?"

"I haven't heard of either," I said.

"The posters are everywhere. You're a bastard if you haven't
seen them."

"Still a bastard, then."

Donggeon sighed. "We've got a jam. Let's lift the reel." He
climbed on top of the table and grabbed the chain that held the
paper roll steady.

"You know, I have heard of *West Side Story*," I said. "Doesn't it have all that singing and dancing?"

"Yeah, so what?" His face reddened as he pulled the chain. The roll was heavy, but he always insisted that turning the wheel was the harder job. "Hurry up."

I checked the paper's hardness and shoved the wheel's stubborn handle with my feet. It turned tight and slow, the paper amassing into a thick, weighty spool. "I don't want to watch a bunch of Americans singing about love," I said. "I want something realistic."

He groaned as he always did when I turned disagreeable. "No movies for you, then."

I was a strange single man to him. To everyone I knew. I didn't like movies except the few that had been released the year before, free of censorship, during our too brief Second Republic. I didn't have a woman. I didn't buy women. "Your dick still work?" Donggeon once asked when we were drunk. I hit him in the face and immediately felt ashamed. It was what Jisoo would have done.

At the end of the workday, Donggeon tightened his cap. "If you change your mind, we're going after dinner." He slapped my back with affection, like an American, and left for the trams.

I didn't like movies, but I had my own obsession. I walked toward it, cutting through the city's thrashing streets. Handcarts, horse-drawn carriages, military junta jeeps, trams, and automobiles crowded the roads without order. The sounds of wooden wheels clattering underneath loads of cabbages, horses breathing in their high, animal way, gas exhaust dusting the pedestrians' legs—these things comforted me. I wanted to fill myself with noise.

At the eastern end of Seoul, where a clutch of paved roads widened into factories and upturned land, the activity quieted to the sounds of machinery and a public speaker spouting Military Revolutionary Committee slogans. *We will rebuild our proud nation! We will eradicate corruption and return to a democratic government!* I entered a garage attached to a tire factory. Unused and slightly defective tires were heaped everywhere. Uncle Park squatted in a rectangle of summer light coming from the open doors. A pile of discarded metal and engine parts lay before him.

"I might get an exhaust today," he said, with a quick glance.

I pulled on my gloves and joined him. We'd already built a chassis, gotten tires from our friends next door, and attached a fork.

He circled his fingers and motioned. "It's this long. Good condition." Uncle Park was fifty-five, widowed, and a father to one son, a lawyer, who'd survived the war. I didn't know why he continued as a mechanic. Mostly he fixed trucks for deliveries, but on his own time he built motorcycles, and I tried to help.

"You work on this." He pointed to a salvaged rear spring. "I'll keep wrestling with the engine."

As we worked, Uncle hummed to block out the slogans that filtered in from the street. "This military coup and their falsehoods. I don't need excuses for what I know and see," he said. "Park Chung-hee will take over and become a dictator, just as Rhee did."

I agreed, but I didn't say this aloud. It was hard to trust any person's political loyalty anymore. Instead, I concentrated on oiling the rear spring and attaching it to an arm. I wasn't good or fast, but I was patient. I wanted to construct a machine with my own hands, one that was better and faster than me. We worked until a delivery boy knocked on the door.

"Eat with me and go home," Uncle said.

The buckwheat noodles were chilled, chewy, mustard hot. They were the only thing I'd ever seen Uncle eat. He slurped without paying me much attention until most of his noodles were gone. Then he looked up. "My son's getting married."

"That's great news." I swallowed. "Who was he matched with?"

"Some woman he met himself. Lee Sunok is her name. She's from here."

"Congratulations," I said. "You must be happy."

He trawled the broth with his chopsticks, looking for any last noodles. "She wears Western clothes and high heels."

I laughed. "So?"

He clucked like an old grandmother. "It's not what I'm used to. She'll have to wear a hanbok for the wedding."

"I don't think that's the style anymore," I said.

"A father gets some say." After finishing his broth, he watched as I ate. I was slow, a habit I couldn't seem to break even now. "My son said he'd pay for your matchmaker."

"Why would he do that?" I asked.

"You work with me when he doesn't want to. He's feeling lucky now that he's getting a wife. Who cares why? Take it. Tomorrow. It's already scheduled."

I slurped my last noodle. "Why so soon?"

Uncle stacked our empty bowls together and laid them by the door for the delivery boy to collect. "You're getting old, that's why. Bring your lineage papers."

As I walked home, I thought about his words. A matchmaker. It was common, traditional. I would be able to buy a house without suspicion. I would have someone to return to in the evenings. A woman to talk to when I woke in the middle of the night, aching with loneliness. Even so, the thought of a wife didn't appeal to me anymore. I no longer belonged to anyone.

Grandmother Song had left me rice, a bowl of spinach soup, and a kettle of tea in the kitchen. Even though I'd just eaten, I took my tray to the inner courtyard. The hanok where I lived was traditional, with the rooms laid out in a square. In the center, the courtyard was decorated with bushes, a small magnolia tree, and a planked wooden porch. I sat by the reading room I rented from the Songs and picked out the spinach leaves, chewing them one at a time. I watched the sky's deep pinks and blues fighting for space. This darkening light was what I most enjoyed about summer.

Across the courtyard, Aejung emerged from her room with her eating tray and a book. She bowed.

"Studying?" I asked.

She crossed and set her tray next to mine. "Mathematics. I don't like it."

I flipped through the pages of her notebook. She had large, graceless handwriting. "I don't think I learned this when I was your age," I said.

"It's boring. Oh!" She snapped her fingers together like a girl in a movie. "I have something for you. Let me get it."

Aejung was beautiful in a youthful way. Sixteen and in high school, with a knapsack stuffed with short, colorful American clothes she wore after class. I'd caught her once in a printed skirt that showed her knees and she'd blushed, begged me not to tell. I had pretended to refuse, until the fury in her face made me laugh and lose my composure.

I ate the leftover pork on her tray and tried to solve one of her math problems. She returned with an envelope. "A post came for you."

I took it and set it aside. "It's probably the matchmaker. I'm meeting one tomorrow."

"On a Sunday?"

I laughed. "Should I be attending church instead? Or seeing a shaman at temple?"

She kneeled beside me, took her notebook, and balanced it on her head. "They make us do this for posture. We even get points."

"That sounds stupid."

"It is. Only the girls have to do it." She made a face. "My parents plan to match me when I'm nineteen."

"You don't want a love marriage like other girls your age?"

She smiled. "Who said I'll listen to them? They're old world." She poured tea from my kettle into her cup. "I'm going to get Oppa to fall in love. If he gets a love marriage, I get one, too."

"I don't know about that. Sons usually get their way, don't you think?"

"We'll see." She drank her tea and fingered the letter. "Open it."

I did. It wasn't from the matchmaker. It was from Haemi.

Kyunghwan,

I've gotten a job. Me, a middle-school failure, a housewife. It isn't much of anything. I work in an orphanage in town. It's where I'm writing you from, with a half-American child sleeping on my lap. I haven't told Jisoo about my working yet, although he might know. I don't have anyone to tell. Mother died earlier this year. It's strange to even write those words. I expected it for years and yet I am stunned by her leaving. Hyunki is in Seoul now, in his last year of high school, about to enter college, and has no time for my small accomplishments. Everyone else in this town, I can't bear.

I've had three children. Three. And you haven't met any of them. Solee is eight. Jieun, six. Mila, eighteen months. I haven't told Jisoo because he will hate it. He will think I am choosing other children over my own. He will say it does not make sense. It's true. Adoption is unthinkable, shameful. He will say I am working to spite him. Do you know why? There was a woman here at this orphanage he used to know. He kept an item of hers hidden among his belongings. A red hairpin. She left for America years ago. Some days, I stink with jealousy, convinced they had an affair. In my dreams, I riffle through her closet searching for an imaginary yellow dress. When I wake, I touch Jisoo as he sleeps and think, this lame-armed, calloused, darkened body is mine. She was sweet-looking in the way found animals seem sweeter for having once been lost. Bright with trust. With straight black hair that shone like it had been soaked in changpo. Other days, I don't care at all. It makes me laugh aloud. The thought of jealousy passes by me, inconsequential, like death in a war. Like the impotent seeds from this year's awful rice harvest. Like jealousy is a feeling that requires too much effort to have ever existed in my body.

When Solee and Jieun are in school, I work at the orphanage with Mila toddling beside me. When they return, I leave Mila with them at our house. Is that terrible? Only for an hour so that I can help Grandmother Lee with dinner. I don't want her to take the job from me because I cannot be there all the time. Sometimes, I bring the girls along. They play and try to give away their toys. Jieun picks fights, and I scold her. She is fierce, and I love her for it when I can. Mila is gentle and dreamy. My little artist. She floats, allowing her sisters to take up space with their need for attention. You'll like Solee. She's smarter than I was at her age.

I'm not a good mother, but I try. How does it come so easily to some? The tending, the giving over of oneself to those who've come out of you. As if we women are nothing on our own.

My mother was like that. Because I am stupid, uneducated, I didn't see this when she was alive. How she was strict and unforgiving and calculating for us, everything for our protection. I pity her, the husk of a person she was, but I'm also grateful. Without her, we wouldn't have survived the war. Without her, I would have married you, and we would have brawled with each other through our poverty. She knew better than to trust my judgment.

Do you remember when we were eight and went in search of chestnuts? We climbed a tree and collected burrs in my hanbok skirt. We jumped from the lowest branch like flying squirrels, and I tripped and dropped the prickly things everywhere. My skirt ripped, so my thighs showed through, and I knew Mother would punish me for being a careless, rough girl. As I was whipped that night, I imagined you roasting chestnuts and eating them all on your own. That was jealousy.

This letter is bulky, I know. It wanders and folds inward. It is ugly, and it is that way because I was not sure what I wanted to say to you when I began. How about this?

It has been eleven years.

If you write here, only I will find it.

Come visit, Kyunghwan. Meet my girls. See your cousin. He misses you. I can tell. I am his wife. Whatever you have there is not enough to keep you from family.

LEE HAEMI

And just like that, the world I had constructed was made insubstantial. Eleven years had passed. Eleven years in which I'd become a new person, a man of the city, someone who ambled unaffected through a quickly changing society. Yet all of it fell away like rice glue with one note from her.

I read the letter again. *I would have married you,* those words more important than anything else she'd written. I burned with a flushing heat, unsteady. She was everywhere, had always been everywhere. I could smell her—the earth's greenness from her run through the fields, the milk-rice scent that rose from her mouth and skin. My head pulsed and tightened, as if I were an object easily squeezed in her hand, not only because of her words but because I hadn't recognized her handwriting at first glance— the hurry that lifted the end of each line so there was always a tiny triangle of space at the bottom of the page, the crooked letters, the slight curl she gave the *n* in my name. I didn't know if it was me who'd changed, or her.

I dropped the letter and watched it fall onto the ground. I was here in Seoul, and Aejung sat beside me.

"Kyunghwan?" she asked. "Who wrote you?"

Haemi was no longer someone I wanted or needed or thought about each day. She wasn't mine. She was his, as she'd written.

"It's the matchmaker." I tried to smile. I flipped through Aejung's notebook. "These mathematics problems are too hard, even for me."

"Bad news?" Aejung asked.

"It's fine. Go study. You don't need to hang around this old man." She gestured to our trays. "Should I take these in?"

"Yes, please."

I concentrated on Aejung leaving. Her pulled-back shoulders, her elbows out as she balanced the plates, the swing of her skirt in rhythm with her widening hips. When I couldn't see her any longer, I walked to my room.

It was easy—moving, walking, talking. Everything would and did continue. I looked around at all I had achieved. An ondol floor to sleep on, money hidden beneath a loose slat in my wardrobe, clean clothes. Books. A few writings of my own on paper I took freely from the factory. Meals that bulged the boundaries of my stomach, the sensation of fullness surprising me each time.

I walked back outside. The sky had already inked over. I sat on the courtyard porch and watched the Song family's shadows move against the white-papered hanok doors. Woolly outlines unrolled sleep mats and blankets onto the floors.

I found the letter on the ground and took it back to my room. With Haemi's words, everything was made small. It was a trick, a manipulation. How she disassembled me.

Eleven years.

I wrote a response and another and then started all over again. I settled on this: *I don't remember what chestnuts you are talking about.*

The matchmaker was thick all around with a jowly face on a fattened neck that led to a boxy body wrapped in a traditional hanbok. The next morning, she questioned me in Uncle's main room. He and I sat beside each other on one end of a large, lacquered wooden table. I wore his son's suit, the sleeves too long. The matchmaker sat across from us and spoke in a charmer's voice. "I've heard all about your intellect, your rising position at the paper factory, Mr. Yun. Do you have your lineage records for me?"

I pushed them toward her. She looked through each sheet. "No family, then? What about education? Salary?" She gave a false smile full of teeth. "We need to get these facts out of the way before I can hear more about what you're seeking in a wife."

I gave her the rest of my materials and flattened my palms against the table. "This is all I have."

She read quickly, her gaze pinpointing the information she needed.

Uncle poured tea. "What he can't prove, I can vouch for."

The matchmaker tilted her head. "But you're not a blood relation?"

"No," he said. "He lost them in the war."

"That won't work." She straightened my papers. "Don't worry, Mr. Yun. There are many men like you in Seoul now." She poured tea and asked more questions. Uncle left the room when she asked what I wanted in a wife.

"You can relax now." She bit into a sesame seed rice cake, and the powder dusted her lips. This imperfection made me feel better about our meeting. "I can tell you don't want to be here. Are you a philanderer?"

I stared. "Excuse me?"

She fanned her documents into a half circle. "These are my eligible prospects, but I only entrust my girls to respectable men. Why do you seem so apprehensive?"

I wanted to leave, but her gaze pinned me to my seat, reminding me that I'd been granted this favor. That she wouldn't be working with me if it weren't for Uncle Park and his son. "I'm unsure of this whole process," I said. "It seems outdated."

"Well, I'm very good. This isn't a job. It's a calling, a serving of the community." She gestured to the rice cakes and placed another in her mouth. "No?"

I raised my tea. "I'm fine with this."

"Business only, then. Based on your status, it may be easiest to match you with a wife who is not originally from Seoul."

"I'd prefer that."

"You're classically handsome."

"I have a scar." I showed her the raised lines on my cheek. "It was from a rat. When I was so poor, I lived in the slums of Namsan. Does that disqualify me?"

"I noticed that. We don't want our men too pretty, and we won't include your past indecencies in the proposal." She nodded, grim but determined. "I'll find a girl who wants a large family to make up for your lonesomeness. Now, any injuries I should know about? From the war or otherwise?"

I looked at her.

She pressed her lips. "It's a formal question."

"There's nothing wrong with me."

"Have more tea. Tell me truthfully. What are you looking for in a wife?"

I was silent. She was a stranger, and I had Haemi's letter in my pocket. I was in the house of Uncle, who was richer than I had thought, with a hanok of his own. And this woman with powder-covered lips wanted me to tell her what I did not know myself.

Uncle's son insisted on lunch. Munsu wore the slim, dark suit of a lawyer. I did, too. When his gaze lingered on my lapels, I realized Uncle hadn't asked before lending me his suit. I pulled at the cuffs and willed myself not to flush. Munsu looked exactly like Uncle, with gangly arms and a long face that framed wide, up-slanted eyes, and a mole high on his right cheek. Sunok was better-looking. She held his hand underneath the table as we picked at our food.

"Munsu says we're celebrating your matchmaking," she said.

"We'll celebrate anything these days," I replied.

"What kind of girl are you looking for?" She leaned on her elbows. Her lips and eyelids were painted the color of Kyoho grapes.

Uncle moved fish bones around his plate with his chopsticks. He seemed smaller in the bright-lit restaurant with his well-dressed son and future daughter-in-law. "He wants a proper wife," he said.

"I have a sister." Sunok clapped her hands. "Wouldn't that be perfect? Munsu says you spend enough time with Father to be a son anyway."

"I seem to say a lot," Munsu joked.

Sunok smiled. "Sunmi's twenty-two. Want to meet her?"

"If she's as pretty as you," I said.

Munsu and Uncle looked up. I scooped the last of the rice into my mouth. Haemi's letter had unsettled me. Images and memories assailed me as I tried to focus on the matchmaker, on lunch, on Uncle, who'd been so accommodating. I wanted to take a bus to Haemi and claim her as my own. I wanted to forget her completely.

Sunok leaned her head against Munsu as if I'd said nothing wrong. "Everyone says she's prettier, except Munsu."

"I want to meet her," I said, avoiding the men's stares. Sunok was forward, rich. I would marry her sister and be done with it.

"Sunmi's studying to be a singer." Munsu tapped his throat. "She wants to be famous. She's good but a dreamer."

"I could meet her next Sunday."

"If the matchmaker doesn't work," Uncle corrected.

"She's supposed to be the best. My colleague used her last year." Munsu raised his sleeve to glance at his watch. "I need to get back to work." He called a waiter and asked for the check.

I brought out my wallet, but Munsu refused. I had to thank him for another act of charity. Sunok pulled out a silver cigarette case.

Uncle coughed. "That's a dirty habit for a woman."

She slid back her chair. "I intend to smoke outside, Father."

Uncle stood, waving the air in front of him even though she hadn't lit the cigarette. "I need to head to the garage."

"Stay a few minutes and we'll leave together," Munsu said.

"No, I can't stand it."

We all bowed and asked him to stay longer without enough effort. Munsu offered to walk him to the tram. "I'll be right back," he told us.

Once they left, Sunok nudged her chair closer to the table. "Do you mind?"

I gestured for her to go ahead. She brushed her hair out of her face and stuck the cigarette in her mouth. She smiled with ease, as if her actions hadn't just caused the elder to leave. "It doesn't seem like Uncle likes you, and you don't seem to care."

She smoked expertly with small, plump lips. "He'll thaw. I come from a good family. I'm a perfect pick for Munsu." She smiled. "Tell me what it was like to be interviewed. I've never been to a matchmaker."

"Can I have one?" I asked.

She slid the cigarette case toward me. I touched its sleek, shiny lid. It was hard, true silver. "Where did you buy this?" I asked.

When Munsu returned, Sunok kissed his cheek and convinced him to drive us to the department store before returning to work. "I told Kyunghwan he has to pay for the matchmaker by helping me with wedding preparations, so don't be cross," she said. I felt Munsu's gaze linger on me, but he assented.

Inside the department store, we wandered the aisles. "An old boyfriend bought the cigarette case from here," Sunok said.

"I won't tell Munsu."

She laughed. "I don't keep secrets."

"That's one you might want to keep."

She ignored me and touched all the glass cases. "Look at this one" coming out of her mouth as we passed necklaces, rings, bracelets. She stopped at the watch section. "Can you help us?" she asked the attendant. "I want to get one for my wedding yedan."

The attendant bowed. "But this isn't the groom?"

"He's a friend. How else would I know if the watch would fit my husband?" She presented my wrist. "Can I see them all on him?"

I tried on leather bands in black, brown, and gray, and linked metal ones with big glass faces. Sunok took her time. "I think the dark green leather will do," she finally decided. The attendant set it in a box and wrapped it with more care than I'd ever spent on any object. She slipped it into a paper bag with curved handles.

"The jewelry," I said, pointing to the section across the floor. "Let's see what they have."

"Already thinking of what to buy your future wife?" she teased, but did as I'd asked.

We stopped at a row of golden bracelets that hung from a velvet log. The attendant, a young woman with a stiff bun, unclasped each one and laid them on the counter. "What's your name, miss?" I asked.

She held up the last bracelet and blushed. "Kim Boyoung, sir."

"Can we see those, too, Miss Kim?"

"Of course." She smiled and turned.

Sunok whispered, "You're a regular bachelor."

Boyoung brought out more bracelets. Gold, silver, delicate links adorned with dark stones. Sunok glided all of them on her wrist and cried out the way I knew she would. "Can I try on those earrings, too?" She gestured to a matching pair behind the counter.

I didn't lift much anymore, but it was easy with Sunok and Bo-young's distracted excitement. They spoke about complementary colors, what jewel to wear for which occasion. I slipped the simplest bracelet up the sleeve of my borrowed suit—a thin gold chain with a single pale jade stone.

Sunok cupped pearl earrings in her hand. "I'm going to ask Munsu to buy me these."

"Let's go before he thinks I've stolen you." I bowed to Boyoung and tugged Sunok's elbow. "Come on."

When she linked my arm, I slipped the bracelet into her bag. It rested, innocent and hidden, beside her purchased watch as we walked past the lone security guard. Outside, I directed us to Munsu and Uncle's home.

"That was fun. Sunmi will love you," Sunok said.

"Even if I work in a paper factory?"

"Don't worry about that. My father will give you a job." She swiveled on her heels to face me. Walking backward, she looked me up and down. "I wasn't lying. She's prettier than me."

"Then I'll like her."

We talked like that, easy and refreshing, albeit temporary. The gold bracelet swung along without her knowing. When she turned to buy sweets from a street vendor, I retrieved the bracelet and slipped it into my pocket. I thumbed the round, smooth jade. I could throw it into the river or pawn it for money. I could give it to Sunmi or Sunok or the matchmaker's choice.

I walked to meet Uncle after parting with Sunok. The government speaker outside the garage had been dismantled, the individual parts scattered on the grass. Through the open doors, I saw Uncle heft the engine onto a workbench. "I only do that to the speaker on Sundays," he said when I entered.

"I won't tell anyone."

"Come see." He gestured to the engine. "I found this cylinder. I want one more, but it could work alone if need be." He smoothed his hands around the motorcycle's body. "Air and a piston here."

"And then we'll attach it to the exhaust?"

"Once we finish with this. I'll show you." He modeled where all the parts would go—the ones we had already and the yet unfound pieces. "The leather belt here, with the spring-loaded pulley and lever here."

I tried to imagine how it would look completed. How it would feel to ride and where I could go. No longer a boy on a bicycle, I could return and save her. "Can I buy it, once it's ready?" I asked.

Uncle rubbed the top of the engine. "The matchmaker said you were a reluctant candidate."

I stopped my daydreaming. "I didn't know what to say to her."

Uncle was precise. He placed the gaskets in a neat row on a side table. He covered the engine with a sheet. "Why are you hesitating?"

I picked up the exhaust. "I'm not. I came here to thank you for setting me up. I appreciate the support." I bowed.

"You were flirting with Munsu's Sunok."

I gazed at Uncle from my half-bent state. A streak of grease had dirtied his nice shirt. I stared at the spot and rose slowly. No words came. I couldn't tell what anyone was thinking anymore. "I've been distracted," I finally managed.

"You went to the department store with her. Munsu came after his meeting to tell me."

"He said it was fine if I joined her. She was looking at watches for the yedan, and I needed to buy something."

"On your salary?" He threw an oil plug into the air and caught it. "Buy what?"

When I didn't respond, he placed the plug in his pocket. "Have I trusted a cat with a fish?"

I still held the exhaust. It was a slim cylindrical pipe with a ridge of rust on its belly. I imagined its place on the motorcycle's body. I imagined what Uncle would say if I told him about my stealing, or about Sunok's previous boyfriend. I was tired. Of our unpredictable world, of being alone among strangers, of their questions and their need to understand everything about me.

I remembered the chestnuts.

I'd known she would get in trouble for ripping her skirt, the pale glare of her thighs bared in public, and I hadn't eaten a single one without her. I'd roasted them until they were golden and tender enough to break with a glancing fingernail, and I brought them to her wrapped in newspaper the next day. Haemi sat at the edge of her neighbor's rice paddy, dipping her welted legs into the cool water. She pitched the whole bundle of chestnuts into the air. "I don't want them anymore," she said with her natural fierceness. I touched the welts gingerly and wanted to lick them, to feel each swell, the heat of her, with the muscle of my tongue.

In the end, it was Haemi who won. I worked, flirted, and slept alone—for her. Her letter confirmed it. She would take me whole, and I would claim her. She wanted me, too. I was sure of it.

I sent her the bracelet wrapped in paper, fresh and blank, and waited for a response.

Part 4

Solee

1963

I COUNTED THE STRAY DOG'S RIBS ON MY WAY HOME FROM school. Five bones stuck out like the rounded claw of a dokkaebi clutching his club. Last month, six bones showed through the skin of his belly. I smiled. I was fattening him up after all.

He nosed my arms and skimmed his yellow-white fur against my stomach as we walked. I gave him a treat every afternoon. Usually, he was so hungry he left a puddle of drool in my palm. This time, when I pulled out my saved chicken bone, he bucked and flattened his ears, frightened by a thunderclap rumbling through the air—a man on a motorcycle, his wheels licking up bursts of dust. He waved and smiled as he passed. I was the only one on the road.

As he disappeared, I waved back.

I heard their laughter before I'd removed my shoes. In the common room, Daddy and Mommy sang with the girls. "Why is everyone so happy?" I asked.

"Come say hello to your uncle." Daddy hugged me with his working arm. He was in a light mood. Alcohol already swam in his mouth.

At the table next to Jieun and Mila and Mommy sat the man

who had scared my dog. With his darkened skin and dusty face, he looked like the farmers in the fields.

"This one's my smartest, Kyunghwan. Like a boy." Daddy guided me into the room.

I tugged on my short hair. I hated it when he called me a boy. "You're the man on the motorcycle," I said.

"You're the girl who feeds the starving dog." He laughed, and everyone joined in.

"Go bow to your uncle," Daddy said. Instead, I hid my face in Mommy's soft stomach. She combed my hair with her fingers as I let my embarrassment fade.

"Say hello like this!" Jieun stood on her chair, bowed, leaned over Mila, and kissed the man on the cheek. Everyone laughed again.

Uncle hugged me like we knew each other. His cheek was softer than Daddy's, and his breath smelled like persimmons. "Hello, Miss Solee."

"Hello," I said back.

They drank as if we girls were invisible. It was nice. Once, on Jieun's third birthday, Mommy and Daddy drank so much they stumbled out of the room. They left us at the table, our hands sticky from miyeok-guk and cinnamon juice. In the doorway to the backyard, they kissed. I hoped they would do that again.

I woke early the next morning and lay still, collecting the floor's coolness inside me before the day heated through with the summer sun. It was my job to make tea in the morning. Daddy drank ginseng and Mommy angelica. Jieun and Mila slept on with open mouths. I imagined dropping seeds down their throats. The kernels settling in their bellies, growing sprouts. Pear blossoms would flow from their lips and crawl up the walls of the room. Then I could puppet them around by their stalks and have *them* prepare the tea.

But I wasn't the only one awake. In the kitchen, Uncle sat at the table with a newspaper laid out before him. Washed and brushed, he didn't look like a farmer anymore. I stared at my feet. My nightclothes were too short in the sleeves and at the ankles.

"Morning, Solee," he said.

"Good morning. Would you like some tea, sir?"

"You're so formal! 'Sir' makes me feel old. Do I look like an old man to you?"

I ducked my head. "I don't know."

"Besides . . ." He pointed to the tea he'd already made, the napkins folded into flowers and tucked beneath each cup. "How'd I do?"

"I like the decorations." I nodded. "I need to bring these to my parents."

"They can get their own tea. Come sit." He nodded at the floor pillow across from him. As I settled onto it, he gave me an American cookie. Rectangular and beige and patterned with small square indents. I licked the creamy middle layer until the sweetness made the back of my ears hurt. I decided he was a nice man after all.

"What are your plans for today, Miss Solee?"

"I have school. I stay late every other day to study extra with the teacher. When I come home, I help Mommy."

He nodded, serious. "You make them tea in the morning. What else?"

"If she's working at the orphanage, I watch Jieun and Mila."

"All that and studying!" He smiled and I could see his nice, square teeth. "Jisoo says you could go to college."

I nodded, my head raised. "I'm the best in class."

He quizzed me with addition and subtraction problems. I started to boast that I even knew multiplication, but no one liked a bragger, even if Mommy told us that girls should show their smarts. That was why the other school kids weren't nice to me.

"What else do you know?" He flattened his newspaper. Stories about the capital ran down its columns. COMING ELECTION. WHO WILL BE OUR NEXT PRESIDENT? A NEW KOREA. I mouthed the words even if I didn't understand them.

"Uncle Hyunki is in Seoul," I said. "He's studying in college." I remembered his funny nose and big eyes, the pencils I liked to count in his room.

"I've heard. I haven't seen him since he was your age."

"I saw him last year, but he didn't come home in time for Halmuni's funeral," I said.

Kyunghwan's face stretched with surprise. "Why?"

"Mommy said no."

He frowned, like I'd said something wrong. "He had to take a test," I tried to explain.

Kyunghwan sipped from Mommy's cup, set it down too hard. Tea sloshed against the rim. He glanced around the room. "What's your dog's name?" he asked, but his attention stayed on the door.

I wanted him to return to me. I thought of a name that would make Uncle Hyunki laugh. He liked it when I was clever in my letters. "He's not really my dog, but I call him Dokkaebi."

It worked. Kyunghwan smiled and shook his head. "Those gremlins gave me nightmares when I was your age." He told me a story about dokkaebis playing pranks on children and old men. He was a good storyteller, using his hands and baring his teeth during suspenseful moments. Soon, it was seven o'clock. I heard Jieun readying for the day. "I have to get dressed," I said.

"I'm going hiking this afternoon. Do you want to come along?" He nodded, like I'd already said yes. "We'll buy you some sturdy shoes. Be good in class, Miss Solee."

"Bye," I said, waving and bowing at the same time.

Outside, I called Dokkaebi as I waited. He nuzzled his snout against my side. When Jieun came to the door, rubbing her fists into her sleepy eyes, I walked her to school and I watched her run to her friends. I smiled. I was glad she and Mila were too young to make tea.

Teacher Han rapped my knuckles twice during mathematics. I didn't mind because that afternoon I would walk up a mountain with Kyunghwan. I played with my hair, brushing it down with my fingers, and I wished Mommy hadn't cut it so short. I could tell Kyunghwan liked long hair. During dinner, his eyes had spiraled as Mommy twirled one long, loose strand.

After the last class of the day, I played gonggi stones with my classmates and waited for Kyunghwan. Chunja was the best. She had her own gonggi set, and her stones were smooth from all her hours of practice. I had just caught them on the back of my hand when the whispers began—

"Look!"

"Who is he?"

"A movie star?"

"Someone's daddy?"

"He's *handsome*," Chunja said.

The boys stared, too. They pointed at his height and the big lump at his throat.

Kyunghwan called my name, waving a pair of small brown

shoes. I dropped the gonggi stones into Chunja's hand and smiled at her surprised face.

We arrived at Whul-ae Mountain. Even before we started climbing, large stains bloomed under Kyunghwan's arms and around his neck. When the boys at school sweated, we made fun of them. But on him, it looked different. *"Movie star,"* I whispered. He pointed to flowers and trees, naming them as we passed. I tried to remember them all, but the words ran away from me.

"You see this?" Kyunghwan pointed to a strange little plant with nubs that curled inward like a ram's horns. "It's Haemi's favorite side dish. Gosari. Wouldn't it be nice if we picked some for her?"

"My favorite side dish is steamed eggs," I said.

"Well, if you help me find these, I'll make my most delicious eggs especially for you. All right?"

I nodded. He opened his bag, made room in the middle. We searched for Mommy's favorite plant. *Gosari.* I plucked one and stared. It looked like a fuzzy caterpillar curled up on my palm, ready for sleep. I wouldn't eat any of them, I decided.

As we searched, he explained that these were babies, that when they matured, the leaves uncurled. When our pile was big enough, we took a break. He lay down with his hands clasped behind his head, maybe drying his armpits. I copied him. He described how he would boil the baby plants, soak them in cold water, and lay them out to dry. "Then we'll dust them lightly with salt and fry them over a fire. With onions and garlic," he said.

"How do you know it's her favorite?"

"Haemi and I were friends a long time ago. I introduced her to my cousin, Jisoo, when the war made us go south. And that's how you and your sisters got to be here."

It was funny, how he called them by their first names.

"What're you smiling at?" he asked.

"I don't know." I rolled over. "Do you have any children?"

He laughed. "I wish I had daughters as lovely as you girls. I missed my chance. Now I'm old and ugly."

"I think you're handsome." I turned my head to his chest so he wouldn't see my blushing face.

Down the mountain and through the town, we walked home. Kyunghwan brought the bag of gosari to the backyard. After boiling and washing them, he found the right spot—out of reach of the roof's and the tree's shadows, where the sun heated the ground all summer long. I kicked a mud clump as Kyunghwan sprinkled salt on the drying plants. The back of my neck prickled. I didn't want to watch the gosari shrivel any longer. "I'm tired," I said.

"We're almost done."

Dokkaebi circled the tree, and I called him over. He snuffled his head into my hands. "No food for you." I broke a mud clump over his back and mixed brown dirt into his fur. "I'm tired," I said again. I knew I was whining, but I couldn't help it.

Kyunghwan looked up. "I'm sorry, Miss Solee. I should have brought you home earlier." He pulled a handkerchief from his pocket. It was the color of potato pancakes, my other favorite side dish. He dipped it into a bucket of water and washed my face, from forehead to nose to chin. He wasn't tickling me, but it felt like he was.

He wrapped the kerchief around my neck, and a trickle of water dripped to my belly. I followed the stain on my shirt with my finger. "I want my special eggs now."

"Go find Haemi for me. I'll finish here. Then I'll cook you up something delicious. You can keep the handkerchief for being such a good partner."

I ran into the house with my chin raised, so everyone could see what Kyunghwan had given me. "Look!"

"My wood nymph." Mommy tugged the kerchief's bow. "How was your hike with Uncle?"

"He picked some baby plants for you. He said they're your favorite and that you like to eat them with your mouth wide open. Like this." I copied Kyunghwan's chewing and smacked my tongue against the roof of my mouth.

Before I could describe Whul-ae's peak and my new brown shoes and the eggs I would soon eat, I saw her eyes close. She swayed. She wasn't listening.

"Mommy?" I shook her, tried to bring her back to me. She did this sometimes. "He's waiting for you."

She smiled slowly, like a goddess returning to her human body. "Watch the girls." She loosened her bun. Raking a hand through her curls, she walked out.

Kyunghwan and I shared a morning game. I rose earlier each day, but he always won. He waited in the common room, the tea hot and ready. Sometimes he had a present for me, like a brand-new Monami pen or speckled quail eggs, already boiled. As we waited for the others, we talked. He touched a small scar on his cheek as

he told me stories, and I touched my scar, too, the one on my knee
shaped like a leaf.

Jieun and Mila awoke next. They always ran to him with their
orange blanket dragging, like an open dress. He gave them pres-
ents, too. He pulled them onto his lap and fed them spoonfuls of
tea. I wanted him to feed me, too, but he winked and I straightened. He thought of me as a grown-up, a friend.

At night, when everyone went to bed, I imagined him holding
me. I wanted to see him. When I snuck into the hallway, no one
stopped me. At Uncle Hyunki's door, I bent down, dusting my ear
against the crack. And then I heard it, the in and out of Kyunghwan's breathing.

On Kyunghwan's ninth day, a Saturday and a special no-school
day, Daddy ate breakfast with us. "Listen," he said between bites of
rice and egg. He smiled and bumped his cup against mine. "When
Kyunghwan and I were boys, he found a secret pond."

"Where the air tastes sweet and the water is clear!" Kyunghwan
sang.

Daddy laughed. "We said we'd never show the pond to any
women, but today, we'll go!"

Jieun jumped up and swung Mila around. Mommy shook her
head, not at them, but at Daddy and Kyunghwan singing a song
we didn't know.

At the pond, we girls pulled off shirts and shorts and ran into the
water in our panties. As we played, the adults baked themselves on
boulders, like squid laid out to dry.

Mommy wore a tee shirt and a pair of Daddy's pants folded up to her knees. I saw the roundness of her breasts where the fabric stretched tight. I looked down. I had two little nipples but no roundness. Little soybeans no one would want to look at. I pushed my chest forward. Nothing changed.

"I'm going to catch a great big fish and fry it over a fire!" Daddy yelled before jumping off a rock. One arm glued to his side, the other in an arc aimed at the water. He made a giant splash and we whistled and whooped and made echoes.

"Don't forget who won the last diving contest!" Kyunghwan started with his back against a tree and ran straight off his boulder. As he fell, he flapped around like a panicked animal.

He sank, screaming.

Mommy shrieked his name.

Silence stretched out in ripples. Even little Mila quieted as we waited for bubbles and his body. But he didn't appear.

"Kyunghwan?" Daddy yelled. "Stop it!"

"Where are you?" I called.

"Are you drowning?" Jieun shrieked.

Kyunghwan bobbed up with a long, high howl. He winked at me and howled again.

"He's a dokkaebi!" I yelled.

His laughter filled the pond and floated all around us. It was contagious. Soon we were laughing, too, chucking our heads above the water to stop ourselves from drowning.

Only Mommy stood quiet, her arms across her chest. "That wasn't funny."

"Oh, come on," Kyunghwan said.

She turned away. We watched Daddy leave to comfort her. She started laughing when he tickled her arms. Kyunghwan shrugged, gulped air, and sank back into the water.

When everyone was happy again, we paired up for a cavalry fight. Jieun on Daddy's shoulders, me on Kyunghwan's, and Mila and Mommy cheering from the rocks. Kyunghwan's hands pushed against my butt, nestling me until I sat with my legs draped against his chest. His body was so slick I thought I'd fall off. He lifted my arms, flapped them up and down until I felt it—I was high and flying.

When the water weighed heavy in our bones and it became harder to float, we headed to the hills above. Boulders crumbled into pebbles. Our skin smelled like pond and sun. Trees thickened to block out the evening light.

"This is where we'd fry fish," Daddy whispered. He seemed so calm and peaceful, with sleepy Mila on his back. There wasn't a fire pit any longer, but he described one until I could almost see it—logs burning and fish crisping in the heat.

"Let's get some wood," Kyunghwan said to Daddy. They left, their bodies hulking together into the forest.

We lay down around Mommy. She sang the apple-cucumber-pumpkin song we liked, squeezing our noses with each new part. We hummed along, rubbed Mila's wide cheeks at the words *Our funny round pumpkin.*

When Daddy and Kyunghwan returned, Mommy went to sit with them. In the dark, Mila drew our family into the sky, using the evening stars to trace our crooked elbows and noses. Jieun snored against my shoulder. I tried to stay awake.

On the first night of Kyunghwan's visit, the adults had told stories. Of the war that split our Korea, of a president who controlled us, and of people now dead. They seemed quieter tonight. When

Daddy went to pee in the woods, Kyunghwan slid closer to Mommy. She looked over at us. I wanted to hear what they were saying, but I felt heavy with sleep. Their whispers twisted together in streams.

The next day, Daddy woke up sick. I brought tea to his room, and he grumbled that his head was wound too tight. He drank in big gulps. He hadn't been in the kitchen to see it, how Kyunghwan and Mommy had smiled at each other with a sliver of shared laughter between their lips. "Come eat breakfast," I said. He pushed the drained cup into my hand and waved me away.

Daddy left the house without saying good morning or goodbye. When he was gone, Kyunghwan turned to me. "Solee, can you do your uncle a favor? Can you watch Jieun and Mila for a few hours?"

"Where are you going?"

Mommy stared out the kitchen window, even though there was nothing there except our tree.

"Whul-ae Mountain. Haemi wants to collect more of those plants she loves. Can you be the ruler of the house while we're gone?"

"Can we go hiking tomorrow, only us?" I asked.

"Of course, Miss Solee." Kyunghwan squeezed my shoulder. "Just you and me."

I smiled at Mommy. I wanted her to see that I was his favorite, but she didn't even look at me. She mussed my hair and glanced at the room where Jieun and Mila slept.

"Are you really going to Whul-ae?" I asked.

She bent down. She was pretty, with big eyes and pale skin the color of eggshells. "Where do you think I'd be going?"

I didn't know, still I thought she was lying.

"Don't worry so much." She smiled. "I'll be back soon with an armful of plants for us."

They didn't come home for dinner. Jieun whined because I burned the rice and said she wanted oxtail soup, not dumplings. "Where's Mommy?" Mila shrieked and shrieked. I gave them pear slices to make them stop, but they only fussed more, now with sticky hands. I told them they were brats and smacked my spoon against the table.

I didn't know where Daddy had gone. I wanted to tell him everything. How Kyunghwan and Mommy had left for Whul-ae. How I was supposed to be the only one hiking up mountains with him.

In our room, Jieun asked for the goddess story. Even little Mila sighed happily when I began. "One day," I said, "when the world was new, a goddess came down from the heavens. A man found her and fell in love. Knees mucky from kneeling in the dirt before her, he asked for her name. 'Lee Haemi,' she said. The man snatched her name from the air and swallowed it. He wrapped her in a piece of silk, scooped her up, and brought her home. Mommy is a goddess from the heavens, and sometimes, when she thinks of the sky, she fades away."

"One more time," they mumbled together. I stroked their heads, told the story again.

When they fell asleep, I climbed onto our desk and slid open the window. It was dark outside. I wondered if Mommy and Kyunghwan could see through the night.

I slept in the hallway, my hand against Kyunghwan's door. When I woke, I was floating. "And who do I love?" I heard him say.

Kyunghwan held me in his arms. Before I could respond, I heard Mommy's laugh.

"Go to sleep, Kyunghwan." Her voice slow and gliding, like a flat river.

"What if I don't want to?" His words sounded strange, like he had gonggi stones in his mouth. It didn't matter. I nudged my face into his shoulder so she wouldn't see my gloating. He loved me.

"Good night, Kyunghwan."

"Good night, Haemi."

In my room, when he pulled my blanket over me, I opened my eyes. "I love you, too, Uncle Kyunghwan."

His laughter washed me with the scent of persimmons. He brushed my hair, too quickly, and left.

I sat up in the middle of the night, unsure of what had knocked me from my dreams. At first I thought it was Kyunghwan returning to me. But it was Mommy and Daddy fighting, the deep snarl in his voice. I tried to sleep despite the noise, a strange thud. Mommy's shouts grew louder. Daddy was silent. It was shameful, and I worried Kyunghwan would hear.

I ran out of the room to yell at them. *How embarrassing!* I would say. The way Teacher Han did when we answered a question wrong in front of the principal. *You are embarrassing yourselves!*

I stopped when I saw her. Mommy hunched low, headed toward Kyunghwan's room, her hair loose and thick with heat. With her nose and mouth smudged by the shadows, she looked like someone else. She closed his door behind her.

I checked on Daddy. He lay on his back, his stomach bulging. One hand between his legs and the other clasping a stick he used against our calves and palms when we were bad. He didn't wake when I shoved his shoulder.

"Mother is in Uncle Kyunghwan's room," I said loudly. I prodded him again. He grunted, and a mess of noise erupted from his mouth. "Did you hear me?" My voice rose higher and higher. "They're in Uncle Hyunki's room together. Wake up!"

The dead-asleep look on his face didn't change.

I sat outside Kyunghwan's door. I thought I could hear them. It sounded like Mommy was crying. It sounded so painful I clutched my stomach. She was sad. He was comforting her. They were whispering each other's names. I imagined. They were kissing. They were naked, with her round breasts and his hairy, musty armpits.

I took off my shirt and pants and laid them out underneath me. I made another person, the sleeves draped over my back and the legs twisted around my ankles. My mouth to the floor, I kissed him. When I stuck out my tongue, dust collected all over. It tasted dirty, not how I'd imagined.

In the morning, I dressed in my best shorts, light blue with orange stitching. Kyunghwan would hike with me after school today, and I would again tell him that I loved him.

When I entered the kitchen, he wasn't there waiting for me. I had won for the first time. I set two cups of tea across from each other and placed the kettle in the middle, the way he did. I tried to fold his napkin into a flower but gave up. A simple square would have to do.

Instead of finding me in the kitchen, he rushed out of the house. I watched as his tall shadow dashed past the window.

I ran outside. "Where are you going?" I grabbed him as he petted Dokkaebi's nose at the front gate.

"I have something to do today. Sorry, Miss Solee." He squeezed my hand. His eyes were misty. He was fading from me, the way Mommy did sometimes. She had infected him.

"Stay," I said.

"I have to go." He lifted his bag and headed to his motorcycle.

"Hiking tomorrow?" I asked.

"Maybe." He shook his head. "I don't know."

"Are you mad at me?"

He untied the handkerchief from my neck. I thought he was going to take it back, that he *was* angry. But he only wiped my eyes.

"I don't want you to go," I said.

"I'll try to come back soon, Miss Solee."

"You don't love me."

When he hugged me, I thrust my face forward so he would kiss me this once, but he shifted and pulled an envelope from his pocket instead. "Can you give this to Haemi? When Jisoo goes to work? I'll bring back a surprise for you."

He shoved the letter into my closed hand.

He didn't kiss me goodbye.

Dokkaebi walked alongside him as he pushed his motorcycle all the way to the end of our road. Kyunghwan turned, a little speck waving. A dog thief. A bad man.

I didn't wave back this time.

I ripped up his stupid letter instead. I threw the pieces into the air. There was no wind and they fell to the ground. I picked them up one by one. I collected his words.

I buried them all.

Haemi

1963

I BLED. YESTERDAY, FROM THE CUTS ON MY HANDS, A careless knife. A week ago, tripping over the stones Mila had placed around the house in the shape of clouds. The sharp taste when I bit down on my tongue the morning Kyunghwan had left, like the discarded C ration tins we used to lick during the war. He'd once dared me to touch the silver, sharp edge with the tip of my tongue. A blood-red river.

I paced the girls' room trying to count the days since I'd last bled between my legs. Mila, surrounded by colored pencils, mumbled at her picture. When I passed, she tugged at the hem of my hanbok skirt.

"I want a cookie." She held up a wet palmful of crumbs. "More for me?" Her hair, the oily stink of it, made me want to retch.

"I don't have any right now." My stomach roiled at the sudden flare of smells—grease, spit, boiled beef bones from the kitchen, a vile sweetness I couldn't place. The thought of the outhouse soured my spit, too. "Mommy needs to go outside."

Mila grabbed my leg. "Take me." Sitting at my feet, she looked tiny. My youngest, a dreamer. I must have been dreaming, too.

Months. Months since I had bled.

"Mommy?"

She toddled after me.

I staggered to the tree in the backyard and retched. Green potato sprigs and white rice, my early breakfast. The acid stench so nauseating I had to lean against the stone wall. The air itself seemed to knock me unsteady. I slid to the ground.

Mila wrinkled her nose and hid her face behind her hands. "Mommy sick?"

"Shush, please." I laid my cheek against the cool stones. "I can't think."

"You going to be all right." She stroked my ankle.

"I don't think so." I cupped her hand with my own. Even gentle Mila had left me suffocating for a year after she was born. I sank in guilt, confusion, fear. How unlike the other mothers I seemed to be. I had never felt more captive than following childbirth.

How could I not have kept track of my bleeding? For months now, I'd been wretched with mourning—my mind like spiderlings bursting from their egg sac, scattering in all directions. Forgetting what I was doing even when I was doing nothing.

I willed myself to bleed. I spat a thick scum of mucus.

"Look!" Mila pried a rock from under one of the tree's roots. It was gray with a small white center, like a nipple or a flower. "I bring in house?"

Our damn house. I walked the length of every room every day. With Mila following, sleeping, slung on my back, hip, or chest, I treaded the wooden floors of our scythe-shaped home. When Jieun and Solee returned, I made dinner. When Jisoo returned, I made more dinner. When I felt as though my mind would disappear, I ate or walked or stared at the sky through the leaves of our one lonely tree. I didn't allow myself to think about him. I was like a mouse in an earthen jar, crawling up sloped, impossible walls.

"What if I ran away right now?" I pointed to the roads beyond the stone wall. "What would you do if I left, Mila?"

She rolled the rock between my toes, up my foot. "Where you going? I hungry."

I wanted to cry and scream and burn the fear that roiled inside me. The air felt all wrong, too thin or too thick for me to breathe. I picked up Mila and threw her stone into my vomit.

"I'm going to tell you a secret." She smiled like an idiot child and grasped my nose. "I think I'm pregnant."

In the kitchen, I held in another swell of spit and stirred a pot of tteokguk. The oval white rice cakes swirled around silvery, shiny broth. In another vat, I skimmed the scum off boiling beef bones. The thick, oily scent made me think of cows. How Kyunghwan and I used to bellow at those lazy, grazing animals on our way to grade school. Queasiness sloshed inside me.

"Not too hot, please." Mila waited at her small table, already holding a napkin. I concentrated on her expectant face. Wide cheeks, like mine. Jisoo's full lips softened into a kinder shape. Wispy, straight hair that she pawed off her face. "Many, many rice cakes, please."

I poured her a bowl of tteokguk. She raised her spoon. "Mommy join?"

"You eat for us both," I said.

"Mommy watch?"

"I'll be right here."

She slurped and hunted for rice cakes with her spoon. Mila always had a good appetite. Like their father, all the girls were such good eaters.

❧

The morning Kyunghwan had left, I returned from my search to find Jisoo waiting for me at the front entrance. He looked hungover and miserable. As I approached—the hem of my hanbok muddy, my feet bare—he turned away from the embarrassment of me, unmoored.

"Have you seen Kyunghwan?" I asked. "Did you see him this morning?"

I stared at his twitching mouth. His eyes slid over mine, refusing to catch. The blurred ankles, ears, silhouette of the man who was my husband. He didn't speak, and I realized. He knew.

I waited for him to drag me by the hair, to call me a whore. I would laugh at him until he released me. Why was it unthinkable for me to love someone, when he slept with other women whenever he desired? He came home smelling of their perfume. Their lipstick smeared on his ears, the back of his neck, along the seams where he couldn't see but the wife could.

I stared at him and readied myself.

He looked beyond me, his shoulders raised. As if there was something worth seeing in the distance. "Kyunghwan left. Some sort of emergency. He told me this morning."

I searched his face. "What kind of emergency?"

"How the hell should I know?"

I tried to think. I didn't understand. My face crumpled and a small gasp escaped my mouth, my body revealing too much. I pressed a hand to my eyes.

Jisoo cleared his throat. "The girls are hungry. I need to go to work. I'll see you this evening?"

I nodded and tried to will myself to walk back into our house. I took a few steps, forcing my feet to rise and land—but I couldn't help myself. I grabbed Jisoo's shoulder. "Is he returning soon? What did he say, exactly? I need to find him." I turned toward town, letting go, hurrying again, lifting my skirt to run.

Jisoo yanked my arm with his thick, stout fingers. Anger fired his cheeks, mouth, and eyes until he looked right at me. "Did something happen last night?"

I tried to rearrange my features into a look of contempt, except my body didn't feel like my own, the fear slippery in my throat. "What do you mean?"

"I'm not an idiot." He shoved me into the stone wall, his hands grinding my shoulders, pinning me. I couldn't breathe. How hard he pushed, until I felt all the bones in my back—a long, curved spine he could break. He wanted to hurt me and was scared of what that meant. About me, us, Kyunghwan. "Don't lie to me, Haemi. What did you do?"

I laughed as hard and loud as I could. "What are you talking about?" I whipped his arm off me, both of us now heaving with fear. "Solee was crying in her room. She said she was supposed to go hiking with him. That's why I'm asking."

I rushed past him into the house.

"Don't walk away from me," he called.

"What kind of uncle leaves after making a promise like that?"

He followed me into our room. The stench of him was everywhere. I pointed at the brimming basin. At his acrid green vomit. "You're disgusting."

I cringed when I thought of that morning. How hurt Jisoo had been to see me undone. How, in the months following, he'd drowned his suspicions with drink, soaring into rages as frightening as the stars. How he'd kissed me in the mornings with a desperate hunger, a sloppy desire for my mouth that made me want to hold him.

I tried to make it up to my husband. After that first morning, I allowed myself to mourn only in the quiet of our home. Alone with Mila, I wept, unraveling until I blamed Kyunghwan, then myself. In Hyunki's room, I lay on the floor and remembered. How I had longed to take pleasure in Kyunghwan's body and how I'd refused to leave with him. His talk of the future. I knew what a life together in Seoul would do to us, and I didn't have the courage.

When the girls returned from school, I frenzied around the house. I tried to be the perfect mother. At night, I reached for Jisoo's body, disgusted with myself. With his lopsided shoulders and his useless arm and the heavy way he panted from the effort of holding himself above me. I wanted the disgust to overtake me so I would no longer think of Kyunghwan. So when I was alone and my mind wandered to his arms muscling over mine, I could conjure my husband instead. The heat of them both and how they loved me too much, and yet not enough.

❦

I touched my stomach, its still-flat surface. A child grew inside me with Jisoo's or Kyunghwan's face.

If only he had waited for me to gather my nerve. If only we had left together.

Here, I couldn't do it again. I knew myself.

Even in my little life, there were things I wanted to do. I wanted to return to the orphanage once Mila started school, if Grandmother Lee would have me back despite my vanishing these past few months. I wanted to visit Hyunki in Seoul. My only brother. Brilliant, forgiving Hyunki had asked me to come see his new world. I wanted to find out what kind of man he had become. I wanted to breathe in the city my girls would leave me for when they were ready for college.

I squeezed my stomach. I wanted things for myself. My daughters. My body.

I dressed Mila in long pants and pulled a knit sweater over her head. She pressed her hands against the orange wool. "Where we going?"

"On an adventure with Mommy." I steered her outside, where the sunlight made me squint. It was too warm for fall. "To a river where lots of plants grow."

Sweat slipped down my back as I swung Mila's arm. She sang a tuneless melody, stringing the words that she knew together. I couldn't recall the last time I had taken her anywhere besides the school or the market.

"You'll help me look for pretty flowers," I said.

"I like flowers." She wiped her wide, sweating face. "I draw good flowers."

"We're going to find some that my mommy showed me once," I said. "Flowers that will help me feel better."

I tried to remember what they looked like. Long stalks, dark blooms. Before the war, before Hyunki was even born, Mother had taken me to a neighbor's house. The woman had lost her baby, and I understood this was a solemn occasion. As we walked, other village women joined us. She did it to herself, a few of them said. She'd eaten plants until blood, clotted and thick, ran between her legs.

Mother had clucked at their gossip. When we reached the

woman's home, she instructed me to wait in the courtyard. I stayed by the door, trying to hear what was happening inside. They spoke over one another in clouds of soothing tones. The woman who had lost her baby wailed.

When a grandmother emerged, I snuck a look. Blood, bright and gashing red, was everywhere. Strips of hemp in a muddled pile, stained crimson. A basin, kimchi water. On everyone's hands and between the legs of the woman lying on the ground. Her skirt the color of chestnuts, jujubes, red pepper.

I screamed. I looked at my hands, scared for one wild moment that the blood had gotten on me somehow. That it was all over me. I had seen the round, hard bellies of pregnant women before. I had seen infants. I had not understood, though, the violence of birth.

"Out!" Mother screamed. One long, stained finger pointing to the door. "Stay outside like I told you."

On the walk home, Mother pulled at my wrist.

"I'm sorry," I said as I tripped along. "I shouldn't have looked."

"It's not you." She unfolded a handkerchief. Inside, a thick green stalk dotted with purplish-black flowers. "She did it to herself."

I combed the ground with my fingers without any luck. Mila collected stones. She had already found a crop of cosmos flowers and stuck them in her hair. I searched the hills, but there were no long-stemmed, night-dark flowers growing on Whul-ae.

As I inspected the mossy slope, I recalled florets the color of pure, unpressed tofu. A little boy, a classmate from grade school, had sucked on the pale yellow petals of a mountain plant and died. Or had he eaten the root? I wished Kyunghwan were with me so we could remember together. So he could watch me chew one petal at a time and bleed out his mistake. I could tell him that if he'd waited one more day, I would have been ready.

Shaded by a canopy of leaves, a chill swept through me. I wouldn't find them here. I didn't even know if I wanted to find them. I lay beside Mila.

She tucked flowers into my hair. "Mommy, you sleepy?"

I squeezed my stomach and saw a child with Kyunghwan's narrow cheeks, a son or daughter. I knuckled my flesh until it hurt, muscling the skin, organs, blood, until I cramped. Sharp slivers slicing whatever was inside me. Maybe I could force my bleeding to come.

"It's not working," I said aloud to the sky, to Mila.

"Mommy?"

I was alone, talking to my three-year-old daughter. Unable to cry or control the workings of my own body.

"What you doing?"

I looked at Mila, my little baby, and hungered for my mother. The woman I'd resented my whole adult life because she too had been molded by her time. Mother had suffered for me when I was too shortsighted to see beyond my own anger. She was a woman who knew how to survive in the world without breaking, the way I seemed to at every turn. She would have known what to do.

"Mommy?" Mila cocked her head. "I tired."

I sighed.

I raised myself up. "All right. Let's go."

She kissed my hand. "Carry me?"

Soon, I would show. I wouldn't be able to hold Mila above my bulging stomach. It didn't matter whether or not it was Kyunghwan's. Our summer would no longer be mine to hoard and hate and love and long for whenever I wanted. I would always have this reminder.

"That bastard." I picked up Mila. Her weight made my arms shake. I twirled her around until she laughed.

Solee and Jieun ran to us with their arms out, ready to embrace, their little orange shorts flapping in the wind. Jieun's thick eyebrows rose in alarm, and I realized how late it was, that I'd forgotten to pick her up from school.

"Mommy!" she cried. "We went searching for you!"

"We looked at the orphanage." Solee cocked her freckled face. "Where did you go?"

Jieun draped her arms around my hips. "You're so dirty!"

I kissed their heads. "Mommy's so sorry she forgot."

"We went to mountain!" Mila thrust flowers at her sisters. "We got many!"

"Which mountain?" Solee asked. "Whul-ae?"

"I wish we could have come." Jieun squashed a large bloom in her shirt pocket. "Stupid school. Why'd you go without us?"

"Can we join next time?" Solee caught a flower as it fell from Mila's hair.

"This weekend, we'll go. We'll picnic by the river and pick all the plants we can find," I said.

The girls danced, cheered. They forgave me so easily.

"How about we cook something delicious? What do my girls want?" I led them into the house.

"Hotteoks!" Jieun twirled her thin wrists. "We can make them together."

"But maybe you should wash first?" Solee pinched my sleeve. "You're dirtier than us."

"I'll wash quickly." I wrapped my arms around my little trio. "Let's make some of Mommy's sweet, delicious hotteoks."

In the outdoor kitchen, we poured flour, sugar, yeast, and salt into a bowl. The girls sifted the softness between their fingers. Mila drew white, powdery circles on Solee's and Jieun's cheeks. When I added water, they squealed and pushed their knuckles in to knead. The girls smacked their sticky hands together until the dough rose on their palms in small, triangular peaks.

"Look, Mommy. Look at the shapes," Mila said.

The wonder my girls had for the world. For something as simple as flour turning into food. These girls were their own beings, bright, and curious. As I watched, they no longer reminded me of my life with Jisoo. I only saw the childlike pleasure of discovery.

I rubbed the stickiness off their palms with a wet rag. "Let's sit outside while the dough rises. I missed my daughters today."

We dragged heavy blankets into the backyard. We lay on the grass in a half circle, our heads touching, our loosened hair a shiny black river, a pond. I forgot, sometimes, how much I loved them. I had been selfish all fall, wound up in my own grief, and yet they went on loving me, their faces turning to mine as if I were their sun.

The yellowing leaves above our heads rippled with the wind. Shifting between the shadow and light, I felt relief for the first time all day. I was glad I hadn't found any plants. No, I had chosen not to find any plants. I had chosen to get pregnant.

"Want to know a secret?" I pulled my hanbok tight across my stomach and placed their hands on me. Their tiny fingers pressed cloth and skin, forming stars on my belly. Hands I had created inside my own body. "Do you feel anything?"

"Grumbling!" Jieun laughed.

"Are you pregnant?" Solee asked.

I smiled. My smart one.

"I have a squash growing inside me," I said. "Big and green and round. I went up the mountain to find it."

I ballooned my hands up around my stomach and they laughed.

"Maybe it'll turn into a baby," I said. "Would you like that?"

Solee nodded shyly. Jieun and Mila rubbed their hands up and down, from belly to breasts and back.

"In here?" Jieun asked. She patted her own small belly. "Squashes turn into babies in here?"

❀

I chose to remember.

When Kyunghwan returned to me, all I had wanted was to touch him. As the girls clambered over his lap, I longed to reach across their heads to graze the scar on his cheek. To feel the raised skin and understand all that had happened to him.

He ignored me whenever Jisoo was in the room. The distance he slipped between us was like tissue paper, filmy and delicate, but still a barrier. I watched his blurred form from the other side. He laughed with Jisoo and acted as if he'd returned only to make amends with his cousin. *He is not even your real cousin*, I wanted to say. *Your fathers were cousins, so what does that make you? Nothing but orphans clinging for family like everyone else.*

He wouldn't look at me. I couldn't stop looking at him. At his high, narrow cheeks and straight nose, his new scar. I wanted to know him again.

One morning after Jisoo had left, Kyunghwan turned to me. He brushed his thumb against my lips. A touch so quick I could have imagined it. We sat across from each other with the table between us. Solee and Jieun were getting ready for school. Mila slept in the corner.

My gaze went straight to the girls. Perceptive Solee, who always seemed to know too much, and Jieun, who was too feisty to be anything but Jisoo's favorite. They crouched over their shoes.

"You have beautiful girls." Kyunghwan smiled at them. They fluttered under his attention. He'd always been a flirt.

As the girls bowed goodbye, blowing kisses at their uncle, I touched my mouth, where I could still feel the pressure of him, how he'd grazed me.

"Have a great day at school, little missies."

"See you later!"

How he exposed me. How I wanted him to expose me.

I stood, moving away, moving toward him, unable to decide. "You haven't looked at me once," I said.

"I have."

"Kyunghwan."

"I've been looking, Haemi." His eyes never leaving mine, he raised my hand and licked a burn along my wrist bone. His mouth found the spot immediately. His tongue searing the heated blur of my skin.

I wore a Western dress that morning, my only one. Striped white and green with a row of buttons down the front. Desperate. Absurd with the desire to make him see me. When he released my wrist, I undid one button and another. He leaned down and kissed my breasts through the thin fabric of my slip. For the first time, I wanted my milk to return so he could taste every part of me.

His slight hands tugged at my underwear. Then I felt his warm mouth.

When Mila stirred in the corner, he pulled back, gasping. For a moment, I wondered if she would wake and see this—her mother standing naked, in pleasure, before a man on his knees. His mouth between her legs as if she were all there was to want in the world.

❀

The girls watched as I pressed brown sugar and walnuts into the dough. I let them pet my stomach. "Squashy," they sang. "Little Squashy likes hotteoks, too."

We plated hot, fried, syrupy hotteoks and ate outside with our propped knees as tables. The brown sugar oozed with each bite. I would eat only sweets, I decided. Rice cakes and red bean shaved ice. I would look only at beauty, at my girls, and I would be hopeful. Whoever came out of me would be better than her mother and these circumstances. This time, the pregnancy wouldn't blanch my mind. I would be a woman who survived, who joyed in the act.

"Hotteoks are the best!" Jieun cried, her mouth crusted with sugar.

We heard Jisoo call from the gate, "Where are my little ladies?"

"Here, Daddy! In the back!" Mila yelled, licking her palms.

He found us outside. "What are you eating? Hotteoks?"

"We saved some for you," Solee said.

"Squashy ate some!" Mila cried.

Jisoo frowned at me. "Why are they eating this now? How're they going to eat dinner?" He unbuttoned the top of his shirt. My husband, so easily rankled, so easily hurt. The one who had stayed.

I picked up a hotteok. "We made them especially for you. Our sweet daddy." I raised one to his lips. "Eat."

"I don't want to."

"Come on," I teased. "Eat for your wife."

"Yeah, come on, Daddy!" Jieun said. "Eat for your beautiful squashy wife!"

I wafted the hotteok around his head until the girls laughed. He smiled, grudgingly, and took a bite.

※

I had licked the freckles along Kyunghwan's right arm, that ocean's wave. I had wanted to swim with him—me, a woman who feared the ocean. I'd wanted to sink into the waters if it meant we could stay together. I didn't care that we weren't alone, that Solee, Jieun, and Mila slept in the same house. That Jisoo could wake from his drunken sleep at any moment. Kyunghwan loved me and I wanted only him, the press of him inside me.

※

My husband carried Jieun on his shoulders through the halls of our home. Jisoo roared and she squealed. At each door, she raised her arms to kiss the frame. Jieun licked her thumb and pressed it to the wood above our heads. Solee and Mila followed them, quiet and smiling.

I watched my family and pressed a hand to my stomach. I would sear this image into me so I could conjure it when needed. If I had to have another child, this was the world it would enter.

They played a game naming as many fruits as they could think of.

"Pears!"

"Peaches!"

"Green plums!"

Yellow melons. Apples. Figs.

I left them and walked to the kitchen. In a wicker basket, I found the fruit Jisoo had brought home a few days earlier—ripe orange persimmons. I pulled off a green cap and sucked on its sweet, fibrous flesh. I would make Jisoo tea with the leaves. I would dry the fruit and stir up punch for the girls. If I couldn't visit Hyunki, swollen with pregnancy, I could at least pour the drink into jars and send it to him as an apology.

I would be happy for this birth. A good, round woman.

Kyunghwan

1964

SHE WAS BEAUTIFUL AND HIS. SHE HATED THAT—THE phrasing and the truth of it.

I had returned to her in the summer.

I saw the child first. The girl's round cheeks, how she played beside her mother in the yard. Beyond them, the house rested on a large, open space bordered by a stone wall. A single tree stood guarding the corner. From the look of the property, I knew right away. He was rich, a landowner. Haemi bent over a jar of soybean paste until the girl's chattering made her turn.

She wore a traditional dress. A hanbok the color of celadon with her hair pulled into a bun. I had never seen her that way. Like the earth, the sky. The cleared neck, her sharp ears in full view.

I gestured to myself. "I came like you said."

She stood there in the morning heat with the tree's shadows streaking her face. The face, I recognized. Bare. Wide and pale. Dark eyes searching mine.

Haemi. The face I had known all my life.

I stepped forward. "What will you do now?"

Before she could respond, the call of my name, deep and happy, and too soon. I turned. Jisoo ran toward us, one arm in a high wave, a smile slathered across his ignorant face.

❀

Twelve years had passed. At first, Haemi avoided being alone with me. When we were, even for snatches of a moment, we were exposed. The children were always there. Or Jisoo. Even so, I didn't want to leave her alone. It seemed she would float into the ether if I turned my back. She laughed in a way that made her pulse. The frenzy buzzed through her, and the girls looked at her like she was an unknown creature. She was unhappy. I wanted her to know that I knew.

"I'm happy," she said, the effort squeezing her face.

She wore expensive-looking dresses. They were impractical in the heat and country. I knew she wore them to show off, to prove to me she was fine.

"That's not what you wrote," I said.

"I changed my mind."

"Why did you ask me to come then?"

"I don't know." Haemi carved the skin off a pear. "To see if you would."

The girls sat around us with their homemade toys. She handed them the ragged, wet slices. We were in the backyard again, surrounded by the tree's shade. I had no interest in the girls that day. Only Haemi. Her sharp beauty. Her refusal to give. I bent to the ground and touched the hem of her pale green hanbok, my fingers following the stitched flowers. I assumed she was punishing me for the lost years, for my foolish, teenage pride. I would make her see me.

❀

Now, I was the one who saw her. Haemi's image followed me everywhere. Summer was coming again to Seoul, the rainy season with its unceasing dampness. I saw her in the thickness of the air, her arms raised, pulling at the strings of her top. Fully clothed, shadowed beneath a tree. Happy. Unhappy. As a Japanese woman, stiff and haughty, pouring tea for a group of diplomats. As a street performer I came across in the night. Even as an American with red hair and milky, freckled skin. It was an uneasy sort of infatuation, one that left me desperate to erase her. Haemi wasn't good for me anymore.

I drove my work truck with the window down and hoped the heavy wind would scatter my thoughts. It was lunchtime and I yelled at the pretty women. "Support the Republic of Korea! Buy domestic beauty products!" Their gazes hung on my face and swept to the truck's bold blue lettering. Manager Kim should have paid me more for that sort of salesmanship.

I bought a coffee for him, a hot tea for me. Manager Kim came out of the front doors as I parked the truck. The building was small, more of a large store than a real factory. We worked in products that appealed to women's vanities. "We're going to make it," he said each morning. I believed him. He had a college degree and had worked in Japan. He taught us how to track revenue, net sales, and gross profit during our weekly meetings.

I jumped from the truck. "The mechanic fixed the back wheels and pumped the front ones."

He drummed his fingers against the pay-phone booth in front of the building. "How much did he charge?"

"Free. He's an uncle I used to work with."

"Good." He sipped the coffee I'd handed him. "Someone called for you. I told you this booth is for emergencies."

"For me? Did the operator leave a number?" I asked.

"He left a Seoul address. Said you needed to check in on a board-

CRYSTAL HANA KIM

inghouse." The pay phone rang just then. Manager Kim sighed. "It'll be for you."

Inside the booth, I picked up the receiver. "Hello?"

"Working hard, cousin?"

Jisoo. I hadn't spoken to him since the previous summer, when I'd left without saying goodbye. The letters we'd exchanged for the New Year had been brief and stilted with reserve. That was the last I'd heard from any of them. I didn't know if he knew. I didn't care. There was no affection between us any longer.

"You can't call here," I said. "I'm at work."

"This is how you greet your elder?" He exhaled in a slow, deliberate way. "We haven't heard from you in a long time."

"My boss needs the telephone."

"Well, *I* need you to check on Hyunki. We heard about the new protests, and he hasn't been writing. Visit him for us."

"Why should I?" Petulance rose in me. I couldn't help it. We were no longer teenagers in a refugee village, yet still he treated me as his lesser. And I, in turn, acted like one.

Jisoo shifted. The phone muffled with his movements, a deep-throated sigh. "If he's protesting, he could get in trouble. You know that."

I imagined Haemi hovering near him, perhaps laughing at me, or worse, pitying me. Outside the booth, Manager Kim clapped his hands and signaled at the work I had to do inside. I nodded. We would get our own telephone soon. He would be able to make his calls in an office, and I wouldn't have to deal with anyone from my old life.

"Make sure he's not getting mixed up in that political shit," Jisoo said.

"You think the students are wrong?" I asked.

· 272 ·

"I think Park Chung-hee's going to fix this country." He laughed. "You need me to explain this to you, little cousin?"

"The Third Republic's just as corrupt as the others. If you were here, you'd know."

He grunted. "You never cared about politics."

"I don't have the leisure to care like you." I opened the door to the booth and poured my tea on the ground. The liquid puddled on a patch of dirt like a beached jellyfish. Specks of dust swirled on the surface. I prodded the curve with my toe, watched the liquid burst.

I gave up and asked what I'd wanted to from the beginning. "How did you know where I worked?"

A fist sliding on wood, a cough. "Who do you think? Do this for us, Kyunghwan."

"Don't call here again." I hung up the phone and relished the sound of the plastic receiver hitting metal.

I wouldn't have been able to find Hyunki even if I'd wanted to. There were more than two and a half million people in Seoul now, and Hyunki was in college. Boys with protest signs and loud, educated voices were everywhere. In the train stations, on public squares, marching the streets. They tried to teach people like me about President Park's censorship, about the government's new proposal to reopen diplomatic ties with Japan. They burned effigies of imperialists and mourned the death of democracy as if we'd ever been one. I had better things to do.

I threw away the address Jisoo had given Manager Kim and went on a date. Insook was soft, with thick wrists, and curves that looked warm and giving beneath her flimsy cotton dress. She held on to my arm as we watched a film, her painted nails pressing into my shirtsleeve. I didn't know her well, but her boldness was a good sign. When I asked her to my room after the movie, she laughed. "Sunmi said you were forward."

"I only want to pick up a restaurant discount. Then we'll get dinner." I raised my arms like an innocent cowboy. "I promise."

She gave me an appraising look. "All right."

When we reached the Songs' hanok, Insook hesitated. "I rent a room," I said. "No one's home."

"I'll wait." She sat on a bench in the inner courtyard. As I walked around the porch, she gestured at the motorcycle. "This is yours?"

"I made it myself." I patted its leather seat. "It'd get stolen if I parked it outside."

Insook considered this with a tilt of her head. "Can I ride it?"

"You don't want to see what a renter's life looks like?"

"Oh, fine." She picked up the hem of her skirt like a girl wading through water. Her heels slipped off easily.

She entered my room, touched the few items I had on display. "I know this." She held up a drawing of Jeju Island. "Sunmi told me you two weren't ever serious."

I shuffled through my papers, looking for the discounts. "Sunmi's sister set us up a couple of years ago, but we were better as friends. She's a good artist."

Insook set down the drawing. "I hardly know you, anyway."

"Let's go to dinner and get to know each other, then."

"Mr. Yun?" Grandmother Song's thin voice rose as she called my name. "Mr. Yun?"

"Oh, no," Insook said.

"It's all right." I opened the door to my room.

Grandmother Song cradled a glossy brown handbag in the middle of the courtyard. She nodded at Insook's shoes. "We've talked about this. It's unacceptable. The neighbors see you. They come to me and I have to handle their complaints."

"We were only picking up a few papers." Insook bowed low with a deferential gaze. "I wouldn't normally come inside like this."

"You're not the one to blame. It's him." She pointed. "I have grandchildren here."

"They're adults now," I said.

"You don't talk to me however you want, Mr. Yun." She walked away.

"Wow," Insook whispered. "Let's go."

Outside the hanok gates, Insook leaned on my elbow and adjusted her right heel. "That's why my brother refuses to rent from hanoks. No family telling him what to do." She nodded at a figure walking up the path. "Is that one of the kids?"

"The granddaughter," I said. "She's in high school."

"I want to meet her." Insook smiled and fiddled with her shoe until Aejung reached us.

Hugging her backpack, Aejung bowed. "Going somewhere?"

"This is Lee Insook," I said. "We're getting dinner." Aejung wore her school uniform, but her lips were painted red. "Your makeup." I pointed. "Better wash that off before you go inside."

"Damn." She touched her mouth and turned to Insook. "Do you have a mirror?"

"You should always carry one around." Insook held one up as Aejung rubbed a tissue over her lips. "Especially if you have a grandmother like that."

"She's in a bad mood," I warned.

"You really should stop bringing women over." Aejung looked at Insook. "He's a dirty bachelor. Three matchmakers gave up on him."

"I don't know what you're trying to imply." Insook wrapped her mirror in a stretch of cloth and tucked it inside her bag. "We're colleagues."

"You work at the beauty products company?"

"And you're in middle school?" Insook gestured at the backpack. "Too young to wear makeup, clearly."

"What are we doing here?" I motioned. "Let's go. These only work before seven."

Aejung sniffed. "Restaurant discounts? I guess it isn't a date after all."

Insook straightened a small pin in her hair that I hadn't noticed earlier. "I'm not very hungry, actually. Kyunghwan, I'm leaving."

"She's just a sassy kid," I said.

Insook turned to Aejung. "You know, that color isn't flattering on you. It brings out the yellow in your teeth."

At the end of the path, Insook slid into a taxi with the ease of a woman who would have let me kiss her after dinner. I was almost angry. "Look what you've done."

"I'm just a sassy kid." Aejung smiled. "What'll you do now?"

I laughed at her eager, obvious face. "I guess I'll have to eat alone like the sad, old bachelor I am." I pretended to turn toward the road.

"I'll come." She hitched up her backpack. "Wait here. I want to change."

"Don't tell your grandmother."

She thrust out her chin. "I'm not dumb."

Aejung was harmless, an easy distraction. She was eighteen and captivated by the political rantings of her older brother. As we ate, she complained about her parents, who'd voted for Park. She praised the recent hunger strikes. These students all said the same things with the same indignant looks, the same shaking fists. They had been children when the country was divided, and now they wanted to be the leaders of the people.

My instinct for preservation took on a different form. Aejung and her brother floated through their lives, padded by their parents' money, shouting their principled indignities. I had only my work, my ability to pass unnoticed.

"I know all about Japan." I cracked open the tab of my beer can. "If they give us a heap of money, so what? Doesn't that help us?"

Aejung twirled a red plastic bracelet around her wrist and complained. "You don't care at all."

"I do, but hunger strikers only hurt themselves."

She sank her chopsticks into the milky-white broth. When she found an ox bone, she didn't wrest off the meat but sucked on it whole. "You wouldn't care if Japan came back and ruled over us one by one, as long as the economy gets better," she said with her mouth full.

"Hey," I said, my voice veering sharp. "You were born after Independence. You don't know what it was like under Japanese rule. It was just as bad as the war."

She raised her nose and sniffed. "Then you should be more upset." She pointed to the open newspaper between us. "I know a lot, anyway. My friends are part of the movement. Things are going to happen, like the demo tomorrow."

I sighed and set down my can. "There have been protests for months."

She glanced behind her shoulder at the other diners. "Not like this one. Park won't be able to ignore us anymore."

I prodded the newspaper. "Why don't you save this talk for your brother and let me enjoy my meal?"

Aejung pretended to pout but set the paper aside. She pulled out a shiny tube and swiped bright red over her lips. "Oppa still thinks I'm ten years old. You don't."

Her clever mouth. I watched her smile and almost wanted to kiss her. She was close enough. A bit more vain and prim, but she had the same willfulness, the same desire to assert herself in the world as Haemi had when she was young. I tugged Aejung's red plastic bracelet, its simple shininess. "How do I think of you, then?"

But as Aejung leaned toward me, I saw only a wide, pale face drenched with rain. Her dark, upturned eyes. The scent of her, a heady mix of rice, salt, grass. The way she had turned to Jisoo in that makeshift bar, years ago, and asked him to take her away.

�

I wanted to erase Haemi, but it wasn't so easy. The night I finally kissed her, when we fell into each other with all the hunger of twelve years, I thought—*At last.* At last, I wasn't alone. At last, the night had untangled itself the way I'd always wanted. Not just the night, but all my years. My life shifted into clarity.

I told Haemi about the strange boredom of the stalemate, and the pulsing rush of fear we felt when the night attacks robbed us of sight, smell, understanding. I told her of the shack along Namsan, Father's death, the failed exam. Memories I thought I'd discarded long ago. How I'd quit my position in the paper factory to return to her, to see her as a woman. That I had a new job selling beauty products waiting for me back in Seoul. That she should come, too.

Haemi unfurled herself beside me. I touched the skin that had always been mine in my mind. Her smooth neck, its paleness rivered by blue veins. The slopes of her tender breasts, the slight slack to their shape from mothering. The dark nipples I held in my mouth, circling with my tongue until they budded for me. I loved the stretch of her stomach, the scars running along the backs of her legs, the cuts on her fingers from careless housekeeping, how the flesh of her inner arm gave way to my grip. My fingers wove with hers, the gasp of us together, and the taste of her, everywhere. I loved her. I had loved her from the beginning. "Tonight. We'll go," she said. It was dark and I could smell her more than see her. The dirt underneath her fingernails, between the creases of her summered neck. The taste of her mouth, full of pond water.

"Tomorrow." I reached for her. "Stay here with me."

"Tonight. We'll come back for the girls." She held my face between her hands. "Do you want me?"

"You know I do."

"Then tonight. I'll lose the courage if we don't. I promise you."

I raised myself up and searched for my shirt. "What about Jisoo?"

She closed her eyes. "He's sick of me."

❀

How much had been true that night? How much had she meant? Why didn't I leave with her right then? I didn't know the answers even now.

Words circled around us, but we wanted to feel each other more than anything. I held her by the throat, the dip where she vibrated with each sound, her collarbone. From outside, we heard the cry of a bird, nothing else. No Jisoo, no children, no world without us together. I lit a candle even though we were burning. I wanted the look of her, how she moved in darkness stained with light. I realized I'd always known this body. Before we even undressed, I had known.

As the hours passed, she trapped herself in the practicalities of our escape, how we would survive. "There's too much in our way." Her hand hovered over the candle's flame. "Jisoo could have us jailed." I tried to convince her that the law against adultery was meant to punish cheating husbands, not wives. She slapped my arm, her palm hot against me. "It doesn't matter. It's me that would suffer. You'd be fine."

She slowly built a pillar of reasons—the law, the impossibility of divorce, the shunning of her daughters, the ruin of poverty. "Even if he let me go, I can't live like we used to." She cupped her hands and held them to her mouth like an animal lapping water. "Remember when we were so hungry we'd eat the lees from the distillery? How tipsy we would be when we got to school? We were seven, eight."

I remembered the thick gray mush that stank of alcohol. Everyone had done it. Red, sleepy faces arriving with loose books and easy smiles. The teachers had smelled our breaths, hit our heads and palms. But we were hungry and they couldn't help us.

I showed Haemi the money I'd brought with me.

"Are you trying to pay me or show me how we'll live?"

"There'll be more. We'll be fine," I said.

She laughed in the way I hated and stood with her dress in her hands.

"Don't leave," I said.

"You already did."

※

The world paled when I thought of her. I couldn't explain her hold on me all these years. I walked Aejung home after dinner and when she looped her arm with mine, I let her. I tried to feel the swing of her weight, this girl who was here and wanted me. She tipped her head against my shoulder. I smelled the clean, common scent of her shampoo. I listened to her hum and felt something release inside me. A desire for a normal life, maybe. No, a determination. For a wife, some children, an end to my aimless flirtations. Haemi had chosen Jisoo. What did that make me?

Aejung slowed our pace at the street that led to our shared hanok. "We're here already?" I smiled down at her, distracted again. "You should go in before your grandmother starts to worry."

"I don't want to yet. Maybe we could go somewhere?" She twisted the toe of her sneaker into the pavement. "To a hotel?"

"Aejung." I dropped her arm. "I can't do that."

She touched her lips, smearing the red. "I'm eighteen."

"Don't do this." I glanced up the road. "You don't know what you're saying."

She pushed out her chest and tilted her head, like a doll cast into a seductive pose. "You watch me." Her lips twitched into a smile. "I see you."

I sighed. I watched her and saw what Haemi could have been. If born a few years later, in a different city, and into a different sort of life. "It's not like that," I said.

"What's wrong with me, then?" Aejung wound her shirt around her finger and I caught a glimpse of pale, soft stomach. "Aren't I as good as the women you bring home?"

A hot wind blew against us. She pulled down the edge of her skirt with a quick, childlike tug. I laughed at the image, not trying to be unkind.

"I'm a terrible person and too old." I tucked a strand of hair behind her ear. She'd painted her lids a shimmering pink. Her eyes were hot with recognition and maybe a little resignation. "You'll find your own person one day, but tonight, you should get far away from me."

She leaned against my chest and blew out a long, slow breath. Her lashes thick, almost wet. "I'll go."

Her desire to be seen still heated her face as she walked away. At the hanok entrance, she bowed.

I roamed the downtown streets, where flickering neon signs advertised bars and coffee shops. A happy flush of noise burst from an open window of a beer hall, but I didn't want a bar girl to pour my drinks and I didn't want to be alone. A group of college boys passed me in a tense roar. "I hope it's a big demo," one of them said. The thought of protests dragged Jisoo's request to the surface of my mind. If Hyunki had been arrested, he would have contacted them. Haemi only wanted to prove that she could still control me. Jisoo wouldn't have called otherwise. I knew it. He did, too. We were alike in this way—beholden to a ruthless, capricious woman.

I passed a row of trees, their branches heavy with shiny green walnut husks. I turned down different paths and tried to convince myself that I wandered aimlessly. Still, I knew where I'd end up.

I entered a neighborhood of apartment buildings and stopped in front of Hyunki's two-story boardinghouse. I'd memorized the address with one read. Haemi. She didn't need me. And with one call, I was reminded of how much I needed her.

I left a note with the landlady and waited at a pojangmacha around the corner. I ordered soju, fish cakes, and broiled sparrows splayed on sticks. I wasn't hungry but gorged myself anyway. I scanned the crowds outside the street bar's clear plastic curtains. Hyunki would come or he wouldn't; at least I had taken care of my end. I wondered if he would recognize me. I glanced at my reflection in the carbide lamp's metal glare. Not yet thirty and I felt ripe with age, pitiful, and alone.

Most of the customers idled at the standing bar—college boys with short hair and clean buttoned shirts; older uncles, already drunk; and grandfathers with long wooden pipes. When Hyunki finally entered, I was surprised at how easily I identified him. Tall and thin, he ducked under the tarp opening and I recognized the serious stare, the strong nose. That same peaked hairline. The small sickly boy I'd once known now stretched into a gangly adult.

I raised an arm. "Here, Hyunki."

"Kyunghwan-hyung." He bowed.

He walked with the unearned swagger of all the college students. These boys who believed they alone were responsible for our country's future. Resentment surged in me, like the vomit that crawled up my throat after downing a shot of soju too quickly.

He bowed again and sat down. "Is everything all right? Is something wrong?" His voice, deep and scratchy, cleared away my bitterness. It was late and I'd scared him with my sudden visit.

"Your nuna and Jisoo wanted me to check on you," I said. "Spare an hour to drink and eat with an old cousin?"

"Thank God." Hyunki coughed into his arm. "It's great to see you."

I examined him. "Are you sick again?"

"It's only a cold." He held the glass I'd given him with both hands as I poured. "Thank you."

"You sure?" Before he could answer, I noticed the green tinge to his face. Across his nose and cheek, his skin was swollen. "Are you sick or beaten up? Let me see."

He turned so I could inspect him and smiled. "It's nothing. Don't tell Nuna. She'll only get mad."

His simplicity reminded me of when I'd first arrived in Seoul—those eager months before I'd failed the entrance exam. "There have always been protests, new republics," I said. "You shouldn't put yourself in danger."

He narrowed his eyes. "You sound like Jisoo-hyung. You don't believe that, do you?"

I didn't know. I had never been able to make up my mind about my political leanings, Haemi, myself.

"You've seen what Park's censorship has done." He quartered an oily fish cake with his chopsticks. "Living in Seoul, you must know."

I cleared my throat. "I'm not some farmer in the fields. You think I was gullible enough to vote for Park Chung-hee?"

He chuckled and raised his glass in celebration.

The soju greased our thoughts and made them easier to share. I couldn't help but like Hyunki. He spoke with an intensity I'd never felt for any ideology. As we ripped into fried fish cakes, he tried to recruit me into joining his college protest meetings.

I swirled soju down my throat as he neared the end of another speech. The ease with which he shared the details of his life made me want to confide in him. He was Haemi's brother, after all. Maybe he would understand if I told him—that I had once loved her, that I thought she had loved me, too.

"Will you come, Hyung?" With his hand on his elbow and his face averted, he refilled my glass. "One demo and you'll see."

"I don't want to talk about our government anymore." I straightened. "I was actually thinking about Haemi. Are you two still close?"

He set down the bottle and I willed him to speak. To tell me some secret that would make me understand her.

"We fought right before I left. She didn't write for two years. She made Mother and Jisoo communicate with me instead." He grimaced. "Then I missed Mother's funeral on Nuna's orders, to take the college entrance exams. But when I went to the tumulus the next day, Nuna refused to see me. I hated her."

Disappointment swept through me. "So you don't talk anymore?"

"We made up, actually. I'm trying to convince her to visit." He sipped, forgetting to turn his head.

"She hasn't yet?"

"I think she's afraid." Hyunki gazed out at the street. It was too dark to see beyond the streetlamp's circled limits. "She's more fearful now than she was before. Don't you think?"

My face rippled with heat. I shrugged. "I'm not sure. I'm not good at staying in touch."

"I feel guilty." The soju smeared his words together. "Working, studying, searching for a job. And then all of a sudden, it's been four years. I'm going back as soon as I finish, though, for the whole winter."

"She'd like that." I nodded so he'd continue, but he seemed caught in his own guilt. His mouth rimmed with worry. I prodded his glass. "What do you two write about?"

He shrugged. "She's written about you before, if that's what you're asking. Wanted to know if I ever saw you around. I tried to explain how big it is here, but she doesn't understand."

"I visited her last year. Saw Jisoo and the girls." I tried to steady myself. My voice sounded tight. "Did she tell you?"

"Yeah, I heard." Hyunki glanced at me. "Did something happen?"

I stared at the table. The oily sparrows, speared through the core with a stick, had soaked through the napkins. I nudged a withered, burned skeleton. "What do you mean?"

"Nuna's been vague these past few months whenever I ask about home. Hyung hasn't written much, either. Maybe they know I'm protesting, but it seems like something else." He crumpled a stale napkin. "Do you know if things are all right between them?"

"Jisoo and I don't talk much anymore." I lined our empty bottles into a tidy row. "Haemi and I were close when we were young."

Hyunki nodded. "Sure, Hyung. You were friends."

"Not just friends." I popped a sparrow off a stick and broke the head and ribs with my thumbs, as if I were a god over its tiny, delicate bones. I rushed on, before I could lose my nerve. "I loved her. Did she tell you that?"

Hyunki's mouth gaped. He scanned the air between us, clicking the story into place. "Haemi-nuna? Does she know?"

I looked down at my hands and wished I could laugh at his question. The undersides of my nails were thick with meat. "She almost ran away with me last year."

He scooted his chair closer. "Who else knows?"

I leaned against the table. My temples throbbed. I couldn't sift through my feelings. There was no point explaining now. "I haven't heard from her since I left."

Hyunki picked up the half-full soju bottle and stared at the liquid inside, the dull, refracted light. "I guess I've been gone a long time."

The pojangmacha owner rang a bell. "One hour till curfew. Get your last orders in while you can."

Hyunki watched me pour soju to the rim. "Hyung, I have the demo tomorrow."

"Drink," I ordered. "And forget I said anything."

He covered the top of his glass when I tried to pour him another. I closed my eyes. "I'm a jealous bastard." I shrugged my shoulders to exaggerate my drunkenness and the movement turned me around. I leaned over, woozy.

The table seemed to swing toward me. Hyunki caught my arm, steadying me as if I were truly old. "Maybe you should go home. Do you live far from here?"

"Don't worry about me." I waved away his concern.

Hyunki hesitated. "Does Jisoo-hyung know? Is that why he hasn't been writing?"

I pulled out my wallet and rubbed the bills in my hand, these thin slips of paper that held such weight in our world. The pojangmacha owner shouted another warning.

"Go back to your boardinghouse before I buy another bottle," I said.

"If it weren't for the demo, I'd stay. I'm sorry, Hyung." Hyunki bowed and hurried out.

My limbs felt heavy. One hour until national curfew, and Haemi had never mentioned me to her precious brother. I ordered another bottle of soju. *Fearful.* A trait I never would have tied to Haemi in the past, when she used to speak of a life beyond our hometown. She had changed into a fearful woman. I had changed, too.

———

The next morning, I didn't go to the protest. I decided to move out of my rented room instead. Haemi had scoffed at my living arrangements last year and I knew she was right. Another family's hanok wasn't enough for a grown man.

In the days afterward, when Park's warning signals burned the air and he imposed martial law, I saw Hyunki. Not in person or on the emptied streets and not in the newspapers scrubbed clean of the protest's violence. I saw him in the absence of demonstrations, crowds, speeches, pamphlets. The late-night gatherings were gone, the schools closed.

I found an apartment building for respectable young men and beginning families. I'd sold the motorcycle, but still my savings weren't enough. A public telephone stood two streets away. I picked up the receiver and asked the operator to connect me to Jisoo's town council. I left a message and waited for the return call. It was pitiful, and I knew there would be pleasure in it for him.

"I need your help," I said.

"Why should I help you?"

"If you do, I won't come back." I held her letters in my hand. The ones from our childhood and the one she'd written two years ago, asking me to visit.

"You think I care if you come back or not?"

I raked a hand over my face. My body felt whittled away, corroded. "I don't know, Jisoo."

He exhaled, measured and slow. "What do you want?"

"I need a cosignature. To rent my own apartment."

"Still too poor to afford a home?"

"I did what you asked me to do."

"How is he?"

I pulled a small jar of cream, our newest product, from my pocket. We claimed it would bring back your youth. Deeper in, a pack of cigarettes. I lit one. I was all smoke and haze now. "Hyun-ki's fine. Safe. I told him to write you."

❀

"If you leave me, I won't forgive you."

She had warned me.

We were sixteen and it was 1951. We were twenty-eight and it was 1963.

I thought we had offered ourselves up to each other. For years, I had no one to claim, and then, finally, I had her. We were all or-phans in this country—I understood this—but I was the orphan who deserved Haemi.

The morning after she said those words, I left her with a final letter. She loved me, and I was sure she would make her way to me, with or without the girls. I was ready. I waited with the dog. She never came. Eventually, I left her again.

Hyunki

1964

I WOKE WITH A HEADACHE, WITH KYUNGHWAN'S WORDS roping my mind. "I loved her. Did she tell you that?" I tried to recall the rest, but the night's edges were smudged with drink. A table covered with sparrow bones, soju bottles. As he spoke, he'd pressed his finger to a scar on his cheek, pushing against the raised white line as if everything he held inside would spill out.

I rose to my knees and fumbled for the glass on my tray table. The wet lash of water slid through me. In a few hours, Gwanghwamun would be filled with students protesting. Whatever Kyunghwan wanted me to do with this confession would have to wait.

A truck outside clattered down our street. I watched it pass by my open window. Piles of lettuce covered the cargo bed, the green heads packed tight. Not a military truck, then. I breathed in, relishing how clean the outside world seemed in comparison to my body. The air was woven with anticipation, textured, as if I could reach my hand across the sky and feel all the hours of preparation that had led to this morning. I imagined Park and the capital officials fleeing, running for their private cars with papers shielding their shamed faces.

I pulled on black slacks, a black shirt. The cotton tee stuck to my back, my skin clammy. At my desk, I shuffled through the love notes Myungsook had slipped between my demo flyers and rolled up the Taegeukgi flag we'd used at the other demos. Kyunghwan still crowded my thoughts, the vague shape of him in our lives. He was Jisoo's cousin, and I'd thought he'd introduced Hyung to Haemi. I wondered if what he'd said was true.

I pulled out Haemi's most recent letter and studied the photograph she'd included. Jisoo stood in the middle of the frame wearing a dark suit. The three girls sat in front, smiling in their matching dresses and frilly headbands. Haemi sat to the right, cradling the new baby. Eunhee had a round, wide face and a tuft of wavy hair. *Jisoo wanted to take a formal photograph for once. What do you think? Eunhee looks just like me, everyone says.* I felt a deep kick of pity. Kyunghwan seemed like the type of man who might imagine a love that wasn't there.

The landlady's cuckoo clock started downstairs, the bird's incessant call like a woodpecker against my temples. Damn Hyung and his drinks. I had an hour before I was supposed to meet Sungsoo, Jinho, and Byungchul. Just enough time to see Myungsook. I pocketed my wallet and identification papers, the flyers and flag, and a handkerchief, and scrambled outside.

As I headed to Myungsook's boardinghouse, I noticed the stains on the rolled-up Taegeukgi. I had coughed up a glob of mucus in the middle of the night and groped for a napkin in the dark. Now a yellow blot marred the corner of the flag. It was almost shaped like a dog, the yolky tail dragging to the frayed edge. I rubbed at it and willed myself to ignore the tight grip around my head. "She almost ran away with me last year." His words were like a burr on a sweater, catching at the thread of my thoughts. Was he lying or dreaming or telling a truth I didn't want to hear? He had visited her last summer. Maybe she loved him back.

I passed a telephone booth with a line of people curled around the corner. Inside the cubicle, a man yelled into the receiver. He banged a long umbrella against the glass and the people in line tensed, looked away.

I felt a wash of guilt at having avoided Haemi's calls, her letters. *You better not be joining the protests, Hyunki. You aren't strong enough. I need you too much.* I imagined her clutching the receiver, her lips pressed tight as she left each message with my landlady. I would call her after the demo. I would tell her about Kyunghwan's strange, drunken declaration, and she would laugh or confide or explain his meaning.

Myungsook snuck out of her boardinghouse with two containers of orange juice and long white strips of yeot. "I dreamed that a horde of crows attacked us." She shuddered, hugging herself with her full hands. "They pecked until we bled all over and one of your eyeballs rolled between their crusty little legs."

"You watch too many movies." I took the juice boxes from her. "Why all the treats?"

She stretched off a piece of taffy, looping it as wide as she could before it broke. "Eat this for good luck."

I groaned. "I can't put anything in my stomach right now. An old uncle made me drink with him for hours last night."

"No wonder you look so tired." She sucked her teeth. "I went out early this morning to buy this for you. Please?"

"I'll have one piece." The sugary yeot inflated my headache, but I chewed until the crease between her eyebrows had smoothed. "I'm all protected now."

We wandered the streets of her neighborhood, our arms brushing in a steady rhythm. Female conductors stepped from packed buses to collect fares, men lined up along a bulletin board pasted with fresh newspapers, and a few aunties lugged metal jugs to the water tank truck. Dense gray clouds, blown in from the north, threatened the skies, and the air was moist, almost brackish. In her short-sleeved dress, Myungsook's skin slid along mine, soft and slick. I caught her pinkie for a moment and she smiled.

"I wish I could go with you," she said, a sudden gust in her throat. She and the others from the women's college had helped distribute information through the activist student groups all week. "Why should the dean get a say in what we do?"

"Maybe he'll change his mind," I offered.

"Maybe we won't listen to him next time." Myungsook slid closer. "Anyway, I don't want to go today. My dream scared me. Please be careful."

I smiled and the bruise on my right cheek throbbed. "I'll be fine."

She sucked her straw, her eyes focused on me. "You don't have to go if you're not feeling well."

I gestured at my face. "This is all superficial. It looks worse because it's healing."

"I mean the coughing." She nodded at my chest, as if she could see through my shirt and skin and bones down to my lungs. "The last few weeks."

It annoyed me, how the women in my life treated me like I was an invalid. I gulped juice and bit off more yeot, as if thirst and hunger equaled health. "Don't worry about me."

We looped back, past a schoolyard full of children and a store selling radios. We stopped at Myungsook's gate. Her landlady's window opened onto the street. We could hear her daughter inside, the high pitch of a young girl around Solee's age.

Haemi had written about Kyunghwan's visit only after Solee had already told me. *Yes, he's here. Do you remember him, Hyunki? I've known him always, since before you were ever sick.* I had thought Haemi and I were knitting in the holes that had formed throughout the years, but she hadn't told me anything.

"Is something wrong?" Myungsook cocked her head. I realized she was waiting for a response. Haemi would like her. Myungsook was smart, confident, a college student. We'd been dating a few months now and I hadn't told Nuna about her. I'd kept the information to myself, just like the river stones I used to shine and hoard.

"I was thinking about my nuna," I said. "She would be like you, if she were here. Helping us get ready."

Myungsook gazed at the third floor, where she shared a room with another classmate. "Maybe I should put on some black pants and one of your shirts. Hide my hair under a cap." She fluttered her hands and presented herself like a magic act. "Jja-jjan! And no one would know the difference."

I laughed and leaned toward her. She cupped my elbow as if even that part of me was hers. "I wasn't joking about the dream," she added. "Promise me, no violence."

I held out my pinkie, even though we both knew yubikiri was Japanese. "Wait, this is what Haemi-nuna and I used to do." I kissed my palm and Myungsook did the same. We slapped our hands together. "Sealed tight."

"Don't be reckless," she said.

"Me? Reckless?"

She smiled. "Go kick Park's ass, all the way to Japan." She blushed even as the curse left her mouth.

I kissed her cheek, quick, before anyone could see. "You're learning my bad habits. I'll come see you after."

Sungsoo, Jinho, Byungchul, and I met at the American restaurant near our college as the rain began to splatter. Sungsoo came in shaking his head, drops falling on his shoulders. He chuckled when he saw me. "You look awful. Sit down. I'll order."

I found a table big enough for the four of us. As Sungsoo spoke to the cashier, Byungchul jumped to Jinho's side, as chatty as Jinho was quiet, and they read through the morning specials together.

Sungsoo joined me first with a tray of cornbread and eggs, two soda bottles. The unnamed leader of our second-year student group, he was squarely built with muscled shoulders and flat feet. He had a flat nose to match and a commanding voice. Grinning, he jerked his head at the counter. Byungchul was speaking in English, as if the cashier weren't Korean. "Our translator's working his charms again," Sungsoo said.

It was Jinho, though, with his glasses and discreet allure, who attracted the most girls. We laughed as the cashier craned her neck to catch his gaze while Byungchul blustered on. Jinho, as usual, didn't notice. A few minutes later, Byungchul sauntered over with three pancakes soaked with syrup. Jinho followed with sliced peaches and watermelon.

"Maybe we should have gone to a place with hangover soup." Byungchul smirked.

"Do I really look that bad?" I pulled at the skin under my eyes. "Better?"

"You shouldn't be hungover for the demo." Sungsoo straightened. Now that we were all seated, he twisted off the soda bottle caps. "Your mind has to be clear."

"Leave him alone," Byungchul said. "We can't all be perfect like you."

I cut into the cornbread with my chopsticks, my stomach roiling at its sweet scent. The dense yellow crumbled and I dabbed at the flecks with my fingers. "An older relative wanted to know if I was protesting. We met at a pojangmacha last night."

"You let an uncle get you drunk?" Byungchul laughed. "Invite me next time."

Jinho's cheek dimpled, the only evidence of his amusement. He pricked his toothpick into a peach slice. "Did you tell him about the fight?"

I shook my head. A week ago, on our way to a demo at Seoul National, Byungchul had insulted a passerby when he cut in front of us. The man threw a punch and I got into my first fight. My classmates thought I'd been beaten at the demo, and none of us corrected their assumption.

Byungchul reenacted the argument, using Sungsoo and Jinho as stand-ins. I heard Kyunghwan's and Haemi's words again over the boys' raised voices and clattering plates.

"I loved her." *Do you remember him, Hyunki?*

Their presence annoyed me. My mind was already foggy, as Sungsoo had said, and the distraction made me feel less pure, less noble than the others. I sliced into my egg. The yolk had already congealed.

Jinho drank the juice from the bottom of his fruit bowl and cleared his throat. "I heard the fourth-years talking this morning." Jinho didn't speak much. When he did, we always listened. "They think this demo will be serious. One of them saw military vehicles heading to City Hall."

"You don't want to go?" Sungsoo glanced at him.

"That's not what I said." He removed his wire-rimmed glasses and wiped them with a cleaning cloth. "We should make sure to stick together. Be vigilant." He nodded at me and Byungchul. "No stupid fights."

Byungchul nudged me across the table. "We'll be on our best, top student behavior. We won't disappoint you, teacher!" From his pocket, he pulled a strange nubbin covered in brown-and-white fur. "My hyung gave me this. They're good luck charms in America."

"What is it?" Sungsoo squinted. "It looks like a dead mouse."

"A rabbit's foot, babo." Byungchul rubbed the fur between his fingers.

"Why would an American charm work on us?" Jinho asked. Sungsoo and I laughed.

Byungchul shrugged, jeering sideways at us. "Lighten up, friends."

We met the rest of our classmates on the main square of campus, where they'd gathered on the wet, mown grass. We assembled naturally according to class, with the fourth-years guiding the front. Atop a stone statue, the student council leader shouted through his cupped hands, "March west and then north to Gwanghwamun!"

We whooped and spread out along the road, blocking trams and pushing against one another in a half jog, more than two hundred of us buzzing with eager insistence. Jinho and I raised the Taegeukgi between us. Sungsoo and Byungchul clutched their signs to their chests to keep them dry. The rain made us unwieldy. We were too frenzied to notice.

Byungchul prodded my back. "How're you feeling now?"

"This is better than any hangover soup," I shouted.

We marched past lingering cars, a grandmother hurrying south. Storeowners watched from windows with splayed fingers, like children ready for a parade. When we reached City Hall, the roads converged into a straight path north and the mass thickened into thousands. Students from universities across Seoul, men in smudgy work uniforms, others with raincoats over their suits, we all came together. Each group chanted its own slogans. We couldn't hear our group's leader over the throng.

"Straight through to Gwanghwamun!" Sungsoo called, reining in the second- and first-years. He waved his sign to hold our attention. "Watch your surroundings!"

We threaded along the eastern edge of the crowd, following Sungsoo's sign. The din vibrated around us. Sungsoo shouted again, only a meter ahead, but his voice was buried too quickly.

Jinho pointed to our right. Soldiers, gripping guns and cudgels, stood packed together. "I told you," he yelled into my ear. I caught a guard's eyes. His expression was blank, removed of all emotion. He had the fatty cheeks of youth, but he didn't flinch when a protester yelled "Our country can't be sold!" right into his face. Whether the soldiers waited from fear or faith in their numbers, I couldn't tell.

Byungchul squeezed into the space on my left. He rubbed his rabbit's foot, his sign propped against his shoulder, the painted words now leaky and distorted with rain. His eyes darted around the crowd. I spoke before he could. "Let's get to the front. That's where the action is." I looped my arm with his. "Stay close."

We tried to steer toward the middle, away from the soldiers, but couldn't make headway. A man in a shiny zippered jacket climbed onto someone's shoulders. "Death to Japanese imperialism!" He jerked his arms, almost spastic, as the others joined in. I felt their anger swell beneath our feet. I let the feeling propel me forward even as I sensed Byungchul's hesitation, the catch in his breath. We watched a military truck spill helmeted policemen holding long black cudgels. A few of them marched with rifles.

"This is bad. This is really bad." Byungchul looked down, then across me to Jinho. "Damn it, Jinho, you broke my charm."

"What are you talking about?" I increased our pace, tightening my hold on him.

He wriggled free. "You all questioned the rabbit's foot! You didn't believe in it!" He shoved his sign at me. I threw it right back.

"Don't be a little shit," I said. "We're almost there."

"I can't do this." Byungchul twisted the charm in his hands. "I can't."

"Park's going to step down today," Jinho said, as if that would convince him. His glasses were flecked with rain. He didn't move to wipe them. "We're taking him down."

Byungchul shook his head. "Do you see what they're carrying? And what do we have? Nothing!" He raised his stupid charm again. "I don't want to be turned into dog meat. I'm leaving."

"Byungchul!" I yelled.

"I'm not an idiot," he said. We watched him turn south, his sign muddy, dragging on the ground.

"Fuck him," I said, when we could no longer see him. "Let's catch up with Sungsoo."

Jinho craned his neck. "He's too far away. Let's dig into the crowd."

We used the Taegeukgi as a leash to hold us together. Jinho followed as I wove through the protesters. Sloshing in our wet shoes,
our shoulders hunched, we sidestepped the scared until we reached
the center. A call-and-response swept past us and we joined in,
shouting "Demand Japanese atonement!" and "Fuck the regime!"
in rhythm with the thrashing bodies. Our collective, magnified
voice thrilled us all. Jinho and I waved our flag, the red-and-blue
taegeuk gleaming darker and rounder as the whiteness around it
drenched sheer with rain.

We thronged toward the gate, pushed by the force of the others more than our own feet. For a moment, I remembered the
start of the war, when we had fled in hordes. How I had clung to
Haemi, reassured by her grip on my shoulder. How she had given
me scraps of food, feigning indigestion. Fifteen and forced to be
brave, putting my life before her own. I had listened to the swish
of hemp cloth and pretended she was sister and father and mother
combined.

"There are a lot of soldiers," Jinho called. He jumped to see
above the other heads. I did, too. Military jeeps and giant shields
guarded the Gwanghwamun entrance. A gap of space, maybe ten
meters long, opened between the military and us. A few of the
braver protesters stepped forward, long signs unfurled.

"Let's get in there," I said.

As we wedged closer, the sound of shattering glass cartwheeled
through the air. A high, sharp crackle. "Someone's throwing rocks
at the soldiers," Jinho yelled.

Around us, students turned to run, twisting around those stilled
with shock. People pushed in all directions, some forward to join
the fight, others fleeing.

"They're using their clubs!" A young man in a yellow shirt, jarring in its brightness, gripped his sign like a bat. "I'm going to get those dogs!"

Someone jostled my shoulder and the flag ripped from my hands, severing me from Jinho. I ducked and snaked between the bodies, trying to catch up, to find him, but I couldn't see through the sea of dark colors, the frenzy of shouts.

My mouth filled with thick, acrid saliva as the day splintered too quickly for me to comprehend. Someone hit my back, and I realized I'd come to a stop, that others were elbowing me around like a top. I wiped the rain from my eyes. I had finally reached the front—protesters swinging signs, and soldiers in domed green helmets, slashing clubs through the air.

I spotted Jinho caught against one of the shields. A soldier held his arm. Sweat or rain or tears streaked his face, and the square panes of his glasses were clouded. He looked strange, almost blind. He threw himself at the shield like a rag doll and tried to yank his arm free. His glasses flew off, disappeared.

"Jinho!"

I ran, too late.

The soldier brought his club down on Jinho's wrist—once, twice, three times. Even with all the noise, I heard the crack of bone. A simple, almost familiar sound, like a branch breaking underfoot.

Jinho raised his arm, the slump of his broken wrist, and screamed. I slid to him, caught his shirt. "I'll get you out of here." But the soldier grabbed his shoulder and pulled until Jinho crumpled backward.

"Let go of him!" I caught Jinho's ankle, pulled against the man's strength. I lunged forward, almost gaining a hold of Jinho's waist, until his voice reached out.

"Left! Your left!"

Wood, long, hard, and unforgiving, slammed into my stomach, then a whip of sound, the air gone, and a new scream in my ears.

Heavy breaths. The cold press of stone against my spine. In a tight passageway at the back of a store with tiled eaves, Sungsoo lifted my shirt. I watched as his fingers probed a red, swollen stomach that didn't feel like my own.

I grabbed a pipe protruding from the wall and remembered why we were alone. "I saw a soldier drag Jinho away." My breath quickened. "We need to find him."

Sungsoo nodded. "They're taking our people to the police station. I'll bring you home and head straight there."

"They broke his wrist." I strained to stand, but my legs gave out beneath me. "You have to go now."

Sungsoo hesitated. The sound of an engine revving made us turn—a paddy wagon, its fenced-in flatbed full of restrained students. "He was hurt. He was screaming," I said. "I'll make it home."

I clung to the pipe and watched as Sungsoo ran off. Bile slid between my teeth, filling my mouth. Slumped on the ground, I realized it was still raining. A fine, damp mist.

As I tracked the slow, silvery clouds crossing the sky, an image of the boy they'd found floating in Masan Harbor came to me. The tear-gas canister that had sliced through his eye. Haemi had refused to let me leave for Seoul because of him, afraid of the protests. I remembered my anger at her power over me, her dramatic tendencies, and my relief when it was finally time to leave.

It shamed me to recall my last night with her. My drunken,

sixteen-year-old self, my blustering words. How I'd called her a bitch.

What did she say to me, that night in the dark, hot kitchen? Dropping the corncob stick, her pregnant belly between us, "You don't know anything. You, Hyunki—you weren't worth this life."

It seemed I'd tugged at the wrong words all day. I had forgotten how she'd always put my life before her own.

I've known him always, since before you were ever sick.

Perhaps she'd been telling me all along.

I blinked up at the sky, the blanket of blue tingeing my sight. Evening had come and I was alone, against a stone wall, unable to stand. Haemi had been right all along. I didn't know anything.

Haemi

1965

A SELFISH PERSON—THAT'S WHAT HE'D CALLED ME. I opened my wardrobe and stuffed hanboks, sweaters, a scarf, socks into my largest rucksack. Jisoo didn't understand why I had to be the one to collect the body.

"Because he's my brother and I'm alone now," I said, walking the perimeter of our room. I grabbed random items—a broken pencil, the scissors I used to cut the girls' hair. I threw them at his feet.

Jieun and Mila sat by the door, pretending to look through my bag. Solee watched us with her exacting concentration. "Want us to pack for you?"

Jisoo pointed to the girls, himself, the room. "You're alone now?"

I found what I needed on his desk—the addresses on a slip of paper, Jisoo's money, the only photograph of Hyunki we had. I folded these items into my bag with care. "You know what I mean," I said.

"You won't know where to go."

"Be good to the girls." I looked at Solee, Jieun, Mila. "Mommy will be home soon."

"What are you doing?" Jisoo pointed to Eunhee. "You're not going to take the baby?" She was curled around a pillow, asleep on top of our folded blankets despite the noise. Eunhee was the best sleeper of my four. Some nights I loved her most just for this.

"You can manage for a few days, Jisoo."

Mila touched my passing ankle. "Where are you going, Mommy?"

"To get Uncle," Solee explained.

They whispered together, my little trio. I heard Hyunki's name and Mila's response. "Who?"

Jisoo followed me from the room. "Now I know why you want to go alone." He carried Eunhee in a careless hold, her head swinging with each stride.

She jolted awake, her lips opening into a cautious cry. "Ma?"

"Watch her neck." I adjusted Jisoo's arm underneath her. "You're going to drop her."

"You're the mother." He thrust her toward me and she rubbed her face against my shoulder, her cries etching higher. By the hallway window, Jisoo grabbed my wrist, his fingers pressing into me in his vicious way. "I know why," he said again. Shadowed by the winter sun, his backlit face seemed unformed, as if I could mold his features anew. I wanted him to stand there forever.

Eunhee cried louder in my arms. Tiny pearled teeth and pink throat. "Ma?"

"He wouldn't want you even if you could find him," Jisoo said.

I twisted from his grasp. "Hyunki's dead and that's what you're thinking about?"

I shouldered past him to our room. Solee, Jieun, and Mila huddled together along the far wall, around a pile of blankets, as if it were a shrine. My girls, looking more like me with each birth. I set Eunhee down in front of them.

I told them to be good, to take care of the baby, and I left.

As I boarded the train that would take me to Seoul, I imagined Hyunki's lungs. The doctor had described their scarring with precise, scientific words. I had pictured rivers—thick white rivers of hard tissue slithering across pink insides.

"It must have been hard for him to breathe for years. These scars were old," the doctor, a floating voice, had said.

Clutching the town's public telephone, I'd wanted to kill him.

"He coughed sometimes, but I thought we had cured the sickness," I said. "Years ago. My husband brought us medicine and said it would work."

A sigh. "Tuberculosis can return if the immune system is weakened. His recent injuries must have exacerbated the illness."

"Injuries?" I wanted to yell at this man who knew so much about my brother. "I spoke to him two weeks ago."

The doctor paused. "Are you or your husband coming to Seoul? Perhaps we could talk in person."

My brother was dead. The disease that had rooted into him during the war had reared up again to speckle his lungs with fresh white dots. Lumps, curdled and full of holes, had slowly taken away his air. Hyunki. Only twenty-one years old. I couldn't collect my thoughts. I couldn't order them into a shape I understood.

"He told me his studies were going well," I said. "He didn't tell me about any injuries."

"Mrs. Lee? When will you arrive in Seoul?"

I hung up. I didn't want to imagine anymore.

"Excuse me, would you like to use this?" The woman seated next to me on the train held out a white handkerchief. Silky and laced at the edges, it looked too expensive to clean my face with. The woman wore matching gloves, the lace frilly across her wrists. A heavy, fur-lined coat lay on her lap. She raised the handkerchief as if to wipe my cheeks for me.

I smeared the back of my hand under my eyes. "I'm fine."

"I don't mind. You can keep it."

"Please, leave me alone. Stop staring at me like I'm some pitiful stranger."

She flinched. It gave me a brief sense of pleasure to see my harshness distort her prim face. She folded her handkerchief into a neat triangle. "I'm sorry to intrude."

"You should be sorry." I turned to the window. "You have no idea who I am."

I looked down at the photograph of Hyunki in his first term of high school in Seoul. He wore a stiff black uniform and looked too serious. Healthy, though, his cheeks full with a roundness he'd never possessed as a child.

The last time I saw Hyunki, he'd climbed onto a bus with *Seoul* written on its glass windshield. I stood behind a tree and watched as he pressed his forehead against the window. A small, frightened face. His gaze swept over the people lined along the road, the women waving goodbye. He was looking for me, and I remained hidden. I hadn't revealed myself until two years later, with my first letter. *You need to forgive me, Hyunki. My only brother. I forgive you, too.*

Oxen, lone shacks, and distant mountains blurred past my window. I followed a bird's flight through tall trees. It was my first time on a train. I had never taken a trip to a neighboring city or gone with Jisoo on his visits to Hyunki. I'd told myself I would go last year, and then Jisoo had refused. I was too pregnant. I was a new mother.

Hyunki had asked again. *Bring the baby. Come and I will take care of you.* I'd laughed when I'd read his words. My little brother all grown up. I'd promised him this year, as soon as I stopped nursing Eunhee.

Always too late or too early, never at the right time.

I curved Hyunki's image into my palm and tried to feel how the earth slid by underneath me, how the train's wheels spun.

A blare of noise overwhelmed me as soon as I stepped off the train. It was cold, mid-February. People and cars crowded the city. I swept a long look around. Even the streets seemed different, paved smoother and wider, crisscrossing everywhere. As if Seoul's roads could prove to the world that we'd recovered.

Buildings with glass windows towered skyward, music twisted out of radios. Boys wore cardboard boxes covered in advertisements, and a man sold American cigarettes from a handmade crate. High school girls released from Saturday-evening classes gathered around a sugar candy vendor woman. With their identical short haircuts and uniforms, they looked like one girl, multiplied.

"Where are you going, Auntie? Need tickets?" A young boy with a brimmed hat waved his papers. "Sungnyemun Gate? Changgyeonggung Palace?" He spoke rigidly, carving the space between his syllables. He spoke like Seoul, like Jisoo when he'd first arrived in my life. The boy glanced at my rucksack. "Do you need a place to stay?"

"I'm a little lost. Can you help me with these directions?" I tried to find the slip with the addresses of Hyunki's boardinghouse and the hospital, but the boy had turned to the next traveler, his papers already flapping.

Passing women and men talked intently at one another. Every-

one looked hurried, walking in half bows for easier greetings and
goodbyes.

As I tried to locate a street crossing, a voice filled with country
drawl filtered through the chatter. I searched for its owner. A girl
in a buttoned coat discussed the best way to preserve radishes, the
inflections pitching her words high and low.

"Excuse me?" I asked.

The girl and a college-aged boy stopped. "Yes, Auntie?"

I showed her the addresses. "I'm looking for my brother. Can
you help me find this place?"

She pointed to buildings and shot her hand down imaginary
streets. The boy touched the girl's shoulder, where her coat was
patterned with purple flowers. He fingered the rounded sleeve,
caught my glance, and sheepishly bowed.

"Once you get off the tram, the boardinghouse should be around
the southern corner," she finished.

"Could you walk me to the right line?" I gestured to the cars.
"I'm not used to this traffic."

"They're over there," the girl said.

In an alcove across the street, trams crowded together. Instead
of wheels or steam, floating wires and grooved tracks guided them
through the city's streets.

"Where do I cross? How do I know which one to take?"

The boy looped his arm with the girl's. From the way he looked
at me, at the wraps and folds of my plain-colored hanbok, I knew
he was native to the city. "We're sorry, Auntie," he said, bowing
again, "but we're late. If you follow the signs, it shouldn't be difficult to figure out."

I didn't understand why they wouldn't help me. As they walked
away, already returning to their own concerns, I wanted to yell

at them. That I was only thirty, that my name was Lee Haemi, and that the way they spoke here—in one timbre through and through—was bloodless.

I held on to a hanging strap on a yellow-and-green tram driven by a kinder man. When we approached a neighborhood of apartment buildings, he whistled. "Jump off here, miss!" I did as he said, hitting the ground hard, and found the boardinghouse around the corner.

The landlady opened the entrance gate before I could even knock. "You must be Mr. Lee's sister. Come in." She wore a tight plaid dress. Her face revealed her middle age, as if her features mocked her attempts at youth. She caught my arm and hurried us across the yard. "I'm so sorry."

She blustered up the stairs to the apartment, almost carrying me by the elbow, wringing her belt with her other hand. "I've prepared a room for you. Of course, it'll be free of charge. Mr. Lee was a sweet boy."

"Did you know him well?" I brushed the bare stairway walls with my fingertips as we reached the second floor, where a single painting decorated the hallway. *The Angelus*. Two figures praying in a field. Hyunki had lived in this simple, clean apartment. "The doctor said he'd been sick for some time. Hyunki never told me. He acted like he was fine."

The landlady hesitated. She opened a door into a dark room. I saw the outlines of blankets and a chest, a desk. A cloying perfume scented the air. "I hope this is enough."

"When did you first notice his illness?" I asked.

She gazed down the hall without speaking, her weight against the doorframe. "After he came back from the demo last year," she finally said. "He didn't recover as quickly as he should have."

The demo. So he'd lied to me. Despite my pleas, he had joined in the protests. On the phone, with his voice distorted by the distance, I had thought he sounded cheerful. "I'd like to see his room," I said.

"Of course." She led me down the narrow hallway, shifting her feet as she described Hyunki's injuries, the coughing she'd heard from his room in the late hours of the night. "I was the one who insisted he see a doctor."

I raised my hand. "I'll stay in here with his belongings. I don't want the extra room. Excuse me."

"Do you need—?"

"Thank you. I'd like to be alone, please."

I shut the door and listened to her hard, clipped footsteps recede. Alone, finally, I felt the tears come.

Hyunki's room was immaculate. I touched the leveled corners of his sleeping mat, the cleared desk, and the folded clothes in the wardrobe. I had tidied for him all those years, and he'd finally taken up the habit.

The air felt dank and clammy. I wondered if my jealous presence was poisoning the space. I should have been the one to tend Hyunki through his sickness these past months. Not these strangers with their undeserving hands, while I sat dumb at home.

I started with the clothes. He was taller than I'd expected. His pants came up to my stomach. I folded each pair at the knee. The shirts were flamboyant—reds, greens, blues, and one with a checkered pattern. I packed everything, even his undergarments.

I found his round white pills in the back of his wardrobe. The medicine was supposed to sturdy his lungs, and yet his illness had curled in on itself and killed him anyway. I packed the useless medicine, too.

Inside his desk, I found his childhood messiness. The hoarding I'd loved and hated. The dregs of his life—movie tickets, a soccer game stub, a photograph of a trio of boys, sketches on exam schedules, a finished bag of puffed rice, crackers wrapped in paper. Underneath all these nothings, I found notes from a girlfriend he'd never mentioned in his letters. Myungsook.

I read each of her notes and tried to picture Hyunki in Seoul. He watched movies with his friends. He met Myungsook at the library to study. There he leaned her against bookshelves and kissed her. Perhaps he had even brought her to his room, laid out his mat, and loved her. At least he had these happinesses.

When there was nothing else to be done, I unfurled his bedding and burrowed in. He had always smelled like Mother. I'd once accused her of washing their clothes in a different river. She'd laughed at my suspicion and worried about my mind. These sheets had that same milky sweetness. I smelled him in, my little brother. I imagined him alive. I would wake and he would walk into this room and laugh at my unannounced visit. He would hurry me out to meet his girlfriend. As I tried to sleep, I worried Mother was right. There was something rotten inside me that turned my mind around.

Jisoo, too, was right. I was selfish. On the corner of a magazine advertisement, I'd written another address and hidden it in my coat pocket. I'd found the address a year ago, scribbled in the margins of a notebook. Beside it, a name.

I recalled the hurt on Jisoo's face when I'd left this morning, his impotence and fear. I hated my callousness. It would have been easy to assure him, to kiss him and say, *No, I won't see Kyunghwan. I will find Hyunki and bring his body home.*

I woke with Hyunki's photo sweat-slicked to my chest. I hid it in my skirtband and left for the hospital. It was early in the morning, but the city was already full. Workingmen hung from wires attached to half-constructed buildings. Down below, vendors claimed their corners. Women hurried along to church, covering their heads with lace. They reminded me of Mother, her religious burial. How the church had refused to change the date of her funeral. Hyunki's insistence on coming home and missing the college entrance exams. My refusal. Mother had been dying for years, and she'd wanted only one thing for her son. Jisoo's accusation: "You are withholding this experience from him. He has a right to mourn. You cannot do this. You don't have the power to do this." But Hyunki was always so good. He listened to his Haemi-nuna.

I didn't know where I was going—too many streets, people, cars, noise, ringing church bells with their hollow echoes. I touched a wall, an elderly vendor's shoulder. "Can you help me?"

"Tea?" The grandfather held up a tray of refreshments. "I have many. What kind would you like?"

His tray was lined with an intricate drawing of children playing with frogs, moles, even tigers. A girl with a long plait of hair rode the back of a boar. "Did you draw this?" I asked.

"It's what I used to do. Would you like some tea?" He lifted a cup.

"Angelica root," I said. "Can you help me find this place?"

As I drank, he drew me a map. A box for the hospital, a curlicued arch for the bridge I should cross, and two small caricatures to represent us. At the top, he sketched a fox's head. "For good luck." He held it in front of his face and yipped.

During the first winter of the war, Mother and I had thought Hyunki was going to die. He'd survived the journey south, but we were convinced he was going to leave us in Busan. We wiped bloodstained phlegm from his lips and told him he would be fine. One night, as I cared for him alone, he tried to sit up.

"I'm the fox you eat," he whispered, and swished his sheets.

I saw the whites of his eyes, his rolling pupils. "You're dreaming." I swaddled him in blankets. "Shush and go to sleep."

Hyunki yelped and wouldn't stop. He was six, the age when boys want to live wild. "I'm the fox!"

I tried to calm him and worried his mind wouldn't come back around. He yowled until his lungs couldn't take it. When he quieted, I held his hand. I kissed his flushed face, his shallow chest, his dirty, quivering fingertips. "You can be the fox tomorrow," I said. "Sleep now."

"I'm the fox," he whispered, his lids already closing.

At the hospital, I stared at Hyunki's face. I wanted him to sit up for me again. If he came back to me, I would even take his hallucinations. On the gurney, only his head and neck were uncovered. The mortician, surprised to find a woman, said this was all I needed to see.

"I did an autopsy," he'd said when I arrived. "There are incisions, stitches. It won't help to look at his body."

But I had seen bodies before. I'd carried Mother's airless, bonelight frame. As the chief mourner, I had pounded my chest and wailed as I watched her disappear into the earth. Just as, years ago, Mother had moaned for Father. Since childhood I had seen so much of the dead. I'd carried an infant Hyunki along a road that teemed with trucks. We had watched as soldiers unloaded bodies from the Second World War. A few were alive, held together by the parts of themselves they were able to keep. When a man emerged whole, everyone had cheered through their jealousy. Hyunki and I had waited. Like the others along the roadside, I was convinced there'd been a mistake. Father would come home to us. He would return for his son.

This body, though, was my only brother. I looked at his pale, petaled eyes and the strange bloat of his cheeks, and convinced myself. This wasn't Hyunki. This was merely a dead thing, someone else's kin.

I almost laughed. I was the only one left alive—cruel, heartless Haemi, a bad mother, sister, daughter, wife.

I walked out of the room. The mortician stopped me in the hallway. He was a short man with a scar ruining his cheek. I'd recoiled when he first greeted me, but he seemed kind.

"I'm done," I said.

"You should sit with him awhile."

"I sat with him for years." I turned to the mortician's office. There were papers I had to sign and a casket to order for the journey home. "He was always sick."

"I was angry, too, when my wife died. It goes away."

There was no blame in his words. I stopped. I couldn't feel my legs or face or hands. Only my thoughts, as if they had a weight and a taste. Like the mist from that smoke grenade I'd unleashed years ago in Busan—metallic, dangerous. Hyunki wasn't alive, in hiding. He was in there, splayed out, dead.

"This will be your last chance," the mortician said.

I let him guide me back to the room. He brought me a chair and sat me down.

I stayed with Hyunki, my little brother, my own.

I no longer knew him, this man before me. I held my hands above his throat, over the knob that declared him an adult. His strange, long face with the high forehead and large eyes that no one could link to Mother or me. He was only twenty-one and he looked like someone else.

I imagined what else had changed. His voice. What I'd heard through the town's one telephone, fuzzy and warped, hadn't been enough. I'd taken care of him since he was born, and I would never know the simple, true sound of his adult voice. Was it dark and low, tinged with a gravelly husk, or higher and delicate, softened at the edges? How did he sound when he laughed? When he spoke in class and whispered to Myungsook late in the night? Did he speak of me, ever?

"Hyunki? Talk to me. Tell me you're a fox."

I dropped the sheet that covered him and looked at his mutilated body. A single cut from the base of his neck to his pelvis, stitched closed with thick thread. A moan, low and vibrating, spilled out of me. My Hyunki, who'd been so carefully protected by Mother, who'd not even been allowed to run outside, now lay here broken.

I touched his shallow chest, his bloated stomach. Imagined it tinged red from a soldier's fists. I hovered above the birthmark that spread across his ribs, and his long, muscleless legs. In between, his penis, like a snail curled in on itself.

The mortician opened the door. "That's enough now."

"Not yet."

This was my only brother. I had been cruel. For two years, I'd refused him a home, a response to his letters. He had forgiven me anyway. He had written cheerful stories and never mentioned his hurt, and I hadn't known enough to ask about his lungs. I hadn't visited or pushed him to come home. I'd lived my life as if he weren't my responsibility. This was my punishment.

I wanted to tattoo the image of his body into my memory, to hurt as he had. I wanted to kiss him, leach death from his lips and store it in my own limbs and lungs.

The mortician gripped my shoulders and tried to pull me away. I wouldn't move. I cupped Hyunki's soft heels, traced the fingers accustomed to pencils and inks. Intelligent and giving, the doctor had said on the telephone. My little brother was intelligent and giving, and he'd died before me. I touched his chest, the space above his heart. I couldn't breathe. I had given him nothing in the end.

Outside the hospital, I dug in my coat pocket. I unfolded a glossy slip of paper and held on to someone else's name. When I arrived at the three-story apartment, I called for Kyunghwan. He would come and we would drink. I would forget Hyunki for a few hours. Kyunghwan would help me pretend. He was good at that, smearing emotions numb with alcohol. I peered through the first-floor windows into other people's lives. "Kyunghwan!"

He wasn't home.

I wandered to the side of the building, where a row of bushes and streetlamps bordered a construction site. A half-built apartment frame stood in the middle of an undone space. I wedged my way through the bushes, past the plastic netting, into a lot full of dirt. One complete wall had been erected. The other three sides were a skeleton of metal beams. I peeled off my shoes and socks and rubbed my soles along the cold concrete floor. In the darkening light, I watched my ghostly imprints fade. I would wait. I would ask all the residents.

And when I finally found him, I would tell him what he didn't know. Hyunki was dead. Jisoo was a drunk. We were losing land. Something was wrong with me. I couldn't rein in my moods, and sometimes I was unkind to my children without reason. I feared they would resent me, the way I'd resented Mother. I had a new, beautiful daughter. Kyunghwan's. Jisoo's. No. She was only mine. Her name was Eunhee—hope and grace. It was true. Of all the girls, she gave me the most pleasure. In moments of frenzy, when Solee wanted to be left alone with her books and Jieun whined for attention and Mila wandered off and I didn't know how to manage, I would squeeze Eunhee's body and feel calm.

I spotted a shadowed figure walking toward the apartment next door. I climbed over the netting, stopped at the bushes, and called out. "Excuse me? I'm looking for someone."

"Haemi?"

Kyunghwan.

Tall and unexpected and handsome. I'd imagined a heavier man, but he was still slender with narrow cheeks, the same thin-lipped mouth and high forehead. He rested one hand against the bushes. In the other he held a dinner pail.

"Haemi, is it you?"

He stood beneath a streetlamp and I laughed. Our nights in Busan returned to me, when he'd waited by the fields with his home-made cigarettes, the lamppost's glow haloing his young, beautiful face—an image from our childhood in this new, unknown space.

"It's me, Kyunghwan."

"What are you doing here? How long have you—?" His anger cut his stride into quick steps. "Why are you here?"

I walked backward, deeper into the construction site. The ragged burr of his voice frightened me. He rushed toward me, quickly bridging the space until he stood close enough to touch. Kyunghwan. Not only of my imagination. Real and alive. I pressed my back into the metal corner. "It's me, Kyunghwan."

He palmed the beam, his arm stretched overhead. Beneath his open coat he wore a gray suit. He pressed his lips together. Silent. I'd seen this before, how he had to pool enough words before he spoke.

I closed my eyes and waited.

"I was going to eat this," he finally said, holding up his pail. I smelled Chinese noodles, black bean sauce.

"That's it?" I pushed him. "You leave, and that's it?" I pushed again. I towed him back to the lamp. "Look at me."

He looked at me in the light, fully, for the first time in two years. At my eyes, nose, at the mouth that had always wanted his.

A floral scent rose from his clothes. I wondered if I looked old, if a woman waited for him inside. If he knew what he had done to me.

"Let's eat." He pointed to a bench in front of his building. "I have a strict landlady."

"It's freezing."

He walked away. Hyunki's pale, closed eyes took his place, floating before me. Dark lashes, a strong brow. A mouth I used to feed, frothing with phlegm and blood and sickness.

"Wait, Kyunghwan."

I followed, resenting myself more with each step. Seated on the bench, Kyunghwan busied his gloved hands with napkins and chopsticks. He balanced the bowl on the armrest between our seats. My neck prickled with cold and I hoped I would catch pneumonia.

"I need you to get me drunk," I said. "I need you to help me."

"I'm hungry and need to think." He ate one noodle at a time, a habit I'd always hated. Black sauce crusted his mouth. The smell of pork masked that earlier flowery odor.

I could fill myself with details of Kyunghwan. I could remember a different, lesser pain, a time when I didn't care about anything but myself. I could tell him how I awoke two years ago, frightened. Not of being found by Jisoo or beaten in public, divorced, or jailed. I'd stared at the ceiling, afraid that what had happened in the night hadn't really happened at all. In the kitchen, I'd leaned against a jar of rice, pulled up my dress, and touched myself. My fingers had turned slick and I was relieved. I'd thought of his face. The small, double-lined scar on his cheek, barely visible, but textured against my tongue. I'd held him inside me and hoped.

I stood, found Kyunghwan's address, and threw it at him. "You stay and eat. I'm leaving."

He set down his noodles. "Don't be angry with me—"

"Forget it, Kyunghwan." I dumped his napkins on the ground and walked away.

"Haemi." He grabbed my arm. I felt the warmth of his hands, the width of his palms. They seemed larger, kinder. As he held me, I knew. I wanted him. Still, I wanted.

"Let's move to Japan," he said. "We can bring the girls."

He didn't know. Not about Hyunki or Eunhee or how his leaving had turned me into a woman who trawled her memories for meaning, signs, misunderstandings. I splayed my fingers against his back and pulled him close. I wanted Kyunghwan to remember me the way I'd been before. When we were young and thought our meager, hungry childhoods were enough.

"What if we went to Japan, just us?" I asked. I rolled a new, foreign name around my tongue. Hibari or simpler—Hisae.

"I'll say they're mine, Haemi."

I followed the straight line of his mouth. I kissed him.

He wouldn't take me to a bar. Instead, we stood on opposite ends of an enormous room. A sea of plush chairs, rooted to the floor in rows, stretched between us. In the Citizen's Center, we faced a shining wooden stage at the end of a sloped floor.

"They hold performances and concerts here. Business events, too. My company's hosting an exhibition tomorrow," Kyunghwan said.

"Your company?"

He pointed. Colorful boxes and bottles filled four tables on the stage, and banners strung above announced KOREAN SOAP! and KOREAN SHAMPOO! "The beauty products company. Remember? We're getting into the export business now. It's not mine yet, but I'm doing well."

I played with a seat's hinge at my side. He'd been in Seoul all this time and he still sold soaps. He didn't own a home. He ate Chinese noodles for dinner. "Let's get onstage," I said.

He followed me up the stairs. "What were you going to tell me?"

At the first table, I picked up a block of soap that was shaped like an oversize grain. I tore through the clear plastic with my nails. Perfume, pungent and floral, rubbed off on my hands. Hyunki was dead, and I couldn't form the words. I opened more boxes, found new bars. One package smelled like sesame seeds, another like peaches, too fragrant.

Kyunghwan held my waist from behind. "The company's expanding to Japan. We're starting a partnership. I could ask them to move us. If I was sponsored, we could do well there." He sifted through my hair, skimmed my shoulder. "A little apartment in Tokyo. What do you think?"

I withdrew from his grasp and sat on the edge of the stage. He followed and sat beside me. I wanted to wash Hyunki's face with one of these soaps, the pink one that smelled like morning glories. I would rub until color stained his cheeks and he returned to me. "Hyunki died. That's why I'm here. I didn't come for you."

Kyunghwan reared back. "When? Why didn't you tell me?"

I pulled out the school photograph. It seemed too small and flimsy in my palm. Panic filled my mouth with spit. I should have taken a photo of the body. I could have found that grandfather and paid him to draw my brother's likeness. Hyunki was dead because of me, and I would never see him again.

"I'm sorry." Kyunghwan stroked my knee, insistent, his fingers digging into my dress. "I'm so sorry."

A streak of anger. "You said he was fine. When Jisoo called, you said he was safe."

"That was—" He drew back his hand. "That was last year."

As he dragged his knuckles across his face, I noticed the sagging skin around his eyes, the new wrinkles. They made me hate him. "Did you know he was protesting?" I asked.

He shook his head. I wished he would turn into Hyunki. That I could tear off his features and replace them with my brother's.

I looked out at the empty audience, at the ghosts in plush seats laughing at the spectacle of us. I knew Kyunghwan, and I didn't have the energy to hate him any more than I already did. "You're lying."

He turned to me. "Hyunki didn't want to worry you. He said the demos were safe. I don't understand. There haven't been any protests in months."

"I hate you, Kyunghwan."

He wrapped his arms around me as a wail tore through the room. I clung to his neck, but I couldn't feel him. His familiar body. His mouth against my hair. Even with him all around me, I was alone.

I would never bury my brother. I would bring Hyunki to my room and sleep beside him, as we'd done throughout childhood, his giggles stitching us together in the night. I would place soaps around his body and cleanse him every day until the scents came to life. Morning glories would blossom around us in thick clusters; grass would grow beneath us, rose balsams, yellow forsythias. Peaches. We would devour them with the juice running down our fingers.

"Haemi? What should I do?"

I pushed my face into his chest. "Make me forget. Tell me about your life here."

I listened to his droning words. About his job, the apartment, how he was going to get rich. He explained how the government was supporting a movement to buy products made in Korea, and that whatever the politics of Park Chung-hee, at least he was helping his people. He spoke as if the company where he worked were important. As if I cared about his small, solitary life. I steadied my breathing until I could sit on my own.

His suit was loose around his shoulders. His shoes were made of more scuff than shine. He didn't have a woman. We were strangers now.

"I think something's wrong with me," I said. "Inside my head.

It leaks into my bones until I feel so heavy. I blamed it on the preg-nancies, but maybe it's me."

"You're mourning. You'll feel better when we get the girls."

A laugh, bitter as pith, rocked through me. No, we weren't strangers. I knew him. He was the same. At sixteen, joining the war to avoid me. At twenty-eight, leaving. At thirty, talking about running off to Japan to hide from his cousin. He was the selfish one.

I pulled myself up. "It's not going to happen, Kyunghwan."

He grabbed the hem of my hanbok. "You look at me now."

I did and saw his earnestness. Seated with his legs dangling off the stage, my hanbok in his fist, like a child. I knew what he was picturing—our perfect, imaginary life.

"We can do this," he said. "I've been waiting for this since we were sixteen. Now we have a way."

"Nothing's changed. I'd go to jail, or if we're lucky, we'd be outcasts. It would be worse than if I were a widow. Take my girls and come live here?"

"We could move to Japan."

"To the country that took my father and ruled over us? Where we couldn't ever be citizens?"

"Why are you doing this?" He stood and reached for my waist. His firm fingers sifted through my hanbok to find the curve of my ribs. The taste and press of him returned to me. How he'd made me gasp, always, with want. "You're thinking too much. What about America then? Anywhere."

I pulled away.

"Tell me," he said.

"You have no money." I stopped at the tables. With my hands outspread, I looked at him, the perfect line of his nose. Those thick eyebrows I loved to touch. Underneath his clothes, the freckles

I'd once traced across his chest, his arms. "I don't want to suffer anymore."

"Why do you always imagine the worst?"

I turned, annoyed at his insistence, and underneath that, at my own stupidity. Kyunghwan would never free me. He and Jisoo only wanted to declare me their own. As if I were barley, soap, a cow, a vessel for birth. Kyunghwan had never been confined, and he couldn't ever understand.

At the table, I balanced scented soaps atop each other, as high as I could go. Orange, pink, yellow. Green, white. He would never see as I did. As my world constricted, he dreamed of silly, impossible futures.

"It won't work," I said. "I gave up already."

He strode to me and pushed the bars over. Color spread across the floor, the soft soaps denting, barely making a sound. "I have a plan. It'll work."

I dug my nail into a white bar that smelled like cream. The shaving butted against my thumb, curling into a perfect wave. "We missed our chance, Kyunghwan. There's no point anymore."

He returned to the edge of the stage and sat down. I loved his back, the way his shoulders sloped and his bones jutted out like wings. I loved the taste of him—salt, musk, a filmy sweetness like persimmons.

"Why did you even find me, then?" His voice slunk low. "If you're going back?"

If only I had his assurance, his confidence in our world. "Because you knew me once," I said.

He let out a small, hurt sound.

I wanted to cradle him, to stroke his head as he fell asleep against my lap. The image stopped me. All I knew was how to mother.

"Kyunghwan," I called.

I would never see him again after this night. I would return home to my daughters. I didn't want to fight. "Let's get drunk. Let's be happy, the way we used to be."

Kyunghwan wanted to sneak me into his apartment or find a makgeolli bar that reminded us of our youth. I wanted to go back to the construction site. I liked the unfinished beams, the risk of collapse, the cold numbing my bones. Kyunghwan bought soju, and we returned to that open space. The soju was too harsh on the tongue, but I took it. Lying beside him and staring at the clouds, I did most of the drinking.

He only wanted to touch me. He concentrated on lining up the bottom scoop of our palms, his thick wrist to my thin. We had the same hands. The shape of our narrow fingers and squat nails, even the palm lines.

"You're frozen. Come to my apartment," he said. "The landlady's asleep by now."

I turned to him, my cheek touching concrete, his face too close to mine. White clouds plumed from his open mouth. "I'm staying here," I said.

He guided our hands through the air like mirrored birds. "Dance with me, then."

"We're not children anymore."

"Do it for me, tonight."

I let him lift me. We moved across the concrete floor, hands around each other's waists, digging into our coat folds for warmth, listening to nothing.

He kissed my hair, still a coward.

I kissed his lips and remembered a long-ago night in a ditch, the way the stars had dusted the night sky. I touched his short hair, the scar on his cheek. I let the alcohol loosen my thoughts.

"Do you remember that dog? When I visited?" he asked.

When he'd finally returned to me, he'd spent too much time with Jisoo and the girls. I had ached at his indifference, the keen gaze he swept over everyone else. One slow day, as he and I circled the land behind the house, I promised myself that I'd stop wanting him. It was almost evening. The clouds were streaky and thin, patterning the air with strips of purple. Solee's dog had trotted toward us. I touched the tree and watched Kyunghwan squat down.

"Feisty boy." He ruffled the dog's hair. "This one needs a wash."

"He's a dirty stray."

"Wash him with me." Kyunghwan looked up with a smile, the same tilted grin he had used on the aunties. "It'll be fun."

I found myself beside him, my hanbok skirt knotted above my knees. We turned a bucket of water over the dog's head and back and tail. We rinsed away the dirt. At first I wasn't sure. The water had numbed my fingers. Threading through the fur, Kyunghwan found my hands. I glanced beyond the house. Jisoo would return for dinner soon, but I didn't care. I'd wanted to stay there with our fingers interlaced, the animal breathing between us.

"I remember the dog," I said.

Kyunghwan hummed and circled us to the outer edges of the construction site. My dress caught on a splintery beam. He touched the bracelet I wore, rubbing the jade between his fingers. When I got home, I would put it away. I would stop thinking about him.

"That dog followed me the next morning, when I left," he said. "He stayed with me while I waited."

We knocked into the one raised wall. Kyunghwan slipped his hands underneath my coat. "I thought you would come," he said.

I pulled my thoughts away from his hands, from the thin cotton between our skins. I focused on his words. "Waited." I stopped. "That I would come?"

He tensed and gripped my hip. "At the bar—like I wrote."

"Wrote?"

I knew that morning. Over the past two years, I'd returned to it so often those early hours were like a film I carried with me. There was no note left behind. No explanation of when he would return, if he'd left for good.

I stepped back and the cold rushed between us. I closed my coat across my throat. "I don't know what you're talking about."

"I gave Solee a letter for you." Shadowed by the wall, in his black coat and gray suit, he was a surface of darkness, a smudged face.

I looked up at the unfinished beams puncturing the sky. There had once been a letter. A piece of paper he'd left with my child and that I'd never received, a thin sheaf, almost insubstantial, almost a bit of nothing.

I drew myself to him until we touched. Kyunghwan kept talking. He stroked my hands, my waist, my hair. Here was the yearning I had wanted from him all those years ago. It was too late.

I didn't want to know anymore. I was tired of the possibilities given to us in this life, and how bluntly even these slight chances burned away. I shifted his hands to hold me. His fingers behind my back, my cheek against his chest.

"Keep dancing, Kyunghwan."

I closed my eyes. I wouldn't open them until I heard movement, the swish of my dress across the concrete.

Solee

1966

AT MY FRIEND KYUNGHEE'S, WE STUFFED OUR SHIRTS with chamoes. Their rippled oval shape made awkward breasts, but it didn't matter. We were movie stars. In her room, we flung open the windows to let in the spring warmth and screamed into the streets, holding up our new chamoe parts. Youngsook and I followed Kyunghee, who shimmied the best. Later, when Kyunghee's mother offered us the fruit as a snack, we crackled with laughter.

Kyunghee held a melon slice to her lips like an oversize white smile. She sucked the seeds and sang along to her LP record. *"Unforgettable woman, I cannot forget her."* With her sticky palms, she grabbed me and Youngsook. "Sing!"

"Watching the raindrops fall, without words, we walked in silence. Unforgettable woman!" We jived to the guitar, stroking the air in front of us with flappy wrists. I mouthed the words, copying Kyunghee's shoulder rolling and Youngsook's hip shaking.

At the end of the song, Kyunghee collapsed onto her raised Western bed. "That is *rock*."

Youngsook draped herself over the bed, too. With her eyes closed and head propped on her elbow, she snapped her fingers to the next song. "I'm going to marry him. He'll teach me drums and then we'll be the rock couple of Korea."

I stood next to the bedside table. There wasn't room for me with them both sprawled out like that, and I couldn't think of anything clever or breathless enough to say. I didn't even know the rocker's name. We were the same age, Kyunghee, Youngsook, and I, but I felt colorless beside them.

"I wonder what kind of girls he likes," Youngsook said.

"He likes *women*," Kyunghee replied. "I saw a picture of him once. He was smoking a cigarette. He kind of looked like Teacher Shim."

"Maybe they're related. Or it's Teacher Shim's secret identity," Youngsook said.

"Teacher Shim?" I looked between them, wondering if they knew. "Why him?"

Youngsook flipped onto her stomach. "Why not? He's handsome."

"Except for his tic." Kyunghee twitched her eye. "If it weren't for that, he'd be perfect."

I laughed. Our science teacher had a boring, square face with his hair always combed and parted, but I knew his secret. Yesterday, I'd returned to class, searching for a barrette, a bright orange hair clip Uncle Hyunki had sent before he died. In the room, Teacher Shim sat on the edge of his desk. A girl I didn't recognize, a high schooler maybe, stood before him, her hand on his knee. He touched the skin of her waist, underneath her white shirt. They broke apart when I entered, but I saw their cheeks color.

"What are you smiling about?" Youngsook asked.

I stared at the ocean-blue stripes on the comforter and shrugged. "I don't think Teacher Shim's that good-looking."

Kyunghee slid a fashion magazine out from underneath her fluffy pillow. A woman in a red dress with a white collar tilted her head at the camera. "I bet he likes women like this. Don't you think?"

I didn't know who she was talking about anymore—Teacher Shim or the rocker—but I nodded, matching Youngsook's excitement.

Youngsook checked the time. "I have to go soon. You promised to let me try it on."

"Try what on?" I asked.

Kyunghee brushed her bangs out of her eyes and swung her feet off the bed. "Youngsook's growing. You better catch up." From her dresser, she pulled out a white brassiere. The cups looked like sleepy, half-closed eyes. "Put it on."

"Here?" Youngsook asked.

"I'll show you mine if it makes you feel better."

Kyunghee wasn't just pretty in a twelve-year-old way. Even teachers stared at her longer than they should. Fathers, boys from the partner school, strangers on the street. It was obvious that she was a student with her short hair, but it didn't matter. The slow tilt to her eyes, the way she scanned the men around her as if she knew what they were thinking, how she walked with her breasts pushed forward—her looks glinted like the sharp edge of a knife.

Kyunghee pulled off her shirt. She wore the same white brassiere underneath. Her breasts looked soft and powdery, like injulmi cakes.

"What if your mother comes in?" I asked.

"She would knock first." Kyunghee shrugged. "She read it in one of her 'Modern Women' articles. Come on."

Youngsook giggled and tossed off her shirt. She was growing, it was true, but her lumps pointed to the sides. Her nipples were brown and too small. "Help me put it on."

Kyunghee clasped the band behind Youngsook's back and surveyed the fit. Her hand hovered over Youngsook's right breast, as if she were about to squeeze or pet her. She brushed the edge of the white cup instead. "You'll need to get a smaller size, but this looks good. Very natural." She turned to me. "What about you?"

I shook my head. There wasn't anything to see and they knew it. "I'm not growing yet."

"Come on, show us." Kyunghee pulled up her straps, so her breasts looked like they were jumping. "You've got to have a little by now."

Youngsook twirled, gliding her chest from side to side. "Don't be a baby about it. You're so boring sometimes." She sat on the bed, still shirtless. Kyunghee did, too. Their stitched brassiere cups and belly buttons looked like faces making fun of me.

"I am *not*."

"You are. You're an angel."

They grinned with their shiny white teeth.

Kyunghee clapped. "I have a tiny brassiere from last year. That might work."

"I have something better than a brassiere. I have a real secret," I said.

Youngsook glanced at me, only half paying attention. She wanted to touch her new womanly parts and the cloth that covered them. I could tell from the way her fingers twitched against her knee. She adjusted her band instead.

"It's so bad I don't even know if I can tell you," I said. "It's about a grown-up doing something *sexy*."

Kyunghee nodded lazily, as if she used that word all the time, but her eyes focused on me. "Tell us, then."

Youngsook hugged a pillow. "What is it?"

I pushed myself onto the bed. They made room for me until we kneeled in a triangle. "Promise to keep it a secret?"

"Tell us," they said. "We promise."

"All right." I took a breath and closed my eyes. I waited until one of them nudged me. "Teacher Shim is having a *sex affair*. With a student."

They gasped the way I had wanted. Youngsook covered her mouth; Kyunghee shrieked with a hand on her forehead like a woman about to faint.

"With who?"

"How do you know?"

"Tell us everything."

When I returned home, the girls and Mother were spread out in the study, which was really Uncle Hyunki's old room. Jieun frowned through her multiplication problems, Mother napped by the windows, and Mila and Eunhee played with their paper dolls.

"Hi, Solee-unnie," Mila said. "I did my homework already."

"Hi, Solee-unnie," Eunhee copied in her garbled way, moving her paper doll up Mila's shoulder. "Rabbit Girl climb mountain."

"This problem makes no sense." Jieun twirled her pencil. "Why are you so late?"

"School stuff," I said.

"Mommy thinks you should have come home to help." Jieun held up her work. "I hate math."

"Mother knows math, too," I said. "She could have helped you."

"She said she didn't." Jieun stretched her thin arms. "Want to finish the rest for me? Please, Unnie? I'll give you a chocolate."

"Jieun." Mother opened her eyes. It was warm with the windows shut, and sweat shined her forehead. "You should have been here, Solee," she said as she picked at her shirt. "Until Daddy comes back, you need to help."

Jieun and I quieted. Father had left without telling us. Even mentioning his name made Mila and Eunhee cry. I avoided Mother's gaze. "I was studying."

"You think you're more important than everyone else, Yun Solee?"

"That's not what I said." I hugged my backpack. I had my own homework to do. Mother didn't see me, but still she asked me for everything.

"That's how you act." She raised herself up slowly and shook her head like an old dog. She flicked an eraser in my direction. She was mean and lazy and picked on me. I hated her sometimes. "Answer me. You think you can do whatever you want in this house?"

"Mama?" Eunhee whispered. I heard Mila and Jieun hush her.

I didn't look their way. I picked up the eraser, twisted its squishy green form between my fingers. "I'm going to change."

"You need to—"

I threw the eraser and turned to the door before she could say anything else. "I'll help them later."

In my room, I prayed with Halmuni's God necklace. The beads were carved with delicate roses and the cross dangled to my navel. The necklace, with its tired-looking Jesus, made me feel like I was praying the right way. I repeated, "Sorry, Teacher Shim," until it turned into a chant. He lent me books and didn't hit me if I turned in a homework sheet with Eunhee's scribbles on the back.

"We promise we won't say anything," Kyunghee and Youngsook had said, before they'd pushed for more details. When I couldn't remember, we imagined them with so much force they'd seemed real. Maybe Teacher Shim and the girl *had* been kissing before I entered. Their faces had been red; their lips, too.

I had the Jesus in my mouth when Jieun walked in. "What are you doing?" She sat beside me.

"Nothing." I slipped the necklace under my shirt and lay on our mat the way Kyunghee had, as if the ceiling held some important, mysterious answer. I made my eyes sleepy and hummed "The Woman in Rain." "I listened to a rock song on an LP machine today."

Jieun scooted next to me on the mat. "What's that?"

"Like on the radio, but you can listen whenever you want because it lives inside this black plate."

"Maybe Daddy will bring one home for us." She threaded her fingers through my hair. "Do you think he will?"

"Maybe." I tickled her knee to distract her from talking about Father. "My friend showed me a picture of a rock star today. You know who he reminded me of?"

"Who?"

"Uncle Kyunghwan." I started singing the words. *"Unforgettable woman."*

Jieun tried to hum along. She lay down, too. Our heads bumped and we giggled. "I only remember him this much." She pinched the air. "He had hair on his arms and I saw him dancing once."

"He was handsome."

"Mommy said you're a selfish girl."

I pulled out the necklace and squeezed the Jesus. I didn't want Jieun to worry about Mother. "She's probably tired."

"I guess." She turned so our foreheads touched. "Can you teach me the song?"

I trilled the words. Jieun bobbed her head against mine. She caught on quickly and we sang together, laughing through the parts we didn't know. "*I cannot forget her.*"

The next morning, I wanted to go to church. My friends attended every Sunday, wearing pretty white veils on their heads. I asked Mother as we cooked breakfast. She boiled potatoes and spinach while I scooped rice.

"Why do you want to go? Are you a sinner, Solee?" She curled her lips at me for a second.

I poured kkakdugi into banchan plates. "Are you mad at me because I was late yesterday?"

Mother laughed, wild, as if something was really funny. She wiped her brows and passed me the bowls. "Halmuni used to bring you to church sometimes. Go if you want, but I'm not taking you. Call your sisters."

The girls collected their meals on individual tray tables. We ate in silence outside the kitchen. Without Father, there was no point in arranging the dining table. Mother still set aside a covered bowl of rice for him, and we couldn't start until she had. The rules remained, just a little unclear.

"Eat," she said.

The food was tasteless. Even Mila shifted the spinach around her bowl. Mother had forgotten to go to the market. I knew it, and she did, too.

"What is this?" Jieun held a wet strand of spinach with her chopsticks.

"I think we need some soy sauce," I said. "Should I get some?"

"Food is for nourishment, to keep you from going hungry. Taste is second." Mother sipped her water in quick, tiny gulps. "Use the kkakdugi for flavor if you need to."

We did as she told us. The red-tinged rice with kimchi radish, blobs of potatoes, and stringy bits of spinach didn't taste much better. Mother was away, her mind folded into thoughts that had nothing to do with us. Sometimes I thought she was happier inside her head.

I'll make lunch, I mouthed to the girls.

"Mama?" Eunhee rolled her spoon so it clattered. She was the only one who still didn't know better. "When Daddy come?"

"Eunhee," Jieun warned.

Mother shook her arm as if we'd been tugging at her and shifted her attention back to the meal. Her voice was murky, as if a screen separated us. "When he's done with whatever he's doing. That's when he'll come back." She rose. "Maybe he's in Vietnam. Maybe he joined the war." She laughed and looked down at us. Her wrinkled hanbok collar exposed a triangle of pale, eggy neck. "You cook next time, Solee."

I rose. "I'm going to take them to church. I'll clean up when we come home."

"You think you're so grown-up." She held my chin tight, until it almost hurt, until her hard, blunt nails grooved into my skin. "Maybe you are. Maybe I'm just the idiot mother. Take them with you, then."

She jerked my head into a quick whip of a nod. I didn't understand the look on her face.

I turned to my sisters in front of the church. We wore matching yellow dresses, black shined shoes. I flattened the collars around their necks. The frilly seaming itched. We'd all complained about them at one point or another, but these dresses were the best we had. "Here." I handed them paper crosses. "I'm wearing this today"—I pointed to Halmuni's necklace—"but we can take turns every week. This is serious business. We have to stay quiet and not fight, okay?"

Jieun and Mila nodded. Eunhee stared at her shoes. She was too heavy for me to carry anymore, but I hefted her into my arms anyway. "Will you be good for me?"

"We sing here?" She rested her head against my neck.

We walked up the steps and entered as quietly as we could. Inside, a rust-red carpet led to a little stage. Families, grandmothers, aunties, and bald-headed grandfathers sat in the wooden pews. I chose the second to last one on the right and ushered the girls to their seats.

"I see my friend." Jieun pointed. "There in the gray shirt."

We played a game, identifying classmates and their families. I found Kyunghee and a few others. When the priest entered in his violet robes, we hushed. The church people stood. I made us stand, too. We copied everyone else. How they held their hands out by their sides, how they swayed just a little and sang from a paper booklet, how they kneeled on the floor to pray. Some had brought cushions for their knees. I wished I had been that smart.

"What do we pray about?" Mila asked.

"Whatever you want. Nothing selfish. Not for candy," I said.

Jieun grinned. "I'm going to, just in case."

I prayed for Father to come home soon, and I prayed for my lying. Mother had raged when she'd found out that he was gone. Still, I'd stayed quiet. I didn't tell anyone how he'd woken me early in the morning eight days ago. When he nudged my shoulder, I thought I'd overslept and sat up right away. "I'm going out of town for work." He placed an envelope on my knee. "Some money, in case something happens. Promise not to use it unless you have to." He held my head between his palms, like he was weighing it. "What do you want to do, Solee?"

"Now?" I whispered back. Jieun shifted next to me, and Father stilled until her breath steadied.

"When you grow up," he said. "What do you want to be when you're an adult?"

I'd never been asked a question like this by him or Mother. I didn't know the right answer. "A mommy?"

"Tell the truth."

A college student like Uncle Hyunki. A teacher. A maker of houses, buildings, bridges. There were things I could have said, but I didn't. My mouth stayed shut until Father shook his head. He petted my hair and told me to go back to sleep.

I prayed he wasn't in Vietnam, as Mother had joked. Teacher Shim had shown us an article about our soldiers going to war there. We'd passed around the paper, careful to hold the edges of the thin gray sheet. I hadn't read the words, distracted by the picture of Korean soldiers. One man stared right at the camera. His eyes were two black gonggi stones surrounded by white, and he had a wilted mouth. His skin looked grimy, as if he'd been speckled with dirt or blood or fear.

The priest hit a small gong and stepped down from his stage. People lined up before him. Women and men opened their mouths. He placed something white and circular on their tongues.

"What's that?" Jieun asked.

"I'm not sure."

"I want to try." She squeezed into the aisle. I grabbed the back of her dress, but she wrenched away. We watched her wait in line. She held up her head like she'd done this before.

When she reached the front, the priest bent to her level. He might have smiled, but he didn't place a white circle in her mouth. Mila and Eunhee held on to the back of the pew in front of us. "Solee-unnie?"

"Don't make a fuss," I said under my breath. "Jieun, you better not."

The people waiting behind her forced Jieun to walk on. She didn't whine or cross her arms, but when a friend of hers tried to catch her attention, she pretended not to notice. She strode with her head raised, right past us, through the doors, and into the street. A few rows ahead, Kyunghee raised her eyebrows at me.

"Oh, Jieun." I brushed the God necklace against my lips. It had a faint rosy smell. "Let's go." I grabbed Mila's hand, who grabbed Eunhee's hand, and we walked down the aisle as fast as we could.

Outside, I yelled at Jieun. "Why did you do that? You embarrassed us in front of all those people!"

She sat on the steps with her back to us. I couldn't see her face, but I knew she was rolling her eyes. She was never afraid of me. "It was boring anyway."

"Then I'll come by myself from now on." I started down the road with Mila and Eunhee. I could hear Jieun coming after us, but I didn't slow down.

"He wasn't mad," she said as she caught up. "He told me we'd have to take classes first."

"What classes?" Mila asked.

"I don't know. Church classes." Jieun tried to loop her arm through mine. I pushed her away. Turning to each of them, I ripped up their paper crosses. That made Eunhee cry, but I didn't care.

We walked on in silence. As we turned the corner past a new clothing shop, Kim Junghee stopped me. She was one of the loudest first-years at my school, always bragging about chewing gum and then getting caught the next second. I didn't notice her until her chubby face was right in front of mine. "So," she asked, "is it true?"

"Is what true?"

She took a step back but stood fast. Whatever she wanted was more pressing than my anger. She tilted her head. "You saw Teacher Shim naked with a student?"

Mila clutched Eunhee and yelled, "That's not allowed!"

"A teacher was naked?" Jieun asked. "How?"

"That's disgusting!" I waved my arms. "That never happened!"

Junghee smirked.

"Who said that?" I asked.

"What did it look like? His man parts?"

I wanted to hit her. Little Eunhee was there. Mila, too. I wanted to call her a dirty girl with a loose mouth, but no words came out. I looked at Junghee's smug face, at my sisters.

"Well?" Junghee crossed her arms. "What're you being so shy about now? Maybe it was you who was naked?"

Jieun stepped between us. "My unnie said she didn't see anything."

Junghee stared down at Jieun. "Everyone's talking about it."

"Tell them they're wrong." Jieun linked my arm in hers and we walked away in a row.

"You're lying!" Junghee called after me. "You saw him!"

"Eat shit!" Jieun yelled back, turning all the way around and placing her hands on her hips.

Jieun squeezed my elbow as we watched Junghee retreat. Happiness washed over her long, thin face, her furrowed eyebrows and sharp mouth. She was breathing hard but grinning. "Remember what Mommy said? When they make fun of us, you say the foulest thing you can think of, or they'll keep coming back."

I felt hot and sick as we walked home. I cried and that made me feel even stupider. Jieun dried my eyes with one of those lacy veils. "Where did you find that?" I asked between hiccups.

"On the ground, outside the church."

"You shouldn't have taken it. It's someone's."

"Who cares?" She wiped some more. "Don't cry."

Mila and Eunhee petted my arms and cooed. They consoled me, my better sisters.

"I didn't say that about my teacher." I wrung the little Jesus and the rosy beads between my fingers. "I didn't see him."

"We believe you," Jieun said.

"I draw you picture," Eunhee said. "Make happy."

"Me too. I will, too," Mila said. "I'll write you a poem."

I stopped them at our front gate. We could hear Mother humming in the back. "Don't tell her," I said. "Keep it a secret, just us?"

We kissed our palms and connected our hands in a circle. "Sealed together," we said, and kissed one another on the lips for extra promise. Then they all ran to Mother.

Cross-legged on a rush mat beneath the tree, she beckoned with open arms. "I missed my girls all morning. Come here to me."

My sisters rolled onto their backs, fighting to be near her, to touch her hand or hair or hip. I felt queasy, my stomach clenching like I had smelled something too strong. I hadn't said anything about a naked anyone. I hadn't said anything like that. I could see the rumor unraveling in all directions. I knew how stories worked. Father had told me. *Even words without feet can travel across the country.*

Mother pinched my ankle, a quick nip, like a mosquito bite. "Frowny Solee. I was under this tree today and I decided. I'll forgive you."

"Forgive?" I rubbed the skin beneath my eyes and wondered if she'd heard about Teacher Shim. "For what?"

Mother hugged the girls closer. She kissed Eunhee's head. "Come lie with us, Solee. Even the grass seems shinier today."

I tried to tamp down my unease, flatten it like a balloon. We lay in a row, tilted our heads to the sun, and tried to drink up the rays in case they disappeared tomorrow. "In case spring decides to leave us," Mother said. The branches threw shadows, slicing us into parts. A bird sang, but we couldn't find it. "There," one of us would say, and then it was gone, singing from another branch. When a fat cloud passed over us, Mother scavenged for white clovers. She taught us how to poke a hole into the base of the stem with our fingernail, to thread another clover in. "Your halmuni taught me this when I was little," she said. "My mother."

We made rings, bracelets, necklaces, and a clover crown. "Next week, we'll picnic at the river," she said. "We'll make a flower blanket." I liked Mother when she was like this, easy and floating, her mind still connected to our world. Her attention homed in on each of us for moments at a time so we felt special, seen.

When we grew hungry, we ventured inside. The tray tables were as we'd left them this morning—empty plates and bowls; hardened, half-eaten rice; chopsticks on the floor. Eunhee ran to the kitchen and reported back to us, her hands clutched to her stomach. "Nothing cooking."

"Put on your shoes." Mother herded us to the entranceway, clapping her hands. "We'll treat ourselves. We can't have you girls hungry."

In town, we ordered instant ramen and bags of juice to go. "I don't want to be around anyone else but you four," Mother said. On our way home, we ran into Auntie Mun. I bowed, my arms weighed down with baskets, and the girls followed. We watched Mother. She didn't like Auntie and the rest of her family.

Auntie Mun clapped at our haul of food. "I didn't think Jisoo was the ramen type."

"He's on a business trip," Mother said. "I'm sure he didn't mention it to your husband. I told Jisoo your family can't keep their mouths shut."

Auntie Mun's eyebrows hiked up. "You don't need to be rude."

"I can be ruder." Mother swung her arm, her baskets thudding with the sudden movement, and thrust out her hip. "Should I show you?"

I saw the prick in Auntie's gaze, how she reared and took in Mother's wrinkled top and mussy bun, and realized she thought something was wrong with us. Her lips tightened into a cluck. I squeezed Jieun, who tugged on Mother. "Let's go," we said.

Auntie looked at me, her smile an invitation. "Is she this unpleasant with her daughters, too?"

Mother laughed. "You know that saying, *You can't spit at a smiling face?* With yours, I can."

"You already have grievances with half the people in town." Auntie steepled her fingers against her temples and widened her eyes. "You don't need to add me to the list."

"Does Mr. Kim's wife have a grievance with you?"

Auntie's hand fell. "I don't know what you're talking about."

"People gossip so freely when they think no one's listening." Mother handed her baskets to Jieun and picked up Eunhee, who'd begun to whine. "About married women and their lovers. About Mr. Kim and a certain ridiculous woman."

Auntie's eyebrows struggled across her face.

"There are laws, you know," Mother said.

"I really don't know what you mean."

Mother stared at her until she won. Auntie ducked her head, her face pink, and walked past us. "Goodbye, Mun Soonhee," Mother called after her.

Back home, we heated a pot of water over an outdoor fire. The conversation with Auntie had loosened the stitches inside Mother. She talked fast, moved with renewed energy. I wanted to be this way, someone who could slant situations to her liking, who felt stronger after a fight.

"What were you talking about with Auntie?" I asked.

"Silly adult things." Mother dumped the hard prepared noodles into the pot. "Don't worry about it even for a moment."

We boiled eggs. She sliced peppers, rice cakes, scallions, and told us stories. "This is how Uncle Hyunki and I cooked with Halmuni."

"Tell us," Jieun said.

"We didn't have enough food. And no instant ramen! But it's the same memory. Spring nights, hot broth." She lugged out the biggest bowl we had, the one Father used on New Year's and Chuseok, and poured in the ramen. We slurped together.

"Tastes like magic!" Eunhee sucked the noodles one at a time, fluttering her eyelids.

Mother cried a little, the tears smearing her face. She hugged Eunhee. "Magic," she said.

I didn't want to go to school the next morning. The balloon of unease had inflated inside me again, and Junghee's rumor about the naked bodies made my palms sweat. Jieun knew without saying. She took over dressing the others and even braided Mila's wispy hair. When they were ready, she opened the bedroom door. "I left Eunhee with Mommy. Ready to go?"

"Yeah." I pulled on my jacket. "Thanks for helping."

"I bet no one's talking about it anymore."

"I don't care anyway." I practiced my blank face. "Do I look like I care?"

Jieun sucked in her cheeks.

"Let's go," I said.

I walked Jieun and Mila to their elementary school. Mila held our hands and talked about her dreams, her favorite drawings, why apples were not a good fruit. At the gate, they both hugged me goodbye. Jieun smiled. "The foulest thing you can think of. Remember?"

"Dumbass," I practiced.

"With more anger. You *dumbass*!" Jieun laughed at her own forcefulness. "Don't worry. No one will be talking about it." She ran to her friends in the yard.

But when I arrived at my school, I couldn't find my friends anywhere. I was late and our classroom was empty. *To the auditorium* was written on the chalkboard. All the first-years were there in a line. Onstage, a woman and a man in white coats sat behind square desks. A teacher in the front yelled at us to be quiet. I looked for

Kyunghee and Youngsook, but Junghee found me at the back of the line. "Do you think this is about Teacher Shim?" She smiled openmouthed, like a dumb ox. "You think they found out? Maybe they'll quiz us on what we know."

A girl between us joined in. "I heard he's going to be fired."

"Why are you telling me?" I tried to look bored. I picked at the skin on my left thumb with my pen point.

"Why do you think?" Junghee whispered.

The girl smiled. "Is it true? That it was Kyunghee you saw?"

I stopped. Junghee caught my Monami pen and twirled it away from me. "You said it was a student with big breasts," she said.

"And she's got the biggest."

"Give it back—I didn't say anything!" I jumped but Junghee was taller and wider.

"Everyone, listen!" Teacher Park clapped her hands. "Pull up your sleeves. All the way. Tuberculosis shots."

Whimpers wove through the room. We all turned to Teacher, our identical black bobs swiveling toward the stage. We'd heard these shots hurt, that they left a scar. I waited for more, but Teacher didn't say anything else.

Junghee raised her hand. "I already have one. I don't need to get it again, do I?"

"You better not be lying, Kim Junghee." Teacher strode to the back, where we stood. The girls in line turned to watch, their heads rippling. Some saw me, pointed, and whispered. They were looking at Junghee. They weren't looking at me. I stared at the podium onstage and hoped.

"Let me see." Teacher Park examined the mark on Junghee's right shoulder. The line loosened a little so the closest girls could see. A glossy, puckered indent marred her skin. It was ugly and craggy and pale, the size of a thumbprint. "Room 202. Teacher Kim will have work for you. Everyone else back in line!"

Junghee jeered at me as she collected her books. She stuck my pen behind her ear. "If they ask, I'm going to tell them you know everything."

"I don't!" I reached for my pen, but she moved out of the way.

"Enjoy the shot. It hurts," she said.

I felt sicker the closer we got to the stage. Girls *were* looking at me, glancing sideways, their short hair swinging around their ears, mouthing things I couldn't hear. Behind Teacher Park and the nurses' backs, they pretended to jiggle breasts, tittering at their cupped hands. I shielded myself with all the curse words I knew. I skimmed the crowds, pretending I was Mother when she'd fought against Auntie Mun. But still I pricked at the whispers. "Naked." "Solee." "Did you hear?"

My shield broke open. All my classmates had heard. Junghee had taken my present from Uncle Kyunghwan. Father was missing. I was going to have an ugly scar.

When I reached the front of the line, Teacher Park rolled my uniform sleeve higher on my shoulder. "How are you doing, Yun Solee?"

I concentrated on the nurse ahead of me, her beige, rubbery gloves. "I'm well, Teacher."

"Is there anything you'd like to tell me?"

"I haven't had this shot before."

"Not about this." She held on to my sleeve. "Anything in private?"

I shook my head.

"Principal Lee wants to speak to you afterward."

I started to cry. It was my turn. The nurse waved me over. She held a plastic tube with nine barbs at one end, ready to puncture my skin. "There's no need to get weepy. You're a big girl now. A middle schooler!"

I prayed to God that I wouldn't get in trouble. That the shot wouldn't hurt. That Principal Lee wanted nothing to do with me. That somehow Father would come home and save me and return everything to its normal shape.

"Look away if you need to. Take a deep breath and count to three."

It more than hurt. It seared. But when I screamed, it wasn't because of the pain.

She strode in through the side doors, yelling my name. Girls in uniforms parted before her. They knew who she was, with her old-fashioned hanboks and her lurching moods, her upturned eyes and smooth, pale skin. The girls had always used Mother's full, wide cheeks against me, saying they didn't understand, with my big chin and slight eyes, how could I come from such a Miss Korea?

I spotted Kyunghee in the crowd, a smile wrecking her face. Youngsook stood on tiptoes trying for a better view as Mother stormed the stage.

"Yun Solee!" She grabbed me in front of everyone, pulled me off the chair in one ragged sweep. I stumbled to my feet, held up by her grip. I felt the bodies around us push back, gasping.

Mother pressed into the swell on my arm, not caring about the audience or her writhing daughter. "Is it true? Are you lying? Are you cutting down another person's life?"

I heard a scream, a high-pitched girl-shriek, but it hadn't come from me. My voice was lost, too afraid of her buzzing body. She wrenched me closer. "You do whatever you want, don't you?"

She doubled, shadowed in front of me. The nurse's strange,

beige fingers grabbed Mother and tried to wrest her off me. "Please! You're hurting her!"

Behind me, somewhere far away, Teacher Park's voice carried across the room, tilting high to rein in all the chatter. "Everyone out! Shut up and turn around!"

Mother continued to shake me, my teeth clattering like gumballs, candy, stones. She pushed away the nurse. "You're a ruiner, Solee. You ruin people."

"I didn't say anything," I spilled out, my teeth too big in my mouth, hitting my tongue, my arm melting into a puddle of heat. "I didn't say anything about Teacher Shim."

She dragged me to the stairs, tumbled me down, my feet barely landing on the wooden steps. My shoes, new white sneakers, like flashes of clouds. "You ruined everything. Where's my letter, Solee?"

I held on to the stage with one hand. She would rip me apart like a doll. I would be armless; the stuffing would fall out of me. I looked around for help—patches of black hair, the sound of feet running away. Mother's face was too close, nearly touching mine, her hair stormy and undone. She crowded everyone out.

"Where's my goddamn letter? What did you do with it?" She didn't let go. She shouted and shouted.

❀

Teacher Shim was dismissed that afternoon and my classmates didn't speak to me for a long time afterward. Not because of my storytelling—the girls envied the power I'd wielded with my words—but because of Mother, her explosion and retreat. I imagined them whispering about us with their slight, satisfied smiles.

I didn't care. What I didn't understand was Mother. I didn't know what she was yelling about, a letter from Father about his leaving? From the school about my lies? She took me out of class that day. She dragged me to the river and wept as I watched the bubble on my arm inflame, red and oozing. She said it wasn't my fault, that it was always her. That she was always too late and too weak. She blamed the world we lived in.

I didn't understand. I concentrated on my arm, too scared to watch her salt the ground. I imagined getting an infection. I remembered Uncle Hyunki. The way Mother had repeated the word *tuberculosis* when she'd returned with his body. I imagined him dying, then me dying. She would regret hurting me if I was dead. She'd weep at my tumulus, unable to stop. The girls alone without me. I was scared for us all.

I figured out what she meant only later.

The letter. My young, simple anger. I had thrown it away years ago. I dug up the ground in the backyard, but all the little pieces were gone. I wanted to tell her I was sorry, to give her that much. But Father had returned by then, and when I approached her in their room and kneeled before her bare, cracked feet, Mother didn't respond.

She only stared at me with dark, blank eyes.

Part 5

Jisoo

1967

I WANTED THEM TO SEE THE OCEAN. HOW IT WAS DIFFER-
ent from the ponds and rivers of their hometown. I wanted them to
feel its strength and want something greater than what Haemi and
I had to give them.

The girls ran screaming into Busan's blue waters. In their red
bathing suits, they plunged and splashed with two plastic tubes to
share between them. Birds flapped high in the same sky Haemi and
I had once stood under. All around us, parents sank into the wet
sand and watched their children swim.

"The water's too cold for them," Haemi said, though it was
mid-July and the sun blazed. A straw hat covered her face. She
tilted its brim so it hit below her ears.

"They'll be fine together," I said.

We sat on towels drinking tea from paper cups. Haemi had
rounded out in the past year, and in the sun, it looked wholesome,
good. I let myself wonder if she was pregnant, only for a moment.
She could tell when I thought this way, and she hated it.

"They'll always remember this," I said. "The time we took
them to Busan."

"You're turning into a sensitive man at thirty-three?" She
cupped my scarred shoulder in a quick, graceless way, as if by accident. "It'll be a good memory."

I wanted her hand on me. She touched easily or not at all these days—mostly not at all. Something flitted within her, from extreme to extreme. I hoped to fix her with this trip, with a reminder of how far we had come. Even Busan, once brimming with war-lost refugees, was now clean and thriving.

"Do you want to go into the water?" I asked.

She scooted into the shade of the tent I'd rented. It was square, white, and rippled in the wind. A red stripe on one of the posts marked it as ours. All the others on the beach had painted bands, each a different color. Families clustered underneath them, some clearly visitors like us, with bags, snacks, towels, fishing equipment. The locals had nothing but a sheet to lie on. Haemi trickled sand through her fingers, forming small anthills around her. "I like the sound from here, the waves."

I touched her knee. She wore the new bathing suit I'd bought—bright blue with a yellow flower on the skirt. I stroked the slippery fabric. I liked how it revealed her body in segments, her limbs pale, unaccustomed to such exposure. "Let's splash around with the girls," I said.

She waved. "I'll cut some apples for when they get hungry. I want to stay here, maybe sleep."

"Come play, Haemi. You can nap later."

"You go." She tried to smile. "I'm tired."

I walked toward our daughters and the ocean. Waist deep in the waves, they took turns on the swim rings. "Be careful with Eunhee," I called from the shore, even though they didn't need reminding.

With small, clumsy fingers, Eunhee wiped the wet curls from her eyes. "I'm okay! Come push, Daddy."

"I'm a shark!" I dove in. Below the current, I gnawed at their legs until even their squeals were spent.

"No more tickling!" Mila, sprawled on one ring, linked her leg through the other to bring Eunhee closer. They tossed their heads back and squinted in the light. Jieun and Solee hung on to the rubber handles with slack arms.

"Look." Mila pointed to a seagull soaring. "I painted a bird for Mommy yesterday."

Jieun lapped around us, popped up behind me, and hugged my stomach. "This is fun, Daddy."

Solee nodded, her freckled chin propped on Eunhee's foot. "This is great."

One after another, they chimed in their agreement. I laughed and loaded two to a tube and pulled them through the deep water. They sang a school song I didn't know. Solee, Jieun, Mila, and Eunhee. My girls were a sufficient world.

When the waves picked up, we made rabbits and turtles in the sand. Haemi woke to us scattered all around her. Jieun and Mila sat at the foot of the tent, while Solee and Eunhee were farther down by me, directly in the sun. Haemi linked her hands over her head and stretched her arms. "What're we making now?"

"Sand creatures," Mila said. "I'm doing fishies."

Eunhee motioned. "Come see, Mama."

"Look at ours first." Jieun kicked and tried to present her turtles.

A small spray of sand landed on Haemi's arms as she crawled out of the tent. She sucked her teeth and swatted at Jieun's feet. "You're getting sand all over me."

"Hey!" Jieun rubbed the top of one foot with the sole of the other. "You don't have to hit."

Haemi reared upright with her hands on her hips. "You knew I was right behind you. And that didn't hurt." She retreated to the tent and touched her toes. "Damn. I'm sunburned."

"It *did* hurt," Jieun said.

Eunhee and Solee stopped patting sand over my buried hands. They were like animals with their instinct for tension. Mila turned slowly from Jieun to Haemi, still clutching pebbles for the creatures' eyes and teeth.

"Come here." Solee beckoned. "Leave Mommy alone."

Mila scrambled toward us, dropping stones, but Jieun stood with her back to Haemi, her hands at her sides, echoing her mother's pose of irritation. She glanced at a nearby tent, where a young family watched us. The mother hastily looked away. Jieun straightened. "Daddy! Tell Mommy she's being mean."

"Come play with your sisters," I said.

"I didn't kick sand on purpose." She trudged to me. "I was showing her the turtles."

"Replace my hand in the mound," I instructed. "No fighting on vacation."

Haemi hugged her knees. "Who's fighting? I just woke up and I'm sunburned." She flexed a red foot at me. Her shoulders were pink, too. "Let's go back to the hotel."

The girls' heads popped up. "No!" They cast sour lips and big eyes in Haemi's direction. "Please? Can we stay?"

"Wrap your feet and you'll be fine." I threw an extra towel at her. "Play a little with your children."

"Jisoo." Haemi stared at the sky. From the way she held her shoulders up by her ears, I knew. The girls knew, too. The goodness from this morning had been sucked out of her.

"Don't ruin a fine afternoon," I said.

"From the looks on your faces, I already have. I'm going."

"But you haven't even done anything with us," Jieun said.

"Stay and spend some time with your children." I was too loud now, almost yelling.

"You're bothering the other families." Haemi pointed to the nosy woman with the child. "Don't be so dramatic."

Mila ran to her. "We can make you new creatures."

"Stay for an hour?" Solee asked. "We won't spray you anymore."

"I look ridiculous in this swimsuit." Haemi brushed sand from her thighs and pulled on her dress. She squatted before Eunhee and rearranged her curls. "Hi, you. Want to come with me?"

Eunhee pointed to her sand animals. "I want to stay."

Haemi pulled herself up. "I'll be ready by dinnertime, then."

She plodded through the sand with unsteady steps, almost as if she were drunk. The girls watched as she wound her way through the families, crossed the main street, and entered our hotel. Then their dark heads turned to me.

"Now what?" Jieun crossed her sandy, slender arms.

"Should we go back, too?" Solee asked.

"We can go fishing." I rummaged through our beach bag for the box of wooden bobbers and picked up the rods we had brought. "We haven't done that yet."

"There aren't any real fishes." Jieun smashed her sand animals. "Everything's ruined."

Mila peered at the waving tent. "It's windy. But we can if you want, Daddy."

"Let's go," Solee said.

They collected their things and I brandished the rods in the air. "Fishing!"

Eunhee patted my hand. "Fishing, Daddy."

A sudden wind had roughened the waters. Nearly all the swimmers had retreated. We waded in anyway. I distributed the rods. Solee tested a hook with her finger. "Is this safe?"

She was right. I couldn't bring bloodied or cut-up girls back to Haemi. "Wait here. Don't move." I returned to our tent and used a paring knife to remove the hooks.

"What's the point then?" Jieun asked when I showed them the blunted lines.

"There are bobbers still." I showed her the wooden cylinders. "Just do it."

We practiced casting with glum faces and stiff hands. Solee arched her rod to the greatest height, and Jieun tried to copy her. Mila rubbed the clear, tight line between her fingers, and around her wrists. I tried to help Eunhee hold her rod steady.

"Too big." She looked up with a bleary face. "Don't want to, Daddy."

I stuck our two rods into the sand so they wouldn't float away and hoisted her onto my shoulders. Even she knew to balance her weight on my stronger side. "Let's watch the others."

She hugged my head. "Watch birds, too."

Chicken-fleshed and shivering, the girls pretended to focus on their imaginary fish. I knew we were all thinking of her. Haemi acted powerless even as she turned our heads around. As soon as she beckoned, they ran to her, no matter how small her offering. A sliver of happiness was enough. I could yell, threaten, shake her, but Haemi only did as she pleased.

Solee lowered her rod. "This isn't working."

I gathered the girls close. Their lips were pale, bluish. The wind whipped strands of thick black hair across their pure faces. "Let's do something else. We'll go to the market."

"Can we all get a treat?"

"Please, Daddy?"

"Or one treat and we'll share?"

"Maybe we can go to the park?"

"But I'm hungry."

"Yes," Eunhee added, from above my head. "Treats!"

They became unwieldy so quickly—four girls, four requests, four bodies to watch over as they rushed from one thought to the next.

We returned to the hotel after the market, our bags laden with too many souvenirs. The girls raced to Haemi as soon as we entered the room. Seated in the middle of the carpeted floor, she summoned them with her arms outstretched, as if nothing was wrong. "Show me what Daddy bought you!"

"We got puffed rice!"

"Candy!"

"Toys!"

"And this silk so you can make a pretty dress!"

"You should have bought more. Then I could have made dresses for all of us," Haemi said.

"Like this one?" Jieun touched the buttons running down Haemi's front. "Or like your hanboks?"

I sat on the raised bed and watched the girls flit around their mother. I couldn't remember the last time I'd seen her wear a modern dress. I recognized the green and white stripes. I'd bought it years ago, to help her fit in with the other women in town. She'd laughed as she tried it on, the fabric tight across her waist and hips.

"I want a dress, too. We can go back." Mila nuzzled the silk against her cheek. "Get more for us."

Haemi rubbed the other end of the fabric between her fingers. "It's so shiny and yellow. I bet Daddy picked this out." She looked at me with a smile I couldn't understand spreading across her lips. "Am I right?"

"Solee picked it out," I said, even though I had. "Our dinner reservation's in an hour."

"Time to wash, then. I'll put these away. You all go to the bathroom. We need to clean up for dinner." Haemi lifted Eunhee's shirt, stopped. "You're still wearing your swimsuit."

"Mine red," Eunhee said, pushing out her stomach.

"They're *all* red, babo," Jieun replied.

Haemi glanced at me. "Why are they still wearing wet suits? They'll get sick." She turned to the girls. "Hands up." She clucked, pulled the shirts off Mila and Eunhee. "Solee and Jieun, take them to the shower. Leave the suits in the sink."

When we were alone, she threw the clothes in the garbage. I picked them out and hung them across the open window. "So they're a little damp," I said.

"You don't have any sense."

"And you do? Where were you?"

Haemi wandered around the two beds. "I had a bad dream on the beach and I didn't sleep well here, either. I hate these Western beds. Sleeping off the ground makes me nervous."

"How was I supposed to know? If you'd told me, we could have reserved one of their traditional rooms."

Haemi lay on the bed closest to the door. The hem of her striped dress rode up, revealing her slip and thick pink thighs. "Well, *I* know more than you think—we can't afford this."

I sat beside her, close enough to feel the heat from her sunburn. "Can't you just enjoy yourself?"

She dug the heel of her hand into my leg. "I was trying to *enjoy* a little sleep and now you're arguing with me."

"You know how many families go on vacation?"

"I keep track of the girls every day. You know how hard that is?" I laughed.

She pushed me off the bed. "Don't. I'm not joking."

"You're ridiculous. Your life isn't that difficult, Haemi." This was the nicest seaside hotel in Busan. She was selfish, yes, and also ungrateful and unaware.

In the bathroom, the girls stood in a line by the showerhead, unaccustomed to its snaking tube. The whole floor was drenched and suds swirled around the drain in the center of the room. Solee coached them under the water one by one. They tilted their heads as she washed the shampoo from their wet strands. Jieun and the younger ones were still flat, sexless, but Solee's body was changing. She reddened when she saw me looking. "We'll be done soon."

"Close the door, Daddy!" Mila splashed. "Cold air's coming in!"

I did as they asked and turned to Haemi. She was still lying down, staring at the ceiling as if focusing hard enough would make me quit. "Something's wrong with you. That's why we're here," I said.

She laughed in a limp way. "I'm fine."

"Solee takes care of them. Not you."

"Why don't you ever buy me yellow dresses?"

"What are you talking about?" I leaned against the bathroom door. I never could follow the strange turns in Haemi's thoughts. "You want me to buy you more clothes?"

"Do you know the last time I wore this dress?" She pinched the green-and-white hem and trailed her hand up to her throat. With quick fingers, she unbuttoned the top to her waist. Beneath her slip, the full white cups of her brassiere.

"What do you want from me, Haemi?"

She sighed. "Forget it. I put on a modern dress for our modern vacation. Leave me alone."

I stared at my hands, angry at her for confusing and arousing me. I pointed to the bathroom. "Go watch the girls. They're making a mess."

She buttoned her dress and lifted herself with exaggerated effort. "Yes, sir, husband," she mocked, saluting. Then she pushed past me into the bathroom, closed and locked the door.

We walked to dinner a few streets away. Even with the extra weight, Haemi was lovely; passing women and men lingered over her face. With her modest smile and straight, unyielding back, she looked like any decent wife. She chattered with the girls about sugar candy dessert and the possibility of a late-night swim.

She cared for them well when she wanted to. I understood what she'd meant about keeping track of them all—how tiresome it was—but she was a mother and this was her burden. I didn't have any pity for that kind of grievance.

When we reached the restaurant, I spread my arms. "We're here. Our first Italian meal."

"Here?" Haemi peered at the menu pasted to the door. Bright illustrations of pasta, fish, cheeses, coffees, and cakes accompanied descriptions. The restaurant's large glass windows overlooked the ocean. "The best and only Italian restaurant that I know of, sir," the hotel woman had said.

"What's Italian?" Jieun asked.

"A country in Europe." Solee pointed. "It's far from here."

"I knew that," Jieun replied. "I was only checking."

I pulled both girls into the restaurant and called to the others. "Let's show Mommy what the food's like."

We entered to classical music and the murmur of servers addressing diners in hushed voices. Women in short black dresses and aprons bowed to us. "Welcome," they said in unison.

"Jisoo." Haemi stopped behind me. "Not here." She gestured to herself. "I feel too old."

"You're wearing a modern dress, like you said."

"It's not the clothes. It's me. I feel old. And I smell cheese."

The girls nodded, wrinkling their noses.

"Cheese is disgusting," Jieun said.

"We don't want that, Daddy," Mila added.

"You think we'll find a restaurant like this at home?" I bent down to the girls. "This will be special."

"I really can't," Haemi said.

"We can't," Eunhee echoed.

Only Solee looked at me with any apology. She squeezed my hand. "Is there somewhere else?"

"You choose, then." I walked out. I wouldn't force them anymore.

They found another restaurant, one that was wooden and familiar. An open stove burned in the kitchen despite the summer heat. Haemi propped her elbows on the table and read the menu aloud.

"Dongnae pajeon, milmyeon, daeji gukbap. Old Busan favorites. How does that sound?" She held Eunhee on her lap and grazed my knee with her perfect fingernails. "Thanks for agreeing."

"It's fine."

She smiled. "I mean it. Thank you. Cranky Haemi's gone now, I promise."

I reminded myself that Haemi was a woman who loosened with familiarity. Maybe I was forcing too much change on her. "Let's order some soju," I said.

We drank, we ate. Haemi attacked her food as if she were a refugee again. She doled out fried baby octopus to the girls and warned them to be careful with their hot stone pots. "You know who loved daeji gukbap? Uncle Hyunki," she said.

"Really?" Solee asked.

Haemi nodded. "On lucky days, we'd get pork bones from the field hospital where I worked. Hyunki would scrounge into my bag before even saying hello!"

I raised my glass. The girls followed with their waters. "To Uncle Hyunki, then."

"And my mother," Haemi said.

"To us also. We met here," I told the girls. "Your mother and I."

We toasted to my parents and sister, our country's lost and missing, and to eventual reunification. To each of our daughters. We drank too much. "One more," Haemi said each time, until Jieun, Mila, and Eunhee had fallen asleep. They nested their heads in their arms. Solee fingered the patterns on the table and listened to our slurred phrasing. Haemi was laughing and fine and I didn't want it to stop. She touched her hair, my fingers. I was confident this was all we'd needed—a trip away from home, a reminder of the happiness we were capable of as a family.

"Have some soju." Haemi pushed a shot to Solee. "We won't tell anyone."

"I don't want to." Solee leaned on her elbows. "I'm too young."

Haemi touched the freckles on her daughter's nose. "We should lighten these. They're ugly."

Solee covered her face with one hand. "Really?"

"I'm joking." Haemi smiled, almost meanly. "Relax." She blew at Solee's bangs. "If you're not having fun, Miss Intelligent, Favorite, Eldest Daughter, we can go."

"Let's stay. We're on vacation," I said.

"Vacation." Haemi stretched the syllables like a noodle. "That's a word I don't think I'll ever understand. Right, Solee?"

I could feel the shift in Haemi's mood, and I didn't want this night to end. I pushed the shot closer to our daughter. "Drink a little. Drink with your parents."

Solee looked at me, her eyes clouding, but did as I asked.

When all the other families were gone, and only the old men were left, we turned to our sleepy, tipsy first daughter. "Go put the girls to bed." We shoved won into her hands. "Walk down the main street and you'll be fine."

"All of them?" She squinted at their soft, lolling heads. "They're asleep."

"Carry Eunhee. You can do it." We woke Jieun and Mila. Haemi fluttered her fingers over their sweaty heads, kissed them on their mouths. They were disoriented and docile. Solee frowned but picked up Eunhee. The others hugged her legs as they walked out the door.

"There are so many of them," I said.

"So many!" Haemi raised her glass. "How did our parents do it?"

"They didn't really. Not ours."

She leaned on my shoulder. "That's true. But still, so many."

"I don't even know how old they are," I said.

She laughed. "You're awful. Three, seven, eleven, and thirteen."

She drank and I followed. "I'm thirty-two and you're almost thirty-four. We're an old married couple."

She was beautiful. I wanted to tell her about the first time I'd seen her—how I'd been caught by her face. The second time, by her hands. The way she had moved her wrists, those bowed moons so white and shiny. Our girls had those hands.

"What're you looking at me for?" She tilted her face, half teasing. I kissed her, not caring what the remaining customers would think. She laughed when I pulled away and touched the scar on my shoulder. "Does it hurt?"

"I'm sorry," I said.

She slid down my arm. "I'm awful, too. I don't mean to be."

"You're unhappy."

She raised her emptied glass. "One more?"

We poured another round and I ordered us a plate of jeon. We chewed on the oily scallion pancakes until our lips puckered from the pepper and soy sauce. She picked out the clams and constructed a small fortress. When there was nothing else left, she dropped them into our mouths one by one. I held her close. The curls she'd smoothed into a bun earlier in the night had loosened. I pulled a strand until it straightened, watched it coil as she slipped it behind her ear. She laid her cheek against my shoulder. This was the Haemi I had always wanted.

"You were right before. Something's wrong." She waved her chopsticks around her head. "Like I can't move in here. Everything's slow or too fast. I'll do better. I'll do that for you and the girls."

"We're here to help you. To get away from home."

"And the neighbors."

I cupped her wide, high cheek. "What you said before, you're wrong. We can afford this. I'll always have enough for our family."

"I'm drunk." She lowered her head into her arms. "Kiss me again and then let's pay and go."

On our walk back, she reached for my hand. The streetlights burned too bright. I wanted to stroll in the dark with my wife. I raised our linked fingers toward the beach. "Let's put our feet in," I said. She hesitated but let me lead her along.

When we reached the sand, she took off her shoes and left them on the wooden pier. She undid her bun. I grasped her hair, the nest of curls and air. She turned to face me. I pretended we were fresh, that the war hadn't cleaved us from our youth.

"I used to come to the beach with these nurses, when I worked at the field hospital," she said, her voice muffled against my chest. "I wonder where they are."

"Do you think any of them settled here?"

"Maybe they're dead."

She broke from me and walked to the water's edge.

"I've always hated the ocean," she said. Waves fell against the sand and crawled back to the sea in a steady rhythm.

"Why?" I stopped behind her, unsure all of a sudden of what we were doing here. How the conversation had shifted so quickly from us to the war to death. It was dark away from the main street and I couldn't see beyond our shadows.

"It's too big, too scary," Haemi said. "The ocean could sweep you away in one swallow."

"Let's go back to the hotel."

She walked in, gasping.

"Haemi?"

Up to her knees, her dress gathered in one hand, the water high and rough. I called her again from the shore. "What're you doing?"

"I don't want our girls to be afraid, the way I'm always afraid."

She fluttered a hand in the air without turning. I couldn't tell if she was walking farther or if the rippling of the water only made it appear so.

I didn't understand her. How she could claim to be afraid one moment and plunge in the next. I tried to raise my voice above the surf, the sudden deafening crashes. I tried to sound angry as I told her to come back to the shore.

A silver film of moonlight rolled off the swollen swells. I didn't know her, my wife. The thought struck me. How strange we were to each other.

I rushed in, the cold lurching into my chest, forcing a ragged gasp out of me.

I reached for her shoulder.

"Haemi?"

"You don't want me." She said it quietly, but I heard. A wave broke around us. She let go of her dress. Wet, it clung to her legs and mine.

The next morning, I woke to a shift in the room. Everything looked the same, with the girls curled together on their bed, their bathing suits folded into an open suitcase. The swim rings and towels stacked by the bathroom door, and a hanbok flung over an empty chair.

Her belongings were here, her children. But Haemi was gone.

I took in our sleeping daughters, the slow curl to Jieun's snores and how Mila always shrouded her head with a sheet. Their mother had finally left. A flash of relief, then a rush of panic, fear.

I went looking for her. An early morning walk, some time away from us. That's all it was. She couldn't have left so easily, not without the girls. The sky was pale and cool and too serene. Down the street, a vendor steamed silkworm pupae in a metal basin, and I suddenly felt starved.

"Can I have some?" I asked.

He rolled a square of newspaper into a cone. "You a visitor?"

"Only here for a few days." I searched the road behind him, but we were alone. "I'd like some of the soup, too."

He poured the pupae into the cone, dipped his spoon in the basin to get at the juice. "You should go to Taejongdae. Magnificent cliffs. I've been here since '51."

"I was a refugee nearby."

He nodded. "The city of refugees. Then you know Taejongdae. It's nicest in the morning."

"Have you seen a woman walking around?" I leveled my hand by my neck. "This tall. Wavy hair. Pretty."

"You're my first customer." He scooped more pupae into my cone. "Enjoy."

I hiked up a hill, hoping to spot her from its peak. Instead, I saw how much Busan had changed. Gabled houses and nail-thin roads butted up against tall, multistory buildings and concrete pavement. Clean streets no longer heaped with sewage and shit. Even the light looked different, filtered through with electricity. Inland, I followed the lines of the Busan Perimeter down to the market where Haemi and I had first met. The makeshift shacks and the tented schools had been razed long ago. I tried to remember where her home had been, that tiny dwelling where I'd sipped tea during the war, when I'd wanted Haemi and the knowledge that life's rituals continued. But I couldn't find the house. There were too many streets, apartments, distractions.

She could have left for good. It seemed easy enough. For her to walk away from us, to walk away from her. *Divorce her. No one will judge you.* I heard this enough to make it sound appealing. But I wasn't that kind of man and Haemi knew it. We were a country of the homeless, the orphaned, and the lost. Abandon her and live with the guilt or hold fast.

I bought juice, a bag of pupae, and returned to the hotel room. The girls were awake, playing with small shells in a circle. It was Jieun, not Solee, who gave me a look. "Where's Mommy?"

"I brought breakfast." I poured the pupae into a bowl. "Come eat."

Solee's gaze followed me around the room. She whispered something to Jieun.

"Street snacks for breakfast?" Mila asked.

"Vacation!" Eunhee said.

They chewed on the waxy, plump bugs and fought over who got to slurp up the brown soup. I passed around juice pouches. "Apple and pear," I said. "We're going to hike the Taejongdae cliffs and go to the beach today."

When we were dressed and fastening sandals, Haemi returned. Still wearing yesterday's striped dress, the bottom thick with the remains of salt. She carried a small purse and a brown bag.

"Where have you been?" I asked.

"The train station." She pulled out tickets. "We're going home today."

The girls' voices soared into a wail. I raised my hand to stop them. "We're not going anywhere. I've paid for three more days."

"I need to leave." Haemi pointed at her ruined dress, at the world outside our window. It was sunny and perfect, the sand golden, the sea lush with color. I wanted to throw her into it. She was a crater of fickleness. It was poisonous, contagious. "I can't be here," she said.

"Leave, then. We're staying."

She picked up Eunhee and spoke to the girls. "Get your bags. I bought new tickets." She turned to me. "We were stupid last night. Letting them go to the hotel by themselves. What if some man had found them? What if they had drowned?"

"That isn't why you want to go," I said. "I know that much."

She dragged our suitcases to the door. "We're stupid when we're drunk. You stay if you want, but they're coming with me."

"I don't want to," Jieun said.

"This isn't fair," Solee said. "This isn't what we agreed on!"

Mila hugged herself. "Why are we going so soon?"

Their voices swelled again. Haemi pushed a knuckle against her eye. Eunhee cried. They all cried, even Solee. I walked to the window. The water was choppy with wind. Whitecaps and blue thrusts. "You really are an awful piece of shit," I said.

"We're leaving." She spoke only to the children. "Your daddy doesn't even know how old you all are. He's the piece of shit."

The night veiled our backyard and though I couldn't see, I sat under our tree anyway. I pictured the property I'd so carefully cultivated since marrying Haemi. The whole swath of land I once had. Over the years, half the fields had been broken off, peddled to tenants by government men who knew nothing about farming. Later, I'd sold the plots willingly, in the hopes of greater compensation. And farther on, the property I should have owned in Seoul, which had been taken from beneath my feet. Packing our bags in

Busan, Haemi had insisted on returning to this leftover, dwindling scrap of land.

The sky had darkened into a summer monsoon by the time we got off the train. We carried our children in silence, drenched from the rain. When we arrived home, Haemi walked to our room and closed the door on me. I listened to her forced, strident breathing, the rush of sound as I walked away. Her unhappiness frightened me. I wanted to tell her I didn't know what to do with her anymore.

The stars shined brighter here, away from all those city buildings. That was something I could say. *You're right. Why do we need to visit Busan when we have stars like these?* It sounded silly even in my mind.

I found the makgeolli jug we kept buried in the summer. Dirt and sweet rice. These smells reminded me of Haemi and the first time I'd seen her drunk, standing as if on a ledge, in a makeshift bar where she shouldn't have been. Dirt and sweet rice—but also anchovies and rain. It was makgeolli that tore my memory open, no matter what I wanted. I poured and drank anyway.

A few weeks before Eunhee was born, in the spring of 1964, Haemi and I had a fight. She was pregnant and I struck her, which made me wrong. I was a bad man, the girls said. They cried and pounded their little fists into my legs. I couldn't handle the noise, so I left.

Haemi found me outside an hour later. I only wanted to stand in our yard and pretend I was alone, but then there she was with that swollen belly brushing against my hand. "Come with me," she said.

She started walking.

At the neighbor's rice field, she took off her shoes and stepped into the paddy.

I stood on the road. "What are you doing?"

"Join me," she said.

Mud, thick from freshly flooded water, clung to her ankles as she balanced between the rows of seedlings. My feet were too wide. The shoots were new and frail. I didn't want the owners to find us here.

Haemi stopped in the center of the field and waited until I gave in. The mud sucked at my shoes, and the water was cold, the wind and air, too. "What are we doing?" I asked again as I reached her. Haemi inspected the ground. Slowly, she lay down. I stared at her red, already swelling face. That moon of a belly accusing me.

"I'm hot. This is the only thing that makes me feel better." She cooled her cheek in the water. "You need to lie down."

She was too still, her limbs too pale. I didn't want to, but I lay down beside her to make sure she was alive. I touched her stomach and tried to feel the baby. When my hand fell to her side, she locked her fingers with mine.

"I want this to be yours," she said.

I did the only thing I could think to do, to show her that I was her husband and that she needed to get Kyunghwan out of her mind.

The whole time I was inside her, pushing into her, Haemi stayed quiet, motionless. Her eyes and mouth shut tight. Her arms crossed against herself. It hurt me. How little she loved me. She rammed her hands into my chest near the end when it was too late. I hunched over her, already out of breath. She wouldn't meet my gaze. I grabbed her and pressed down on her stomach with our fingers entwined.

"Listen carefully," I said. The water was everywhere. She wasn't crying or she was. "I know what you did. But this?" I felt movement between us and pressed until the baby kicked. "This son is mine."

I understood why she had wanted to leave our vacation in Busan. For her, it wasn't the city where we'd met, or even where she'd survived. It wasn't where memories of Hyunki or Mother or the war overtook her. It was Kyunghwan, always him, taking up all the space in her mind.

I drank the last of the makgeolli. I passed the girls' room, where they slept, exhausted from the train ride and their protests. Their suitcases were heaped around them, half-open and slopping out clothes. I entered our room, where Haemi slept on her side with her hands cupped beneath her cheek. I kneeled beside her and kissed her, shook her. My fingers sank into her sunburned arms, so soft and thick. "Haemi."

"What?" She jerked awake, blinking slowly. "What do you want?"

I stroked her face. "I thought you had left us this morning."

She nestled farther into her pillow. "I didn't. I couldn't, even if I wanted to."

"We need to get better." I brushed the blanket off her. "Listen to me."

"We're fine, Jisoo. We're exactly like everybody else."

I clenched her shoulder. She'd changed back into her hanbok, a plain white dress. "We fix this or I divorce you," I said.

She sat up, cradling a pillow against her chest, her face fierce. "I'm going to die here as your wife. All I want is for you to do your job."

"I'll try harder, but you need to also." I held her. "You can't keep on like this. I'm trying, Haemi."

"Did you really think Busan would be a good idea—to go there after the war?" She rose and her voice did, too. "You think I'm the one who needs to be fixed? You don't fuck me. None of your other women have brought you a son." She circled me like the snake she was. Toxic, fickle, savage. She was all of it, an undertow of everything I'd tried to swim away from. "You're a cripple. That's what you're bitter about. Not me."

I struck her. The breath loosened out of her rough and quick.

"You bastard." Hands by her side, her cheek pink, that straight, unyielding back. "You're the one who'll never change."

Haemi

1967

MY GIRLS FIND ME AT THE RIVER, THEIR WHITE UNDER-
things and shirts gathered in my arms. I am up to my ankles in
water. It moves against me.

They stand in a fearsome row. Wild hair and bright colors, each
wearing shorts that show the knobs of her knees.

"Mother," Solee calls. "Come here to us." She motions with
both hands, waving arms wide and high, as if I were on the other
side of an ocean.

I wade back to my daughters. Jieun and Mila and Eunhee mimic
their eldest sister, their fingers netting me in.

I know which rocks to glide over, how to balance my body
against the current's flow. They know, too. This is our river. We
have spent all our fall weekends here.

They wait above on a hanging ledge of grass. I show them the
wet clothes. "I was washing. All done."

They don't remind me that we have a sink in our home now. A
basin large enough for all our laundry. With one twist of a metal
handle, water gushes out. When Jisoo first installed the tap, the
girls marveled at its force. They cupped their palms under its flow
and drank like animals.

I climb to them. Solee plucks the wet clothes from me and lays them out on the grass. Yellow, dry blades poke through holes in the fabric.

"Remind me to stitch those spots," I say. "Can't have you looking like orphans at school."

Solee glances at my shoulder and cheek, where my skin is still red from Jisoo's morning anger.

"Right," she says.

"Right," they say.

"We brought gimbap." Jieun pulls long rolls of seaweed-wrapped rice from her rucksack. They are perfect and cylindrical and gleaming.

We find our spot of earth, where the ground has molded to our forms. Mila sets bojagi cloths before us, and Eunhee claps her approval. We huddle in a circle.

In another rucksack, a knife waits for me, handle first. My girls know they are not allowed. They could hurt themselves.

"Thick slices, please!" Eunhee asks.

They lean in and watch with their easy wonder. Vinegar scents the air with each slicing. The smell lingers on the pads of my fingers, and I let them sniff in the sharpness until each of them turns away, noses wrinkled and aching.

We eat. Perfect rounded gimbap, the white gleam of sticky rice.

When all that remains are the seaweed bits stuck between our teeth, Mila overturns her swollen bag. "There's more."

Dusty orange globes tumble out, one after another.

"Persimmons," Solee says.

"We didn't steal them," Jieun says.

"There was a tree with too many," Mila says. "We took all the ones on the ground."

"When did it turn into persimmon season?" I ask.

They do not respond. I touch my lips—closed—and I do not know if I've spoken aloud.

"Look at all these goodies," I try again, eyeing the plump orbs full of juice. "So many!"

Eunhee cups one below her nose. She pulls off the hardened green cap and offers the fruit to me. It smells too ripe, almost turned.

I let them eat anyway. I wonder if their small bodies will feel the fermentation, if they will dream up fantasies. I want them always to be full, bursting.

I choose one with cracked skin and bite in. I have always loved persimmons. How the furry, bitter taste of the unripe turns so quickly into unreserved sweetness. The scent holds me, heavy on my tongue. "I have an idea. Let's eat as many as we can," I say.

"That's silly." Solee takes mousy, furtive bites. She is an almost-woman now and too serious.

"So what?" I show her my already empty hands, the mushed pulp filling my mouth.

The other girls try for me—Jieun and Mila and Eunhee. Green caps fall and fingers stain orange. Their cheeks bloat as they chew on the slippery fruit. I am on my fourth when—

"I can't," Eunhee says, her hands to her lips, her eyes curving into worry. My Eunhee, who is composed of features that belong only to me. "I don't feel good."

"I told you," Solee says quietly.

"I was wrong. Mommy was wrong."

The girls nod slowly, the ruined persimmons in their palms.

We lie on the grass with yellowed, sticky mouths. Eunhee pats her bloated belly, and Mila groans on her side, her lips burbling.

Jieun, ever eating and thread thin, piles the rest of the fruit in the center of our circle.

"Sunday already," I say. "What will I do when you go back to school tomorrow?"

"Cook! Sleep!" Mila says. "Draw!"

"Come with me, Mama." Eunhee yanks fistfuls of grass. "I hate school."

"Nursery isn't real school," Jieun says to our littlest. I cannot tell if she is teasing or reassuring or merely being herself. She raises her face to the sun. "I hope it stays warm so we can keep coming here."

As the light hits the girls, their sprawling bodies, I see how dark they have become. Toasted and warm like chestnuts. Good. I have shored up my wretchedness, have spilled only cheer onto my children these past weeks.

Because they are too pure for me to ruin, I remind myself, because I don't want to cast blame on them. Because I want to tend them like they are the best fruit.

Because I want them to love me.

Solee rolls onto her back. Staring at the color-changing sky, she touches my hand. "We'll come home quickly, right after school. We'll help you."

I move to the other side of the circle, where Eunhee lies, listless. Solee is like Jisoo, with his chin and eyes, his personality. Too practical. Too full of knowing. Relentless no matter how absent I am. She is his spy, I think. I heave Eunhee onto my lap. She nestles her face into me, leaves a trail of tacky saliva on my skin.

Today, I see and hear clearly.

The river rushes below us. The water's thundering sounds louder now that I am not wading through its rhythms. The heat clings to the afternoon air. My girls are like pasque flowers in their purples and reds. Mila braids the grass together, patterning the ground. Jieun hums a song that sounds almost familiar and nods at Solee to join. Eunhee, I hold her.

A bird calls from a high tree. I recognize it, iridescent with green-black feathers and a wisp of a crown rising from its head. I lift a hand into the air, trying to get its attention. A swallow lands on top of our persimmon mountain instead. Brown-bodied and common, swallows remind me of a man I no longer know.

Jieun twitters, pats a patch of dirt. The swallow ignores her, cocks his head, and eyes the fruit.

"Eat it," I say.

He hops and ruffles. He nips at the persimmon's wounds, where we bit and broke flesh. We watch as he pecks. We are mesmerized, all except Eunhee. She moves against me in her sunbaked languor.

"Eat more," I say. "Eat, eat, eat."

He rips open the skin with his sharp, hungry beak. Our little swallow. He will gorge. I will force him. Until his belly swells with fruit meat and drunkenness, until his wings fracture under his weight as he tries to fly back home.

I wonder who taught Solee to be so good. She reminds me that a man is coming for dinner. We are standing in our kitchen with its faucet and sink. With a mountain of the yeontan briquettes Jisoo has tried to invest in. We have so many to use now. We can heat our house through winter. We can cook all the food we want.

"Daddy said tonight was important." Solee dumps a bowl of rice into a boiling pot. Bubbles break on the surface as the grains sift down. She arranges salted blue crabs in our prettiest bowls.

"Who's coming again?" I ask.

"Get out the kimchi." She reaches for the engraved chopsticks and spoons.

My child telling me what to do, a little expert.

"I already did," another voice says from behind me. Jieun. She flattens the belt on her dress.

"What happened to your shorts?" They are wearing matching dresses, sun-dappled yellow with red ribbons in their hair. Solee's top is too tight across her growing chest.

"Mother." Solee touches my hand. She is always touching my hand. "Eunhee picked out a hanbok for you, the light green one with flowers at the bottom. She asked if you could wear it. She thinks you look pretty in it."

"We can finish here," Jieun says as she tidies the kimchi.

Solee lifts the lid of another pot on the stove. As the thick scent of meat rises, I remember that I braised the galbi ribs this morning. Solee stirs and Jieun hovers. They sigh and raise their heads up and up, not wanting even the slightest cloud of the savory smell to go to waste.

I take out a bowl of cooked chestnuts. "You can have one each," I say, "for being such good helpers."

They smile at me and exchange a look I don't want to understand. "Thanks, Mommy," one of them says, but I have already left.

I call Mila and Eunhee to my room. They come, yellow and fluttering. I touch the hem of the pale green hanbok they've laid out, where the pink- and orange-stitched flowers rise and fall in waves. I touch the wall. I touch my girls' darkened foreheads. Wide-cheeked, full-lipped Mila—my sweet third, always passed over because of her quiet, dreamy wonder. How obedient she is, without me ever noticing. I squeeze her extra in apology.

Eunhee pushes between us. "Me too. I want hugs, too."

"We can both have hugs," Mila says, allowing her space. "Let's get Mommy dressed."

The air bristles, shifts. No, it has been a good day.

"Should Mommy wear some jewelry with her hanbok?" I ask. "My stylish, pretty girls."

"Fancy time!" Mila swings Eunhee around the room as I unwrap and change. My two youngest are gentle, soft beings. They find my jewelry box and rattle it between them.

"I bought this hanbok with my own money. I earned it when I worked at the orphanage before I had Eunhee in my belly," I say. "Isn't that nice?"

Their heads are together, ignoring me. Their hands sift through the pieces I have left. A necklace found on a woman by the roadside during the war. My first earrings, smoothed stones made to look like jade. A present from Mother, when I was heavy with Solee. "For good luck," she'd said. Always, luck.

I comb Mila's slick-straight strands, Eunhee's curls. My baby is the only one with hair like mine. She stares up at me as if I am hers alone; she holds a golden bracelet. Delicate chains link together, a real jade at its center. A small, smooth eye. "This, Mama?"

No. That's not right.

"It's too plain," I say.

"Green and gold go nicely together." Mila nods. "If the jewelry is too showy, it makes you look uglier. A fifth-form girl told me so."

"Mama's not ugly." Eunhee points to the stone. "Green in bracelet, green in dress. Put it on, Mama."

I have fattened and the bracelet no longer fits. "Should we try something else?" I ask.

"I can do it." Eunhee squeezes my fingers together and forces the loop up to my wrist.

When the evening's darkness rolls in, Jisoo comes home. "Mr. Baek will be here soon." He pulls on a collared shirt, a jacket, and black socks with clear elastics.

"Must be a special man." I run my fingers along his neckband, where his hair is razored off in a straight, flat line. I try to kiss him.

He rustles his shoulders. His elbow knocks into me. "What did you cook?"

"Galbi-jjim," I say.

We walk to the dining room. The girls have laid out the dishes in perfect order. He sniffs, goes to the cabinet where he keeps his soju. He turns over two glasses and pours.

"They've prepared this." He sets the soju on the table and points to the water cups. "They should be doing their homework."

"What are you talking about?"

"Get the tea."

Of course. The girls and their cold water. The adults and their need for heat.

"And—" He points to the shadows behind the papered door. Four humps are hunkered together, unmoving.

"I don't know what you're saying." I line up the chopsticks that are perfectly straight already. "It was hot today. I thought you'd want a cup of cold water. Take Mr. Baek somewhere else then."

"Girls!"

The shadows don't move.

Jisoo slides open the door. They scramble apart. My girls look at their father and then me, blinking slowly as if we've disturbed them from their slumber.

"Daddy." Mila bows.

"We came to say hello before dinner," Jieun says, moving closer. She knows she is his favorite, his plucky one.

He shakes his head, strokes their cheeks. "Go do your homework. We'll be fine."

As they scurry away, he calls, "Solee—make sure. I don't want to see you out of your room until I say so."

When we are alone, he turns. He is a good actor with everyone but me.

"You let them run around all weekend, and then they're tired at school."

"That's not why you're mad," I say.

"Tonight's important. Mr. Baek could hurt us if he wants to. You're so—" He holds me by the head, his palms against my temples. I want him to squeeze harder, to crush this sudden headache wrapping itself around my brain. "You think only your world is collapsing."

He walks the length of the room and back. "This is important." His thick lips twitch, like a pair of mice rustling beneath a layer of hay.

I try to kiss him. He pushes me away.

"More tea?" I pour steaming cups for my husband and Mr. Baek. He is a man I do not recognize. A ring of hair salutes his shiny bald crown. His features are boring, except for his eyes. Thick, doughy lids bulge like overstuffed rice balls. His eyes below flit from object to object, like a drunken bee.

He slops the tea down as if it were soju. "Why don't you leave us to talk? Go join the little girls?" He rubs my wrist when I refill his cup. I jerk away.

We three are too close together around our low, square table. Between Jisoo and Baek, the odors overwhelm me, the stink of their feet and oil. I want to tell this man he smells like ginkgo nuts left out in the sun.

"I wouldn't want to embarrass a man in front of such a beauty." Baek laughs and I see all his rotting teeth.

I pick up my chopsticks, sliver my meat. "Embarrass?"

"You don't need to know." Jisoo smiles, but I see his lips twitch. "It's all business talk. You can go now."

I don't leave the table. Instead, I push my hand through Jisoo's still-thick hair and slither toward him like a bar girl. "I would think my husband would be the one embarrassing you, Mr. Baek."

"Maybe you should be stroking me, not him. I own his land, you know." Baek touches my feet under the table. I feel his fingers clench my toes in a tight, cold grasp. "He owes me."

"Enough." I stand too quickly, drop my chopsticks. "Jisoo? What is this?"

He smiles along with Baek. A cracked, teeth-showing grin I want to ruin.

All men are disgusting creatures. I say it. "You are disgusting."

Jisoo grabs my wrist and shakes it at our guest. "Apologize."

"It's fine." Baek lounges, stretching his shoulders and rolling his neck. A laugh. "I like a woman with a bad mouth."

"You can have her, then," Jisoo says. He throws my wrist as if it weren't a part of me. "Get out."

I want to push my husband's thick body into the earth until he's buried and lost.

Instead, I leave.

I walk out of the house without my shoes, in rubber slippers and then bare feet. I always go to the same place. A rice field we don't own. Where I once lay with Jisoo, where I went to cool my pregnant mind, where the neighbors scream when they see me and claim I am a ghost.

During my last pregnancy, I dreamed a baby would come out of this wet earth fully formed. A ghost of Kyunghwan. In the dream, the naked baby cried alone in the field. Wet, sallow, and alive. I ran to pick him up, fearing the rice field water would seep into his mouth and choke him.

But when I clutched him to me, his head began to tilt. It swung around and around, until the neck tightened into nothing, until his head rolled off with a squelch—in its place, a hole, an empty space. Slowly, a new bulge grew out. Not a face but something misshapen and puckish, with a wide-open mouth.

I didn't scream. I didn't leave. I kissed this new creature and searched for its tongue with my own.

Jisoo wakes me as he enters our room. Still dressed, he crawls closer until the sour smell of soju routs any lingering sleep from my head. He has gotten drunk with Baek, has found a bar girl who purrs as they please. I tuck my blanket tighter around me, but he tries to tunnel into the sheets like a dog.

"I meant it," I say. "I was saying it to you." I turn away from his drunken body as he collapses beside me. "You are disgusting."

He doesn't react the way I expect.

I open my eyes to his damp cheek against mine, his hands pulling on my underwear.

"Take it off," he says. His belt buckle unclasps. A snake of leather whizzes through the air and onto the floor.

I don't care. I go back to sleep.

I pretend he is someone else.

Kyunghwan.

I confuse my senses. I blur shapes, sounds, colors, tastes—the slight bridge of Kyunghwan's nose, how the skin crinkles around it when he's upset and, when he's overjoyed, summons the pale pink insides of salmon. Incandescent. When I last saw him, he stood soaked in lamplight, glowing and flimsy. A swallow.

Both of these men are invading me. I see Jisoo's eyes, violently dark, and a surge of sour lemon stings and scratches at the back of my throat.

I love you, when whispered by Kyunghwan, is pale green. By Jisoo, harsher, it is white.

"Look at me."

A hand grips my face. The heat of a sweat-slicked body presses into me. It is Jisoo. It is always Jisoo.

The girls are gone at school. I will be alone all day, all week. "I don't want to do this anymore," I say to no one, to the crow in the tree above me. It preens with its wretched beak.

I am tired of red pepper paste stinging my cuts, staining the underbeds of my nails. The limp cabbages have been soaked and pummeled in enough paste for one day. I set the kimchi jar aside in a patch of darkness, where the leaves and branches above provide safe shade.

My fingers, tainted red, leave marks on the clay. The sight of my carelessness, of myself, bothers me. My long, thickened joints and rumpled knuckles.

I want to plunge my hands into the dirt, to clean the red from them with the earth. Then I see it. I am still wearing the bracelet. That pale green eye.

I pull and tug, but it won't come off. My hands are too fat, too swollen.

And I want it all to fall away—my bracelet, the red paste on my skin, the cottoning in my mind, the sounds and tastes of today and yesterday, and even the girls.

They, too, will slip from me, like leaves from a tree.

I will slip, too. Like a heel on a mossy rock—one misstep leading to another until the body is only a buoyant thing floating away with the stream. I can imagine it, the whiteness of arms and legs, of her face. The water, mineral and cloudy, paints her until she is no one, until she is only mine.

Laundry stretches from the tree to the house, folded over a length of twine. I trail my fingers from one sun-dried piece of cloth to another, leaving stains behind.

I stop at the row of jars lining the back wall of our home. Earthen brown, formed from clay and sand. They hold expected and unexpected items—soybean paste, rice, kimchi, but also seeds, another for spades, and one for the superstitions that come with each birth.

I find the kumchul rope that Jisoo hung around the house the last time I was pregnant. I pull off the red peppers and pine needles. It is difficult. He knotted each piece in tight with his eager hopes. It is bad luck to prepare the rope before birth, but he did it anyway, for every pregnancy, for each dream of a boy.

He has saved them all. And at the bottom of the jar, two carved ducks. I throw the birds into the air and listen as they plunk onto our neighbor's land. I braid the four ropes together until there is a new object in my hand. Thick and sturdy, my fingers don't meet when I hold its body. The bristles are smooth and the color pleases me. It reminds me of old barley fields, dried out in the summer heat.

I wrap this new rope around my arm and pull down until Kyunghwan's bracelet is forced from my wrist, until it is nothing but a bit of metal and stone on the ground.

I stand beneath the tree. Gold glints in the grass. Burned skin turns red, a wet pile of kimchi waits for me.

In my hand, a rope. An opening I have made, with its perfect circle.

Here is what I imagine: a thick, smothering cloud escaping my open mouth.

"Mama?"

Eunhee shakes my shoulder. I awaken, still under the tree. She wipes my face with a fist. Her knuckles press into my eyes, the sweep of my cheeks. Her rucksack lays open and abandoned, its tongue flapping in the middle of the yard. The sun is gone, painted over by evening blues.

"We're home. Unnies are inside," she says.

"Sit with me." I pat the ground. "Did you eat?"

She crawls into my lap and her knees dig into my hips. She

swings her arms across my neck, pushes her face against my chest. "You're sweaty."

"Let's stay here together for a while."

She lifts my arm, examines the rope I still grip in my hands. She follows the lines of my wrist, where the bristles chafed my skin. "What are you doing?"

"It's a game." I hold the circle above my head. "A crown for Mama."

She grabs it and puts it around her neck. "Do you like my jewelry?" She dabs the remnants of pepper and pine. She preens and smiles like a lady.

"Beautiful," I say. "Can I try your necklace, too?"

She touches my wrist again, pauses at the peeling skin. "But the bracelet was too small?"

"Yes, Mama didn't realize." I hold her closer. I brush heat-swollen curls from her face. My perfect Eunhee. She has harnessed all the best parts of her sisters, of me, inside her body.

"Hey." She swats my arms. "Too tight."

I kiss her. "Tell me, Eunhee. How was my baby's day?"

"I got this. My nose was running." She wriggles to face me, points to a handkerchief pinned to her shirt. "I learned a song. Can I teach you?"

"Let's put the game away first." I lift the rope from her neck and set it on the ground.

The circle loosens, loses its shape. One thick rope unravels into four.

"Don't cry, Mama."

"Sing for me."

And she does.

And I listen. I listen to my daughter sing.

Kyunghwan

1967

"YOU'RE MEANT TO BE ALONE." A WOMAN TOLD ME THAT once. My last matchmaker, a grandmother with lines rivuleting her face. With my papers spread across her table, she'd shrugged. "There's nothing I can do with you."

"What do you know?" I had swept up my jacket, almost yelling at her. "I don't need your help."

Her words followed me, though, a portent I pushed away only to have it return again and again. I realized the truth after a dance in the night. Across a concrete floor, with my hands on Haemi's hips, I knew.

"Find someone else," she'd said.

"If you leave me, I'll be alone." I'd sunk to the ground. "I know it."

"You'll forget me."

We were both right. Haemi would always be an ache inside me, a reminder of my loneliness, but now I was thirty-two and for the first time, almost happy. I lived in Seoul and made good money as a supervisor for a beauty products company. I had managed to push aside any thoughts of her, and him, and everything I'd done to my family. I had found someone.

❀

The loud trill of the phone shook us awake. "I still can't get used to that sound in our apartment." Miyun pulled the blanket across her face. "Go get it."

I pressed my forehead into the pillow. "It's probably a misdialed call."

"Oh, fine. I'll go." She took the blanket with her.

I met Miyun while I was overseeing a shipment of soaps to a fancy women's shop near her university. She was considering a scarf, holding it against her chest to see if it matched her shirt. She was too young, I could see that right away, but something in her easy movements had excited me. She was unimaginably rich and from the city. You could tell from the way she stared at you, all bluntness. Like she owned everything she saw. There was a naïveté to her privilege that I liked. Sometimes I'd find myself thinking of her in a more permanent way and I'd panic. But I was nearly happy.

"You were right," Miyun said, returning to me. "Wrong call."

"It's *my* apartment." I sat up against the pillows. "Mine. Not ours."

She stood there, her naked little body shivering even with the blanket caped across her shoulders. I don't know what pushed me to say things like that to her.

"I paid for the telephone," she said.

"Get in bed."

"Why should I?"

I turned over. I didn't want to watch her decide if she'd stretch this out into a fight. Or maybe I was scared that she would finally realize I was a shit, and I didn't want to see it all fall apart. She eventually slid in beside me, rubbed her face against my back, and called me a dog. I turned over and put my mouth on hers, on her breasts, and stomach, between her legs. When I pushed inside her, she forgave me.

Miyun woke early the next day. Her parents had gone to Tokyo for an anniversary trip, and I had her to myself for two weeks. Each morning, she sang the same tune as she did her makeup, her alto voice a little off on the higher notes. It was a nice picture to wake up to. She smelled like a better life. I knew it was the aromatic oils she used, but I liked to imagine some of that richness emanating from me as well. Before she left, she crawled on top of me. I felt ready, all of a sudden, for the panic.

"I have study group for my midwinter exams." She kissed me. "I'll see you after?"

"I'll do it," I said.

She tilted her head. "See me?"

"See your parents."

"Really?" She kissed me again, her mouth splitting into a smile so wide our teeth clicked.

"Really," I said, carrying her into the kitchen. We laughed and couldn't stop touching each other. I felt the way you did when you're scared and praying to something out there that you're ready.

"Let's celebrate. Let's start right now," she said. I lifted her onto the table and she raised her skirt, her hand already guiding mine.

We went out and she bought me a new suit. We planned how she'd introduce me to her parents. She was their only living child. They were pliable, she said. They wanted a son again, even if it was me. I told her to savor one accomplishment at a time.

In the evening, Miyun rolled ground beef in egg yolk and I opened our third bottle of soju. As she placed the patties on the frying pan, the phone trilled again. She handed me the receiver. "Can you?"

I cradled the phone against my neck as I poured two glasses. "Hello?"

After some static, a buried voice seemed to wade toward me. A man panting out words and air. The sounds distorted by his heaving, loud and wet, like an animal.

I set down the bottle. "Who is this? Who are you?"

He spoke quickly. About a body, water, currents, the police, someone skipping stones, a discovery. "The river, Kyunghwan. They found her."

I gripped the receiver. I felt bodiless, a hand and an ear, nothing else. I tried to palm the kitchen wall. Muted flowers and vines, Western wallpaper. But my hand shook, looked strange, like someone else's.

"She's dead."

And I knew. I knew who was calling and who had left and who was I to know all this so soon? Before he started to wail, beating her name into my ear, I knew.

Miyun's fingers were alarmed on my neck. "What's wrong?"

I caught sight of her earrings. I focused on their white sheen, how they swung from her lobes. Pearls rimmed with silver. I held on to the receiver and stared at those orbs, trying to disappear all sound, to collapse everything around me—Jisoo's crying, Miyun's questions, and eventually, my own strange gurgling. I tried to push away these swelling feelings, to deny them, but in the end, the line disconnected, Miyun stopped holding me, and only my choked breathing was left.

A chicken clucked in the back of the train. I wanted to shove it out a window. I'd never liked farm animals. Haemi, though, she had loved them. One afternoon, when we were young, we'd found a hen pecking at my lunch tin. I threatened to pluck out its feathers, but Haemi scooped the bird into her arms and kissed its sharp yellow beak. She sat on the road, skirt splayed, holding the animal above her head, away from my reach. She dared me to kiss the hen, too, and when I refused, her laughter shook the fields around us.

"That's a nice suit." The woman seated next to me nodded. She looked about my age, but when she smiled, a missing tooth aged her. "What are you going down for?"

I ignored her and stared at the frosted winter landscape as it passed by—bare branches slapping in the wind, a cloudless sky. The emptiness of the fields reminded me of Haemi and I had to turn away. She'd taken this train home two years ago. I had let her.

An accident, Kyunghwan.

Haemi, the ache of her, in my chest.

"Is everything all right?" The woman reached out her hand.

Her touch, a stranger stroking my shoulder, unmoored me. I had harbored my want and anger and regret all these years. Finally, I wept out the words. I was too late. Haemi was dead. Fierce, unknowable Haemi—was gone.

The last time I saw her, in a half-built structure in Seoul, she told me how she felt. I didn't want to listen. The misery, she said, clouded her mind and took up all the space inside her. She felt heavy, not right, as if snatches of her being had been stolen. Then she had laughed. "What am I saying?"

As she spoke, I had only watched her lips. How they were slightly bitten, pink, wry with beauty. I watched her all night, savored every sense of her. She still walked the same, with that light lope that swayed her body from side to side. She looked older at thirty. A mother. Those three girls had pulled her body into a different shape, but even so, I wanted her.

"An accident," Jisoo had said. A river. A drowning. I thought of her body and mouth and laugh and mind as I walked from the train station to her home. I hadn't wanted to listen to her, worried that it would ruin my time with her, worried that she would blame me. I had been too absorbed with my own selfish wants.

When I reached the house, I found Jisoo in the back, hacking at a tree with an ax. He hewed, thrusting back and forth, yet the ax landed soft and aimless on the trunk. He kept his bad arm loose and shifted with each swing to maintain his balance.

"Jisoo?" I stood, unsure, as he straightened. He looked away as soon as he recognized me, but I saw how his jaw clenched. "I took the earliest train."

"What are you doing here?" Jisoo, still gripping the ax, cut me with a quick glare. "Why are you on my property?"

I hadn't thought of what I'd say to him if he didn't want me here. "I came for the funeral," I said, steadying my words.

He tested the trunk with one hand. His body, still like a boxer's, was square and squat and stronger than mine. His voice, though, shook. "I didn't ask you to come."

"You shouldn't have to prepare everything yourself." I walked toward him, trying to buoy my tone. I slid a smile onto my face. "I can help."

"Don't bullshit me." He met my gaze, finally, and leaned the ax against his shoulder. The weight tugged at his shirt, revealing the scar that roped his right arm. "You're not here for anyone but yourself."

I shifted my feet, suddenly aware of how alone we were. "You're the one who called me." Jisoo had Haemi for all these years, and he'd failed, so what did it matter who I was here for? I turned to the house. "Where are the girls? I'm their uncle." I started toward the rear kitchen. "I can console them if I want."

He circled around me quick, his ax out, the thick blade pointing at my chest. "You don't get to come here like this."

I stopped in the middle of his yard. He was right. There wasn't any use in lying. "Let me go to the burial," I said, "and then I'll leave."

He fell into a growling laugh, the gray blade shuddering with his movement. His voice unhinged. "You think I'd be stupid enough to call you before the funeral? It's done. You're too late. She's buried."

"You didn't—" Jisoo lifted the ax when I stepped toward him. I threw my hands up. He laughed again.

"You're pathetic." He spat the words, his measured face slipping. "Go home, Kyunghwan."

He threw down the ax. It bounced, almost hitting him, before it slashed the earth. He staggered to the tree, a low cry ugly and thick in his throat. Without the ax, he started clawing the bark with his hands, peeling with his fingers, scattering splinters around him. He split through the middle, like a seed, and I saw myself from the night before. How his words had cored me. Here was steady Jisoo, undone.

I put my arms around him, his muscled and damaged shoulders, and squeezed. Using the whole of me, I held fast against his pawing, his shoves against my chest. We butted against the trunk, my arms still encasing his, both of us crying. I held him as hard as I could until he yielded, until he closed his eyes and grew quiet.

Slumped against him, spent and shadowed, I looked up at the tree. Its raw, gouged trunk. *Chop it down,* I wanted to say. *Take me down, too. Take me to her.*

I promised Jisoo I'd get him drunk. Really, I was desperate for a drink myself. The bar was nearly empty when we arrived and we chose the table closest to the exit. A waitress came over, rested a hand on Jisoo's shoulder.

"Everyone consoles me to my face." His gaze traveled up her hand. "Then they gossip about my wretched family once I've left."

The woman, sheepish, rolled her finger along the hem of her apron. She glanced back at the kitchen, where two other waitresses stood, watching us. "What would you like to eat today?"

I ordered for us both. Soju and lemons, samgyeopsal, boiled blood sausage. "Bring the drinks first," I said.

Jisoo jerked his head as she retreated. "They're saying Haemi walked into the river on purpose." He shredded a paper napkin in front of him. "They're filling their mouths with shit."

I watched denial paint over his features. "She knew how to swim," I said, as careful as I could manage. "It's winter."

He leaned across the table, his whole being on edge. "Don't talk about what you don't know. Don't be an idiot like the rest of them."

I steadied the tipped table and tried not to flinch. "You're right, Jisoo. You're right."

"Fuck you all." He pushed back his chair, but he didn't get up and leave. "She was doing the laundry."

We didn't speak to each other again until the waitress returned. As we drank, Jisoo steered the conversation to business. He spoke about how agriculture as a way of life was dying in our country. "The government only cares about producing rice, not about us," he said. Farmers were leaving to become city-dwelling industrialists like me. I thought it strange, how he'd forgotten what it meant to be from Seoul, but I nodded along. When he grunted at me to say something, I mentioned Miyun. We emptied bottles at an even pace and skirted any talk of Haemi. Jisoo and I hadn't spoken in years, and I thought, stupidly, that we were united in our grief.

When the air around us trembled, Jisoo looked at me. "So." He squeezed the juice out of a lemon, wringing its round body. He poured soju on top of the pulpy liquid. "Haemi turned strange after you left."

I popped a slice of sausage into my mouth. As the thin skin broke between my teeth, I concentrated on the taste of cellophane noodles, pork blood, barley. "Oh?"

"You can say it."

I shook my glass, watched the lemon juice and alcohol mix.

"We would get drunk some nights," I said.

He swung his shot into his mouth. He grabbed mine and drank it, too. "Tell me something else."

"I don't have anything else to say."

"Liar."

He pushed my head against the wall, his knuckles driving into my temple until we tipped to the ground. I wanted to let him hurt me, but I couldn't give him even that. He lifted his leg into a swing and I rolled away. He was clumsy, his bad arm hampering his speed, but still he pinned me down. Hit me with a cross. I tried to grab his crippled shoulder. He had always been faster, stronger.

The drunks shouted. I saw a flash of the waitress's black apron. She jittered in frantic side steps. We pushed and shoved each other in a tight circle. He punched me until I felt bruises stretch the skin on my face. "I didn't," and "Liar," the only words either of us could manage. His breathing, quick and deep, took up all the space in my head.

When I was ruined enough, he left.

The waitress held cabbage leaves against my swelling skin and guided me to a seat. "He's having a hard time." She slid a chunk of ice over my cheek. "You know about his wife?"

"I can take care of myself," I said.

As soon as the bleeding stopped, I headed to his house. I didn't know what I wanted to say. I only knew that I wanted him to hurt me again.

When I reached his land, I heard the girls crying. I stood in the neighbor's field and listened. The high, constant howl of children in mourning. Solee. Jieun. Mila. I remembered their names, their faces. Behind the stone wall, they wept for her.

Their sounds swept through me and I understood. I hadn't thought about the girls and their future, about Haemi as a mother and what it meant to have her gone. They would be alone, orphans in an already motherless country. Those girls and their unfathomable fates.

One of them had found her in the river while skipping stones.

I imagined the screams, the confusion and torture of seeing her body wedged against the rocks, drenched and unmoving.

I made myself listen.

I found my way to the river. Jagged gray rocks lined the banks as the current rushed on, slipping south toward some open mouth. Standing there, I understood why Jisoo had hacked down the tree. There was nothing you could do to revenge against water.

I walked in, gasping at the cold. I trudged to the center, where the land gave way and the water deepened. Almost slipping, I waded in to my chest. I didn't know if I was in the right place. The river had already erased her.

I had missed it all. I hadn't mourned or bowed or called her name. I hadn't helped bathe or bury her body.

I wanted to tell her I was sorry and that I missed her. I only stood there, unable to breathe, imagining what it would feel like to let go, wondering if she had loved me in the end. If she knew how much I had loved her.

When I could no longer control my shivering, I climbed out.

It took a lot of begging and wandering around town before I found a store that would let me use their telephone. Wet and still drunk, I dialed. After the second ring, I heard Miyun's voice. Sometimes, when I woke her in the middle of the night, gauziness cobwebbed her words together. I wanted her to talk to me in that voice and tell me everything would be all right. My words came out all wrong.

"I'm a dog," I said. "You should leave."

"Kyunghwan?" Her voice was sharp, awake. It was only evening after all. "I've been waiting all day."

"I made a mistake with you. Get out of my apartment."

"Stop fooling around. Are you drunk?"

I wanted to hurt her and myself. "Even for all that money, I wouldn't marry you," I said.

"You don't mean that."

"I've had you. You're a rag. Dirty. Disgusting. You're nothing to me."

"You dog." Her voice tilted. I imagined her trying to tamp down her hurt, not wanting her weakness to cut through the line. "Why are you saying all this?"

"Take the telephone with you when you leave."

I told myself I was saving her. But really, I wanted to hurt someone. I wanted to push the pain in me onto another.

After the call, I paid for a woman. She was younger than I requested. A slender girl who looked too scared for what I needed. Her eyes were large against her anemic face. In a brothel room behind a cluster of bars, I told her to close her eyes and turn around. Afterward, she pulled up her skirt. I stopped her and asked for one more.

"There's no discount," she said.

She had the hands of a child. Those thin fingers took the bills from my wallet. Only then did she drop the skirt and step out of its circle. She slipped underneath me, facedown into the blanket the way I had placed her the first time. I turned her over. She let me fix the hair around her forehead. I tried to make her look older, softer.

"I want you to do something," I said. "Slide your hand across my neck, like this, until I open my eyes."

She looked at me for a long time, my face already bruising and red, then gave a simple "All right." She was careful and exacting, but her fingers were cold.

I pulled her on top of me. "Put your mouth on my temple. Down my nose."

When she leaned over, the curtain of her hair covered me, and I asked her to stay this way for a while.

"Don't ask. Just tell me."

She did it all, even the hushed strain of her voice against my ear. She roamed my back with her hands and crossed her ankles with mine. She did everything, but the requests hung in the air, turning it all thick and false. When we were done, she didn't leave to empty my come in the bathroom. Instead, she turned toward the wall and slept. Her skin smelled thick and metallic. I kissed the space between her shoulder blades, and I let myself pretend.

I woke hungover and alone. I crawled to the public bathroom, heaved into the basin of shit and piss, and lay there until the smell made me retch once more. Outside, the clouds hung heavy with snow. I wanted a storm, a blinding both clean and monstrous.

At the market, I sat at a food stall and ordered a bottle of makgeolli, some pig's feet, anchovies, sweet potatoes, gosari—her favorites. I set a plate across from me and pretended I was waiting for someone, even going so far as to lay some food aside for my date. I looked around for the girl from the night before, or the waitress, or even the woman from the train. There was no one.

I thought about the first night of my visit four years ago, when we'd gotten drunk together. Jisoo had slung his good arm around Haemi, and I'd wanted to strike him, to feel my fingers smart with the impact of hitting bone. Mila had clapped and said, "Kissy, kissy," until Jisoo leaned over and kissed Haemi on the cheek. I remembered how the girls had squealed with embarrassment and excitement.

I should have turned away right then and let them have each other. But I was in love and certain I had a right to her. I had found her first. She was mine.

I walked to Haemi with flowers. I would leave them at the house and say goodbye. In the backyard, on the steps leading to the kitchen, I found Solee crying, still dressed in the white hemp of her mourning clothes. The thin fabric wasn't enough. It didn't cover her throat or wrists or feet. Her fingers twirled something small around and around.

"Solee," I called. "It's too cold for you to be outside."

She gasped at the mash of purple and red on my face. The item she held, a piece of jewelry, fell into her lap.

I lifted the flowers to hide my bruises and remembered my knuckles were swollen, too. "I fell."

She folded into herself, as if I could hurt her. "You fell on your face?"

"Don't be smart." I started to sit, but she raised her hand. With her lips set and eyebrows drawn together, she looked too much like Jisoo. A plain, square face without any hint of Haemi's grace.

She bared her teeth. "Father says you're not allowed here. We're leaving for the burial soon."

"The burial?" I started. "The funeral's today?"

"You're not invited." A hard edge in her voice. "You can't come."

I looked past her for someone else who might confirm this news. The funeral hadn't happened yet.

"Do you know what this is?" Solee picked up the object in her lap and slipped it on her wrist. A thin gold bracelet.

I recognized it immediately. I had lifted it for Haemi, folded it in the whitest paper. I had tasted the stone in my mouth as I'd kissed her limbs.

"This used to be hers. She drowned. She drowned herself." Solee shook her wrist. The bracelet slid up and down without making a sound. Her skin was chicken-fleshed and too pale.

"Solee—" But my tongue was too thick. I didn't know what to say, how to comfort her.

"We went to the river all the time, and now she's dead." She pushed the bracelet up, trying to reach her elbow. "You told me you'd come back."

"I'm sorry."

"*I'm sorry*," Solee mimicked. "She hated you. I heard her say it. She gave me the bracelet and said she didn't want anything from you anymore."

I sat beside Solee, ignoring her attempts to push me away. I tried to adjust the bracelet, scared for some senseless reason that it would cut off her blood flow. She hit me, against the fresh bruises. It hurt and I must have groaned because her eyes widened. For a second, I saw the girl from the night before, the same fear. The thought of harming Solee passed through me. She had never given Haemi my letter. But I was the stupid one. I had trusted a child with my hopes.

"I'm all right." I clutched my cheek and tried to smile. "I know it was an accident."

"I hit you on purpose." She slid to the other end of the steps. "Because you said you'd come back and you didn't. Because you—" She pressed her nails into her palms until it looked like it hurt. I was scared she'd cut into her skin.

"Solee—"

"Go away." She tucked her head between her knees. "You don't belong here."

I stood and set down the flowers beside her. They were white, their smell too strong. "Take these in at least. Do that for me."

"Go!" she yelled.

But I couldn't bring myself to leave. I watched as she pulled off the flower heads until only the green stalks remained. Round bulbs rolled at her feet, shedding petals. Her sniffling was the only sound between us. I stared at the stone wall that gated their home. I would go. I wouldn't speak to them again.

I turned to apologize one last time, to tell her that she wouldn't have to see me anymore, to ask her to say goodbye for me, to say I was done—but when I turned, the words finally ready after all these years, I saw him.

Jisoo ran to the back steps. He pulled Solee up by the arm. "Get inside now."

She scrambled away, her face and body a blur, the bracelet rolling onto the ground as her bare feet kicked at the door.

Jisoo, dressed in white, surged toward me. "You"—he pointed— "should have left yesterday."

I squared myself, ready. "You said the funeral was over. I should be allowed."

He grabbed my arms and I waited for his fist. I would take his anger, if it meant I could see Haemi. He worked his jaw, the bones moving as he ground his teeth.

"I'm going with you," I said. "I deserve to say goodbye."

"You think you deserve anything?"

"Wait!" Solee appeared at the back door and ran toward us. "Come," she yelled.

The girls rushed out of the house, half-dressed, confused. "Stop arguing!" Young bodies invaded the space that separated us, their small hands pushing us apart and wrapping around our legs.

"No fighting," one of them said.

"No fighting."

"No fighting."

They swarmed around us. Jisoo tried to steer them to the house. With his arms outspread, he worked to shift the girls behind him. But I saw. There were too many faces, too many bodies. A little girl held on to Solee's leg. She had the round face of her mother, the same loose curls. There were four of them now.

The way he grabbed her, holding her close to his chest, hot with some fear as he glanced back at me—it made me understand.

"When? How old?" I reached out to them. I turned to Solee. "Somebody tell me."

Jisoo gripped the child tighter, tried to walk up the steps. The other girls yelled, flashes of white holding on to our legs, sliding between us. They slowed him down.

"Let me see her." I reached over Jieun's or Solee's head. I grabbed one soft arm. Jisoo shouldered me, but I held on to what I could of the girl. "Let me see her face. If—"

"She's mine." Jisoo swung a sharp elbow. A scab across my nose cracked open, a rush of tears hitting me on impact, a smear of red on his sleeve. I didn't let go.

I shoved one hand under the girl's bottom for leverage. I could take her from him now, if he only loosened. She was slick, sweating, her head tucked into his chest. I pried at his fingers. Her face was shaped like Haemi's, but the eyes. I caught her right shoulder and one leg by the knee. I almost had her, and then—she screamed.

All of them, shrieking.

"You're hurting her!" Solee yelled.

The girl's face was red, fully red, and wet with tears. "Don't," she whispered. Her limbs, where I held her, streaked pink.

I let go.

Jisoo shrouded her, hoisted her closer. He murmured to her, forgetting me, and stroked her arms and legs and stomach and hair. She gripped him, buried her face into his neck. Our white imprints faded from her skin.

I stepped back, a swell of acid in my throat, my awful hands. "I'm sorry."

Jisoo stood under the shadow of the roof holding the child. The girls ran to his side. They petted their sister's pale, bare feet, shushing and soothing, even though they were crying themselves. The back door, behind them all, opened into a house where I had once slept.

It was winter, cold, and we were shivering. I squatted down. I beckoned to Solee, Jieun, Mila. To the little girl. I wanted to hug their little waists. I wanted to be forgiven.

Coda

Solee

SOME DAYS, WE LOOK FOR HER.

In the beginning, we searched the corners of empty rooms, the fields she'd walked when lonesome, each other's growing faces. The tree we used to lie under together cut down, we searched the skies above and wondered where she could have gone. Now, we look for her in our work, our partners, our children. We fret, especially, over our own girls. And when we are alone, we examine ourselves for all the ways we can and cannot be her daughters.

Our mother left us. She slipped. She let go. In a white dress, she dragged herself into the winter river. No shoes on the bank, no basket of clothes, no morning-glory soap. There was no sign for us to follow, but Jieun knew. She rushed to the river alone that day, an excuse tucked inside her pocket. Once, years later, while angry with me, Jieun told me what she'd seen. How Mother's face had been covered by her wet black hair, how the pink of her tongue poked through, like a dead limp fish. I pushed my fist into Jieun's face again and again when she told me. She didn't cry or fight back. I cannot forget the image now, of my sister lying in the grass, one cheek reddening from my blows, yelling, "I shouldn't be the only one."

After Mother's death, we turned inward. The four of us as one, like a flower petaling in on itself in the night. Father, separate, rotated on his own mournful axis. Kyunghwan vanished, nothing but a specter haunting the capital. In the room we shared, my night-time stories changed. Lee Haemi was still a goddess from the heavens, but in the end, she was never meant for this world, where a name, a life, a woman, could be taken whole.

Some of us have forgiven her and some of us have not. Jieun, with her temper that flares like a switch, rides the train every year, and climbs the hills to visit Mother's tumulus. She weeps the most for all of us.

I try to hold on to them, the way we clasped together those first nights without her. Our fingers laced, our legs locked. We slept with our cheeks on each other's backs. Now we are separate. We slip through days and months without speaking. Like water, without shape or hold. Mila calls each of us, frets she cannot be closer. Eunhee maintains her distance, flitting from country to country, never still for a moment, never coming home. Mother loved her most, but it is Eunhee who has forgotten her completely.

I hunger for them, my sisters. To know they thrive is to remind myself. Look, Solee. We are alive.

Look, Mother.

We are still here.

Acknowledgments

FIRST, ALWAYS, THANK YOU TO MY PARENTS, KIM JUCHON and Kim Aelee, for your strength, sacrifice, and understanding. I have felt your love and support every step of the way. Appa, you are my foundation. Your generosity and quiet devotion to your family, friends, and the mountains do not go unnoticed. Umma, I admire your passion for the world. You've taught me to embrace all challenges with fierce confidence. Thanks to my best sister, Diana Beena Kim, for being my earliest listener and friend. Thank you also to my grandmother, Park Soonnam, and to my Kwak family in Korea and my Kim family here in the States.

Thank you to Juliana Chyu and David Whitney for embracing me as a daughter. Love to the rest of the Chyu, Whitney, and Leonard families.

Thank you to my inimitable agent and advocate, Katherine Fausset, for believing in this novel since its infant stages. I am grateful for your faith in me and my words. And to the rest of the Curtis Brown team, for their support and kindness.

I am grateful to my brilliant and fierce editor, Jessica Williams, for guiding me with such care, wisdom, and grace. You have helped make my dream possible, and I am forever indebted to you.

Acknowledgments

I feel so lucky to have worked with you on my first book. Thank you. Huge thanks to everyone at William Morrow, especially Sharyn Rosenblum, Katherine Turro, and Ploy Siripant, and to Laura Cherkas and Laurie McGee.

Many thanks to the Bread Loaf Writers' Conference, Hedge-brook, the Kimmel Harding Nelson Center, the Bread Loaf Bakeless Camargo Fellowship, the James Jones First Novel Fellowship, and PEN America. These communities have provided me time, friendship, and support along the way. A special thank-you to Emily Nemens for selecting "Solee" for *The Southern Review* and for cheering me on ever since.

A profound thank-you to everyone at Columbia University for making me a stronger and more thoughtful writer, particularly Nicholas Christopher, Stacey D'Erasmo, David Ebershoff, Deborah Eisenberg, John Freeman, Gary Shteyngart, and Elissa Schappell. Special thanks to Ben Metcalf for insisting I write *this* novel and to Richard Ford for his wisdom and encouragement throughout the years. To my MFA women—a coven I admire and am so grateful for—Kerry Cullen, Sanaë Lemoine, Alexandra Watson, Diksha Basu, Essie Chambers, Andrea Morrison, and Naima Coster.

And to all my friends who have fed me, housed me, laughed with me, and reminded me of a world outside of writing, I give you all my hugs and thanks. Special cheers to Sujean Park, Deborah Ma, Steven Shlivko, Rohan Sud, Sam Rothschild, Dave Williams, Mickey Brener, Michael Vieten, Rachel Hall, Kate Sandlin, Dave Resnick, Taylor Simeone, Kyle Snow, Amy Ahn, Jinee Lee, Jennifer Kung, Annie Bae, and Ashley Kim for listening to me talk about this novel for many years.

Acknowledgments

Thank you, finally, to my love and greatest champion, Eric Whitney. For reading all of my drafts, for your unwavering faith in me even when I doubted myself, for always being my person. Without you, I would not have written this book. I love you, always.